Thomas and Rebecca Vaughan's

AQUA VITÆ: NON VITIS
(British Library MS, Sloane 1741)

MEDIEVAL AND RENAISSANCE
TEXTS AND STUDIES

VOLUME 217

AQVA VITÆ: NON VITIS.

Or

The Radical Humiditie of Nature:
Mechanically, and Magically dissected,
By the Conduct of Fire,
and Ferment:

As well in the particular, specified Bodies
of Metalls, and Minerals:
As in her seminal, Universal Formă,
and Chaos.

MS. 1614

By   M. B. 1741

Thomas Vaughan Scrip:

Dixit Heb: Hamed,

Novit Creator Creaturarum, quod Sermo de
salibus, et de His, quæ sunt, de Fenici Eorum,
fugat à me Tristitias mias, et exultat in ijs
Anima mia, & requiesco inde à Tædio, quod patior
a Naturâ.

— Et sic de multis alijs.

Title page from Sloane 1741.
By the kind permission of The British Library.

Thomas and Rebecca Vaughan's

AQUA VITÆ: NON VITIS
(British Library MS, Sloane 1741)

Edited and Translated with an Introduction

by

DONALD R. DICKSON

Arizona Center for Medieval and Renaissance Studies
Tempe, Arizona
2001

Library of Congress Cataloging-in-Publication Data

Vaughan, Thomas, 1622–1666.
　　　[Aqua vitae, non vitis. English]
　　　Thomas and Rebecca Vaughan's Aqua vitae, non vitis : (British Library MS,
Sloane 1741) / edited and translated with an introduction by Donald R. Dickson.
　　　　　p. cm. (Medieval and Renaissance texts and studies ; v. 217)
　　　Includes bibliographical references.
　　　ISBN 0-86698-259-0 (acid-free paper)
　　　1. Alchemy—England—Early works to 1800. 2. Vaughan, Thomas, 1622–
1666. 3. Vaughan, Rebecca. I. Vaughan, Rebecca. II. Dickson, Donald R. III. Brit-
ish Library. Manuscript. Sloane 1741. IV. Title. V. Medieval & Renaissance Texts
& Studies (Series) ; v. 217.
　　　QD25.V2813 2001
　　　540'.1'120942—dc21   00–045356

∞

This book is made to last.
It is set in Garamond Antiqua typeface,
smythe-sewn and printed on acid-free paper
to library specifications.

Printed in the United States of America

TABLE OF CONTENTS

ACKNOWLEDGMENTS

Work on this edition first began during the course of a research fellowship provided by the Alexander von Humboldt-Stiftung. I remain indebted to their generosity as well as to the genial support of Karl Josef Höltgen at the Institut für Anglistik at the University of Erlangen-Nuremberg. A semester fellowship provided by the Center for Humanities Research at Texas A&M University (formerly the Interdisciplinary Group for Historical Literary Study) made it possible to study the manuscript for an extended period at the British Library. Travel grants provided by the College of Liberal Arts and the Center for International Programs at Texas A&M University enabled me to complete this research in a timely fashion.

I am indebted to many librarians who patiently answered my inquiries: particularly, the librarians at the Manuscripts Students Room of the British Library. I also wish to acknowledge the kind assistance of James Collett-White, archivist with the Bedfordshire Record Office; Betty Chambers, a Meppershall historian; and the Saunders family of Wanstead Park for their continuing generosity and friendship.

For his careful scrutiny of the manuscript and many helpful suggestions, I am much indebted to David Crane, who devoted countless hours to this project and saved me from many errors. For consultation with translation problems, I wish to thank Craig Kallendorf and Edward H. Thompson. Alan Rudrum, the dean of Vaughan scholars, has helped in many ways. I must also especially acknowledge the great care that one of my readers for Medieval and Renaissance Texts and Studies, Leslie S. B. MacCoull, took with my manuscript. The depth of her Latinity and the breadth of her learning enriched this edition a great deal—*ago vobis gratias*.

College Station, Texas

INTRODUCTION

A. BIOGRAPHICAL INTRODUCTION

Thomas Vaughan

Thomas Vaughan (1621–1666) was descended from an ancient Welsh family and was related through his grandmother to the Somersets of Raglan, one of the most powerful families in South Wales. His paternal uncle Charles inhabited the family's imposing home at Tretower Court, situated about half a mile from the river Usk on the Brecon-Crickhowell Road.[1] The great round tower of the castle keep (early thirteenth century) was fortified as late as 1403 during the Owen Glendower uprising, though by 1300 the lords had begun to build a fine house enclosing a courtyard, the remains of which are still preserved.[2] In 1611 his father—likewise a younger brother and also named Thomas—married Denise Morgan, heiress to a much more modest estate along the Usk in Llansantffraid parish, valued at £400, called Trenewydd or Newton in English, a part of Scethrog Manor in the county of Brecon (or Brecknock). In this eight-room house, twin sons were born in 1621, Henry, the elder, and Thomas. The exact date of birth is unknown. A third son, William, was born in 1628, whose death in 1648 was memorialized by both brothers. Little is known of the profession of Vaughan's father; he appears as justice of the peace in 1624 and as under-sheriff in 1646. He was often before the law with petty suits, as was the case with many of the smaller gentry, and a distant kinsman,

---

[1] A full biography of Thomas Vaughan has not yet been written, though shorter accounts of his life appear in E. K. Chambers's edition of the *Poems of Henry Vaughan, Silurist*, 2 vols. (London: Routledge, 1896), 2, xxxiii–lvi; F. E. Hutchinson, *Henry Vaughan: A Life and Interpretation* (Oxford: Clarendon Press, 1947), 141–55; *The Works of Thomas Vaughan*, ed. Alan Rudrum (Oxford: Clarendon Press, 1984), 1–31; Donald R. Dickson, "Thomas Vaughan" in *Dictionary of Literary Biography*, vol. 131: 310–17, *Seventeenth-Century British Non-Dramatic Poets*, ed. M. Thomas Hester (Detroit: Gale, 1993); and Stevie Davies, *Henry Vaughan* (Bridgend, Wales: Seren, 1995).

[2] C. A. Ralegh Radford, *Tretower Court and Castle* (Cardiff: Her Majesty's Stationery Office, 1969).

the Oxford antiquary John Aubrey, described him as a "coxcombe and no honester than he should be—he cosened me of 50s. once."[3] Whatever the size of the Newton estate (some estimates run as high as two hundred acres), Henry and Thomas Vaughan did not expect to be supported by it and both sought professions.[4]

Anthony Wood and Aubrey provide the few anecdotes and passing details about the Vaughans upon which later biographers have relied. According to Wood, both Henry and Thomas were "educated in Grammar Learning in his own Country for six Years under one *Matthew Herbert* a noted Schoolmaster of his time." This tutelage probably took place from 1632 until 1638. Both boys later dedicated verses to Herbert, rector of nearby Llangattock. Herbert may also have been represented as the Amphion in Henry's "Daphnis: An Elegiac Eclogue" who first instructed them in "dark records and numbers nobly high / The visions of our black, but brightest bard."[5] Whether the boys' curiosity about the natural world was nurtured by Herbert as well is not known. From an autobiographical recollection amidst his speculation on the interaction of fire and water in Thomas's *Euphrates* (1655), we know that one of the texts he was taught to read was the book of Nature:

> This *Speculation* (I know not how) surpris'd my first youth, long before I saw the University, and certainly *Nature*, whose pupill I was, had even then awaken'd many *Notions* in me, which I met with afterwards, in the *Platonick Philosophie*. I will not forbear to write, how I had then fansied a certain practice on water, out of which, even in those childish dayes, I expected wonders. ... This *Consideration* of my self, when I was a Child, hath made me examine Children, namely, what thoughts they had of these *Elements*, we see about us, and I found thus much by them, that *Nature* in her simplicity, is much more wise, than some men are with their acquired parts, and *Sophistrie*.[6]

The poetry of Henry likewise reveals a fascination with the *res creatae*. In this, as in other things, the boys were much alike. Based on the evidence of the opening lines of Thomas Powell's dedicatory poem to *Olor Iscanus*,

---

[3] *Aubrey's Brief Lives*, ed. O. L. Dick (London: Martin Secker, 1949; Penguin, 1972), 356.

[4] See Hutchinson, *Henry Vaughan*, 16–20.

[5] Henry Vaughan, *The Complete Poems*, ed. Alan Rudrum (New Haven: Yale University Press, 1981), ll. 60–61. In *Olor Iscanus* (1647), Henry Vaughan included "Venerabili viro, Præceptori suo olim & semper Colendissimo M[ro]. Mathæo Herbert" and Thomas Vaughan dedicated *The Man-Mouse taken in a Trap* (1650) "To my Learned, and much Respected friend, Mr. MATHEW HARBERT."

[6] *Works*, 521.

"Upon the Most Ingenious Pair of Twins, Eugenius Philalethes, and the Author of these Poems," which celebrate their likeness, we can surmise that they were identical twins. Stevie Davies has theorized that "Henry's psyche was forged in the crucible of twinship," and her conjectures have sparked considerable interest in the nature of that relationship.[7] Unfortunately, there is little evidence, i.e., intertextual references in their writings, of this bond. The evidence from *Aqua Vitæ* to be discussed below suggests that his wife Rebecca played a more important role in his spiritual life.

In his seventeenth year Thomas went up to Oxford. On 4 May 1638 he was admitted to Jesus College—where 59 of the 99 men then on the college books were from Wales—and matriculated on 14 December 1638. At some point Henry joined him there, though he did not stay to take a degree.[8] At Oxford Thomas "was put under the tuition of a noted tutor; by whose lectures profiting much, he took one degree in arts."[9] A later poem tells us that he also studied with William Cartwright, reader in philosophy and a popular preacher.[10] At Jesus College he won academic honors (a scholarship in May 1640) and took the B.A. degree on 18 February 1642. The Senior Bursars' Accounts, which include lists of stipends paid to fellows, graduate scholars, and undergraduate scholars, show that he changed ranks from commoner to scholar in May 1640, and then again from undergraduate to graduate scholar in February 1642. Much later Henry Vaughan would claim in a letter to Aubrey that his brother took the M.A. degree and was made a fellow of Jesus College, staying some ten or twelve years.[11] (Thomas's academic achievements were reported in Wood's *Athenæ Oxonienses* on the strength of Henry's letter to Aubrey.) There is no record of Thomas's paying fees for an M.A. degree in the annual accounts of Jesus College; it should be noted, however, that a lacuna exists for the period 1644–1648, thus not excluding the possibility altogether. The Senior Bursars' Accounts, on the other hand, do show that he continued to receive a graduate scholar stipend until 1648, so Henry's memory may not have played him false.[12]

---

[7] Davies, *Henry Vaughan*, 32. See also her chapter, "The Crucible of Twinship," 28–55.

[8] The archivist of Jesus College, Brigid Allen, "Henry Vaughan at Oxford," *Jesus College Record* (1997/1998): 23–27, has argued recently that new evidence shows that Henry may have entered three years after his brother did (i.e., in 1641).

[9] Anthony à Wood, *Athenæ Oxonienses*, ed. P. Bliss, 3rd ed., 4 vols. (facsimile rpt. of London, 1817; New York and London: Johnson, 1967), 3: 722.

[10] See "On the Death of Mr *WILLIAM CARTWRIGHT*," in *Works*, 581–83.

[11] Letter, Henry Vaughan to John Aubrey, 15 June 1673, from Brecon, Bodleian MS. Wood F 39, fol. 216, in *The Works of Henry Vaughan*, ed. L. C. Martin, 2nd ed. (Oxford: Clarendon Press, 1957), 687.

[12] Jesus College Archives, BU.AC.GEN.1 (Senior Bursars' Accounts, Vol. 1, 1631–1650), Outgoings, passim. Brigid Allen, archivist at Jesus College, has kindly supplied these details.

In the spring of 1642, when Vaughan took his baccalaureate, the nation was lurching toward war, and many were obliged to alter their plans. Vaughan was no doubt still at Oxford when the king entered on 29 October 1642, after which time his studies were interrupted by the rush toward civil war as the college records show. The usual stipend for undergraduates was £5 *per annum*, £10 for graduate scholars. According to the reckoning of Brigid Allen, archivist at Jesus College, Vaughan received £4.5s. for 1642, the year in which he was graduated B.A., and in 1643, £6.14s.7d. (instead of £10 each year).[13] During the five-year period from 1644 to 1648, he received £26, which suggests that while he was in residence for a substantial portion of the time, he was also absent for a considerable time. This was not unusual, according to Allen; of the six graduate scholars in residence during 1644–1648, only one earned his full £50.

That Thomas Vaughan took up arms for the king is clear, since the Propagators in 1650 evicted him for being "in armes personally against the Parliament" (see below). To what extent he was involved in the fighting is largely unknown. After the royalist defeat at Naseby in June 1645, King Charles himself had come to Brecon, lodging with Sir Herbert Price at the Priory on 5 August, to raise support for a campaign to hold the north of Wales. Evidence suggests that Vaughan fought with Price's Breconshire regiment of horse at Rowton Heath near Chester, 24 September 1645, where the royalists again suffered a great defeat. Among the list of captains from Price's company taken prisoner is the name "Tho. Vaughan." After the Restoration, his name also appears on a claim made for the relief of the king's "truly loyal and indigent party" as captain of Price's company.[14] The five Latin poems on Col. John Morris's capture of Pontefract Castle (in 1648 during the last phase of the war), published in his brother's *Thalia Rediviva* (1678), do not necessarily reflect personal involvement in the latter fighting.

As a younger brother, Thomas was intended for the church and may have begun to read divinity and acquire oriental languages at Oxford after his arts course. Henry told Aubrey that Thomas "was ordayned minister by bishop Mainwaringe and presented to the Rectorie of St Brigets by his kinsman Sir George Vaughan."[15] Since Thomas attained the canonical age required for ordination as a priest in 1645, he would not normally have been installed until that year as rector at Llansantffraid—St. Bride's or Bridget's in English.[16] Since the Jesus College records show that he was still

---

[13] Personal letter from Brigid Allen, 9 March 1999, Jesus College, Oxford.
[14] Hutchinson, *Henry Vaughan*, 64–65.
[15] *Brief Lives*, 356.
[16] Hutchinson, *Henry Vaughan*, 92.

resident in Oxford roughly half of the year, he must have hired a curate to assist him, a not uncommon expedient. He could certainly afford to do so, for his native parish offered a living worth £60 *per annum*, an income several times as much as the average Welsh parish. With it went a substantial rectory and a glebe of perhaps twenty-five acres. We know from a 1649 Chancery suit brought by Thomas Vaughan junior against some trespassers on these arable lands that Thomas Vaughan senior was "fformer [i.e., farmer] of the said Rectorie of Llansantffread under the plaintiff his son" and would continue to farm the glebe until his death in 1658.[17] This raises the possibility that the father's financial interest in the living at Llansantffraid may have propelled the son toward a career in which he seems to have had little interest. When he was formally evicted under the "Act for better Propagation and Preaching the Gospel in Wales" in 1650, the document for his case read as follows: "Tho: Vaughan out of Lansantfread for being a common drunkard, a common swearer, no preacher, a whoremast^r, & in armes personally against the Parliament."[18] In the account of Vaughan's case in *Sufferings of the Clergy* (1714), John Walker observed that the motivating force behind the other charges was political:

> He was Turned out by the *Propagators*, for *Drunkenness, Swearing, Incontinency*, being *no Preacher*; and what was in their Opinion *worse* than All, for having been in *Arms* for the *King*: And perhaps *this last Article*, was the only *Proof* and *Evidence* of *all the Rest*.[19]

Indeed, accusations against the "scandalous life" or "drunkenness" of incumbents were quite common—leveled in over twenty percent of the cases reported by Walker—suggesting that such charges may have been inserted to cover partisanship.[20] On the other hand, Vaughan himself professed a certain fondness for drink. In *Aqua Vitæ* he records a dream on 9 April 1659, in which he saw a "certaine person, with whom I had in former times revell'd away many yeares in drinking," though he also avers that his life has been since then "much amended."[21]

His brief career as pastor at Llansantffraid (1645–1648) would have

---

[17] Hutchinson, *Henry Vaughan*, 91.

[18] Hutchinson, *Henry Vaughan*, 93.

[19] John Walker, *An Attempt Towards Recovering an Account of the Numbers and Sufferings of the Clergy of the Church of England*, 2 vols. (London, 1714), 2: 389.

[20] In neighboring Herefordshire, for example, twelve of the fifty incumbents were so accused; in Bedfordshire, seven of thirty-five. See A. G. Matthews, *Walker Revised: Being a Revision of John Walker's Sufferings of the Clergy During the Grand Rebellion 1642–60* (Oxford: Clarendon Press, 1988), 64–67 and 191–96.

[21] Sloane 1741, fols. 103^r, 18^r (45, 234 below). Hutchinson, *Henry Vaughan*, 95, speculates that this "certaine person" may have been his cousin John Walbeoffe who was "of a gay and extravagant turn."

taken place in a time of great turmoil in his native land, with the war, the monarchy and many friends having been lost. F. E. Hutchinson is surely correct in pointing to numerous passages in the poetry of Henry Vaughan and to a lesser extent in the writing of Thomas, expressing horror for the bloodshed of the Civil War.[22] As a result of these dislocations, Vaughan withdrew from the *via activa* and returned to Oxford, where he sought the "Acquisition of some naturall secrets, to which I had been disposed from my youth up."[23] Inasmuch as he never applied for reinstatement to St. Bridget's after the Restoration, it seems likely that he had discovered his true life's work in chemical research. As Wood explained, "the unsetledness of the time hindring him a quiet possession of [St. Bridget's], he left it, retired to *Oxon*, and in a sedate repose prosecuted his medicinal geny, (in a manner natural to him) and at length became eminent in the chymical part thereof at Oxon, and afterwards at London. ..."[24] Since the dedication to his first book (later published at London in 1650) is dated "Oxonii 48," we also know that he began to write. If we can accept as accurate his statement from the preface to *Aula Lucis*, dated 1651—"I have lived three yeares *in Regione Lucis*"—then he moved to London in 1648, where he would remain.[25] Indeed, he is last listed as a resident graduate scholar in the Buttery Books at Jesus College in the eighth week of the quarter, i.e., about the end of February 1648.[26]

The 1650s was one of the most intellectually turbulent decades in early modern England, when more treatises on chemistry, natural magic, and hermeticism appeared than in the entire century before.[27] By 1650 Vaughan had taken up residence with Thomas Henshaw (1618–1700) in Kensington, where together they formed a research *collegium* of chemists

---

[22] Hutchinson, *Henry Vaughan*, 56–58. See, e.g., *Anima Magica Abscondita* in *Works*, 134: "Above all Things, avoyd the *Guilt of innocent Blood*, for it utterly separates from God in this Life, and requires a timely, and serious Repentance, if thou would'st find Him in the Next."

[23] *Works*, 588.

[24] *Athenæ Oxonienses*, 3: 722.

[25] See *Works*, 453. A single letter from one Thomas Vaughan to a London solicitor, Charles Roberts, dated 8 February 1654 (Ash Wednesday) from Newton, has been interpreted by some, e.g., A. E. Waite, *The Works of Thomas Vaughan: Mystic and Alchemist* (London: Theosophical Society, 1919), xi, as evidence that Vaughan returned for a time to Wales. Hutchinson, *Henry Vaughan*, 116–18, argues persuasively that this must be Thomas Vaughan's father, who held possession of the Newton estate until his death in 1658. A comparison of Bodleian MS. Rawlinson A. xi., fol. 335^r with Sloane 1741 shows that they were written by different hands.

[26] Jesus College Archives, BB.a.5 (Buttery Books), 242. Brigid Allen has kindly supplied these details.

[27] John Ferguson, "Some English Alchemical Books," *Journal of the Alchemical Society* 2 (1913): 5, states that "Between the years 1650 and 1675 or 1680 more alchemical books appeared in English than in all the time before and after those dates."

known as the *Christian Learned Society*. Vaughan's statement in the preface to *Aula Lucis* about having lived "three yeares *in Regione Lucis*," which was written in "Heliopolis," most likely a reference to the mythic locale of anther utopian brotherhood, Campanella's *La Città del Sole*, may fix his tenure with Henshaw between 1648 and 1651. One of the founding fellows of the Royal Society, Henshaw was born in the parish of St. Lawrence Jewry but lived most of his life at the ancient manor of West Town in Kensington, called Pondhouse or Moathouse, which his father Benjamin Henshaw, a captain of the City of London, had leased from the owners of nearby Holland House. From 1634 to 1638 Henshaw studied at University College, Oxford, where he was tutored by the famed mathematician William Oughtred, then entered the Middle Temple but left off his legal career at the outbreak of hostilities.[28] Henshaw and Vaughan could have met as early as 1638 at Oxford, and some have speculated that they were comrades in arms for the king. While the list of captains taken at Rowton Heath, 24 September 1645, included the names Vaughan and Henshaw,[29] it seems unlikely they were imprisoned together. In Henshaw's own account of his life for the *Athenæ Oxonienses*, he indicated that he had joined the king at York (January to September 1642) and was taken prisoner upon his return to London to outfit himself with money and arms. Given the gentleman's option of pledging not to fight again or being confined for the duration, he travelled on the continent (from 1644–1645 with John Evelyn in Italy). Henshaw returned "a little before the Kgs murther" and was called to the bar (24 November 1654), but confessed that "my long absence and ye sowre complexion of ye times quite discouraged me from ye practice of that profession."[30] With a small income from his family that was perhaps supplemented by money from his second wife—according to the memorial tablet along the nave of St. Mary Abbots, Kensington, Henshaw had married an heiress, Anne Kipping of Twedley, Kent (d. 1671)— he was able to devote himself to the pursuit of experimental chemistry.[31]

---

[28] See *Alumni Oxonienses: The Members of the University of Oxford, 1500–1714*, ed. Joseph Foster, 4 vols. (Oxford, 1891–1892), 1: 694; he did not take a degree. He matriculated on 21 April 1638: *Register of Admissions to the Honourable Society of the Middle Temple*, 3 vols. (London: Middle Temple, 1949), 1: 135. See also K. Theodore Hoppen, "The Nature of the Early Royal Society," *British Journal for the History of Science* 9 (1976): 243-46.

[29] Thomas Willard, "The Life and Works of Thomas Vaughan," Ph.D. Diss., University of Toronto, 1978, 31.

[30] Letter, Henshaw to Anthony Wood, 21 June 1693, Bodleian MS. Ashmole Wood S.C. 25216, fol. 181; ed. by Stephen Pasmore, "Thomas Henshaw, F. R. S. (1618-1700)," *Notes and Records of the Royal Society* 36 (1982): 177-80. In this letter to Wood, Henshaw stated that his brother, Major Nathaniel Henshaw, and a cousin named Thomas Henshaw were both soldiers. One of these men may have been captured at Rowton.

[31] Henshaw, in a letter to Sir John Clayton at Oxnead, 29 August 1671, Norfolk Record Office MS, Bradfer-Lawrence, 1c/1, stated that he had about £200 a year from his father.

Both Vaughan and Henshaw were royalists, but science was their common bond.[32]

The purpose of Henshaw and Vaughan's *Chymical Club* was to make available manuscripts and translations of philosophical works and to promote learning. Prominent among them were Obadiah Walker and Abraham Woodhead, two Oxford dons, both recently ejected from their fellowships, who had tutored and befriended Henshaw at University College. What most of them had in common was an interest in experimental science and mathematics that had been cultivated by the leading mathematician of the age, William Oughtred (1575–1660), whose *Clavis Mathematicæ* (1631) was hailed for introducing Hindu-Arabic notation, algebraic symbols, decimal fractions, and algorithms and for teaching the mathematical operations fundamental to scientific research.[33] Vaughan was also associated with the circle of Samuel Hartlib, educational reformer and utopian idealist. It is from Hartlib's daybook that we learn:

> Hinshaw is about to put in practise a Model of [Chri]stian Learned Society in joining hims[elf] with 6. other friends of his owne familiars[,] men of qualities and competencies, that will have all in comon, dedicating thems[elves] wholly to devotion and studies and separating thems[elves] from the World by leading a severe life for diet apparel. etc.; Their dwelling-house to bee about 6. or 7. miles from London; They will have a Laboratorie and strive to doe all the good they can to their neighbourhood.[34]

---

[32] The political background of Vaughan and his circle has been clouded by a misattribution in the catalogue of the British Library. The author of a royalist political pamphlet in the Thomason collection (dated 29 September 1654), *A Vindication of Thomas Henshaw Esquire, Sometimes Major in the French King's Service ... concerning a pretended Plott for which J. Gerharde, Esquire and Peter Vowell, Gent., were murthered on the 10th of August, 1654*, is given in the BL catalogue and hence in the *Short Title Catalogue* as "Thomas Henshaw, barrister." The "Major Henshaw" involved in the so-called Gerard Plot to assassinate Cromwell, however, was not Vaughan's roommate but rather his cousin, as Henshaw himself later explained to Wood in a 1693 account of his life (Bodleian MS. Ash. Wood. S.C. 25216 fol. 181): "My bro: Major Henshaw and my cousin Tho. Henshaw were during ye whole warre in Kg Charles's service, but it was ye last of them was in the plot against Cromwell." Also, Ronald Hutton, *Charles II: King of England, Scotland, and Ireland* (Oxford: Oxford University Press, 1989), 82, reports that when a "Major Henshaw" proposed assassinating Cromwell to Charles, the king approved but then "received information that Henshaw was a double agent and disowned him." If this is so, then Charles II would hardly have rewarded Henshaw with the diplomatic posts that came his way after the Restoration.

[33] For a full account of the activities of this group, see Donald R. Dickson, *The Tessera of Antilia: Secret Societies and Utopian Brotherhoods in Early Modern Europe* (Leiden: Brill, 1998), chap. 6.

[34] *Ephemerides* (1650), Sheffield University Library MS, Hartlib 28.1.65a.

Others in Vaughan's ken who shared his interest in hermeticism, the Rosicrucians, Cornelius Agrippa, Jakob Böhme, and chemistry may have included his publisher Humphrey Blunden, Henry Pinnell, John French, William Backhouse, and Elias Ashmole.[35]

Furthermore, we know that Vaughan's writings or personality had antagonized one of the most colorful personalities of the time, the alchemist George Starkey, who was then lodging with a member of the *Chymical Clubb*, a Mr. Webbe. Born in the Americas and educated at Harvard College, Starkey was also a member of the Hartlib circle from 1650–1653.[36] From a remark made by Sir Robert Boyle to Hartlib, we know that Starkey was preparing a refutation of Vaughan's work.[37] Though this refutation is no longer extant, we can speculate about its direction since fundamental methodological differences separated the two. As a follower of Jan Baptiste van Helmont, Starkey held that all the elements originate from water, while Vaughan, who adhered to the tradition of Agrippa and Michael Sendivogius, reduced all to "elemental earth" by using *sal nitrum*. Moreover, as William R. Newman has recently discovered, Starkey believed Vaughan had cheated others out of large sums of money.[38]

At what point Vaughan began his more important association with one of the principal architects of the Royal Society, Sir Robert Moray (F.R.S., president 1661–1662), is not known. Wood described Moray as a "noted chymist" who had devoted himself to chemical experiments during his exile in Maastricht (1657–1659) and Vaughan's patron; Aubrey reported that he was a "good Chymist and assisted his Majestie in his Chymicall operations" at the royal laboratory in Whitehall; Henry called him Thomas's "great friend ... to whome he gave all his bookes and MSS."[39] Thomas Willard has argued that Moray may have even provided Vaughan access to the translation of the Rosicrucian manifestos (published with a preface in 1652), thus placing their association in the early 1650s.[40]

---

[35] *Works*, 14–15.

[36] See R. S. Wilkinson, "George Starkey, Physician and Alchemist," *Ambix* 11 (1963): 121–52, and "The Hartlib Papers and Seventeenth-Century Chemistry, Part Two," *Ambix* 17 (1970): 85–110; and William R. Newman, "Prophecy and Alchemy: The Origin of Eirenaeus Philalethes," *Ambix* 37 (1990): 97–115, and *Gehennical Fire: The Lives of George Starkey, An American Alchemist in the Scientific Revolution* (Cambridge: Harvard University Press, 1994).

[37] *Ephemerides* (1651), Sheffield University Library MS, Hartlib 28.2.7b: "Hee [Starkey, marginal note] is about to refute Vaughan as likewise to translate a Chymical Booke into Engl. out of Latine."

[38] Letter, Starkey to Boyle, 3 January 1652, Royal Society Library, Boyle Letters, fol. 131ᵛ; ed. Newman, *Gehennical Fire*, 222.

[39] *Athenæ Oxonienses*, 3: 722; *Brief Lives*, 282, 356.

[40] Thomas S. Willard, "The Rosicrucian Manifestos in Britain," *Papers of the Bibliographical Society of America* 77 (1983): 489–95.

Through Moray, Vaughan was likely employed by the Crown during the last five years of his life. When the king left London for Oxford to escape the plague in 1665, Vaughan was part of the entourage. According to Henry Vaughan's letter to Aubrey, Thomas was "vpon an imployment for his majesty" when he died on 27 February 1666 after a laboratory accident.[41] He was buried in the village churchyard in Albury at Moray's expense. All his remaining manuscripts were left in Moray's hands (along with his library); only his notebook of experiments, *Aqua Vitæ: Non Vitis: Or, The radical Humiditie of Nature: Mechanically, and Magically dissected By the Conduct of Fire, and Ferment*, now in the British Library (Sloane 1741), is extant.

Rebecca Vaughan

Precious little has been known about the identity of Thomas Vaughan's wife, whom he married on 28 September 1651, other than her Christian name, Rebecca. Efforts to discover her identity through a marriage license have been frustrated because the Vaughans were married during the Interregnum when episcopal records simply were not kept, and were married in London where many parish registers were destroyed in the Great Fire.[42] Vaughan biographers have all surmised that she hailed from a village in Bedfordshire called Meppershall, because her corpse was transported over fifty miles for burial there (she died in London on 17 April 1658 but was buried at Meppershall on 26 April).[43] Recently another valuable clue to her identity was discovered in a 1652 letter to Robert Boyle from one of her husband's chief adversaries, the American alchemist George Starkey, who revealed that Vaughan had recently married the "daughter of a certain cleric, of no fortune."[44] It is very probable, therefore, that Rebecca Vaughan was the daughter of Dr. Timothy Archer, rector of Meppershall.

Timothy Archer (1597–1672) was born in Bury, Suffolk and took the

---

[41] Letter to Aubrey, 15 June 1673, from Brecon, Bodleian MS. Wood F 39, fol. 216, in *The Works of Henry Vaughan*, 687. Hutchinson, *Henry Vaughan*, 144, also agrees that Thomas was employed by the crown.

[42] In the *Allegations for Marriage Licenses Issued by the Bishop of London*, Harleian Society, vol. 26 (London, 1887), there is a hiatus between 14 December 1648 and 24 January 1661. Nor are the Vaughans listed by the *Vicar General of the Arch-bishop of Canterbury 1600–1679*, Harleian Society, vols. 33, 34 (London, 1886), or in Joseph Foster's *London Marriage Licenses, 1521–1869* (London, 1887).

[43] See Chambers, *Poems of Henry Silurist*, 2: xxxviii; Hutchinson, *Henry Vaughan*, 142–43; and Rudrum, *Works*, 16–17.

[44] The letter, Starkey to Boyle, 3 January 1652, was discovered among the Boyle letters at the Royal Society Library by Newman, *Gehennical Fire*, 222: "Philosophus maximus Thomas Vaughan nuperrime uxorem duxit, clerici cujusdam filiam, nullius fortunam. . . ."

B.A. (1617) and M.A. (1620) from Trinity College, Cambridge.[45] He was installed as curate of St. Mary's in Meppershall in 1624 through the good graces of his uncle, who held the living. Thomas Archer, D. D., also of Bury (1554-1631), fellow of Trinity and chaplain in ordinary to James I, was a clergyman of some stature. Timothy later became rector at Meppershall after his kinsman's death and also at nearby Blunham, where John Donne had preceded him.[46] The relationship between Thomas and Timothy Archer was apparently close: not only did Thomas provide employment, he also bequeathed his books and papers to Timothy and a sum of money to the four Archer children living when the will was made. In all likelihood, Timothy named his first son Thomas in his honor. Another relation, Richard Archer, then became Timothy's curate. Thus in the village of Meppershall the Archers enjoyed a considerable presence. In an area known for Puritan leanings, Archer was a staunch royalist, whose predilections no doubt were enhanced when the king conferred a doctorate (*Sacræ Theologiæ Professor*) upon him while passing through Blunham in 1632. However, he eventually paid dearly for this allegiance. According to *Sufferings of the Clergy*, Archer was dispossessed by the Parliamentarians sometime before 15 October 1644 and imprisoned in the Fleet for eighteen years, then eventually restored to St. Mary's (1660-1672).[47]

Archer married Rebekah Beedelles or Beedles of Cambridgeshire on 17 December 1621 at Chesterton.[48] Based on information about the Archer family gathered by Walker, we have good reason to believe that theirs was a fruitful union with eleven children in all. Walker's source was a grandson, also a minister, who inherited Dr. Timothy Archer's books and manuscripts, which may have included a family Bible.[49] The christening records for only nine of these children, however, can be verified. We know

---

[45] *Alumni Cantabrigienses: Part I, from the Earliest Times to 1751*, eds. John Venn and J. A. Venn, 4 vols. (Cambridge: Cambridge University Press, 1922-1927), 1: 38.

[46] *Fasti Ecclesiae Bedfordiensis, Blunham*, fol. 3, and *Meppershall*, fol. 3. Normally, the duke of Kent held the rights to Blunham and the earl of Peterborough to Meppershall, but they granted Elizabeth Archer the right to present both to her kinsman *pro hac vice*; see C. W. Foster, "Institutions to Ecclesiastical Benefices in the County of Bedford, 1535-1660," *Publications of the Bedfordshire Historical Record Society* 8 (1924): 144, 154. See also the *Dictionary of National Biography* article on Thomas Archer, D. D., 2: 73.

[47] Matthews, *Walker Revised*, 64.

[48] Since Mrs. Archer signed her will "Rebekah," I use this spelling.

[49] Walker's source of information about the Archer family was a grandson, "G. Wateson"; see Matthews, *Walker Revised*, 64. George Watson, the son of Frances Archer Watson (born 3 September 1654 at Ampthill; died 9 June 1742), would have been the best source for such information, since (according to Rebekah Archer's will, Bedfordshire Record Office, ABP/w 1685/90) he inherited his grandfather's papers. Walker's notes, Bodleian MS. Walker, c.5, fol. 311, unfortunately do not list the children's names.

a daughter, Elizabeth, was born in 1623 at Litlington, a small village in southwest Cambridgeshire; the other ten were born at very regular intervals from the time Archer was appointed curate at Meppershall in 1624 until 1641. As is so often the case, the parish register has many lacunae, and even the records for the family of the rector are not complete. For example, a daughter named Marie must have been born before All Souls' Day in 1630 when Dr. Thomas Archer left bequests in his will to the "fower children of my coosen Timothy Archer vide[licet]. Elisabeth, Francis, John, and Marie, to each of them in monie fourtie shillings."[50] Yet there are no extant records for Marie Archer, who could have been born elsewhere and whose baptism accidentally left unrecorded. In like manner a convincing case can be made that Rebecca Archer, *filia*, was the eleventh child despite the absence of records definitively establishing this identification.

The original parish records for Meppershall no longer exist; for his edition of the registers, F. G. Emmison used the Bishop's Transcript, which was missing the crucial years of 1636 and 1637. Following are the recorded baptismal dates of the Archer children (with Marie's probable data in brackets):[51]

NAME	CHRISTENING DATE	BIRTH INTERVAL
Elizabeth	10 August 1623 at Litlington	20 months
Thomas	15 May 1625 at Meppershall	21 months
Richard	10 September 1626 at Meppershall	16 months
Frances	27 March 1628 at Meppershall	18 months
John	6 July 1629 at Meppershall	15 months
[Marie	before November 1630]	
Timothy	30 January 1632 at Meppershall	31 months
	*	
Ann	6 November 1634 at Meppershall	33 months
	*	
Sarah	4 April 1638 at Meppershall	42 months
Robert	27 January 1641 at Meppershall	34 months

Assuming that Dr. Thomas Archer's will was accurate—and we know from the parish burial register that the two children not mentioned, Thomas and Richard, had already died in infancy—we can assign a birthdate to

---

[50] Bedfordshire Record Office, ABP/w 1630/129, fol. 4. Thomas Archer's will was made on 1 November 1630.

[51] *Bedfordshire Parish Registers: Meppershall*, ed. F. G. Emmison, vol. 38 (Bedford: County Records Committee, 1948), B2. Elizabeth Archer's data was taken from the International Genealogical Index (1994 edition).

Marie sometime before the autumn of 1630. (A birthday in October 1630 would mean an interval of fifteen months after John's birth.) The order of the children mentioned in their uncle's will—"Elisabeth, Francis, John, and Marie"—would also reflect the order of their birth. The most likely time for the missing eleventh child's nativity would be either in 1633 (when an interval of thirty-three months between births occurred) or in 1636–1637 (when the interval was forty-two months). Anomalies in the records make each period possible. In the case of the former, as Emmison explains, the Bishop's Transcript is headed 1633, but it is "not clear if the entries are for 1632/33 or for 1633/34," thus introducing the possibility of confusion (and error) on the part of the transcriber; the Bishop's Transcripts for 1636 and 1637 are simply missing.[52] Since the Archers seemed especially fond of using family names, a daughter christened in honor of her mother would be fitting; indeed, its absence is telling for there was a daughter named Rebecca in every generation of every branch at this time.[53]

Rebecca Archer Vaughan would have had ample reasons to want to be laid to rest at St. Mary's, Meppershall, where her father and uncles had served for so many years. At least two infant siblings had already been interred in the churchyard, Richard (14 January 1627) and Thomas (23 May 1628); John, who had spent most of his life in London, was later buried there (4 May 1680). Others may have been since only two children, Elizabeth and Frances, were alive when Rebecca Archer's will was proved in 1685. Although Elizabeth Archer Emery lived nearby in Ampthill parish, five of her own children were likewise buried there (Timothy and Elizabeth in 1657, John in 1660, Archer in 1661, and Frances in 1677), as were both she and her husband (1683 and 1696). We also know that Dr. Timothy Archer was enshrined at St. Mary's on 2 December 1672, and his wife requested that her mortal remains be interred "in the Chancell of the Parish Church of Meppersall in the said County of Bedford soo neare the body of my loving & deceased husband as the same may be placed."[54]

---

[52] *Bedfordshire Parish Registers: Meppershall*, B2.

[53] The children of Elizabeth Archer Emery and Richard Emery were named Rebecca, Richard, Elizabeth, Timothy, Archer, John, Sarah, Elizabeth, Francis, and Frances. The children of Frances Archer Watson and John Watson were named John, George, Charles, Rebecca (who would name her first daughter Rebecca; when she died in infancy, the second child was also named Rebecca), Henry, Mary, and perhaps Ann. The children of John and Mary Archer (of St. Dionis Backchurch Parish, London) were named John, Mary, Katherine, Anna, Timothy, Anna and Rebecca. All data were taken from the *Bedfordshire Parish Registers: Ampthill*, ed. F. G. Emmison, vol. 17 (Bedford: County Records Committee, 1938); the *Bedfordshire Parish Registers: Meppershall*; *The Reiester Booke of Saynte De'nis Backchurch Parish*, ed. Joseph Lemuel Chester, Harleian Society, vol. 3 (London, 1878), 109–15; and the International Genealogical Index.

[54] Rebekah Archer was buried on 4 December 1685. Her will is in the Bedfordshire Record Office, ABP/w 1685/90.

Though the churchyard has one or two gravestones from the late seventeenth century, none can be deciphered bearing the Archer name (nor are any listed in a register of monuments at St. Mary's). At this time burial was still by rotation: bodies were interred first at the southern wall of the churchyard; when the northern wall was reached, burial took place at the southern end again. Wooden grave-boards and simple linen shrouds were the norm; only the wealthy had headstones and coffins. The absence of any family markers is thus not surprising, despite Dr. Archer's position and the monument to him in St. Mary's (closely resembling that of Dr. Thomas Archer at Houghton Conquest). On the south wall of the chancel, his half-length figure resting on a cushion can still be found. The canopy is surmounted by the Archer coat of arms—three broad arrows, points down—and below a marble tablet bears the following inscription:[55]

TIMOTHEVS ARCHER
SACR: THEOL: (PROFESSOR PER 42 ANNOS)
RECTOR HUIVS ECLESIÆ ET DE BLVNHAM
MVLTOS EXPERTVS CASVS
SAQUESTRATVS ET POST LONGUM RESTITVTVS
HÎC TANDEM IN PACE REQUIESCIT
OBijT 2DO * DECEMBERIS * 1672 *
ÆTATIS SVÆ * 75 *

So Rebecca Archer Vaughan's attachment to this Bedfordshire village is quite understandable. The parish register, accordingly, shows the burial on 26 April 1658 of "Rebecka, the Wife of Mr Vahanne."[56]

Meppershall lies about fifteen miles south of Bedford along the Bedfordshire and Hertfordshire boundary. In the seventeenth century the village was small and poor with forty-one households paying some sort of hearth tax; the population has been estimated at 174. As described in a terrier of 1607, the rectory was the largest domicile in the parish; the two-storied timber-framed building had fifteen bays or windowed sections with grounds of about an acre surrounded by a moat with a drawbridge. The living was worth £60 *per annum* and included a glebe with two large barns and stables.[57] The church rests on the summit of a hillock that affords a pleasant air and fine prospect of the Chiltern Hills to the west. This setting was such that a dedicated man of the cloth could have enjoyed the simple, fulfilling life of a country parson described in Herbert's *A Priest to the*

---

[55] The wording varies slightly with the version given in *Bedfordshire Notes and Queries* 3 (1893): 365.

[56] *Bedfordshire Parish Registers: Meppershall*, B20.

[57] I am indebted to V. H. Chambers, *Old Meppershall, A Parish History* (Meppershall: privately printed, 1979), 42–43, for these facts on the early history of Meppershall.

Temple. By the end of their days, the Archers had even accumulated a considerable estate: Rebekah Archer left bequests of property (of unspecified value), a share of the White Hart Inn in Ampthill, legacies totaling about £450, along with the usual plate and linen.[58]

When Dr. Archer was ejected from his living and confined at the Fleet Prison in London, however, the family's circumstances changed dramatically. A Parliamentary order was made in 1644 for the support of Rebekah Archer and her children, but it amounted to only one-fifth of the parish tithes.[59] Without the shelter of the rectory and the yield of the glebe, this amounted to a pittance especially to a family that had some aspirations to gentility. The Archer monuments at Meppershall and Houghton Conquest bore coats of arms.[60] We know that two of the daughters married local men of standing: Frances married John Watson of Little Park in the parish of Ampthill; and Elizabeth married Richard Emery, a widower from Meppershall whose estate was called Ewe Greene.[61] (Nothing is known of the fates of Timothy, *filius*, Ann, Sarah, or Robert.)

The fifth child, John Archer, also prospered, though not at Meppershall. Shortly after his father's ejection, he went to London where he was apprenticed as a draper in 1645.[62] He was aided in this endeavor by an uncle, also named John Archer (d. 1678), who lived in Fenchurch Street, near St. Dionis Backchurch. Since other relations lived in the same parish, London was a logical refuge during this time of crisis. The senior John Archer was a prominent member of the drapers' guild, in fact a member of the "court" most of his career.[63] The younger John Archer also thrived as a draper and was even elected master (1659–1660). Like his par-

---

[58] Bedfordshire Record Office, ABP/w 1685/90.

[59] British Library, Add. MS. 15,669, fols. 104^v and 113^v.

[60] According to J. H. L. Archer, *Memorials of the Families of the Surname of Archer* (London, 1861), 50, this family was a branch of the Archers of Umberslade, Warwickshire, a prominent landed family.

[61] In her will, Bedfordshire Record Office, ABP/w 1685/90, Rebekah Archer referred to both sons-in-law as gentlemen; so did the Ampthill parish register.

[62] *Roll of the Drapers' Company of London: Collected from the Company's Records and Other Sources*, ed. Percival Boyd (Croydon: Gordon, 1934), 5.

[63] According to John Stow, *A Survey of the Cities of London and Westminster*, ed. John Strype, 6 vols. (London, 1720), 2: 152–53, John Archer was a major contributor towards the rebuilding of St. Dionis after the Great Fire (i.e., he gave more than £100). He was listed on a table of benefactors hanging in the church, but this tablet was lost after the church was deconsecrated in 1878. He also presented the company with a silver ewer and basin, weighing 191 ounces, that was considered among its most important pieces of plate. He was apprenticed in 1624, then was listed among the "livery" from 1639 to 1655, then became a warden (2: 453); see A. H. Johnson, *The History of the Worshipful Company of Drapers of London*, 5 vols. (Oxford: Oxford University Press, 1922), 2: 474, 476.

ents and siblings, he wished to be buried at Meppershall, where the register characterized him as a "gentleman and citizen of London."[64]

Rebecca Archer likewise found herself in London, where her brother was prospering, where her father was incarcerated, and where she met a former minister, also lately ejected from his living (of a similar class), then pursuing his true vocation in experimental chemistry. I believe she married Thomas Vaughan on 28 September 1651 (perhaps at St. Dionis Backchurch), a union that produced no children. If she had been born in 1633, she would have married at eighteen; if born in 1636, she would have married at fifteen—an unusually young age. The commonest age for first marriage by women was then about twenty-two, but young brides and grooms were certainly not uncommon. In the Archer family, Rebecca Watson, granddaughter of Timothy and Rebekah Archer, married Edward Houlden, rector of Ampthill, on 3 April 1673; since she was born on 1 January 1656, she married a few months after her seventeenth birthday.[65]

The notebook provides only a few clues about the circumstances of their married life. It seems likely that Rebecca Vaughan died at Wapping, a rough and tumble dockland east of London, and her effects were left with a Mr. and Mrs. Highgate, judging from the entries on folios 106^v and 107^r. It may be that Highgate was the "certain Apothecary in Wapping" with whom the Vaughans conducted experiments (folio 76^v), but a search of the records of the Worshipful Society of Apothecaries of London at the Guildhall Library proved fruitless.[66] Likewise no parish records can be found for the "Mr. Coaleman" of Holborne (at St. Andrew's, St. Etheldreda's or St. Dunstan's), with whom the Vaughans lodged (folio 104^v) before moving into an inn in the parish of St. Pancras called the Pinner of Wakefield (folios 12^r, 86^r, 87^v, 104^v, 105^v, and 106^v). Nothing significant is known of Sir John Underhill, with whom Vaughan took refuge for a while after leaving Wapping, other than that he was one of the many knights created by the Stuarts.[67]

---

[64] He was buried on 4 May 1680, *Bedfordshire Parish Registers: Meppershall*, B19. John Archer may have been a draper like his uncle John, who was mentioned in Dr. Thomas Archer's will as a London draper (BRO, ABP/w 1630/129, fol. 3).

[65] See Peter Laslett, *The World We Have Lost: Further Explored*, 3rd ed. (New York: Scribner, 1984), 81–84. Laslett reports that in his sample of over a thousand licenses between 1619 and 1660, nearly 85% married after the age of 19; but one woman gave her age as 13, four as 15, and twelve as 16. On 16 January 1647, one John Archer married Mary Collings at St. Dionis Backchurch, London (then located at the south-west corner of Lime Street and Fenchurch); since their children bore the common Archer family names (see note 11), he may very well have been the son of Timothy and Rebekah. If so, he married at eighteen.

[66] No apothecary named Highgate or from Wapping was listed. Neither tax records from Wapping nor parish records list the name Highgate.

[67] John Underhill was entered among the Knights Bachelor on 22 July 1626. See William A. Shaw, *The Knights of England: A Complete Record from the Earliest Times to the Present Day*, 2 vols. (London: Sherratt and Hughes, 1906), 2: 191.

B. REBECCA VAUGHAN AS
RESEARCH PARTNER AND IDEALIZED MUSE

What can yet be discerned about Rebecca Vaughan's work with her husband derives chiefly from the memorials and anecdotes Thomas recorded in his alchemical notebook, which was intended as a tribute to her and a record of their accomplishments. Evidence from this source indicates that she was involved in the discovery of the "aqua vitæ" mentioned in the notebook's title as well as an "Aqua Rebecca," and that she played a significant role in their alchemical experiments at London in the 1650s.

The odd format of the notebook can perhaps be attributed to Rebecca's influence. The entries on folios 3^r–39^v were made right side up, predominantly on the rectos; however, the remainder of the volume was filled in from the rear, with the retrograde text written upside down on the versos. That is, he turned the book to facilitate writing in it. The occasion for the fresh beginning was plainly the death of his wife, as the first reversed entry indicates:

> My most deare wife sickened on Friday in the Evening, being the 16 of April, and dyed the Saturday following in the Evening, being the 17. And was buried on ye 26 of the same Moenth, being a Monday in the Afternoone, att Mappersall in Bedfordshire. 1658.[68]

At this point he also created a new title page (folio 107^v), bearing the inscription *Ex Libris Th: et Reb: Vaughan* with the motto *Deo duce: comite Naturâ*, which identified the book as the joint intellectual property of Thomas and Rebecca Vaughan. He then constructed a distinctive monogram combining the initials T., R., and V. to mark most of the entries in the notebook.

From his inventory of her goods made at this new beginning (folio 106^v), it is clear that she was literate, that religion was important to her, and that she had only a few worldly possessions. Besides two trunks, her clothes, linen and pillows, a table and chairs, some silver spoons, and some fireplace implements (that would have served an alchemical furnace as well) were her Bibles, her copy of Bayley's *Practice of Piety*, and a few other devotional works. She had three Bibles: a pocket Bible, her "mayden Bible" (presumably a childhood gift that Thomas kept "by mee" for sentimental reasons), and a "greate Bible."

In what I believe was the second entry, Vaughan made clear not only that Rebecca had assisted him in his research, but that their work together from 1651–1658 produced a number of conceptual breakthroughs:

---

[68] Sloane 1741, fol. 106^v.

To the End wee might live well, and exercise our Charitie, which was wanting in neither of us, to our power: I employ'd my self all her life time in the Acquisition of some naturall secrets, to which I had been disposed from my youth up: and what I now write, and know of them practically, I attained to in her Dayes, not before in very trueth, nor after: but during the time wee lived together att the Pinner of Wakefield, and though I brought them not to perfection in those deare Dayes, yet were the Gates opened to mee then, and what I have done since, is but the effect of those principles. I found them not by my owne witt, or labour, but by gods blessing, and the Incouragement I received from a most loving, obedient wife, whome I beseech God to reward in Heaven, for all the Happines, and Content shee affoorded mee. I shall lay them downe heere in their order, protesting earnestly, and with a good Conscience, that they are the very trueth, and heere I leave them for his Use, and Benefit, to whome god in his providence shall direct them.[69]

Closer inspection of the manuscript reveals that Rebecca Vaughan had more than just an "incouraging" part in the experiments that were first assayed during that fruitful period when most of Thomas Vaughan's books were also written.

It was long assumed that the patriarchal gender relations of early modern Europe prevented women from playing any role in science, though that myth has since been laid to rest. In the first place, not all women were without education. Before the dissolution of the monasteries in Tudor England, convent schools flourished as centers of learning. Afterwards, a fortunate few, for example, the women of the Sidney family, received a private education at home that was as comprehensive as any public school's. Judging from the profession of Rebecca Vaughan's father and her own small library, we can presume that she received her education at home through her family. Secondly, since universities did not have formal curricula in the sciences or mathematics, those without university education were not automatically excluded from the practice of science, which was in many respects dominated by amateurs. Some women of talent and birth, such as Margaret Cavendish, Duchess of Newcastle, gained access to the world of learning through their family's circle. Other women, as Londa Schiebinger and Stanton Linden have shown, gained entrée to science in household

---

[69] Sloane 1741, fol. 105ᵛ. They lived at an inn, the Pinder of Wakefield, in Grays Inn Lane in the parish of St. Pancras; see Hutchinson, *Henry Vaughan*, 196–97.

workshops as assistants to their husbands.[70] Such was the case with Rebecca Vaughan, whose position alongside her husband in the laboratory was not without precedent. We can presume he encouraged her intellectual interests in that direction, judging from his comments on the suitability of women for laboratory work, published just before their marriage: "For my part I think *women* are fitter for it than men, for in such things they are more *neat* and *patient*, being used to a small *Chimistrie* of *Sack-possets*, and other finicall *Sugar-sops*."[71]

Sloane 1741 offers specific evidence that she in fact worked on experiments with him. As one would expect with laboratory formulas, the imperative mood was used most often. This convention gave us the familiar sign for chemists and pharmacists, ℞ for *recipe*, i.e., "take [the following ingredients.]" On occasion, however, Vaughan employed the first person plural forms, e.g., *facimus, scripsimus, diximus*, to indicate that together they had done something; and he signed half a dozen entries *Inquiunt* or *Dicunt, T. R. V.*, thus averring that they together said or proved such and such.[72] He also recorded some joint discoveries, notably an "aqua vitæ, which I found, when I lived with my deare Wife, att ye Pinner of wakefield." He named this compound *Aqua Rebecca* in her honor, "since my dearest spouse showed it to me from this sacred text. She showed it to me, I say, though I have otherwise never found it again."[73] Similarly, he repeatedly used the formulation *ut in diebus Conjugis meæ Charissimæ inventa est* to assert that a formula had previously been proved or tested with Rebecca during his married days. Even after her death, he continued to sign most of the entries with their combined initials.

Since Rebecca Vaughan was an active partner in alchemical experiments during their marriage, she may have been a part of the *Christian Learned Society* with Henshaw and her husband. Hartlib recorded that Henshaw's mother was also a chemist.[74] Because Anne Henshaw negotiated for the

---

[70] Londa Schiebinger, *The Mind Has No Sex?: Women in the Origins of Modern Science* (Cambridge: Harvard University Press, 1989), 66–101. For an interesting case in point, see Stanton J. Linden, "Mrs Mary Trye, Medicatrix: Chemistry and Controversy in Restoration England," *Women's Writing* 1 (1994): 341–53.

[71] *Magia Adamica: or, The Antiquitie of Magic, and the Descent thereof from Adam downwards, Proved* (London, 1650); in *Works*, 220.

[72] British Library MS, Sloane 1741, fols. 97^v and 100^v. He used *inquiunt* or *dicunt* on fols. 22^v, 24^r, 27^v, 35^r, 58^v, 75^v and 98^v. He also claimed on occasion (using first person singular) sole responsibility for an action. Twice he stated specifically that she had taught him some mystery or technique (fols. 86^r and 91^v).

[73] British Library MS, Sloane 1741, fol. 101^v: "Quam sic voco, Quoniam hanc ex sacrâ Scripturâ ostendebat mihi Conjux mea Charissima. Ostendebat (inquam) nec unquam aliter invenissem."

[74] In his *Ephemerides*, Sheffield University Library MS, Hartlib 28.1.43b, Samuel Hartlib recorded Henshaw's first visit to his Duke Street residence on 30 January 1650. He noted

new lease to their manor house in Kensington, called Pondhouse or Moat-house, in 1650, she almost certainly was living there when the society flourished in the early 1650s. Two women, therefore, may have been active.

While Thomas—older, formally educated, and more experienced—may have played the lead role, he attributed much of their joint success to her rather than to his own sagacity. At the end of one entry, he declared: "I discovered all this in the days of my dearest Wife, about whom I can say, what Solomon said about his wisdom: all good things came to me in like manner through her."[75] Like many alchemists, Vaughan believed success in the great work was always a *donum dei*. Success came, he confessed, "not by my owne witt, or labour, but by gods blessing" and he reproached himself for his own shortcomings on several occasions. Several anecdotes attest to this phenomenon and hence to her special talents. On the very day she was taken from him in death, for example, he recounted how he was gifted with the memory of a formula long since forgotten:

Memoriæ Sacrum.

On the same Day my deare wife sickened, being a Friday, and at the same time of the Day, namely in the Evening: my gracious god did put into my heart the Secret of extracting the oyle of Halcali, which I had once accidentally found att the Pinner of Wakefield, in the Dayes of my most deare Wife. But it was againe taken from mee by a wonderfull Judgement of god, for I could never remember how I did it, but made a hundred Attempts in vaine. And now my glorious god (whose name bee praysed for ever) hath brought it againe into my mind, and on the same Day my deare wife sickened; and on the Saturday following, which was the day shee dyed on, I extracted it by the former practice: Soe that on the same dayes, which proved the most sorowfull to me, that ever can bee: god was pleased to conferre upon mee ye greatest Joy I can ever have in this world, after her Death.

The Lord giveth, and the Lord
taketh away: Blessed bee the Name
of the Lord. Amen! T. R. V.[76]

---

that "His Father is dead a great chymist and so is his Mother who is yet alive. Hee keepes there [at Kensington] a Laboratorie and is not shye to ackn[owledge] to haue the Alchahest."

[75] British Library MS, Sloane 1741, fol. 100ᵛ: "Hæc omnia inveni in Diebus Vxoris meæ Charissimæ: de Quâ dicere possum, quod de Sapientiâ suâ dixit Solomon: Venerunt mihi paritèr cum Eâ, Omnia Bona &c."

[76] Sloane 1741, fol. 12ʳ.

Vaughan plainly regarded God's gift of the formula as recompense for taking Rebecca.

Similarly he regarded the two dreams that occurred on successive nights near the first anniversary of her death as *dona dei*. On the evening of 8 April 1659, suffering from a "suddaine Heavines of spirit, but without any manifest Cause whatsoever," he prayed contritely for pardon from his sins and to be reunited with his wife. That night it was revealed through a dream that God had foreordained their special relationship (to be discussed below); the second night, "after prayers, and hearty teares," his wife appeared in an enigmatic dream that hinted at the length of time before their reunion. She was arrayed "in greene silks downe to the ground, and much taller, and slenderer then shee was in her life time, but in her face there was so much glorie, and beautie, that noe Angell in Heaven can have more."[77] She appeared to him, that is, as the divine Thalia from his *Lumen de Lumine* (1651), who was attired "in *thin loose silks*, but so *green*, that I never saw the *like*, for the *Colour* was not *Earthly*."[78] Thalia, the attendant spirit at the Temple of Nature, guides Eugenius Philalethes'to the mythical source of the Nile, Ptolemy's *montes lunæ*, from whence flows the *prima materia* for the *magnum opus* out of a "stupendous *Cataract*, or *Waterfall*." Because Eugenius has been her servant for so long, she offers him her love, admits him to her *Schola Magica* to teach him its secrets, and gives him the privilege of publishing an emblematic representation of her sanctuary.[79] For Rebecca to be associated with the divine Thalia—be it for her spirituality, intuitive insights, or laboratory skills—is high praise indeed and commemorates her special contributions.

In addition to documenting the extent to which Rebecca Vaughan was active in pursuing alchemy, Sloane 1741 also affords us an intimate glimpse of a truly companionate marriage. Along with conventional tokens of affection—such as a "lock of my deare Wifes hayre, made up with her owne Hands" safeguarded in a small box, or the tenderness evident when he evoked her memory—we find a remarkable dream near the anniversary of her death that reveals the depths of their spiritual and emotional attachment. In the dream he declared to his friends that his father had chosen him a beautiful mate, with whom he immediately fell in love. In a marginal note, he clarified that "This was not true of our temporall mariage, nor of our natural parents, and therefore it signifies som greater mercie,"

---

[77] Sloane 1741, fols. 104ʳ, 103ʳ, and 102ʳ.

[78] *Lumen de Lumine*, in *Works*, 305. Rudrum, in a note in *Works*, 753, comments on this connection. See also his "Alchemy in the Poems of Henry Vaughan," *Philological Quarterly* 49 (1970): 472.

[79] *Lumen de Lumine*, in *Works*, 305–17. The emblem of the "Scholæ Magicæ Typvs," engraved by Robert Vaughan, is reprinted on p. 316.

which can only mean he believed that God himself had designated Rebecca for his eternal companion:

> I went that night to bed after earnest prayers, and teares, and towards the Day-Breake, or just upon it, I had this following dreame. I thought, that I was againe newly maried to my deare Wife, and brought her along with mee to shew her to some of my frends, which I did in these words. Heere is a wife, which I have not chosen of my self, *but my father did choose her for mee*, and asked mee, if I would not marry her, for shee was a beautifull Wife. Hee had no sooner shewed her to mee, but I was extremely in love with her, and I married her presently. when I had thus sayd, I thought, wee were both left alone, and calling her to mee, I tooke her into my Armes, and shee presently embraced mee, and kissed mee: nor had I in all this vision any Sinnfull desyre, but such a Love to her, as I had to her very soule in my prayers, to which this Dreame was an Answer. Hereupon I awaked presently, with exceeding great inward Joy. Blessed bee my God, Amen.[80]

This dream also gives greater point to the tag-phrase adapted from the wedding service used in signing some of the entries—*Quos Deus conjunxit, Quis separabit?*—for he believed they would soon be reunited in spiritual marriage. Her comeliness may thus be interpreted spiritually, as the dream of his wife as the ravishing Thalia in green silks would indicate. This combination of spiritual beauty and research acumen made his science possible.

One further matter that sheds light on the close relationship of Rebecca and Thomas Vaughan was his belief that she communicated intelligence about his future. In the months immediately following her death, he was visited by a series of premonitory dreams in which she presided as his spirit-world messenger. When she appeared on 13 June 1658, announcing she would die again in a few months' time, he recognized that she now figured or represented himself: "my mercifull god hath given mee this notice of the Time of my Dissolution by one that is soe deare unto mee, whose person representing mine, signified my death, not hers, for shee can dye noe more."[81] Later that month she appeared in a dream to predict, correctly as it turns out, his father's death: a letter arrived shortly after informing him that Thomas Vaughan, senior, had passed away in early June 1658.[82] On 16 July the presentiments of his impending death seemed even stronger when he was beset by the same ominous dream that troubled

---

[80] Sloane 1741, fol. 104ʳ.
[81] Sloane 1741, fol. 90ᵛ.
[82] Sloane 1741, fol. 89ᵛ.

Rebecca just before her death: he was pursued by a "stone-horse" [i.e., stallion] and consequently was "grieveously troubled all night with a suffocation att the Heart."[83] Then on 28 August he received, "after a wonderfull maner," his first assurance that she was resting with God, at which time "those mysterious words" of St. Paul about things temporal as opposed to things eternal were unveiled for him ("For we know that if our earthly house of this tabernacle were dissolved, we have a building of God, an house not made with hands, eternal in the heavens" [2 Corinthians 5:1]).[84] Though not every significant dream involved his wife—the vision of his father and younger brother William removing his body's corruption by sucking the sores of his feet is the most notable exception[85]—both the frequency and character of the dreams involving Rebecca suggest that theirs was an unusually close relationship. Sloane 1741 shows not only how strong their ties were during the days of their married life, but how vital she was to him psychically after her death: as tutelary spirit through the medium of his dreams, as spiritual lover who teaches him the sublime mysteries of eternal versus earthly love—in the tradition of Dante's Beatrice or Petrarch's Laura—and, perhaps most importantly, as an idealized muse.

C. THE VAUGHANS AS "EXPERIMENTAL PHILOSOPHERS"

"Spiritual" vs. Experimental Alchemy

Because fundamental questions about the nature of Vaughan's intellectual activities have remained unanswered, our understanding and appreciation of his achievements has been impeded, especially the degree to which he was an "experimental philosopher" as opposed to a "spiritual" alchemist. Certain passages in his published writings make it clear that he had little regard for those who *tortured metals*, thus lending support to the idea that he was interested only in mystical alchemy as opposed to work in the laboratory. This view of his activities has been fostered in this century through the editions of A. E. Waite, whose other works helped fuel the late Victorian mania for theosophy, hermeticism, and secret societies. While Waite acknowledged that Vaughan had experimented with metals,

---

[83] Sloane 1741, fol. 107[r]. The key to the symbolism here may be the fourth horseman of the Apocalypse: "And I looked, and behold a pale horse: and his name that sat on him was Death, and Hell followed with him" (Revelation 6:8).

[84] Sloane 1741, fol. 90[r].

[85] Sloane 1741, fol. 105[r]; also in *Works*, 591. Cf. the vision of whitish flames breaking out of the toes of his left foot, fol. 17[v].

he believed Vaughan's true subject was the union between God and the soul; thus, he regarded Vaughan as one in a long line of "spiritual" alchemists.[86] The conception of alchemy as primarily a form of spirituality was further popularized in this century by Carl Jung, who was interested in alchemy to the extent that it seemed to mirror his theories of psychological transformation. The writings of Thomas Vaughan, indeed, continue to enjoy a certain celebrity among those interested in esoteric philosophy. Waite's edition of *The Works of Thomas Vaughan: Mystic and Alchemist* has been frequently reprinted (whereas Rudrum's scholarly edition had only a meager print run and is virtually unavailable). Yet when the evidence provided by Sloane 1741 is set alongside the record of his activities with the *Christian Learned Society*, it is clear that the Vaughans were "experimental philosophers" involved in iatrochemical experiments and that the passages in Thomas Vaughan's writings bearing on "spiritual alchemy" need to be considered anew. Since Sloane 1741 has largely been ignored, the precise nature of Vaughan's own research consequently has thus remained obscure. Before looking closely at his public writings, it is helpful first to place them in context with the great issues of the time being raised by Bacon and Descartes.

Vaughan began his public career, brief though it was, during the turbulent 1650s. His writings ought to be seen as a part of the firestorm sparked by the work of Descartes. In his first two treatises, Vaughan aimed his vitriolic barbs at the idea of an atheistic, mechanistic universe, or as he later put it, at the "*Whymzies* of *des Chartes*."[87] He devoted considerable efforts to refuting the notion of a lifeless universe. As a youth he was fascinated with the hidden forces of the natural world—which "(I know not how) surpris'd my first youth, long before I saw the University."[88] With his first works, *Anthroposophia Theomagica* and *Anima Magica Abscondita* published together in 1650 under the pseudonym of Eugenius Philalethes, he established himself as an anti-Aristotelian and a defender of divine immanence in the universe.

Vaughan declared his allegiance to the new science by using the well-known epigraph from the title page of Bacon's *Novum Organum* for *An-*

---

[86] Thus in his edition of *The Magical Writings of Thomas Vaughan* (London, 1888), 9, Waite stated: "Vaughan was a mystic, and though he seems to have had some practice in alchemical work, his proclivities were mainly in the direction of mystical rather than of physical Alchemy." See also his introduction to *The Works of Thomas Vaughan: Mystic and Alchemist*, xxv–xlviii, and Stanton J. Linden, *Darke Hierogliphicks: Alchemy in English Literature from Chaucer to the Restoration* (Lexington: University Press of Kentucky, 1996), especially 224–46.

[87] *Anima Magica Abscondita* in *Works*, 137.

[88] *Works*, 521.

throposophia Theomagica: "Many shall run to and fro, and knowledge shall be increased" (Daniel 12:4).[89] Like Bacon he too was committed to the idea that the way to break open the sealed fountain of truth was empirical investigation:

> But it will be question'd perhaps, how shall we approach to the Lord, and by what means may we finde him out? Truely not with words, but with workes, not in studying ignorant, *Heathenish Authours*, but in perusing, and trying his *Creatures*: For in them Lies his secret path, which though it be shut up with thornes and Briars, with outward worldly Corruptions, yet if we would take the pains to remove this luggage, we might *Enter the Terrestriall Paradise*, that *Hortus Conclusus* of *Solomon*, where God descends to walk, and drink of the sealed Fountain.[90]

At the same time as he declared his commitment to the new empirical methodology, Vaughan dedicated the work to the most notorious of the mystical brotherhoods in early modern Europe, *Illustrissimis, et vere Renatis Fratribus R. C.* ("to the most illustrious and truly reborn brothers of the rosy cross"). These positions are not as cross-purposed as they might at first appear to modern readers, because the Rosicrucian manifestos were written as part of a campaign to foster a similar renewal in the early years of the seventeenth century.[91] Comparable historical exigencies, Vaughan maintained, compelled *him* to write, for as he observed in the preface to his first work, "It is an *Age* wherein *Trueth* is neere a *Miscarriage*, and it is enough for me that I have appeared *thus far for it*, in a *Day* of *Necessity*."[92]

When Vaughan brought out two years later the first print edition in English of the Rosicrucian manifestos and wrote an introduction defending their ideals, he became infamous as England's leading Rosicrucian, despite his repeated avowals that he had no personal acquaintance with the Rosicrucians.[93] While the *Athenæ Oxonienses* would identify him as a "great chymist, a noted son of the fire, an experimental philosopher," it also

---

[89] Rudrum, *Works*, 597, citing Charles Webster's *The Great Instauration* (London: Duckworth, 1975).

[90] *Anima Magica Abscondita* in *Works*, 115. As he indicated in the subtitle of his research notebook, he believed Nature must be "Mechanically, and Magically dissected, By the Conduct of Fire, and Ferment" (Sloane 1741, fol. 1ʳ).

[91] For a fuller account see Dickson, *The Tessera of Antilia*, chaps. 2–3.

[92] *Anthroposophia Theomagica* in *Works*, 53.

[93] Vaughan published *The Fame and Confession of the Fraternity of R.C., Commonly, of the Rosie Cross. With a Præface annexed thereto, and a short Declaration of their Physicall Work* (London, 1652), under his pseudonym Eugenius Philalethes, though he was not the translator. For his avowals see the Preface to the *Fame and Confession*, in *Works*, 483, 498. See also Linden, *Darke Hierogliphicks*, 266, 268, 278–79.

would characterize him as a "zealous brother of the Rosie-Crucian fraternity." This public perception would later be made indelible through the
satire of Samuel Butler and others.[94] During his pamphlet war with
Henry More in the early 1650s, Vaughan was further tarred with the brush
of *enthusiasm*.[95] As a result, his writings have been removed altogether
from their context in the intellectual debate of the time, and Vaughan himself turned into a caricature.

The problem of appreciating Vaughan's intellectual activities has since
been compounded by the marginalization of alchemy itself within the
academy, which viewed alchemy as either merely a metaphor for "spiritual" processes or, more typically, as intellectual fraud. Scholars now recognize that not all of those who pursued alchemical secrets in early modern
Europe were the sort satirized in Chaucer's figure of the Canon or Jon-
son's Face and Subtle. By the late sixteenth and early seventeenth centuries, alchemy had become an intellectually respectable, if controversial,
branch of natural philosophy that had little to do with gold-making. To its
adherents, alchemy offered insights into and a method of exploring the
fundamental processes and relationships of the universe, especially in the
new field of chemical medicine. From alchemical laboratories came knowledge of such basic compounds as alcohol, ammonia, nitric acid, and hydrochloric acid. For many respectable "scientists" and fellows of the Royal
Society, such as Sir Isaac Newton and Sir Robert Boyle, alchemy was a life-
long passion.[96] If a typology of alchemists were established, it would include in its broad spectrum the charlatans, the vulgar who sought gold for
personal enrichment, those who delved into nature's secrets using chemical
principles, and the mystics who pursued an esoteric philosophy. The com-

---

[94] *Athenæ Oxonienses*, 3: 723. Samuel Butler's sketch in *Characters*, ed. Charles W. Daves
(Cleveland and London: Press of Case Western Reserve University, 1970), 144–45, of the en-
thusiast who adores the *Brethren of the Rosy-Cross*, those *"Philosophers Errant*, that wander
up and down upon Adventures, and have an enchanted Castle, invisible to all but themselves," was probably based on Vaughan. So too was Sir Hudibras's Squire Ralph, in *Hudibras*, ed. John Wilders (Oxford: Clarendon Press, 1967), I.i.519–616; II.iii.613–40.

[95] See Noel L. Brann, "The Conflict Between Reason and Magic in Seventeenth-Century
England: A Case Study of the Vaughan-More Debate," *Huntington Library Quarterly* 1980
43(2): 103–26; and Frederic B. Burnham, "The More-Vaughan Controversy: The Revolt
Against Philosophical Enthusiasm," *Journal of the History of Ideas* 35 (1974): 33–49.

[96] See Betty Jo Teeter Dobbs, *The Foundations of Newton's Alchemy: or "The Hunting of
the Greene Lyon"* (Cambridge: Cambridge University Press, 1975) and *The Janus Faces of
Genius: The Role of Alchemy in Newton's Thought* (Cambridge: Cambridge University Press,
1991). On Boyle see the recent essays in *Robert Boyle Reconsidered*, ed. Michael Hunter
(Cambridge: Cambridge University Press, 1994) and Lawrence Principe, *The Aspiring Adept:
Robert Boyle and His Alchemical Quest* (Princeton: Princeton University Press, 1998). See
also Donald R. Dickson, "Thomas Henshaw, Sir Robert Paston and the Red Elixir: An Early Collaboration Between Fellows of the Royal Society," *Notes and Records of the Royal Society* 51 (1997): 57–76.

paratively rigorous program of research recorded in Sloane 1741 reveals that Vaughan, as an alchemical practitioner, sought scientific advances in a manner consistent with the other researchers of his age.

Certainly, some of Vaughan's contemporaries would agree with Patrick Scot's assertion in *The Tillage of Light* (1623) that alchemy was nothing more than an allegory for perfecting wisdom. However, many would strenuously disagree, notably Robert Fludd, who countered Scot with *Truth's Golden Harrow*, breaking his points down into twelve "furrows" that were in turn "harrowed" to find their "truth." Fludd also considered transmuting base metals into gold *chymia vulgaris*. While he believed (with Scot) that the true philosopher was concerned with the transmutation of the soul, he also maintained that the sought-after elixirs were materially real and not metaphorical.[97] Had Vaughan drafted a response, it would have been essentially the same as Fludd's, though Vaughan's stand on the issue of experimental alchemy is complicated by comments made in his published works, which castigated certain alchemists as *vulgar* precisely because they had lost sight of the higher dimensions of the work. He tagged them "broylers," faulting their preoccupation with transmuting metals, which, in his view, revealed an unsophisticated grasp of the mysteries of nature:

> The *common Chimist* dreams of *Gold* and *Transmutations*, most noble and *Heavenly Effects*, but the *Means* whereby hee would *compasse* them, are worme-eaten, dustie, mustie *papers*. His *Study* and his *Noddle* are stuff'd with *old Receits*, he can tell us a hundred *Stories* of *Brimstone* and *Quick-silver*, with many miraculous *Legends* of *Arsenic* and *Antimonie*, *Sal gemmæ*, *Sal prunæ*, *Sal Petræ*, and other stupendious *Alkalies*, as he loves to call them; with such strange *Notions* and *Charms* doth he *amaze*, and *silence* his *Auditors*, as *Bats* are kill'd with *Thunder* at the *Eare*. Indeed if this *Noyse* will carry it, let him alone, he can want no *Artillery*. But if you bring him to the *field*, and force him to his *Polemics*, if you *demand* his *Reason*, and *reject* his *Recipe*, you have laid him as *flat* as a *Flounder*. A rationall, methodicall *Dispute* will undoe him, for he studies not the whole *Body* of *Philosophie*: a *Receit* he would find in an old *Box*, or an old *Book*, as if the *knowledge* of *God* and *Nature* were a *thing* of *Chance*, not of *Reason*.[98]

The key to this puzzle lies in recognizing that alchemical research meant

---

[97] C. H. Josten, "*Truth's Golden Harrow*: An Unpublished Alchemical Treatise of Robert Fludd in the Bodleian Library," *Ambix* 3 (1949): 97–98.

[98] *Lumen de Lumine* in *Works*, 345–46.

more than turning base metals to gold. There was considerable interest in chemistry in England at the time (discussed further below) centered on producing medicaments in the wake of the revolution brought about by Paracelsus. To Vaughan and his circle, the true philosopher sought to discover the mysteries of the prime matter and the formation of the elements by experimentation in order to use these secrets for the benefit of mankind (the Creation too they regarded as essentially a divine chemical separation). He conceded that "in *metalls* there were great *secrets*, provided they be first reduc'd by a proper *Dissolvent*; but to seek that *Dissolvent*, or the *matter* whereof it is *made*, in *Metalls*, is not onely *Error* but *Madness*."[99] Without the evidence of Vaughan's practical applications and experiments, this statement appears to renounce experimental in favor of spiritual alchemy. To understand it properly, we need to place his theory in the context of his practice, i.e., Sloane 1741.

The issue is further complicated by the fact that the transmutation or radical transformation so central to alchemy has much in common with the promise of spiritual regeneration (of the microcosm) sketched out in the New Testament as well as with the creation of the macrocosm in Genesis. Luther noted as much in his *Table Talk*: "The alchemical art is in fact the natural philosophy of the ancients, which pleases me exceedingly, not only for the many benefits it conveys with itself in melting metals, likewise in distilling herbs and subliming liquids; I like it also for the sake of its allegory, which is exceedingly fine, on the resurrection of the dead at the last day."[100] Vaughan was certainly aware of alchemy's rich symbolism—its potent homologies with religious experience—and made use of this metaphoric relationship in his writings for the spiritual edification of his readers. As his private notebook everywhere reveals, he and his wife were deeply religious. For the theoretical foundation for his understanding of Nature, he was indebted to the account of the creation in Genesis, where "all *secrets Physicall* and *Spirituall*, all the *close Connexions*, and that *mysterious Kisse of God* and *Nature* is clearly and punctually discovered."[101]

His first work, in fact, which sought to defend the principle of divine immanence, *Anthroposophia Theomagica* (or "the divine-magical wisdom of mankind"), can be read as an exegesis of Genesis to show that the mysteries at the heart of alchemy are the same as those within the Trinity. The

---

[99] *Euphrates* in *Works*, 513.

[100] Martin Luther, *Tischreden*, 6 vols. (Weimar: Hermann Böhlaus Nachfolger, 1912), I, 1149: "Ars alchimica est vere illa veterum philosophia naturalis, quae mihi vehementer placet, cum propter alias multas utilitates, quas secum affert in excoquendis metallis, item herbis et liquoribus distillandis ac sublimandis, tum etiam propter allegoriam, quam habet pulcherrimam, resurrectionem mortuorum in die extremo."

[101] *Anima Magica Abscondita* in *Works*, 120.

original act of creation, he explained, was brought about through the "Processe of the *Trinity* from the *Center* to the *Circumference*" with the Father as supernatural foundation, the Son as Idea or Logos, and the Holy Spirit as agent.

> No sooner had the Divine *Light* pierced the *Bosom* of the Matter, but the *Idea*, or Pattern of the whole Material World appeared in those *primitive waters, like* an *Image* in a *Glasse*: by this Pattern it was that the Holy Ghost fram'd and modelled the Universal Structure. This Mystery or appearance of the *Idea* is excellently manifested in the *Magicall Analysis* of Bodies: (For he that knows how to imitate the *Proto-Chymistrie* of the Spirit, by Separation of the Principles wherin the Life is Imprisoned, may see the Impresse of it Experimentally in the outward naturall vestiments.)[102]

After the *Spiritus Opifex* and the divine Logos first informed the *primitive waters* or prime matter, a series of separations or reductions took place. A *"thin Spirituall Cœlestiall substance"* was extracted and given a "tincture" of heat and light, which provided bodies for the angels. The next separation produced the *"Inter-stellar skie"* and so on. The creation of sublunary Nature was accomplished by an active masculine principle and a passive feminine one, figured as earth and water with the agency of light, but in actuality the prime alchemical materials, sulphur and mercury.

> Remember the *practice*, and *Magic* of the *Almightie God* in his *Creation*, as it is *manifested* to thee by *Moses*. *In principio* (saith he) *creavit Deus Cœlum et Terram*: But the *Originall* if it be truly, and rationally *renderd*, speaks thus, *In principio Deus miscuit Rarum, et Densum*; In the Beginning God *mingl'd* or *temper'd together the Thin* and the *Thick*: for *Heaven and Earth* in this *Text* (as we have told you in our *Anima Magica*) signifie the *Virgin Mercury* and *Virgin Sulphur*.[103]

The separations and rarefactions that occurred in the alchemist's alembic—*chymia* usually was defined as "the art of separating pure from impure, and of making essences"[104]—thus imitated the primal creative act.

Vaughan believed, therefore, that the *"Primitive, Original Existence"* of

---

[102] *Anthroposophia Theomagica* in *Works*, 58–59.

[103] *Lumen de Lumine* in *Works*, 334–35 (referring to *Anima Magica Abscondita* in *Works*, 120); *Anthroposophia Theomagica* in *Works*, 61–65.

[104] Gerhard Dorn, *A Chymical Dictionary: Explaining Hard Places and Words Met withal in the Writings of Paracelsus and Other Obscure Authors*, trans. John French, 2nd ed. (London, 1674), 319.

the alchemical mystery was found in God himself.[105] From this fundamental understanding followed a series of further correspondences. As an
amalgam of base earth and mud with spirit, the human body similarly
needed to be reborn by water and fire.

> The *Laws* of the *Resurrection* are founded upon *those* of the *Crea-
> tion*, and those of *Regeneration* upon those of *Generation*, for in *all
> these* God works upon *one*, and the *same Matter*, by *one* and the
> *same spirit*.[106]

Or as he put it more succinctly, "*Salvation* it self is nothing else but *transmutation*."[107] He found ample references to the "*Christian Philosophers
stone*" throughout Scripture: the mysterious rock whose waters sustained
the Israelites in the wilderness (Numbers 20:7–11), the stones of fire in Eze-
kiel (28:14), the stone with seven eyes upon it in Zechariah (3:9), and the
white stone with the new name written upon it in Revelation (2:17).[108]
He noted, too, that in his mission on earth Christ worked miracles on
bodies even though he was more interested in souls.[109] Vaughan's understanding of alchemy was thus predicated on the mystery of the creation.
The emphasis he placed on the many biblical types and analogues to alchemy suggests how important it was for him. Or as he put it in his last
work, *Euphrates* (1655), "*Experience*, and *Reason* grounded *thereupon*, have
taught me, that *Philosophie* and *Divinity* are but one, and the same science."[110] Yet as potent as these biblical origins and correspondences were
for Vaughan, alchemy was not simply a metaphor for him. The comparatively rigorous program of research recorded in Sloane 1741 demonstrates
clearly that Vaughan, as an alchemist or chemist, sought scientific advances
in a manner consistent with other scientists of his age.

Vaughan's laboratory record illustrates the degree to which the technical aspects of what has been called the "most flourishing laboratory tradition" before the scientific revolution had been raised.[111] Terminology
and procedures were becoming more standardized and (somewhat) demys-
tified with the publication of such student's manuals on the *techne* of

---

[105] *Magia Adamica* in *Works*, 155.

[106] *Magica Adamica* in *Works*, 185.

[107] *Lumen de Lumine* in *Works*, 357.

[108] *Anima Magica Abscondita* in *Works*, 132–33.

[109] *Magia Adamica* in *Works*, 167–68.

[110] *Euphrates* in *Works*, 519.

[111] Dobbs, *Foundations of Newton's Alchemy*, p. 64. On the competition between the
iatro-chemists and the Galenists, see Charles Webster, "English Medical Reformers of the
Puritan Revolution: A Background to the 'Society of Chymical Physicians,'" *Ambix* 14
(1967): 16–41; and Harold J. Cook, "The Society of Chymical Physicians, the New Philosophy, and the Restoration Court," *Bulletin of the History of Medicine* 61 (1987): 61–77.

chemistry as Jean Beguin's *Tyrocinium Chymicum* (1610), a text that appeared in more than forty editions during the seventeenth century.[112] Studies by historians of science have made it increasingly clear that alchemy was virtually indistinguishable from chemistry in the seventeenth century, as the examples of Newton and Boyle show. While the record provided by Sloane 1741 is ample evidence of the experimental nature of Vaughan's own research program, we also know that Vaughan's quondam partner Henshaw boasted to Hartlib of possessing the *alkahest*—or universal solvent of prepared mercury—that would yield the prime ingredient for the work and thus the secrets of nature.[113]

A further glimpse into his research activities is provided by the meager evidence of his association with the chemical circle at the court of Charles II. We know that Vaughan's patron Sir Robert Moray played a role in setting up a royal laboratory at Whitehall and served as an intermediary for the king with the Royal Society. As a result, Vaughan may very well have been part of these experiments. We know that Vaughan was in the entourage when the king left London for Oxford to escape the plague in 1665; according to his brother, Thomas was "vpon an imployment for his majesty."[114] He and Moray took lodging at the rectory in nearby Albury (perhaps at the laboratory Oughtred had set up when he was rector) where they conducted experiments, during which "as it were suddenly, when he was operating strong mercury, some of which by chance getting up into his nose killed him."[115]

The Vaughans and the Iatrochemical Revolution

A careful examination of the Sloane manuscript reveals that the Vaughans were part of the most important development in medicine in a millennium, the advent of chemical medicaments. Medical theory until this time was dominated by the Galenic notion that disease was a general imbalance in the body's humoral system that could be remedied by its contrary—e.g., an excess of the "hot" quality could be tempered with something "cold." Paracelsus started a revolution when he insisted that all di-

---

[112] Allen G. Debus, *The French Paracelsians: The Chemical Challenge to Medical and Scientific Tradition in Early Modern France* (Cambridge: Cambridge University Press, 1991), 82.

[113] Samuel Hartlib, *Ephemerides* (December 1649), Sheffield University Library MS, Hartlib 28.1.37a: "One Hinshaw about Kensington a Gentl[man] of 2. or 300. a y[ear] a universal Schollar and pretty communicativ. Hee pretends to have the Alchahest or a true dissolvent." Henshaw acquired a manuscript of J. B. van Helmont's formula for the *alkahest* that had been given to Sir Hugh Platt when van Helmont was in England.

[114] Letter to Aubrey, in *The Works of Henry Vaughan*, 687. Hutchinson, *Henry Vaughan*, 144, also agrees that Thomas was employed by the crown.

[115] *Athenæ Oxonienses*, 3: 725.

sease was localized in a part of the body. "Seeds" of disease grew in the body in the same way that metals were propagated from "seeds" and nurtured within an aliment in the earth. The basic treatment, moreover, ought to be homeopathic: like cures like, or *similia cum similibus* as it was usually put.[116] That is, he assumed that the poison that caused a disease would also cure it if administered properly (as twentieth-century immunization theory upholds). The task of the chemist was to remove the toxic quality of the drug, which Paracelsus accomplished, for example, by using mercury compounds instead of the metal itself.[117] Within thirty years of the death of Paracelsus in 1548, a school of "Paracelsian" physicians existed which advocated the use of chemically prepared remedies from mercury, arsenic, and, most controversially, antimony. These principles, usually called *iatrochemistry*, were championed in England by the chief physician to the court, Turquet de Mayerne.[118] At the heart of Paracelsus's philosophy was a belief in an empirically observable chemistry as the foundation of Nature, rather than in the mathematical abstractions or the study of motion taught in the schools. While he referred to the four Aristotelian elements in his writings, he believed a second set of elementary substances to be more significant, the *tria prima* of mercury, sulphur, and salt. Paracelsus's ideas, therefore, presented a multifaceted challenge to the medical establishment and universities of Europe, which were predicated on traditional Aristotelian elemental theory.

The stock of the apothecary in earlier times had been nearly all herbal in origin. After the flowering of iatrochemistry in the late sixteenth century, apothecaries, using the principles of Paracelsus, began a search in their laboratories for chemically prepared medicaments. Chemistry was gradually accepted in the seventeenth century for its practical pharmaceutical value. The Royal College of Physicians included a section on chemical medicines in its first *Pharmacopœia Londinensis* (1618)—and had intended such a section for its earlier (unpublished) pharmacopeia of 1585. While English physicians were willing to use chemical remedies, Paracelsus him-

---

[116] Walter Pagel, *Paracelsus: An Introduction to Philosophical Medicine in the Era of the Renaissance*, 2nd ed. (Basel: Karger, 1982), 129–48.

[117] For a full account, see Allen G. Debus, *The English Paracelsians* (New York: Franklin Watts, 1966) and *The French Paracelsians*.

[118] Mayerne (1573–1655), French-born physician and Baron of Aubonne, studied at Heidelberg and Montpelier (M.D. in 1597) and practiced at Paris. When his interest in iatrochemistry earned him the censure of the French College of Physicians in 1603, he moved to London in 1611, becoming a fellow of the College of Physicians and royal physician to James. Biographical articles may be found in the *Dictionary of National Biography*, 37: 150–52, and the *Dictionary of Scientific Biography*, 13: 507–9. See Brian K. Nance, "Determining the Patient's Temperament: An Excursion into Seventeenth-Century Medical Semeiology," *Bulletin of the History of Medicine* 67 (1993): 417–38.

self, however, was looked on with suspicion and was scarcely mentioned in the *Pharmacopœia Londinensis*.[119] By mid-century even the Royal College of Physicians had established a chemical laboratory at its Physic Garden in Chelsea in the charge of William Johnson ("chymicus noster"),[120] and Sir Thomas Browne would include the writings of Beguin, Daniel Sennert, and Heinrich Crollius in his list of essential writings for the medical student.[121]

With their experience in the laboratory and their familiarity with Paracelsian principles, the potential allies of apothecaries and the so-called chemical physicians, as one might suspect, were the alchemists. Indeed the connection was often close.[122] The stereotypes of gold-making charlatans persisted, however, prompting Beguin's caution at the opening of his chemical handbook, *Tyrocinium Chymicum*:

> how egregiously they are deceived, who, hearing the name of an Alchymist, presently conclude that Man imploys himself in nothing else, than the transmutation or Metamorphosing of Metals, and meditates on no other thing than the wonderful Mystery of the Philosophick Stone; Whereas the intention of this Artist, is to prepare most sweet, most wholesome, and most safe Medicaments.[123]

Medicine was, in the opinion of Vaughan's brother the poet, who had declared, in response to queries from his kinsman Aubrey, with whom he had begun to correspond when Aubrey was collecting biographical data for Anthony Wood's *Athenæ Oxonienses*: "My brothers imploym^t was in physic & Chymistrie. ... My profession allso is physic."[124] Like his twin brother, a practicing country doctor who translated two iatrochemical works, namely Heinrich Nolle's *Hermetical Physick* (1655) and *The Chymist's Key* (1657), Thomas Vaughan utilized the principles of chemical medicine throughout his notebook.

---

[119] Debus, *English Paracelsians*, 153–54.

[120] H. Charles Cameron, *A History of the Worshipful Society of Apothecaries of London, Volume I: 1617–1815*, rev. ed. (London: Wellcome Historical Medical Museum, 1963), 93.

[121] Frank Livingstone Huntley, *Sir Thomas Browne: A Biographical and Critical Study* (Ann Arbor: University of Michigan Press, 1962), 70.

[122] On the competition between the iatrochemists and the Galenists, see Charles Webster, "English Medical Reformers of the Puritan Revolution: A Background to the 'Society of Chymical Physicians,' " *Ambix* 14 (1967): 16–41; and Harold J. Cook, "The Society of Chymical Physicians, the New Philosophy, and the Restoration Court," *Bulletin of the History of Medicine* 61 (1987): 61–77.

[123] Jean Beguin, *Tyrocinium Chymicum: or, Chymical Essays Acquired from the Fountain of Nature, and Manual Experience*, trans. Richard Russell (London, 1669), 2–3.

[124] Letter, Henry Vaughan to John Aubrey, 15 June 1673, from Brecon, Bodleian Library MS. Wood F 39, fol. 216, in *The Works of Henry Vaughan*, 688.

Though Vaughan was accused by More and others of uttering, like Hamlet, only wild and whirling words, his fundamental positions on natural philosophy were internally consistent, based on authoritative sources, and reasonably simple (even if they seem difficult for modern readers). About the influences on his thinking and the direction of his chemical research there is little doubt, for he proudly announced in print that Cornelius Agrippa, whose picture adorned his first work, Johannes Trithemius, Johannes Reuchlin, and Michael Sendivogius were his masters, calling himself "an *Usher* to the *Traine*, and one borne out of due time."[125] William R. Newman has ably traced the lineage of Vaughan's ideas from Agrippa and Sendivogius.[126] From his frequent invocation in his notebook of the authority of the pseudo-Lullian *Testamentum* (ca. 14th c.) and the Polish alchemist Sendivogius, we can also locate his research within the framework of contemporary theory. Most natural philosophers believed that metals were propagated from "seeds" and nurtured (in the same fashion as the human fetus) in the earth in an aliment known as *sophic mercury* that was considered the mother of all metals. Just as in natural generation, where seed was multiplied into corn by the husbandman, so in minerals was there a sperm for multiplying; most chemists failed because the earth or vessel in which the seed was buried was too cold or the heat used to nurture the seed was too hot.[127] The *Testamentum* considered philosophic salt a substance necessary to every stage of the alchemical opus, because it was the medium through which nature produced metals from the *sophic mercury*.[128] To the common belief that the great work of transformation meant uniting the fixed with the volatile principles (i.e., *sophic sulphur* with *sophic mercury*), Sendivogius emphasized especially the role of "centric salt" (*sal nitrum*) within the earth in nurturing these metallic "seeds."[129] In fact many chemical philosophers, such as Bernard Palissy, Joseph Duchesne, Robert Fludd, Johann Glauber, and Nicolas Le Fèvre, believed the life force or *spiritus mundi* was actually an aerial saltpeter within the grosser air that turned into arterial blood. For example, recognizing that air was essential for both fire and life, Le Fèvre believed saltpeter to be the

---

[125] *Magica Adamica* in *Works*, 154.

[126] See *Gehennical Fire*, 213–21; and "Thomas Vaughan as an Interpreter of Agrippa von Nettesheim," *Ambix* 29 (1982): 125–40.

[127] Preface to the *Fame & Confession* in *Works*, 505–6.

[128] See Michela Pereira, *L'oro dei filosofi: saggio sulle idee di un alchimista del Trecento* (Spoleto: Centro Italiano di Studi sull'Alto Medioevo, 1992), 166–73.

[129] "By *Earth*, I understand not this impure fæculent *body*, on which we *tread*, but a more simple pure *element*, namely the *naturall centrall salt* Nitre. This *salt* is fixed or permanent in the *Fire*, and it is the *sulphur* of *Nature*, by which she retains and congeales her *Mercurie*" (*Euphrates* 538–39). See Zbigniew Szydło, *Water Which Does Not Wet Hands: The Alchemy of Michael Sendivogius* (Warsaw: Polish Academy of Sciences, 1994), 93–125.

"universal salt," possessing within itself the *spiritus mundi*.[130] (Since Le Fèvre was the royal chemist of Charles II, Vaughan, through the offices of his patron Sir Robert Moray, may even have worked with him at the king's laboratory.) All in all, there was significant interest in the mid-seventeenth century in the role of salts in the procreation and sustenance of life, e.g., in dissolved salt from dung as a fertilizing agent. Vaughan's quondam research partner Henshaw, we know, signed at least one letter to Sir Robert Paston as "Halophilus," i.e., "salt-lover," and was involved in such research and spoke before the Royal Society on the history and manufacture of saltpeter.[131]

So too were the Vaughans within the chemical mainstream in their use of various salts in their laboratory experiments, including sodium chloride, borax, saltpeter, a salt they called *scarabæus*, and, very frequently, *sal ammoniac* for washing or purifying processes.[132] (Any solid that was soluble in water was considered a salt; hence there were neutral salts as well as acids and alkalis.) Roughly half of their experiments involved work of this kind; nearly all of the research involved substances that were used as medicaments, as the notes and the glossary will show. The notebook also catalogues a wide variety of recipes from favorite authors, such as Ramon Lull, Paracelsus, Sendivogius, and Basil Valentine, as well as their own discoveries, notably an "aqua vitæ, which I found, when I lived with my deare Wife, att ye pinner of wakefield," and several versions of an "Aqua Rebecca."[133]

More than fifty of the experiments (about half) clearly involved the preparation of medicines—either involving herbal preparations for scammony, rhubarb, larch fungus, senna, cassia, jalap root, the sap of panax,

---

[130] Nicolas Le Fèvre, *A Compleat Body of Chymistry*, 2nd ed., 2 vols. in 1 (London, 1670), 2: 251–55. See Allen G. Debus, *The Chemical Philosophy: Paracelsian Science and Medicine in the Sixteenth and Seventeenth Centuries*, 2 vols. (New York: Science History Publications, 1977), 1: 109; 2: 495.

[131] Letter, Halophilus [Thomas Henshaw] to Sir Robert Paston at Oxnead, 5 November 1663, Norfolk Record Office, Bradfer-Lawrence MS, 1c/1. See British Library MS, Sloane 243, a copy of the first Register Book of the Royal Society: Nr. 18: "The History of the Making of Salt Peeter. By M^r. Henshaw" (fols. 43^v–48^r); "The Manner of making Salt Peeter" (fols. 48^v–51^r); "To Refine Saltpeeter" (fols. 51^v–53^r); "The History of making Gunpowder" (fols. 53^v–57^r). See Dickson, "Thomas Henshaw, Sir Robert Paston and the Red Elixir," 57–76.

[132] Vaughan's experiments with saltpeter were known. The alchemist William Backhouse remarked (June 1651) to Elias Ashmole that Vaughan was working "upon the spirit of salt-petre / and of late he added May-dew to it"; see *Elias Ashmole (1617–1692): His Autobiographical and Historical Notes, His Correspondence, and Other Contemporary Sources Relating to his Work*, ed. C. H. Josten, 5 vols. (Oxford: Clarendon Press, 1966), 2: 575. For a discussion of the theory underlying Vaughan's alchemy, see Newman, *Gehennical Fire*, 213–22.

[133] Sloane 1741, fols. 87^v, 101^v, 97^v, and 93^v.

narcotics, such as opium, or mineral compounds used as medicaments, such as *crocus metallorum*. The Vaughans used alcohol to separate the essences of mercury and sulphur from the plant salts by extraction (as opposed to fermentation). The Paracelsian term *arcanum* was also used (on thirty-seven separate occasions) to denote a medicine whose secret "virtue" allowed it to act directly (as opposed to Galenic medicines that balanced or tempered the elements). Paracelsus believed that each of the four elements contained a fifth, the quintessence, an ethereal substance that constituted its "virtue" and was the vehicle for the special powers in herbs or iatrochemical medicines.

While Vaughan may very well have supported himself by preparing such medicaments, he was further driven by altruistic motives, judging from the private thanksgiving he recorded for a dream in which God revealed "A Notable Medicine to Reduce Fever":

> I dreamed that I had intended to fashion a certain medicine mixed from nitric salt and crystals of tartar. ... I hope that God has shown and shared this to me, a most unworthy sinner, in solace of those suffering fever. For which gift of His mercy, eternal praise be to Him.[134]

Such sentiments in a work not intended for the public eye help us see that his interests lay in medicine, just as his experiments show he had nothing to do with gold-making.

As discussed above, Vaughan held vulgar alchemy in little regard. Even so, metals such as antimony, lead, tin, and the like, were used in some experiments. A curious biographical disclosure in one of his published works may explain this inconsistency. After the invective and ridicule he suffered publicly at the hands of Henry More, he was silent for nearly four years. Then, in *Euphrates* (1655), he reminded his readers of his previous writing, or "Judgements of *Philosophie*"—as he called them—"I say of *Philosophie*, for *Alchymie* in the common acceptation, and as it is a *torture* of *Metalls*, I did never believe; much less did I study it." He went on:

> But to acquaint thee how *ingenuous* I am, I freely confess, that in my *practise* I waved my own *principles*, for having miscarried in my *first attempts*, I laid aside the *true subject*; and was contented to follow their *Noise*, who will hear of nothing but *Metalls*. What a Drudge I have been in *fœtid* and *fœculent School*, for three years to-

---

[134] Sloane 1741, fol. 54ᵛ: "Somniabam me medicam quandam mixturam ex Anatro et Crystallis Tartari intentasse. ... Hoc mihi peccatori indignissimo, in solatium Ægrorum febricitantium, monstrasse Deum, et impartivisse spero: Pro quo Misericordiæ suæ dono, sit illi Laus Æterna."

gether, I will not here tell thee, it was well that I quitted it at last, and walk'd again into that *clear light*, which I had foolishly forsaken.[135]

This confession may shed some light on one of Vaughan's most puzzling episodes: his action at law with Edward Bolnest, who had brought a Chancery suit against him in May 1661, alleging that four or five years before Vaughan had promised to instruct him in "naturall phylosophy and Chimicall physicke" in exchange for £300.[136] Having learned the principles from him, Bolnest had reneged and forcibly tried to recover £30 in expenses. Vaughan then agreed to "make known to [Bolnest] a certain physicall receipt of . . . great use" in exchange for being released from all further obligations. In 1661 Bolnest finally decided to bring Vaughan to the Court of Marshalsea, claiming that he had often "most solemnly vowed and swore he could at his leasure produce and make" the philosophers' stone. No record of the judgment has been found, and Rudrum's suspicion of fraud on Bolnest's part seems likely. Nonetheless, if Vaughan was casual in his deposition with the dates, and we can push them back a year or so to 1655, the Bolnest affair would nicely explain the sudden break. So too would it jibe with George Starkey's claim that Vaughan had cheated some people out of considerable sums of money.[137] The notebook itself offers some corroborating evidence of his activities with metals.

As befits one who placed himself in the Baconian vanguard, Vaughan carefully recorded the details of his experiments. The text gives evidence of having been amended with new material being added at a later time. These modifications show the care he took in recording procedures and correcting mistakes. He specified the proper operation, the necessary apparatus, the quantities of materials, and, to a lesser extent, the grade of heat and the duration of each operation. He differentiated between *assation*, roasting or incinerating a substance in a glass vessel to desiccate it; *calcination*, heating a solid substance at a high temperature to reduce it to a fine powder; *cohobation*, repeated distillation; *decoction*, separation of pure from impure substances through a gentle heat; *distillation*, heating a substance to convert it into a vapor, then cooling it to extract its essence by condensation; and *putrefaction*, decomposing or disintegrating a substance, usually by chemical means. He frequently specified the apparatus required: alembic, athanor, crucible, glass spheres, matrass, retort, *sextum barbatum*, or even a common iron pot. As the subtitle to Vaughan's notebook—*The Radical Hu-*

---

[135] *Euphrates* in *Works*, 513.

[136] Rudrum, *Works*, 17–21, discusses the case and transcribes the relevant Chancery documents.

[137] Newman, *Gehennical Fire*, 222.

miditie of Nature: Mechanically, and Magically dissected, By the Conduct of Fire, and Ferment—indicates, the key to success in most operations lay in controlling the heat, which was accomplished by using various sources (the thermometer being not yet available). The lowest grade was produced by a warm water bath, the *balneum Mariæ*, named for its inventor, the legendary Maria the Jewess or Maria Prophetissa. The next grade was produced by a fire kindled under a pan of ashes or cinders. The third grade was compared to boiling sand or iron filings. The fourth grade, the fiercest, was produced from coals and a bellows.[138] While Vaughan sometimes specified a *balneum Mariæ* or *balneum roris* (a steam bath) or instructed that something be heated *in cineribus* or *in arenâ*, more often than not he indicated only that it be done *igne modo, igne moderato, igne fortissimo*, or *igne violento*. He took less pains to indicate the duration of experiments, which were indicated in hours or days.

Typically Vaughan gave the quantities of the ingredients using a ratio of parts, as for example in his recipe for the spirits of common mercury:

Place [equal] parts vitriol and mercury in a retort; pour in aqua fortis in an equal weight of mercury. Decoct with the heat of the ashes for two days. Then distill, and if the fumes do not wish to be resolved into a vapor, pour in a little distilled water, and immediately it will succeed. Dissolve new mercury often in this rectified spirit, and proceed until you have enough.[139]

Occasionally he used weights as in a recipe for a calcinated water, attributed to Ramon Lull.[140] These examples from Sloane 1741 show that the Vaughans' chemical experiments in the 1650s were empirically rigorous, even in comparison to many of those performed before the Royal Society the following decade.

To modern readers the language of the notebook may seem encoded in exotic and unfamiliar ways. Because of its origins in Greco-Roman Egypt as a metaphysical as well as physical inquiry into the innermost secrets of

---

[138] Vaughan discusses of the various grades in *Magica Adamica*, 221–23; see also Martin Ruland, *A Lexicon of Alchemy*, ed. and trans. A. E. Waite (London: 1893; rpt. Kila, MT: Kessinger, 1991), 180.

[139] Sloane 1741, fol. 9ʳ: "Olei vitri & Mercurii partes pone in Retortâ: affunde Aquam fortem ad pondus Mercurii. Digere in Cineribus per dies duos. Tunc distilla, & si fumi nolunt in Humorem Resolvi, affunde parum de Aquâ distillatâ, & statim succedet. Hoc spiritu sæpius rectificato solve novum [mercurium] & procede donèc satìs habeas."

[140] Sloane 1741, fol. 55ᵛ: "Aluminis & vitrioli calcinatorum lib[ram] 1. nam vitriolum viride valet loco vitrioli Azoquei, in confectione Aquæ n[ostr]æ primæ. Cinnabaris, vel magnesiæ Cinnabarinæ lib[ram] 1. salis nitri lib[ram] 1. Distilla nudo igne, sed relicto spiraculo, et fiet."

God's creation, alchemy's practitioners relied on symbolic language to protect their mysteries from the unworthy. This symbolic tradition also has epistemological roots, as Lyndy Abraham has observed:

> Alchemical symbols expressed the philosophical properties residing in matter as well as the outer form of that chemical matter. Such a philosophical experience of matter existed beyond the scope of the rational mind, and could only be adequately expressed in symbol, emblem, paradox and allegory.[141]

Alchemical writing had much in common with the Renaissance emblem tradition. Both arts were predicated on the underlying unity in the created universe; both the alchemist and the emblematist delighted in simultaneously discovering and concealing these correspondences through symbols.[142] As was customary for his day, Vaughan always used alchemical symbols for metals based on the celestial analogues of the seven prime metals—gold, silver, iron, mercury, tin, copper and lead (e.g., ☉ for gold); he sometimes used standard notations for chemical operations, such as ⧧ for firing in a crucible; and he frequently used coded names or alchemical *Decknamen* to refer to certain substances postulated by alchemists, such as *aquila* for the volatile principle, or *lac virginis* for the *prima materia*. Especially typical was the use of the adjective "philosophical"—e.g., *plumbo philosophico* (fol. 5ᵛ), *stybii philosophici* (fol. 7ʳ), or *flores philosophicos* (fol. 10ᵛ)—attached to certain substances. While the use of such exotic language in part served the same function as symbolic notation or abbreviations do for scientists today—convenience—it also enabled adepts to control access to secret knowledge, to protect trade secrets, and to enhance the mystery of their art. While I do not credit the notion that all alchemical language is intrinsically paradoxical and hence unfathomable, we should still recognize the language of alchemy is often steeped in mystery for a reason.[143]

Vaughan's notebook shows that he was a master of these secret vocabularies, just as his printed work demonstrates his skill in the interpretation of difficult allegories. He had remarked in *Anthroposophia Theomagica* that since most people were accustomed only to seeing the "Barke of *Allegories*," his own explanations of nature's hidden mysteries would seem

---

[141] Lyndy Abraham, *A Dictionary of Alchemical Imagery* (Cambridge: Cambridge University Press, 1998), xvii.

[142] Abraham, *Alchemical Imagery*, xviii. See also Don Cameron Allen's classic study, *Mysteriously Meant: The Rediscovery of Pagan Symbolism and Allegorical Interpretation in the Renaissance* (Baltimore: Johns Hopkins University Press, 1970).

[143] For an overview of the languages of alchemy, see Gareth Roberts, *The Mirror of Alchemy: Alchemical Ideas and Images in Manuscripts and Books from Antiquity to the Seventeenth Century* (Toronto: University of Toronto Press, 1994), 65–91.

strange. He observed further that many texts could only be understood allegorically:

> I will now digresse a while; but not much from the purpose, where-by it may appear unto the Reader that the *letter* is no sufficient *Expositor* of *Scripture*, and that there is a great deal of difference between the *sound* and sense of the *Text. Dionysius* the *Areopagit* in his Epistle to *Titus* gives him this Caveat. *Et hoc præterea Operæ prætium est cognoscere: Duplicem esse Theologorum Traditionem, Arcanum Alteram, ac mysticam: Alteram vero manifestam, et notiorem.* And in his Book of the *Eclesiastical Hierarchie* written to *Timotheus,* he affirms, that in the *primitive, Apostolical times,* wherein he also lived, the mysteries of Divinity were delivered *partim scriptis, partim non scriptis Institutionibus.*[144]

Oral traditions have long been associated with sacred texts: for example, accompanying the Torah were the oral commentaries known as the *Mishnah,* which according to Jewish tradition Moses had received on Mount Sinai and transmitted to Joshua (and were not written down until 200 A.D.). Implicit in these traditions, especially in what came to be known as *prisca theologia,* was the necessity to conceal esoteric wisdom from the vulgar.[145] The belief that some knowledge ought to be reserved only for an elite was in earlier times far more widespread than now. In every guild or craft in the Middle Ages, masters safeguarded the "mysteries" for the good of all.

Secrecy was certainly used to conceal the sharp practices of the charlatan, but so too was it common for persons to form partnerships for commercial ventures, licensed in the Patent Rolls, which bound the principals to confidentiality. For example, among the papers of Dr. Robert Plot, the first professor of chemistry in the University of Oxford, is a draft agreement, dated 1677, concerning a partnership to prepare and sell chemical medicines. In return for the secrets of preparing the *elixir, alkahest,* and *grand arcanum* to be supplied by Plot, the agreement bound his partner to secrecy and held him responsible for production and sales.[146] And such confidences were taken seriously. Henshaw would later quarrel with his

---

[144] *Anthroposophia Theomagica* in *Works,* 74: *Et hoc* . . .: "Furthermore, it is worth knowing that the tradition of the theologians is twofold: the one part secret and mystical, the other revealed and better-known; *partim* . . .: partly in written, partly in unwritten canons."

[145] See D. P. Walker, *The Ancient Theology: Studies in Christian Platonism from the Fifteenth to the Eighteenth Century* (Ithaca: Cornell University Press, 1972).

[146] British Library MS, Sloane 3646, fols. 77–81. See F. Sherwood Taylor, "Alchemical Papers of Dr. Robert Plot," *Ambix* 4 (1949): 67–76.

patron who had betrayed a confidence by revealing certain secrets entrusted to him.[147]

The penchant for secrecy was especially pronounced in the *demi-monde* of alchemy. So strong had the habit of reading texts allegorically become, that Henshaw explained to a patron puzzled by a passage in an authoritative text, "who knows but Sendiuog [Sendivogius], myght safely enough conceale his meaning in a litteral sence, where all ye world expected an Enigmaticall."[148] To ensure the continued succession of the art, some would entrust their secrets orally to a worthy *"Heire* unto this *Science,"* as Elias Ashmole explained in *Theatrum Chemicum Britannicum*.[149] When Ashmole himself was selected for tutelage by an adept in 1651, he wrote an ode—"To my worthily honour'd William Backhouse Esqr Upon his adopting me to be his Son"—celebrating his initiation into the alchemical mysteries by a man he called "father" thereafter.[150] A single statement placed near the new beginning of *Aqua Vitæ* suggests that Vaughan may have intended his manuscript notebook as a book of secrets or *testamentum* to be handed down at such a time when God saw fit: "I shall lay them downe heere in their order, protesting earnestly, and with a good Conscience, that they are the very trueth, and heere I leave them for his Use, and Benefit, to whome god in his providence shall direct them."[151] It seems highly significant that only here on the title page of this notebook would Vaughan use his own name, whereas for all his printed works he employed the pseudonym Eugenius Philalethes, the well-born (i.e., noble) lover of truth.

While Vaughan was in many ways the typical Baconian who empirically tested all hypotheses, his notebook *Aqua Vitæ* stands Janus-like in this transitional age: with its codes and exotic language, it hearkens backwards to traditions of esoteric secrecy; with its attempts at precision, it looks forward to modern laboratory practice. As an historical document it shows that Vaughan quite clearly was involved in experimental philosophy; any sketch of his life and work, therefore, ought to take this into account.

---

[147] See Dickson, "Thomas Henshaw, Sir Robert Paston, and the Red Elixir," 65–66.

[148] Letter, [Henshaw] to Paston at Norwich, 9 September 1671, NRO Bradfer-Lawrence, 1c/1. Henshaw likewise counseled Paston on 2 September 1671 (NRO Bradfer-Lawrence, 1c/1) to be circumspect in concealing their work from an outsider: "put a mist before his eyes, or else a strong obligation of Secresy on him. but aboue all conceale from him ye use y^u mean to make of it, and take heed least hee picke any thing out of y^r discourse before him wth Sr John but use French or Latine when there is any thing of secrecy."

[149] *Theatrum Chemicum Britannicum* (London, 1652), 440–41.

[150] See Josten, *Elias Ashmole*, 1: 77–78.

[151] Sloane 1741, fol. 105^v.

D. TEXTUAL INTRODUCTION

Sloane 1741 is a quarto volume, consisting of one hundred and eight numbered leaves, gathered into eighteen quires of unequal length (from six to ten leaves each). Each page measures approximately 151 mm x 202 mm. About twenty percent of the folios are blank. The few personal anecdotes and memorials to his wife are in English; the alchemical notes and recipes are chiefly in Latin. In the first thirty-nine folios, memoranda were entered right-side up in the normal fashion (predominantly on the rectos, with some of the versos blank); the remainder of the volume was filled in from the rear, with the retrograde text written upside down on the versos. That is, he turned the volume to make writing in it easier once he decided to rededicate the notebook to his wife. This method of entry strongly suggests that he was writing in an already bound book. Sloane 1741 was foliated twice (each time, a few blank leaves were not numbered) and was rebound in September 1961.

Since many of the entries are dated (66 from 1658, 38 from 1659, and 4 from 1662), we can learn something about how and why Vaughan compiled the notebook. We cannot be certain how much it was used before Rebecca Vaughan's death on 17 April 1658. To signal this fresh beginning, he created a new title page that identified the book as their joint intellectual property, *Ex Libris Th: & Reb: Vaughan* (fol. 107^v). On the reverse of the new first entry about her death (fol. 106^v), he recorded a prayer from Amos (5:8) that encouraged the search for God in the Book of the Creatures; on the next page, he declared that their many conceptual breakthroughs were hers alone (fol. 105^v). For the reasons given more fully above, the notebook is clearly a tribute to her. When we take into account the number of times he confesses to losing or forgetting something—e.g., "And yet I doubt, I shall bee much troubled, before I finde, what I have lost, soe little difference there is, betweene Forgettfullnes, and Ignorance" (fol. 85^v)—we can also recognize his perceived need to record the details of his experiments, now that Rebecca Vaughan was no longer there to assist him. The many revisions and additions to the text show his struggle to recover these details. Nearly all the entries that follow in the reversed or back portion of the volume date from 1658. Thus, when he wrote on fol. 60^r, *ut supra dixi*, he is referring to the *secreti occultissimi* listed on fol. 62^r—which are "above" only if the book is read backwards. Once he reached the halfway point (at fol. 54), he began to use the front portion of the book. The first dozen folios all bear the date 1658. Nearly all the entries dated in 1659 are contained in fols. 14^v to 53^v. The few entries dated in 1662 demonstrate that he worked on the notebook for some years.[152]

---

[152] E.g., fol. 45^v is dated 8 August 1662; fols. 49^v and 50^v are dated 1661=2, i.e., between 1 January and 24 March 1662.

There are a few exceptions to this method. His account of the dream of the stallion foreboding his own death on the night of 16 July 1658, which is technically the first entry in the rear of the book, was added later—for aesthetic reasons, I believe. Though it occurred several months after, it matched the dream Rebecca had shortly before her own death so it was placed on the recto (i.e., 107ʳ) opposite her death notice. Similarly the dreams described on fols. 104ʳ and 103ʳ–102ʳ, which took place on 8 April and 9 April 1659, were added much later on the empty versos near the other anecdotes of her. Thus, most of the biographical material can be found together at the back of the book.

Before the notebook was acquired for the Sloane collection, it was owned for a time by one Edward Reynolds who added his name above the Vaughans' on the rear title page. Nothing is known of his identity. The entry on fol. 108ᵛ for "Balsamus Sulphuris Rulandinus" is most likely not Vaughan's. Not only is it in a different hand—perhaps it is that of Reynolds—but it also uses abbreviations and notations that are not used anywhere else.

§

In editing this manuscript journal, I have followed the long-established principle, articulated cogently by G. Thomas Tanselle, that to modernize the text of documents not intended for publication "is to conceal the essential nature of the preserved document."[153] As Tanselle points out,

> Errors and inconsistencies are part of the total texture of the document and are part of the evidence which the document preserves relating to the writer's habits, temperament, and mood.[154]

Since readers of Thomas Vaughan's notebook will be interested in the composition process, an edition of Sloane 1741 must reproduce in print the characteristics or texture of the manuscript that bear on that process. At the same time, I have been mindful of Michael Hunter's admonition that modern editors should not try to "produce a type facsimile of a manuscript." Seventeenth-century typesetters routinely imposed a house style on texts (i.e., capitalization and punctuation) and otherwise eliminated many of the vestiges of scribal culture. Hunter reminds us that Joseph Moxon's *Mechanick Exercises on the Whole Art of Printing* (London, 1683–84) made clear that compositors were expected to amend texts "to render the Sence

---

[153] G. Thomas Tanselle, "The Editing of Historical Documents," *Studies in Bibliography* 31 (1978): 10; also 48–51.
[154] Tanselle, "Editing," 48.

of the Author more intelligent to the Reader."[155] In preparing this print edition, the needs of a general audience for a readable text (and translation) have been balanced against the needs of scholars interested in Sloane 1741 as an historical document.

The transcription, therefore, is a diplomatic one that preserves the original spelling, capitalization, paragraphing, punctuation, and spacing on the page. To make this a more readable text, however, the use of *i, j, u, v,* and long *s* has been regularized to conform to modern usage. The thorn is retained as part of document's "total texture." Vaughan's characteristic macron at the end of a line—the u has a swirling tail ascending to the left or right—has been silently expanded. Abbreviations for the enclitic "-que" ("q;") and the commonly superscripted ending "-ur" have likewise been silently expanded and moved to the line. For Vaughan's &c., I have used the common abbreviation for *and so forth* (i.e., etc.). Other abbreviations are expanded in brackets with Vaughan's punctuation omitted: e.g., "part. 1:" is rendered "part[em] 1" in the text. In the Latin text I have included the superscripted case endings for the symbols of the seven prime metals within the brackets: e.g., $\odot^i$ is rendered as [auri]. Where a Latin word appears to be misspelled, the probable intended form is given in a note. The pagination of the original is indicated within brackets, e.g., [fol. 136^v]. On five occasions (fols. 70^v, 86^r, 92^v, 103^r and 105^v), Vaughan did not have room to finish an entry on a single page and continued writing on another page; in each case this happened in the reversed portion of the notebook. Since readers of this edition would then encounter the continuation before the beginning, I have changed the order of these pages for their convenience.

I have otherwise preserved the practices of Vaughan's scribal culture that may shed light on his meaning, such as punctuation, initial capitalization, spelling, underscorings, marginal notes, and other indications of emphasis. Vaughan's occasional revisions have been preserved by using **emboldened text** to mark material that was added at a later time on the grounds that such re-working is important evidence of the care he took in recording laboratory procedures accurately. Such revisions are recognizable in the Sloane manuscript by the different ink, or by having been squeezed into a space, or by being added with a caret above the line. To indicate emphasis, he placed in the margin the common abbreviation for *note bene* or some form of *maniculum* (i.e., a "little hand" or arrow pointing to the text). The former are left untranslated as *NB.* in the margins; the latter are indicated by an asterisk within braces {*} and the words or phrases inserted into the margins {within braces} at the bottom of the page. Simi-

---

[155] Michael Hunter, "How to Edit a Seventeenth-Century Manuscript: Principles and Practice," *The Seventeenth Century* 10 (1995): 288–89.

larly I have included all the passages that were later ~~crossed through~~ to help convey the sense that the notebook was a work in progress.

Based on the evidence of his youthful Latin poems,[156] Vaughan was a competent Latinist, though he did not always conform to the practice of classical authors in his private notebook. When he translated Latin quotations in his printed works for the benefit of his readers, he paraphrased quite freely. In my translation, however, I have tried to render as literally as possible Vaughan's comparatively simple Latin. The syntax is typically straightforward and the style is unadorned—quite different, in fact, from the copious style he used in his English prose. The few occasions when I have departed from what might be considered classical Latin practices, e.g., using a participle instead of a gerund, are indicated in the notes.

I have relied primarily on Cooper's *Thesaurus Linguæ Romanæ & Britannicæ*, Lewis & Short's *Latin Dictionary* and the *Oxford Latin Dictionary*, supplemented by Latham's *Revised Medieval Latin World-List from British and Irish Sources* and Souter's *Glossary of Later Latin to 600 A.D.* I have now and then been guided by Vaughan's own translation of terms in his published works. In light of the practice among alchemists to use secret or fanciful names for various substances—over a hundred terms for mercury have been identified—it is sometimes difficult to determine exactly what is intended. While Vaughan generally eschews fanciful or secret names, some terms in the text are left as he and his wife employed them. Unfamiliar words that are used more than once are defined in the Glossary and are marked in the text with an asterisk preceding the word. If a word is used only once or appears in only a single entry, the gloss is given as a footnote to the text. To make some sense of the text, I also had frequent recourse to the various medical or hermetic treatises listed in the bibliography, especially Dorn's *Chymical Dictionary*, Ruland's *Lexicon of Alchemy*, and Johnson's *Lexicon Chymicum*.

---

[156] See Dickson, "Thomas Vaughan," 131: 310–17.

My most deare wife~ sickened on Friday in the Evening, being the
16 of April, and dyed the Saturday following in the Evening,
being the 17. And was buried on y 26 of the same Mo:nth,
being a Monday in the Afternoone, att Mappersall in Bedfordshire.
1658. Wee were maried in the yeare 1651, by a minister
whose name I have forgott, on y 28 of September.

    God, of his infinite, and sure Mercies in Christ Jesus,
bring vs together againe in Heaven, whither shee is gone
before mee; and with her my Heart, and my faith not to bee
broken, and this thou knowest oh my God! Amen!

Left at M^{ris} Highgates.

1. One flatt Trunk of my deare wifes, with her maydin Name vpon
   it.

2. Another Cabinet Trunk of my deare wifes in which is her small
   pocket Bible, and her maydin Bible I have by mee.

3. One greate wodden Box of my deare wifes, in which is all her best
   Apparill, and in that is her greate Bible, with her practice of
   pietie, and her other Bookes of Devotion.

4. Another wodden Box, with pillowes in it, and a sweet Basket of
   my deare wifes.

5. One large Trunk of my deare wifes, with my name vpon it, in
   which are the Silver Spoones. And in the Drawers are two small
   Boxes, one with a lock of my deare wifes hayre, made vp with her
   owne Hands; and another with severall small Locks in it

6. One paire of greate Irons with Brass-knobs, and a single paire with
   Brass-knobs. a fire-shovell, Tongs, and Bellowes: my deare wifes
   little chaire, a round Table, Joynt stooles, and Close stoole,
   with a great glass full of eye-water, made att the pinner of
   wakefield, by my deare wife, and my sister vaughan, who are both now with god.

Thomas and Rebecca Vaughan's

AQUA VITÆ: NON VITIS
(British Library MS, Sloane 1741)

AQUA VITÆ: NON VITIS:

Or

The Radical Humiditie of Nature:
Mechanically, and Magically dissected,
By the Conduct of Fire,
and Ferment:

As well in the particular, specified Bodies
of Metalls, and Minerals:
As in her[1] seminal, universal Forme,
and Chaos.

By

Thomas Vaughan. Gent.

Dixit Heb: Hamed,

Novit Creator Creaturarum, quod Sermo de
Talibus, et de His, quæ sunt, de Genere Eorum,
fugat à me Tristitias meas, et exultat in iis,
Anima mea, & requiesco inde à Tædio, quod patior
a Naturâ.
  —Et sic demulceo Vitam.

[fol. 1ᵛ blank]
[fol. 2ʳ blank]

---

[1] *Its* was added above the line with a caret, though *her* was not crossed out.

AQUA VITÆ: NOT OF THE VINE.[2]

Or

The Radical Humiditie of Nature:
Mechanically, and Magically dissected,
By the Conduct of Fire,
and Ferment:

As well in the particular, specified Bodies
of Metalls, and Minerals:
As in her seminal, universal Forme,
and Chaos.

By

Thomas Vaughan. Gentleman.

Hebuhabes Hamed said:

The Creator of creatures knows that discourse on
such matters—and on these things which are on
their kind—drives my sorrows from me, and my
soul exults in them, and I rest thence from the
tedium which I suffer from nature.
—and thus I soothe my life.[3]

---

[2] Throughout Vaughan uses *aqua vitæ* for common alcohol, but in the title he plays on the biblical metaphor of the waters of life, which is picked up in the epigraph on fol. 2ᵛ: "As the hart panteth after the water brooks, so panteth my soul after thee, O God. My soul thirsteth for God, for the living God: When shall I come and appear before God?" (Psalm 42:1–2 [AV]).

[3] *Platonis Libri Quartorum ... cum commento Hebuhabes Hamed*, prologue to Book III (in Lazarus Zetzner, ed., *Theatrum chemicum*, 6 vols. [Strasbourg, 1659–1661], V.136); identified by Rudrum, *Works*, 752.

[fol. 2ᵛ]   Ex Libris Th: & Reb: Vaughan.
                                  1651. Sept. 28.
                             Quos Deus conjunxit: Quis
                                    Separabit?

                        Sitivit Anima mea ad Deum Ælohim: ad Deum
                        El vivum; Quando-nam veniam, et visitabo
                             Faciem Dei Ælohim![4]
                                    T. R. V.
                                    1658.

---

[4] Vaughan cites this passage (Psalm 42:1–2) many times in his notebook. His text is somewhat idiosyncratic: e.g., he preserved the Hebrew word for God as an appositive and used *visitabo* instead of *apparebo* (Tremellius) or *videbo* (Vulgate). Like many writers of this time, he often relied on memory for familiar texts from the Bible. *Elohim* is the plural form of the Hebrew *eloah*, God, that expresses the general notion of the deity, which I have translated as an intensive, "my God."

From the Books of Thomas and Rebecca Vaughan.
1651. Sept. 28.
Whom God has joined: Who
Will separate?

My Soul has thirsted for God, my God, for God,
the living God. When shall I come and visit
the face of God, my God?[5]
T. R. V.
1658.

---

[5] Psalm 42:3.

[fol. 3ʳ]   Ars Tota:

Ut inventa est in Diebus Conjugis meæ Dulcissimæ: Una
cum variis Nitri, et salium Præparationibus.

Via Universalis una tantum est, fitquè ut sequitur, nec alio modo. ℞. A-
quam de B[alneo] & congela illud cum sulphure suo præparato, proprio, et
pontico. Congelatum Aerem, abjecto prius phlegmate, sublima, et habebis
Salem Armoniacum Philosophorum.

Modò.

℞. Arsenicum nostrum: fluat per Resinam, eleveturque in Cubilibus, igne
moderato. Elevatum contere cum magnesiâ excoriatâ, & coque in Cinnabarin.

Huius Cinnabaris

Partem 1ᵐ. conjunge cum mediâ parte salis nostri Armoniaci: et inspissetur
mixtura cum proprio phlegmate, distilleturque igne nudo, et fiet. Hic est
Mercurius, et menstruum universale, & Aqua prima philosophic, sine quâ
nihil fit.

T. R. V. 1658

Tibi vero soli, Deus noster Altissime, et
misericors, sit Laus omnis, et gloria! Qui
fons es Aquarum viventium, et Aqua
vitæ vera, saliens, et surgens in vitam
Æternam; Amen! & Amen!

The Whole Art:

As it was discovered in the days of my sweetest wife:
Together with various preparations of *nitre and salts.

There is one universal way, that is all, and it is made as follows, nor by
any other way. Take water from the bath[6] and congeal it with its prepared *sulphur, proper and briny. Sublime the congealed *air, after the
fluid has been first cast off, and you will have *sal ammoniac of the philosophers.

Now

Take *our arsenic; let it flow through resin, and be rarefied in its chambers
with moderate *fire. Grind what has been rarefied with caustic *magnesia,[7] and concoct it into *cinnabar.

Of this Cinnabar

Join one part with a half part of our sal ammoniac; and let the mixture be
thickened with proper *phlegm, and distilled with a bare flame, and it will
be made. This is *sophic mercury, and the universal *menstruum, and first
philosophical water, without which nothing is made.

T. R. V. 1658

To you alone in truth, our most exalted and merciful
God, be all praise and glory! You who are the fountain of
living waters, and the true water of life, springing and
surging into eternal life.[8] Amen! & Amen!

---

[6] I.e., hot water. A distillatory furnace or warm water bath was a common piece of laboratory equipment.

[7] I have translated *magnesiâ excoriatâ* as "with caustic magnesia," though Vaughan had
a particular compound in mind, described below, fol. 104ᵛ, as "the Excoriation, or philosophicall sublimation of the red Magnesia by Corrosives, I found, while wee lodged att Mr
Coalemans in Holborne, before wee came to live att the Pinner of Wakefield."

[8] John 4:14. See Donald R. Dickson, *The Fountain of Living Waters: The Typology of the
Waters of Life in Herbert, Vaughan, and Traherne* (Columbia: University of Missouri Press,
1987).

[fol. 3ᵛ]   Alius Mercurius *Vegetabilis.

Sulphur nostrum *ponticum imprægna cum spiritu nostro ardente. Tunc distilla igne fortissimo, & habebis.

Alius Mercuris Mineralis.

Sulphur nostrum ponticum imprægna cum Aquâ forti, donec nolit bibere de Animabus. Tunc distilla igne violento, et fiet.

[fol. 4ʳ]   1.
Mercurius vegetabilis.

℞. utrumqùe sulphur: contere seorsim, et misce ad pondus. Mixturam calcina, sicut scis. Calcem solve in Aquâ vitæ, & procede ad sublimationem
NB.   salis, ut docet Lullius. Notabis tamen, quod si calx solvatur in aquâ communi, habebis in distillatione Aquam vitæ ex ipso sulphure, et sale, et est
Res admiranda; est enim Aqua ardens, & Aqua sulphuris vegetabilis.

2.
Mercurius mineralis.

Fit dupliciter, & primo quidem sìc Aquilæ partem 1ᵐ. cum mediâ parte
Scarabæi contere, & projice in Crucibulum ignitum, et candens. Solve
NB.   filtra sicca, & cum oleo vitri distilla. si distillatione crystallos Tartari adjun-
gas, fiet menstruum mirabile: puta mediam partem Crystallorum, ad unam
Aquilæ.

Another Animating[9] Sophic Mercury.

Impregnate our briny sulphur[10] with our burning *spirit. Then *distill it with a very strong fire, and you will have it.

Another Mineral Mercury.

Impregnate our briny sulphur with *aqua fortis, until it does not want to drink from the spirits. Then distill it with a very fierce fire, and it will be made.

1.
Animating Sophic Mercury.

Take each sulphur; grind separately, and mix equal weights. Calcine the mixture, as you know. Dissolve the *calx in the *aqua vitæ, and proceed to the *sublimation of salt, as Lull teaches.[11] You will note, however, that if the calx should be dissolved in common water, you will have aqua vitæ in the distillation from the sulphur itself and from salt, and it is a wonderful thing; for it is a burning water, a sulphurous animating water.

2.
Mineral Mercury.

It is made doubly, and at first certainly in this way; grind one part sal ammoniac with a half part *scarab, and cast into an ignited and glowing crucible. Dissolve, filter, dry, and distill with *vitriol. If you add crystals of *tartar in the distillation, a wondrous menstruum will be made, that is to say, a half part crystals, to one of sal ammoniac.

---

[9] See *vegetabilis* in glossary.

[10] See *pontic water* in glossary.

[11] *Sal petra* was (with *argentum vivum* and *vitriolum azoqueum*) one of the fundamental principles for Pseudo-Lull, for whom the unity of the cosmos was depicted by a triangle with God in the middle. See the *Practica*, chapters VIII–IX, in *Theatrum Chemicum*, IV: 140–43.

Aliter sic fit.

Aquilæ partem 1. cum mediâ parte Sacchari contere, & combure sicut scis. Solve, filtra, sicca, et cum oleo vitri distilla. Sic fiet ex Aquilâ oleum nobile, et potens.

T. R. V.

[fol. 4ᵛ]

NB.   ~~Fluat Talcum per Resinam. Tunc conjunge cum Aquilâ per Scarabæum præparatâ: vel per Resinam cum grano Talci. Vel Talcum per Resinam fusum conjunge cum Aquilâ crudâ, iterumque Fluat per Resina, et fiet.~~

Nota de Nitro.

Omne Sulphur, sive minerale, sive vegetabile, figitur cum Nitro: et post deflagrationem, extrahi potest tinctura eius, cum Aquâ vitæ. Sed in proportionibus, cavendum est. &c.

Aliud *Arcanum de
Nitro.

NB.   Addatur illi pars minima de Alkali, vel Talco: postea tere cum Sulphure, et per Vices projice in Crucibulum candens. Sic erit optimè præparatum, sine Scarabæo, & nullis ferè sumptibus. ~~XXXXXXXXXXXXXXXXXXXXXXX~~
~~XXXXXXXXXXXXXXXXXXXXXXXXXXXXXXXXXXXXXXXXXXX~~[12]

Expertum est in Diebus Conjugis meæ Charissimæ, fidissimæque.
T. R. V.
1658.

---

[12] Two lines were crossed out too heavily to be deciphered.

Otherwise It Is Made So.

Grind one part sal ammoniac with a half part sugar, and heat it, as you know. Dissolve, filter, dry and distill with vitriol. Thus the noble and potent oil will be made from sal ammoniac.

T. R. V.

B. ~~Let *talc flow through resin. Then join it with sal ammoniac prepared through the scarab. Or through resin with a grain of talc. Or join the melted talc through resin with crude sal ammoniac, and again let it flow through resin and it will be made~~.

Note Concerning Nitre.

Every sulphur, whether mineral or animating, is fixed with nitre; and after destruction by fire, its *tincture can be extracted with aqua vitæ. But it is necessary to be careful about the proportions, etc.

Another *Arcanum Concerning
Nitre.

3. Let a very small part from the *alkali, or from talc, be added to it; afterwards grind with sulphur, and by turns *project into a glowing crucible. It will be prepared best in this way, without the scarab and with scarcely any expense.

Tested in the days of my dearest and most faithful wife.
T. R. V.
1658.

[fol. 5ʳ]   ~~Oleum ex Alkali.~~

~~℞. Talci part[es] 2. Alkali part[em] 1. Aquilæ partes duas: vel ℞. Talci &~~
~~Aquilæ partes æquales. fluant per Resinam &c. Huic mixturæ adjungas par-~~
~~t[em] 1. vel mediam partem Alkali, et fiet.~~

De Nitro.

NB.

Præparatur variis modis: puta cum omnibus rebus combustibilibus. Si vero
sunt ex vegetantibus, præparatum stringit, nisi per Resinam fluat, quod notandum erit.

Atque hæc sunt,

Quæ in mineralibus secreta reperii, in Diebus Conjugis meæ Charissimæ:
Quam iterum in Cœlis videre, et Alloqui, dabit Deus meus misericors.
Amen, Domine Jesu! Lux, et vita mundi: Filius Dei, Filius et Redemptor
Hominis!

Trahe me post Te:
Curremus.[13]
T. R. V. 1658.

---

[13] These lines from the Song of Solomon 1:4 are usually attributed to the maiden who
is speaking to her beloved. Vaughan's punctuation of this text is curious: he joins the prepositional phrase *post Te* to *Trahe me* twelve of the seventeen times he uses this phrase, whereas both the Vulgate and the Tremellius translations place a comma after *Trahe me*, thus
joining the prepositional phrase to *curremus*. Vaughan may have been influenced by the KJV
translation (which follows the Targum), "Draw me, we will runne after thee." Modern
translators generally follow the Massoretic text, e.g., the RSV, "Draw me after you, let us
make haste," which is how Vaughan usually punctuates the text. The difference is slight,
but it raises the question of whether Vaughan had enough Hebrew to consult the original.
The Hebrew verb *mâshak* is used elsewhere in Scripture for the drawing power of divine
love (e.g., Jeremiah 31:3; John 6:44). I have preserved Vaughan's punctuation and translated
curremus literally as "we shall run," though "let us hasten [after Thee]" may be closer to his
meaning.

~~Oil from Alkali.~~

~~Take two parts talc, one part alkali, and two parts sal ammoniac; or take~~
~~equal parts talc and sal ammoniac. Let them flow through resin, etc. You~~
~~join one part or a half part alkali to this mixture, and it will be made.~~

Concerning Nitre.

It is prepared in various ways; that is to say, with all combustible things.
If in truth they are from growing things, the preparation binds, unless it
B.   flow through resin, which will be noted.

And Indeed These Are,

those secrets I found in minerals in the days of my dearest wife, whom
my merciful God will grant that I see and speak with again in heaven.
Amen, o Lord Jesus! Light and life of the world, Son of God, Son and
Redeemer of Mankind!

Draw me after Thee:
We shall run.
T. R. V. 1658.

[fol. 5ᵛ]   Aqua Caustica.

℞ Talci, et Alkali partes æquales. Conjunge cum Aquilâ ad pondus utriusque & cum oleo vitri distilla, et fiet pro certo. **Sit autem *Aquila cum scarabæo purgata, et sic forsan cum solo Talco conjuncta faciet mirabilia,
pondere tamen observato; Nec opus erit *Collâ, Alkali marino, Terreo,
aut Fontano.** NB. NB. NB.

NB.   Quandcum¹⁴ [plumbo] philosophico opus incipis, pone cum eo Talcum
           & Aquilam pari pondere, simul fusa, soluta, filtrata, siccataque. Et hæc est
           vera via, quâ oleum habebis fervidum, & incombustibile. Expertum est in
           diebus Conjugis meæ charissimæ, fidissimæque.

NB.   Compositum solvere potes in Aquâ causticâ supradictâ, quæ eo præstan-
           tior erit, si Aquila priùs per Scarabæum, vel per Resinam cum grano Talci,
           purgata sit: vel per se fusa, et in Aceto soluta, siccataque.

                                    Oleum Alkali.

NB.   ℞ Talci part[em] 1. Alkali marini partes 2 vel 3. distilla cum oleo vitri, et
           fiet. si loco Alkali marini, ponatur Alkali Terræ [vel Colla maris, vel Al-
           kali fontarum],¹⁵ longè plus olei, et spiritus impetrabis, quos expertus
           sum, quando ista duo corpora cum Alumine conjuncta distillavi.

---

¹⁴ Sic, for *quandocumque.*
¹⁵ This phrase was added in a marginal note.

Caustic Water.

Take equal parts talc and alkali. Join an equal weight of each with sal ammoniac, and distill with vitriol, and it will be made for certain. **But let the sal ammoniac be purged with scarab, and perhaps in this way joined with talc alone it will make marvelous things, if the proper weights are observed. Nor will there be need for *colla, or sea, earthen or aqueous alkali. Note well. Note well. Note well.**

NB.   Whenever you begin the work with philosophical *lead, place equal weights of talc and sal ammoniac with it, melted, dissolved, filtered, and dried together. And this is the true way, by which you will have the fiery and incombustible oil. It was tested in the days of my dearest and most faithful wife.

NB.   You can dissolve the composite in the caustic water described above, which will be the more excellent if the sal ammoniac be purged before either through the scarab, or through resin with a grain of talc; or melted by itself and dissolved in *vinegar and dried.

Oil of Alkali.

NB.   Take one part talc, two or three parts sea alkali, distill with vitriol, and it will be made. If earthen alkali be used instead of sea alkali (or *colla maris or alkali from well water), you will obtain much more oil and spirit, which I proved when I distilled those two bodies joined with *alum.

[fol. 6ʳ]   Cabala Metallorum:
                              Sive Lapis de
                                 Rebis.

Herbæ Saturninæ Succum exprime, et evapora, ut habeas terram eius purissimam. Hanc cum suo Compari pari pondere conjunge, et utrumque solve cum Humore metallico crudo. Putrefac per dies 40, & habebis lapidem Animalem per viam siccam.

   Terram supradictam solo igne Calcinare potes, & conjungere cum Arsenico sublimato, eritque Arcanum maximum pro Corporibus humanis.

                                   Vel

Calcina totum compositum cum veneno albo mecuriali: Calcem solve in aquâ Aquilæ minerali, vel in Oleo ex Alkali, et fiet. Hæc est Via Humida, et verè Universalis.

                          T. R. V. 1658.

NB.   In extracione succi, parum sulphuris mercurialis multa comburit dura Corpora.

[fol. 6ᵛ]   Alius Mercurius
                               Metallicus.

Sulphur n[ost]rum ponticum acuatum cum spiritu vegetabili, pro Corporibus Humanis: Pro Metallis vero, cum spiritu minerali, vel cum sublimato ignito: vel cum Utroquè: sepeli in ventre mercurii: Digere in Humorem lacteum: multiplica, putrefac, distilla, et fiet.

Cabala of Metals:
or the Stone from the
*Rebis.

Press out the juice of the Saturnine herb,[16] and evaporate it, so that you
have its purest *earth. Join this with its like in equal weight, and dissolve
both with a crude metallic humor. *Putrefy for forty days, and you will
have the *animated stone through the dry method.

You can calcine the earth described above with fire alone, and join it
with sublimated arsenic, and it will be the greatest arcanum for human
bodies.

Or

Calcine the entire composite with a white mercurial venom: Dissolve the
calx in mineral water of sal ammoniac, or in oil from alkali, and it will
be made. This is the wet method and certainly the universal one.

T. R. V. 1658.

B.   Note well. In the extraction of the juice, a little of the mercurial sulphur
consumes many hard bodies.

Another Metallic
[Sophic] Mercury.

[Take] our briny sulphur sharpened with animating spirit for human
bodies; or indeed for metals, sharpened with mineral spirit or fired
*sublimate, or with both. Bury in the belly of mercury. *Decoct into a
milky humor; multiply, putrefy, distill, and it will be made.

---

[16] According to Ruland, *Lexicon*, 375, a "Vegetable Matter from which the Hermetic
Philosophers know how to extract their Mercury."

Mecurius Metallicus
alio modo.

℞. Terræ fœtidæ per se, vel cum Arsenico conjunctæ, part[em] 1. Aquilæ
præparatæ, vel Salis Alcali, sicut scis, part[em] 1. Misce, et cum Oleo Vitri
per Retortam pelle, et fiet.

[fol. 7ʳ]   Abbreviatio Mercurii
Metallici Secundi.

Stellæ nostræ nubibus suis obductæ, impone magnesiam. Contere cum igne
mercurii, et calcina. Tunc solve in oleo Aquilæ, aut Alkali, & habebis rem
nobilem in medicinâ.

Aliter.

Magnesiæ, vel Lithargyrii part[em] 1. funde per Resinam, cum duabus
partibus Arsenici. Corpus hoc nigrum calcina cum sublimato: Calcem
solve in Oleis supradictis, vel in Aquâ forti ab oleo vitri rectificatâ, et fiet.

T. R. V. 1658.
Quos Deus conjunxit: Quis
separabit?

Ut vero mercurium primum metallicum facili labore acquiras, sic facito.

NB.   ℞ stybii philosophici q[uantum] v[is]. tere cum [sulphure] vulgari, & in
patellâ terreâ super carbones calcina, vel si vis in crucibulo. Calcem cum
Arsenico per Resinam purgato contere, & cum Talco, et Aquilâ misce, &
in aquâ Causticâ solve, &c.
T. R. V.

[fol. 7ᵛ blank]

Metallic Mercury.
By another method.

Take one part fetid earth by itself, or joined with arsenic, and one part prepared sal ammoniac, or sal alkali,[17] as you know. Mix, and drive with vitriol through a retort, and it will be made.

Diminution of Sophic Mercury's
Second Metal.

Put magnesia in our star, covered by its clouds.[18] Grind it with fire of mercury, and calcine. Then dissolve in oil of sal ammoniac or alkali, and you will have a noble medicine.

Otherwise.

Melt one part magnesia or *litharge through resin, with two parts arsenic. Calcine this black body with sublimate. Dissolve the calx in the oils described above, or in aqua fortis rectified from vitriol, and it will be made.

T. R. V. 1658.
Whom God has joined, Who
will separate?

But to acquire the first metallic mercury with easy effort, you must do it this way.

B.   Take any quantity of philosophical *antimony, grind with common sulphur, and calcine in an earthen bowl over coals, or, if you wish, in a crucible. Grind the calx with arsenic purged by resin, and mix with talc and sal ammoniac, and dissolve in caustic water, etc.
T. R. V.

---

[17] I.e., potash (K_2CO_3). In *Lumen de Lumine* in *Works*, 326–27, Vaughan wrote that the "the *secret Candle* of *God*" was purest and most abundant in sal alkali, or *Halicali*. "This *substance* is the *Catholick Receptacle* of *spirits*, it is *blessed* and *impregnated* with *Light* from *above*, and was therefore *styl'd* by the *Magicians, Domus signata, plena Luminis et Divinitatis* [a house shut up, full of light and divinity]."

[18] When heated with iron filings, then cooled, crystals of antimony will form with "branches" that may be arranged into a star-shape; see *antimony* in glossary.

[fol. 8ʳ]   Arcana quædam particularia
                             ad Rem medicam facientia.[19]

Contra Hydropem.

Olei vitri & Crystallorum Tartari partes æquales distilla, et fiet.

Alia Aqua.

Sacchari & crystallorum Tartari partes æquales distilla cum oleo supradicto, et fiet.

Alia.

Tartarum & Camphoram ana distilla cum eodem oleo, et fiet. **Idem fiat
cum Tartaro, & Ammoniaco. Item cum Tartaro & Sale communi.**

Aqua mirabilis.

Sulphur nostrum ponticum contere cum sublimato, & eleva quoties potes.
Tunc Resolve per Deliquium, vel in Vesicâ in Balneo tepido, &c.

[fol. 8ᵛ]   Oleum Salis communis.

Aquæ fortis, & Aquæ collæ marinæ partes æq[ales]: commisce, & rectifica
aliquoties. Hac aquâ, vel menstruo salem Collæ, vel Communem, vel gemmæ putrefac per dies 40. Tunc distilla, et invenies.

---

[19] Here and elsewhere (fols. 10ʳ, 19ʳ, 24ᵛ, 94ᵛ), I have translated *facientia* as if it were a
gerund. As a participle it agrees with the substantive *Arcana*; literally, this title should read
"certain particular secrets bringing into existence a medical thing" but "for making medicine" is far more idiomatic, especially in the presence of "ad," which presumes a gerund.

Certain Particular Arcana
For Making Medicine.

Against Dropsy.

Distill equal parts vitriol and crystals of tartar, and it will be made.

Another Water.

Distill equal parts sugar and tartar crystals with the oil described above, and it will be made.

Another.

Distill equal quantities of tartar and camphor with the same oil, and it will be made. **The same may be made with tartar, and ammonia. Likewise with tartar and common salt.**

A Wondrous Water.

Grind our briny sulphur with sublimate, and rarefy it as many times as you can. Then resolve it by a cold bath,[20] or in a vesica[21] in a tepid bath, and so forth.

Oil of Common Salt.

Mix together equal parts aqua fortis and colla of sea water, and rectify several times. In this water or in a menstruum, putrefy salt of colla, or common or rock salt, for forty days. Then distill, and you will discover it.

---

[20] *Per deliquium*: a method by which impure calxes "included in a bag are suspended; that moistning by the humid Air, they may let go their pure juice," according to Beguin, *Tyrocinium Chymicum*, 30.

[21] A covered egg-shaped vessel, made of copper, for elevating, congealing and condensing.

Si Aqua fortis

Priùs cohobetur super Talcum & Alkali ana, melius, et citiùs succedet. In digestione post paucos dies, ascendet super faciem menstrui oleum salis albissimum, instar Butyri. Hoc expertus sum in diebus Conjugis meæ Charissimæ, & Butyrum istud in Medicinâ Arcanum esse scias.

Si Aqua Collæ

NB.

Haberi non possit, sufficit Aqua pluvia, quâ ipse usus sum: Collam enim tunc Temporis, nondùm vidissem. Salem fusum projice in istud menstruum, et citiùs fiet.

[fol. 9ʳ]   ### Alia Aqua.

Spiritum Tartari ex crystallis eius, et oleo vitri, funde super Terebinthinam, et in Cineribus distilla, et fiet.

Alia Terebinthinæ
Aqua.

Terebinthinam solve in Aquâ forti, et distilla, &c.

Spiritus Mercurii vulgi.

NB.

Olei vitri & Mercurii partes pone in Retortâ: affunde Aquam fortem ad pondus Mercurii. Digere in Cineribus per dies duos. Tunc distilla, & si fumi nolunt in Humorem Resolvi, affunde parum de Aquâ distillatâ, & statim succedet. Hoc spiritu sæpius rectificato solve novum [mercurium] & procede donèc satìs habeas.

{*}   ### Oleum Aquilæ aureum.

Aquilam fusam projice in [aquam fortem], & digere in Cineribus per dies 12, vel 40, si vis. Tunc distilla, et habebis.

{* symbol for *acetum distillatum [distilled vinegar]* in margin}

If Aqua fortis

Be first *cohobated upon equal quantities talc and alkali, it is better, and will succeed sooner. After a few days in decoction, a very white oil of salt will ascend upon the surface of the menstruum, like butter.[22] This I tested in the days of my dearest Wife, and you should know that butter is an arcanum in medicine.

If Water of Colla

Cannot be had, rain water suffices, which I myself have used; for I would not yet have seen colla at that time. Cast the melted salt into that menstruum, and it will be made sooner.

Another Water.

Pour the spirit of tartar from its crystals and from vitriol upon *turpentine, and distill with the heat of the ashes, and it will be made.

Another Water of
Turpentine.

Dissolve turpentine in aqua fortis, and distill, etc.

Spirit of Common Mercury.

Place [equal] parts vitriol and mercury in a retort; pour in aqua fortis to the weight of the mercury. Decoct with the heat of the ashes for two days. Then distill, and if the fumes do not wish to be resolved into a vapor, pour in a little distilled water, and immediately it will succeed. Dissolve new mercury in this often rectified spirit, and proceed until you have enough.

Golden Oil of Sal Ammoniac.

Cast melted sal ammoniac into aqua fortis, and decoct with the heat of the ashes for twelve days, or forty if you wish. Then distill, and you will have it.

---

[22] The consistency of a substance was sometimes used to name or describe it.

[fol. 9ᵛ]   Præparatio miranda
                                       [Mercurii] Sublimati.

Sublimati, & olei vitri partes æq[uales] commisce. Mixturæ [aquam fortem] affunde: Affusam in Arenâ abstrahe, donec sublimatum in Collum Retortæ ascendat; Quem iterum affusâ [aquâ forti], reduc ad suum oleum, & toties cohoba, donec in venenum Igneum abeat. Hoc venenum Mercurium occidit, & aurum ipsum radicitùs calcinat, & destruit; præsertim si aurum incorporetur cum Mercurio crudo. Brevitèr, Arcanum est admirandum, et si cum [sulphure] pontico misceatur, fiet inde Ignis infernalis.

Christe Jesu! Lux et Vita Mundi: Filius Dei: Filius, et Redemptor Hominis: Trahe me post Te: Curremus!
                                       Amen!

                                       T. R. V.
                                       1658.

[fol. 10ʳ]   De Spiritu Vitrioli quædam
                                       Notabilia,
                                       Ad rem Medicam facientia.

Cum isto spiritu corrigi potest Antimonium per Resinam prius purgatum. Quin & omnia purgantia corrigit, puta Scammonium, Rheubarbarum; Agaricam, Senam, Cassiam &c. Quin & omnia Narcotica, & præsertim Opium. Correcta vero solvi possunt in spiritu nostro Ardente &c.

A Wonderful Preparation
for Sublimate of Mercury.

Mix together equal parts sublimate of mercury and vitriol. Pour aqua fortis in the mixture. Draw out what has run out in the sand,[23] until the sublimate ascend into the neck of the retort; after aqua fortis has again been poured in, reduce it to its oil, and cohobate as many times as necessary, until it changes into a fiery venom. This venom kills mercury and utterly *calcines gold itself and destroys it; especially if the gold be incorporated with crude mercury. In brief, this is a wonderful arcanum and if it be mixed with briny sulphur, an infernal fire will thence be made.

O Christ Jesus! Light and Life of the World: Son of God: Son, and Redeemer of Mankind: Draw me after Thee: We shall run!
Amen!

T. R. V.
1658.

Certain Notes
On the Spirit of Vitriol
For Making Medicine.

Antimony can be set right with that spirit if the antimony is first purged by resin. And furthermore it sets right all purgatives, that is to say, scammony, rhubarb, larch fungus, senna, cassia, etc.[24] And furthermore all narcotics, and especially opium. The amended matter can in fact be dissolved in our burning spirit, etc.

---

[23] See *fire* in glossary.

[24] All these herbs were simples used as purgatives. Scammony leaves were macerated to produce a milky juice, which, according to Gerard, *Herball*, 867–69, "clenseth and draweth forth especially choler." Because scammony is so harsh, Pliny, *Natural History*, XXVI.xxxviii, recommended that it be taken with aloes to prevent nausea. Rhubarb was widely valued as an herbal medicament; see *Herball*, 393–96, and the note below for fol. 96ᵛ on rhubarb. *Agarica* is a mushroom-like fungus that grows upon the larch and was also thought to draw forth humours (*Herball*, 1366–67). The leaves of cassia (or *cassia fistula*), also known as senna or sene, was likewise used as a cathartic or emetic (*Herball*, 1297–98, 1431).

Item gummi, & Aromata omnia in dicto spiritu solvi possunt. Solutioni affunditur Aqua vitæ nostra, donec omnis tinctura extrahatur. Hac viâ tincturæ Rerum, specierumque Calidarum mitescunt, quin et ipsa Vitæ Aqua corrigitur, præsertim vero sulphureitas eius calida, et inflammans.

Brevitèr, est Secretum maximum in Re medicâ, attestante ipsâ Experientiâ, Rerum omnium Magistrâ. Laus vero sit Deo Datori! Amen, & Amen!

T. R. V.
1658.

[fol. 10ᵛ]   Fixatio quædam Mercurii.

Memini me olim, in diebus Conjugis meæ Charissimæ, contrivisse sulphur vulgi cum Lapide Rebis in primâ suâ Compositione. Trituram vero in Crucibulo positam combussi, & mercurium fixatum inveni. Si vero igne fortiori urgeatur, dabit forsan flores philosophicos, aut Basilii Valentini Salem, febribus accommodatum quibuscunque.

Credo sane,

Quod, si combustio ista cum sulphure, aliquoties repetatur, totum Compositum in Calcem rediget: nam post primam deflagrationem, Corpus inveni rarefactum valde, et foraminosum instar spongiæ. Repete ergo, et ex hac Calce, extrahe salem n[ost]rum, cum Aceto distillato, Ut docet Basilius, & sic habebis febrifugum philosophicum.

T. R. V.
1658.

Likewise gums and all aromatics can be dissolved in the said spirit. Our aqua vitæ is poured in the solution, until every tincture is drawn out. In this way the tinctures of things and of fiery forms become mild, and furthermore the aqua vitæ itself is set right, and especially its fiery and inflaming sulphurity.

Briefly, this is the greatest secret in medicine, with experience itself attesting, the Mistress of all things. Praise indeed be to God the Giver! Amen, and Amen!

T. R. V.
1658.

A Certain *Fixing of Sophic Mercury.

I recall once, in the days of my dearest wife, that I ground common sulphur with the rebis stone in its first composition. What was ground I then indeed heated in a crucible, and I discovered fixed mercury. If indeed it be plied hard with a stronger fire, it will perchance yield philosophical *flowers, or the salt of Basil Valentine, proper for fevers of whatever kind.

I Believe certainly,

That, if that combustion with sulphur be repeated several times, it will reduce the entire composite to calx; for after the first burning, I found the body exceedingly rarefied and full of holes like a sponge. Repeat therefore, and from this calx, draw out our salt, with distilled vinegar, as Basil [Valentine] teaches, and in this way you will have a philosophical medicine to reduce fever.

T. R. V.
1658.

[fol. 11ʳ]   Aqua [mercurii] vulgaris.

℞ Arenæ nostræ part[em] 1. Jovis²⁵ optimi part[em] 1. misce: & per Cribrum Vulcani fac omnes sordes, & paleas leviculas ascendere: quas aufer, donec Jovis Sydus inclarescat. Hoc Jove *Junonem metallicam copula, & utrumque ciba cum Veneno albo Mercuriali. Tunc pone in Thalamo vitreo, & generabunt filiam candidissimam, quæ Ros Jovis est, & pluvia Junonis Argentea &c.

Jupiter etiam per Descensum post Cribrationem, vel ante, purgari potest: & denuo cum novâ Arenâ conjungi. Sed frustrà fit per plura, quod fieri potest per pauciora.

T. R. V.

Arcanum [Sulphuris].

℞. de eo trito lib[ram] 1. pone in Retortâ: cui affunde lib[ram] 1. olei Terebinthinæ, cum pari pondere olei vitri. Distilla, et ascendet primò in collum Retortæ substantia quædam fætida, quam exime. Tunc fortifica ignem, et exibit lac spissum, et valde odoratum, quod sicca, et serva; valet enim in Hydrope, & capitis Defluxionibus, et Catharris. T. R. V.

[fol. 11ᵛ]   NB. NB. NB.

℞. Talci part[em] 1. Aquilæ per Scarabæum præparatæ part[em] 1. Alkali partes 4. Distilla cum oleo vitri, et fiet. Hæc est Aqua Salis trium generum. Sufficit Aquila cruda.

Aliter.

℞ Talci part[em] 1. Alkali partes 1. vel 2. Scarabæi filtrati, siccatique partem mediam. Distilla cum oleo vitri, & forsàn fiet. Processus vero Supra-scriptus Certissimus est, et expertus in Diebus Conjugis meæ Charissimæ.

T. R. V.
1658.

---

²⁵ Jove and Juno were *Decknamen* for sulphur and the mercury of the philosohers; see Vaughan's *Anthroposophia Theomagica* in *Works*, 69.

Water of Common Mercury.

Take one part of our sand and one part of the best sulphur, and mix; and by the sieve of Vulcan make all the impurities and light chaff ascend; take these away until the star of sulphur be clear. Mate the metallic mercury to this sulphur, and feed both with a white mercurial venom. Then place them in a glass chamber, and they will generate a radiantly white daughter, which is the dew of sulphur, and the silvery rain of mercury, etc.

Sulphur also can be purged through its descent after sieving, or before, and once more be joined with new sand. But it is to no purpose to do through more operations, what can already be done through fewer.

T. R. V.

An Arcanum of Sulphur.

Take one pound of this ground up sulphur; place in a retort; into which pour one pound of oil of turpentine with an equal weight of vitriol. Distill, and a certain fetid substance will ascend first into the neck of the retort, which [you] take away. Then fortify the fire, and a thick and exceedingly odorous milk will go out, which dry and save; for it is efficacious for dropsy, and defluxions of the head and catarrhs. T. R. V.

Note Well. Note Well. Note Well.

Take one part talc, one part sal ammoniac prepared with scarab, four parts alkali. Distill with vitriol, and it will be made. This is water of three kinds of salt. Crude sal ammoniac suffices.

By Another Way.

Take one part talc, one or two parts alkali and a half part of filtered and dried scarab. Distill with vitriol, and perchance it will be made. The process described above in truth is the most certain and was tested in the days of my dearest wife.

T. R. V.
1658.

[fol. 12ʳ]   Memoriæ Sacrum.

On the same Day my deare wife sickened, being a Friday, and at the same time of the Day, namely in the Evening: my gracious god did put into my heart the Secret of extracting the oyle of Halcali, which I had once accidentally found att the Pinner of Wakefield, in the Dayes of my most deare Wife. But it was againe taken from mee by a wonderfull Judgement of god, for I could never remember how I did it, but made a hundred Attempts in vaine. And now my glorious god (whose name bee praysed for ever) hath brought it againe into my mind, and on the same Day my deare wife sickened; and on the Saturday following, which was the day shee dyed on, I extracted it by the former practice: Soe that on the same dayes, which proved the most sorowfull to me, that ever can bee: god was pleased to conferre upon mee ye greatest Joy I can ever have in this world, after her Death.

The Lord giveth, and the Lord taketh away. Blessed bee the Name of the Lord. Amen! T. R. V.

[fol. 12ᵛ]   {*}

Menstruum
Universale.

℞ Aquilæ fusæ, & Scarabæi purgati partes æquales. Solve in Aquâ ultimâ
de B[alneo] et digere per horas aliquot. Tunc distilla, et repete cum novâ
minerâ, donec acescat omninò. Tunc cohoba, donec Aquila in mare transeat, cum Scarabæo. Hæc Aqua solvit omnia Corpora, & si fermentetur
cum ovo Colubrino, & terrâ fœtidâ, miranda faciet.

Quando vero incipit acescere, Tunc solve in eâ Salem, aut Farinam Lithargyrii, & habebis menstruum nobile pro Corallis resolvendis.

T. R. V.
1658.

[fol. 13ʳ]   NB: Secretum Admirabile, et
verissimum inventum in Diebus
Conjugis meæ Charissimæ.

{*}

℞ Aquilæ crudæ, vel fusæ part[em] 1. Scarabæi optimi partem etiam: 1.
Tere subtilissime, & in Aceto distillato solve, vel in spiritu nostro ardente.
Tunc distilla, & habebis menstruum nobile pro calcibus metallicis resolvendis, & in spiritum volatilem sublimandis: sive sint Auri, vel Argenti,
vel Mercurii, vel cuiuscunque metalli calx sit. Idem menstruum valet in
Resolutione perlarum, Coralli, Bezoar, omniumque lapidum pretiosorum.
Quin et in ipsis salibus resolvendis, sublimandisque modo repetitis distil-
lationibus exuberetur cum novâ minerâ eiusdem generis. Probatum est in
reductione, et sublimatione Calcium metallicarum in aquam viscosam, volatilem, igneam, et valde Acetosam.

Laus vero sit Deo, Domino nostro misericordi, et excelso: in te Jesu justis-
sime: Animarum Peccatricium Redemptor Clementissime Deus, et Homo:
Deum Homini, & Hominem Deo Uniens, et concilians: Amor Magnus:
Fœdus novum, & æternum: vita vera: via, et Lux viæ: Trahe me post Te,
Curremus! T R V.

{* symbol for emphasis used}

[fol. 13ᵛ blank]

{*}

Universal Menstruum.

Take equal parts of melted sal ammoniac and purged scarab. Dissolve in
the hottest water of the bath and decoct it for several hours. Then distill,
and repeat with a new mineral, until it turns sour altogether. Then
cohobate, until the sal ammoniac with the scarab is transformed into salt
water. This water dissolves all bodies, and if it be fermented with an adder
egg and fetid earth, it will do wonders.

When indeed it begins to sour, then dissolve salt in it, or powder of
litharge, and you will have a noble menstruum for resolving corals.

T. R. V.
1658.

Note Well. An Admirable and Most True Secret,
Discovered in the Days
of My Dearest Wife.

{*}

Take one part crude or melted sal ammoniac, also one part of the best
scarab. Crush very gently, and dissolve in distilled vinegar, or in our burning spirit. Then distill, and you will have a noble menstruum for resolving
and subliming metallic calxes into a volatile spirit: whether it be a calx of
gold, or silver, or mercury, or any kind of metal. The same menstruum is
efficacious for the resolution of pearls, coral, *bezoar, and all precious
stones. And furthermore in resolving and subliming salts themselves, just
by repeated distillations, let it be made abundant with a new mineral of
this very kind. It was proved in reduction and sublimation of metallic
calxes into viscous, volatile, fiery, and exceedingly acidic water.

Praise indeed be to God, our merciful Lord and most high; in thee, o most
just Jesus, redeemer of sinful souls, most clement God and Man, uniting
and reconciling God to man and man to God. Great Love, new and eternal
bond, true life, the way and light of the way. Draw me after Thee, We
shall run! T. R. V.

[fol. 14ʳ]   Aqua Calcinativa
                                    Ray: Lullii.

Extrahe Succum Lunariæ, sintque [mercurius] & [sulphur] ana. Succum extractum cum veneno suo albo calcina. Calcinatum cum vitriolo, et nitro
distilla.

                                        Vel

Calcina lacertam cum A[quâ]F[orti]. calcinatam cum Cinnabarii crudâ
conjunge, & fiet.

                                        Vel

℞ fæcem ex qua Succus extractus sit: tere, et distilla cum vitriolo, et nitro,
et fiet.

                                      Forsan

Etiàm Sola Cinnabaris valet, quamvis Raymundus in practica magni Testamenti Lacertam enumerat, si non addit. Sed in his Experientiam consule:
credo tamen lacertam valere cum nitro, quamvis per se nihil potest contra
argentum vivum vulgare, sed ar[gentum] vivum commune confundit, et
destruit, tamen non sine sale.

Ramon Lull's
Calcinated Water.

Extract the juice of *lunaria, and let there be equal quantities of mercury and sulphur. Calcine the extracted juice with its white venom. Distill what has been calcinated with vitriol and with nitre.

Or

Calcine *colcothar with aqua fortis. Join what has been calcinated with crude cinnabar, and it will be made.

Or

Take the dregs from which the juice has been extracted; grind, and distill with vitriol and nitre, and it will be made.

Perchance

Even cinnabar alone is efficacious, although Ramon [Lull] in the *Practica* of his great *Testamentum* lists colcothar, even if he does not add it.[26] But in these matters, consult experience. I believe nevertheless that colcothar is efficacious with nitre, although by itself it can do nothing against vulgar quicksilver, but it diffuses and destroys common quicksilver, though not without salt.

---

[26] The pseudo-Lullian *Testamentum* (ca. 14th c.) was a well-known alchemical source; its divisions into a *Theoria* and a *Practica* were much imitated. According to Michela Pereira, *The Alchemical Corpus Attributed to Raymond Lull*, Warburg Institute Surveys and Texts, vol. 18 (London: University of London Press, 1989), 1–20, the large corpus of alchemical works ascribed to Lull (143 mss) are all forgeries, mostly written in the late 16th century. An *aqua calcinativa* (or *aqua corruptibilis* as pseudo-Lull called it), made from the juice of lunary, is discussed in chapter XV (*Theatrum Chemicum*, 4: 146). For a fuller version, see *Philosophical Experiments of that Famous Philosopher Raymund Lully*, trans. Robert Turner (London, 1657), 143–57.

[fol. 14ᵛ]   1659. Die Aprilis 17.°
                    In Ipso Anniversario, Sive Die Solemni
                        Nativitatis suæ Æternæ.

                              T. R. V.

                      Spiritus quidam philosophici
                        et secreti, inventi in diebus
                    Conjugis meæ Charissimæ, et hic
                    in suum ordinem reducti. 1659°

                        Quos Deus conjunxit,
                          Quis separabit?
                    As God decreed: so wee agreed.

            Christe Jesu! Lux, & vita mundi: Filius Dei Filius, & Re-
            demptor Hominis: Trahe me, post Te: Curremus. Amen!

                              T. R. V.
                               1659.

                      Propriùs, quam Priùs.

1659. On April 17th.
On the very Anniversary, or the Solemn Day
of her Eternal Nativity.

T. R. V.

Certain philosophical and secret
Spirits, discovered in the days
of my dearest wife, and here
reduced to their order. 1659°

Whom God has joined,
Who will separate?
As God decreed so wee agreed.

O Christ Jesus! Light and life of the world: Son of God,
Son and Redeemer of Mankind: Draw me, after Thee: We
shall run. Amen!

T. R. V.
1659.

Properly, rather than First.[27]

---

[27] The sense seems to be: I do these things properly rather than quickly or carelessly.

[fol. 15ʳ]   De Aquis mineralibus,
                                et metallicis.

Fit Aqua regis ex nitro cum duabus, aut tribus Scarabæi partibus cocto, et
combusto, et postea cum oleo vitri distillato.

Fit

Etiam aqua ex Crystallis Tartari ut supra distillatis, puta cum oleo vitri.
Quin et dicti crystalli conteri possunt cum Talco, et in simul distillari, et
fiet Aqua nobilissima, cum dicto oleo vitri.

Aliter.

Tartari Crystallos contere cum Talco. Trituram distilla cum vitriolo, et
Alumine calcinatis, et habebis spiritum Bonum. Vel idem facito cum Talco,
NB.   et Sale communi, et Halinitro, et habebis spiritum philosophicum, adjectis
adjiciendis.

[fol. 15ᵛ]   Aqua nobilis.

℞. Talci, Halinitri, vel Salis communis, & salis petræ cum Scarabæo correctæ, o[mn]ium ana partes æquales. Terrantur[28] cum Cerusâ, calce Draconis, et Vitriolo, & Alumine calcinatis. Trituram macera, et digere in
spiritibus corrosivis per horas 24. Tunc abstrahe spiritum ad perfectam sic-
citatem. Materiam siccatam tere diligenter, et nudo igne distilla per horas
6, et habebis. Potes loco Salis petrae, addere Halinitrum, et Salem communem, et sic habebis oleum Salis.

Potes etiam istis omnibus addere Salem Petræ.

---

[28] Sic, for *terantur*.

On mineral and
metallic Waters.

*Aqua regia is made from nitre prepared with two or three parts scarab, then fired, and afterwards distilled with vitriol.

The Water is Made

Also from crystals of tartar distilled as above, that is to say with vitriol. And furthermore the said crystals can be ground with talc and distilled together in it, and a very noble water will be made with the said vitriol.

By Another Way.

Grind tartar crystals with talc. Distill what has been ground with cal-
B. cinated vitriol and alum,[29] and you will have a good spirit. Or do the same with talc, and common salt and *saltpeter, and you will have a philosophical spirit, after the things that need to be added have been added.

A Noble Water.

Take talc, saltpeter, or common salt, and rock salt corrected with scarab, all equal quantities. Let them be ground with white lead, calx of the *dragon, and vitriol, and alum, all of them calcinated. Soften what has been ground, and decoct it in corrosive spirits for twenty-four hours. Then draw off the spirit to a perfect dryness. Grind the dried material diligently, and distill with a bare flame for six hours, and you will have it. In place of rock salt you can add saltpeter and common salt, and thus you will have oil of salt.

You can also add saltpeter to all these things.

---

[29] When alum ($AlK[SO_4]_2 \cdot 12H_2O$) is calcined or heated, it yields sulphuric acid (H_2SO_4) and aluminum oxide (Al_2O_3).

[fol. 16ʳ]   Ignis contra naturam.
                                              1.

Cinnabarin ex magnesiâ dulci, tere cum sale nitro, et vitriolo calcinato,
cum Alumine. Trituram nudo igne distilla, et fiet. Addi possunt pennæ
Draconis, vel *sputum eius.

                                          Aliter.
                                              2.

℞ vitrioli, & Aluminis calcinatorum. lib[ram] 1. Cerusæ uncias duas; Draconis per Resinam purgati, vel cum [sulphure] calcinati uncias sex; vel calcina Draconem cum nitro per Scarabæi halitum correcto: Tunc adde Talci
partem tertiam. Misceantur omnia per minima, et nudo igne distillentur.

                                      Ignis naturæ.

Magnesiam cum [aquâ forti] excoriatam, vel per descensum sicut scis, pur-
gatam, et solo igne calcinatam: Tere cum sputo fixato: vel cum rubea Draconis minerâ. Trituram solve in oleo Salis, et peracta digestione distilla.

     Cum oleo vitri, ex Talco, sale communi, et Halinitro, extrahitur Aqua
singularis pro solutione sputi fixati, &c.
                              T. R. V. 1659.

Unnatural[30] *Fire.
1.

Grind cinnabar from sweet magnesia with salt nitre, and calcinated vitriol with alum. Distill what has been ground with a bare flame, and it will be made. The *feathers of the dragon can be added, or its *spittle.

By Another Way.
2.

Take one pound of vitriol and alum, both calcinated, two ounces of white lead; six ounces of dragon purged by resin, or calcinated with sulphur; or calcine the dragon with nitre corrected through the vapor of scarab. Then add a third part talc. Let all be mixed only a little, and distilled with a bare flame.

Fire of Nature.

Grind magnesia made caustic with aqua fortis, or purged through its descent, as you know, and calcinated with fire alone, with fixed spittle; or with red lead. Dissolve what has been ground in oil of salt, and distill after decoction is completed.

With vitriol a singular water is drawn out from talc, common salt, and saltpeter, for a solution of fixed spittle, etc.

T. R. V. 1659.

---

[30] The great work was in itself considered *contra naturam* in that the alchemist had to "destroy" or dissolve the matter into the *prima materia* of the original creation. See Abraham, *Alchemical Imagery*, 139.

[fol. 16ᵛ]   Triplex est modus corrigendi
                                   spiritum nigrum, Typhonem
                                   puta, sive Fratricidam.

Primus cum Resinâ, ut docet Democritus: Secundus cum Anatro, sitque
Anatri pars media, ad unam Draconis. 3ⁱᵘˢ Cum pulvere nostro albo stellato, et splendido &c.

Quod si ad unam Draconis, et mediam Anatri partem, Resinæ pars addatur, & omnia comburantur in simul, egregie parabitur: vel post deflagrationem cum Anatro fluat per Resinam: sed præstat priùs.

                          Lithargyrium etiam per
                   Resinam combustum volat, et est
                        Secretum admirandum.

[fol. 17ʳ]   NB. De Salibus
                                        Sublimatis.

℞. Aquam supradictam ex Talco, et nitro per Scarabæi Halitum correcto
&c. Solve in eâ Crystallos Tartari, solutos sublima in Glaciem clarissimam.
Sal fixum, quod in fundo remanet, calcina, et repetitis solutionibus purga.
Purgatum conjunge cum glacie suâ, sive sale volatili, et utrumque sublima,
donec figantur. Hæc est medicina nobilissima et contra podagram specifi-
cum potentissimum. Si glaciem in spiritum acetosum reducas, et cum isto
spiritu salem fixum, et novam glaciem solvas, et omnia simul figas, præstantior erit medicina.

                                   De Nitro.

Separa spiritum suum album ab oleo suo rubro, sicut scis. Salem dealbatum
in spiritu solve, et sublima. Vel sublima cum Aquâ supradicta, et habebis
medicinam universalem, si omnia debito modo figantur.

                            T. R. V. — 59.

Threefold Is the Way of Correcting
Black Spirit, *Typhon
For instance, or Fratricide.

First, with resin, as Democritus[31] teaches; second, with nitric salt, and let
it be a half part nitric salt to one part dragon; third, with our white powder, sparkling and splendid, etc.

But if to one part dragon and a half part nitric salt, one part resin be
added and all be fired together, it will be prepared excellently; or after the
destruction by fire, let it flow with the nitric salt through the resin; but
the first method is better.

Litharge also flies through
fired resin, and it is
a wonderful secret.

Note Well. On Sublimated
Salts.

Take the water described above from talc and nitre corrected through the
vapor of scarab, etc. Dissolve in it crystals of tartar; sublime the dissolved
crystals into a very clear glass. Calcine the fixed salt, which remains in the
bottom, and purge with repeated solutions. Join what has been purged
with its glass, or volatile salt, and sublime both until they be fixed. This is
a very noble medicine and very potent specifically against gout. If you reduce the glass into an acidic spirit, and with this spirit you dissolve the
fixed salt and the new glass, and you fix altogether, the medicine will be
more excellent.

On Nitre.

Separate its white spirit from its red oil, as you know. Dissolve the
whitened salt in the spirit and sublime it. Or sublime with the water
described above, and you will have a universal medicine, if all be fixed in
the proper way.

T. R. V. 1659.

---

[31] The oldest recognized alchemical text was the *Physika kai mystika*, ascribed to Democritus of Abdera (fifth cen. B.C.), whose teacher was the great Persian *magus* Ostanes. Now
fragmentary, this treatise was once comprised of books on gold, silver, precious stones, and
purple. Both Pliny and Annaeus Seneca knew of the recipes of Democritus.

[fol. 17ᵛ]   April the 16ᵗʰ. at night 1659.

I dreamed that a flame, of a whitish colour should breake out at the toes
of my left foote, and this was told mee in my dreame by a strange person,
and of a dark Countenance. It is to bee noted, that this was the very night,
on which my deare wife died 1658: it being a Saturday night, and but one
day short of the number, or true Accompt.[32] It may bee the Disease that
shall occasion my death, was shewed mee; on the night wherein shee dyed,
for true it is, that in my left foote there is even now a dangerous humor
fallen downe; and lodgeth under my very heele, & upon the lifting of my
leg upward, it paineth mee strangely. It fell first into my knee, and what
it may come to, I know not, unless it will end in a gout: but it first of all
troubled mee in the Sinewes, and caused a Contracture of them, and then
I had a dull paine, and still have in the uppermost Joynt of the Thigh.
T. R. V.

[fol. 18ʳ]

Many yeares agoe, at Paddington, before my distemper in the Liver seized
mee, there appeared to mee twice in the same night in two severall
dreames, a young, strange person, not unlike to him, who appeared in a
strange manner to mee at Edmond Hall in Oxford. His Countenance was
dark, and I believe it is the Evill Genius, but in this last dreame, I saw him
not soe clearely, my life I blesse god for it, being much amended. The evill
hee so gladly signifies to mee, frights mee not, for I am ready for Death,
and withall my heart shall I wellcome it, for I desyre to bee dissolved, and
to bee with Christ, which is farr better for mee, then to live, and sinne, in
this sinnfull Body.[33]

T. R. V. 1659.

God is T. R. V. Amen! & Amen!

[fol. 18ᵛ blank]

---

[32] His wife died on Saturday, 17 April 1658.
[33] Philippians 1:23–24.

[fol. 19ʳ]   Experimenta quædam particularia
                              ad rem medicam facientia.

{*}

Oleum fellis Terræ.

Valet ad calculos deturbandos, tam renum, quam vesicæ: sed absque
Corrosivis extrahi debet, inquit Paracelsus. Teratur ergo cum Colcothare
duplicato, sicut scis, et nudo igne distilletur.

{*}

Oleum Resinæ, Picis Burg[undicæ]
et gummi omnis generis.
Item Ceræ.

Terantur cum colcothare pulverato, et distillentur in Arenâ. Spiritus su-
bacidus Hepaticum est nobilissimum, et in febribus valet. Quod si sal commune cum colcothare misceatur, habebis spiritum acidissimum, et oleum
magis defæcatum. Olea [septies] rectificata valent contra podagram: et si
cum oleo fellis Terræ misceantur, valebunt etiam contra calculum, et intrò
sumi possunt.

Si Salia

Ita præparentur, ut in aquâ lactescant, nec resolvantur, tunc in dictis oleis
solvi, et sublimari possunt in medicamenta nobilissima.

T. R. V. 1659.°

{* symbol for *oleum* [∴] used}

Certain Particular Experiments
For Making Medicine.

{*}

Oil of Common Centaury.[34]

It is efficacious for expelling stones, as well as stones of the kidney or bladder; but it ought to be extracted without corrosives, says Paracelsus. Let it be ground therefore with doubled colcothar, as you know, and distilled with a bare flame.

{*}

Oil of Resin, of *Burgundy Pitch,
and of every kind of gum.
Likewise of Wax.

Let them be ground with pulverized colcothar, and distilled in the fire of sand. A sour spirit is a very noble liver medicament and is efficacious for fevers. If common salt be so mixed with colcothar, you will have a very acidic spirit and an oil more cleansed. Oils rectified seven times are efficacious against gout; and if they be mixed with oil of common centaury, they will be also efficacious against the stone, and they can be taken internally.

If Salts

Be thus prepared, as they turn milky in water, yet not be resolved, they can then be dissolved in the said oils and sublimed into very noble medicaments.

T. R. V. 1659.

---

[34] A plant whose medicinal properties were said to have been discovered by Chiron, the centaur (OED). Pliny, *Natural History*, XXV.xxxi, explained it was also called *fel terræ*, or gall of the earth, because of its extreme bitterness.

[fol. 19ᵛ]   Oleum Talci.

Talcum optimum tere cum Anatro, et per horas aliquot combure igne fortissimo. Tunc extrahe cum Aquâ vitæ, et fiet.

Tincturâ Plumbi nigri
Pictorum.

Combure ut supra, cum Anatro; tunc extrahe cum spiritu vini, et habebis.
si in combustione non salìs rubescat, adde plus Anatri, et iterum calcina.

Oleum Universale.

℞ Terram optimam: cribra diligenter, ut a lapillis, & sordibus liberetur.
Tunc distilla in Arenâ, et separa oleum ab aquâ. Oleum rectifica per se, et
valebit ad extrahendas rosarum Tincturas, et Essentias odoratissimas. Idem
fiat cum Luto, sive Terrâ pingui, et aliquantulum tenaci, sed non cum Ar-
gillâ.

[fol. 20ʳ]   Additio ad Aquas philosophicas
                                      Supra-scriptas.

Nigrum nigrius
Nigro.

Typhonem reducito cum Resinâ, et unciis aliquot Anatri in substantiam
pinguem, Resinosam, et nigerrimam. Hanc cum Sericone tere, et coque in
[crucibulo] clauso in massam Lapidosam, quam iterum solve, et distilla, et
habebis aquam vitæ metallicam. Idem facito cum sputo, si pecunia suppetit.

Oil of Talc.

Grind the best talc with nitric salt, and heat for some hours with a very strong fire. Then extract with the aqua vitæ, and it will be made.

With Tincture of Painters'
Black Lead.

Heat as above with nitric salt; then extract with spirit of wine, and you will have it. If none of the salt redden in combustion, add more nitric salt and calcine again.

Universal Oil.

Take the best earth; sieve diligently, so that it is freed of pebbles and impurities. Then distill in the fire of sand, and separate the oil from the water. Rectify the oil by itself, and it will be efficacious for extracting the tinctures of roses and the most odorous essences. Likewise it may be made with clay, or with a fatty and slightly sticky earth, but not with potter's clay.

An Addition to the Philosophical Waters
Described Above.

A Black Blacker than
Black.[35]

Reduce Typhon over and over with resin and with some ounces of nitric salt into a fatty, resinous, and very black substance. Grind this with red lead, and concoct for ten days in a closed crucible into a stony mass, which [you] dissolve again, and distill, and you will have a metallic aqua vitæ. Do the same with spittle, if money is available.

---

[35] Each stage of the alchemical operation had its proper color, which together formed the *cauda pavonis*, or peacock's tail. Black was the sign of putrefaction, the first stage, which was signified by various degrees of blackness; white was the second stage, followed by red. Vaughan's phrase *nigrum nigrius nigro* suggests total putrefaction.

Aqua mineralis.

Nigrum Resinosum tere cum Sericone: Trituram cum Anatro misce, et cum vitriolo & Alumine calcinatis. Mixturam nudo igne distilla, et sic Anatron exibit sine magna violentia: saltem impetus iste ventosus aliquantulum sed abitur. Idem fit cum Typhone per solam Resinam purgato.

Aqua Mercurii.

Nigrum Resinosum et sericonem misce æqualiter: vel sint tres partes nigri ad duas Rubei. Adde sublimati partem unam, vel duas. Solvantur omnia in Urinâ saturni, et distillentur, & habebis.

Laus Deo! Amen!

T. R. V. 1659.°

[fol. 20ᵛ]   Sal plumbi.

Lithargyrium projice in [aquam fortem], secundum notam proportionem: Adde primam matrem et agita bene, sic totum resolvetur, et in salem purum transibit. NB. NB. NB.

{*}

Arcanum Pul[chrum].

℞ Sacchari candi et Sulphuris partes æquales. Distilla in Cineribus, et fiet.

1658.

{* symbol for *oleum* [∴] used}

Mineral Water.

Grind the resinous black substance with red pigment; mix what has been ground with nitric salt and with calcinated vitriol and alum. Distill the mixture with a bare flame, and in this way the nitric salt will reveal itself without great fierceness: or at any rate that little rush of wind will soon go away. The same is made with Typhon purged by resin alone.

Water of Mercury.

Mix equally the resinous black substance and red lead; or let there be three parts black to two of red. Add one part of the sublimate, or two. Let all be dissolved in the *urine of Saturn, and let them be distilled, and you will have it.

Praise Be to God! Amen!

T. R. V. 1659.

*Salt of Lead.

Cast litharge into aqua fortis, according to the known proportion. Add the first mother[36] and agitate well; in this way the whole will be resolved, and it will turn into pure salt. Note Well. Note Well. Note Well.

{*}
A Beautiful Arcanum.

Take equal parts white sugar and sulphur. Distill with the heat of the ashes, and it will be made.

1658.

---

[36] I.e., some form of *sophic mercury* or *menstruum*.

[fol. 21ʳ]   Aqua prima Philosophica
                    ex Draconibus crudis, et absque Corrosivâ.

Cruda lacerta non valet, sed calcinata, & cum leone crudo conjuncta,
Secretum [Præparatis] est secretorum. NB.

Tere semilibram Lacertæ **calcinatæ** cum unciâ Leonis nigri. Trituræ adde
tantundem Aluminis, & vitrioli calcinatorum. Hæc omnia commisce cum
Librâ unâ, Anatri purissimi. Distilla nudo igne, & habebis.

                                Potes addere

Uncias tres, aut quatuor Lacertæ **calcinatæ** ad unam Leonis: sufficit enim
ista quantitas, et Residuum suppleat vitriolum &c.

                            Aliter. NB.
                                NB.

               ℞. rubeam mercurii mineram instar Cinnabaris apparentem. Item ℞ Auri
NB.   nigri ignem non experti mineram optimam, quam reperire poteris. Te-
               rantur in simul pari pondere, et cum Aquilâ distillentur. Experire priùs in
               Crucibulo. Gratiæ sint Christo!

                    T. R. V.   T. R. V. 59.º

[fol. 21ᵛ blank]
[fol. 22ʳ blank]

The First Philosophical Water
From the Crude Dragons and without a Corrosive.

Crude colcothar is not efficacious, but calcinated and joined with crude lion it is the secret of secrets. Note Well.

Grind a half pound of **calcinated** colcothar with an ounce of black lion. Add just enough alum and calcinated vitriol to what has been ground. Mix all these with one pound of very pure nitric salt. Distill with a bare flame, and you will have it.

You can add

Three or four ounces of **calcinated** colcothar to one of the lion; for that quantity suffices, and may supply a residue of vitriol, etc.

By Another Way. Note Well.
Note Well.

B. Take red mineral of mercury appearing like cinnabar. Likewise take the best ore of black gold you can find, untouched by fire. Let them be ground together in equal weights, and distilled with sal ammoniac. Test first in the crucible. Thanks be to Christ!

T. R. V.   T. R. V. 1659.

[fol. 22ᵛ]   Sequitur, adversâ paginâ, Synopsis apertissima, et
              verissima Arcanorum totius Artis: prout inventa,
              et experta sunt, in Diebus Conjugis meæ Cha-
              rissimæ: Quam iterum videre, et alloqui, in Cœlis
              suis Sanctis, dabit Deus meus,

Misericors.

Christe Jesu! Lux, & vita mundi:
Filius Dei: Filius, et Redemptor Hominis:
Trahe me, post Te: Curremus! Amen!

Inquiunt

T. R. V.
As God decreed: so wee agreed.
1651.°

Quos Deus conjunxit, Quis separabit?
1659.°

There follows on the opposite page a very open and true synopsis of the arcana of the whole art, just as they were discovered and tested in the days of my dearest wife, whom my merciful God will grant that I see again and speak with in his holy heavens.

O Christ Jesus! Light and life of the world:
Son of God: Son and Redeemer of Mankind:
Draw me, after Thee: We shall run! Amen!

Thus say

T. R. V.
As God decreed: so wee agreed.
1651.

Whom God has joined, who will separate?
1659.

[fol. 23ʳ]   Totum opus, ut

Inventum est in diebus Conjugis meæ Charissimæ R: V:
Anno Domini nostri Jesu Christi, 1659.°

Aqua prima:

Fit [tripliciter]. 1° sic: ℞ Alvitri calcinati, et Anatri partes æquales. Terantur in simul cum mediâ parte Draconis per Resinam et Anatron præparati.
vel sit pars purgata per Anatron, et pars per Resinam. Distilla nudo igne,
et habebis.

2° sic fit.

Rubeam mercurii mineram tere ad pondus cum Astro Solis nigro: Distilla
cum Anatro, et fiet.

3° sic fit.

Sputum Draconis cum Sale Lithargyrii tere; Adde Anatron, et nudo igne
distilla.

NB. NB. NB.

Resina Draconem mirabiliter præparat, et valdè volatilem facit, ita ut in
Distillatione facillimè transeat.

The Whole Work, as

It was discovered in the days of my dearest wife R: V:
In the year of our Lord Jesus Christ, 1659.°

The First Water:

It is made in a threefold manner. First in this way: Take equal parts calcinated *alvite and nitric salt. Let them be ground together with a half part
dragon prepared by resin and nitric salt. Or part may be purged by nitric
salt and part by resin. Distill with a bare flame, and you will have it.

Secondly it is made in this way.

Grind red ore of mercury with an equal weight of the black star of the
sun.[37] Distill with nitric salt, and it will be made.

Thirdly it is made in this way.

Grind the *spittle of the dragon with the salt of litharge. Add nitric salt,
and distill with a bare flame.

Note Well. Note Well. Note Well.

The resin prepares the dragon wonderfully and makes it exceedingly volatile, so that it is transformed very easily in distillation.

---

[37] I.e., with the *regulus of gold.

[fol. 23ᵛ]   Aqua Mercurii.

℞. Cinnabarin ex Magnesiâ excoriatâ, vel crudâ: Tere cum Alvitro calcinato: Trituræ adde Anatron ad pondus omnium, et distilla igne nudo.

Alius modus
præstantissimus.

℞. mineram Cinnabaris, ut supra: Tere ad pondus cum Nigro Resinoso,
per Resinam & Anatron præparato: vel cum Dracone calido per solum
Anatron rubifacto: Vel cum Chalybe purissimo, **vel cum sputo**. Adde
Anatron ad pondus omnium, & nudo igne distilla, et habebis pro Certo.
&c.

T. R. V.
1659.°

[fol. 24ʳ]   Habitis, et rectificatis his

Aquis, procedere potes ad sublimationem [mercurii] philosophici, quem si
nosti, benè est, Sin aliter, parum efficies in hac Arte.

Oleum Stibii per

Viam particularem. Sputum Draconis fige cum A[quâ] f[orti]: Fixum solve
in Aquis suprascriptis: vel in Aquâ factâ ex sale communi, et Halinitro ana
commixto: Adde parum Aluminis Hispanici, et cum oleo vitri distilla. Sic
habebis spiritum nobilissimum. **Idem facit oleum ex Arenâ Tartari duplicati, cum Alvitro combusto distillatum: NB: Adde Talcum, aut Halinitrum, vel utrumque.**

{*}

{* symbol for emphasis used}

Water of Mercury.

Take cinnabar from caustic magnesia or crude magnesia; grind with calcinated alvite. Add nitric salt to what has been ground in an amount equal to the weight of all other ingredients, and distill with a bare flame.

Another Most Excellent Way.

Take ore of cinnabar, as above; grind with an equal weight of black resin, prepared by resin and nitric salt; or with the hot dragon, made red by nitric salt alone; or with very pure *chalybs, **or with spittle**. Add nitric salt in an amount equal to the weight of all other ingredients, and distill with a bare flame, and you will have it for certain, etc.

T. R. V.
1659.

Once these waters have been obtained and rectified

You can proceed to the sublimation of philosophical mercury, which if you have learned is well, but if otherwise, you will effect little in this art.

Oil of Stibium[38]

By a particular way. Fix the spittle of the dragon with aqua fortis. Dissolve what has been fixed in the waters described above; or, in water made from common salt and mixed with an equal quantity of saltpeter. Add a little Spanish alum, and distill with vitriol. In this way you will have a very noble spirit. **The same makes oil from sand of doubled tartar, distilled with fired alvite. Note Well. Add talc, or saltpeter, or both.**

*}

---

[38] See *antimony* in glossary.

De Anatro.

Corrigitur, et dealbatur spiritu suo corrosivo: Item cum Scarabæo. Si vero cum Tartaro calcinetur, Solutumque siccetur: Siccatumque cum Talco ana teratur, iterumquè cum novo Tartaro calcinetur, repetititis[39] solutionibus, & congelationibus, fiet sal fusibile, fixum ex quo fit Aquila volans cum Batrachio.

Laus Deo, optimo, maximo!
Amen dicunt T. R. V. 1659.°

[fol. 24ᵛ]   Sequuntur Quædam Particularia
                              ad rem medicam facientia.

                                   T. R. V.
                                    1659.°

                              Acetum particulare
                               nobilissimum.

Succum Lombardi misce ad pondus, cum Corpore suo albo. Distilla in cineribus, et habebis. Hoc Aceto solve novum Succum incorporatum, et putrefac per dies aliquot. Tunc distilla, et paratum est. Hoc Aceto vegetabili solvi potest Magnesia, quin et Corallia, et perlæ, et lapis Bezoar, estque Arcanum nobile ad Medicinam.

                              Corpus Lombardi
Teratur cum sulphure, distilleturque in oleum pro Pulmonibus.

---

[39] Sic, for repetitis.

Concerning Nitric Salt.

It is corrected and whitened with its corrosive spirit. Likewise with scarab. If it may indeed be calcinated with tartar, and the solution dried, and what has been dried be ground with equal quantities of talc, and again calcined with new tartar with repeated solutions and congelations, a fixed, fusible salt will be made, from which volatile sal ammoniac is made with borax.

Praise be to God, incomparably good and great!
Amen say T. R. V. 1659.

Certain Particulars Follow
For Making Medicine.

T. R. V.
1659.

A Particular,
Very Noble Vinegar.

Mix juice of *Lombard in a weight equal to its white body. Distill with the heat of the ashes, and you will have it. With this vinegar dissolve new incorporated juice, and putrefy for some days. Then distill, and it is prepared. With this animating vinegar magnesia can be dissolved, and furthermore corals, pearls, and bezoar stone, and it is an noble arcanum in medicine.

The Body of Lombard

May be ground with sulphur, and distilled into oil for the lungs.

[fol. 25ʳ]   Oleum Universale.

℞ Saturnum vegetabilem ex Latio, vel ex Monticulis: Distilla in Cineribus,
et separa aquam ab oleo: Oleum rectifica per se, et extrahet odores, &
Q[uinta] Essentias ex Aromatibus, et floribus quibuscunqùe &c.

Oleum Resinæ
contra Podagram.

Teratur cum Alvitro calcinato, et in Cineribus lento igne distilletur: sitque
Recipiens amplissimum. Habebis oleum tenue, et rubeum instar sanguinis,
et ita tenue, ut nunquam in gummi redeat, quod in pice Burgundicâ, aliis-
que Resinosis Succis, contingit. Rectificetur⁴⁰ [septies], et paratum est.

Cum eodem

Alvitro distillari possunt Rhabarbarum, Aloes, Jalop,⁴¹ Opium, Scammo-
nea, et reliqui succi, radicesque purgantes, quod summoperè notabis, et
retinebis.

[fol. 25ᵛ]   Purgatio [Saturni]
Pro Cinnabari faciendâ, ad
Aquam primam philosophicam.

Hæc purgatio, non est illa, quâ utuntur philosophi in succo Lunariæ fa-
ciendo: sed quædam est abbreviato, quâ non tantùm sumptus, sed et labor
etiam diminuitur, & alleviatur. fit autem sic. Amalgametur [saturnus] cum
NB.   mercurio, fluantque ambo in Crucibulo: Fluentibus pulveratum sulphur injice, et paratum est.

    Potest etiam A[malgam]a conteri cum [sulphure], et demum comburi,
et liquifieri. Tandem calcina cum sublimato, et habebis Cinnabarin bonam.

Laus Deo!
Amen!

T. R. V. 1659.ᵒ

---

⁴⁰ Sic, for *rectificietur*.
⁴¹ Sic, for *jalap*.

Universal Oil.

Take animating Saturnine herb from the plain or from the hills. Distill with the heat of the ashes, and separate the water from the oil. Rectify the oil by itself, and it will extract odors and quintessences from the spices and any flowers whatsoever, etc.

Oil of Resin
Against Gout.

It may be ground with calcinated alvite, and distilled with a slow flame in the heat of the ashes; and let the container be very large. You will have a thin oil, and red like blood, and so thin that it will never return to gum, which happens in Burgundy pitch and other resinous juices. It will be rectified sevenfold, and thus it is prepared.

With the Same Alvite

Rhubarb, aloes, *jalap,[42] opium, scammony, and the remaining juices and purgative roots can be distilled, which you will note very much and retain.

Purgation of Lead
For Making Cinnabar, for
the First Philosophical Water.

This purgation is not that which the philosophers use for making the juice of lunaria. But it is a certain abbreviation, by which not only expense but also labor is diminished and alleviated. It is made however in this way. Let lead be amalgamated with sophic mercury, and let them flow together in a crucible. Cast pulverized sulphur in the fluids, and it is prepared.

The *amalgam can also be ground with sulphur, and at length heated and liquefied. Finally calcine with sublimate, and you will have a good cinnabar.

Praise be to God!
Amen!

T. R. V. 1659.

---

[42] Jalap is a variety of bryony found in Mexico that was used as a purgative. Gerard, *Herball*, 873, likened it to scammony.

[fol. 26ʳ]   NB. NB. NB. NB.

Si dictum A[malgamatum] [plumbi] sive Cinnabaris teratur cum [sulphure] vulgari, et descendat per Kymam, erit proculdubio Arcanum nobile: Sed Ecce toties Artis Encheiria absolutissima!

    Fac unguentum ex Sulphure, Mercurio, Arsenico, sicut scis. Coque in Cineribus per horas 24: sitque Mercurii pars una ad duas Sulphuris, et Arsenici. Succum serva, est enim Argentum vivum ex latebris deauratis. Arenam nigram tere cum sublimato, et calcina inter duo vascula. ℞ huius calcis uncias 4. Anatri lib[ram] 1. Alvitri tantundem. Misce in simul, & distilla igne nudo, & habebis. Arena ista nigra, est [antimonium] Artefii,⁴³ Saturninum, et Eudica Morieni,⁴⁴ et fæx vitri. De hoc dixit Zadith, Clavis ei una tantum existit, vilis radicis, et quod in operatione projicitur ignorando, magis est vile. Et Sendivogius, Multi projiciunt, quod philosophi amant.

NB.   Notandum tamen, Quod si argentum vivum sit ex stanno, tunc primum Argentum vivum, secundum æstimatur. De isto stanno dixit Turba: *Æs, et plumbum pro nigredine, et stannum pro liquefactione sumite. Et alibi, Non tamen fit de illâ nigredine Tinctura, sed Clavem Esse, vobis intimavi.

                                   T. R. V. 1659.

---

⁴³ Artefius or Artephius, a legendary Jewish alchemist of the Middle Ages, was the author of the widely regarded *Clavis Sapientiæ* and the *Liber Secretus*, which appeared with an English translation by Eirenæus Orandus of Flamel's *Exposition of the Hieroglyphicall Figures* (London, 1624). Artephius's *Secret Book* held that antimony was a mineral with a saturnine nature, containing both the principles of *sol* and *argent vive*.

⁴⁴ Morienus is thought to have been a Byzantine monk and pupil of Stephanos of Alexandria, who taught Khālid ben Yazīd (d. 704), the Arabic philosopher and alchemist, whose *Liber de compositione alchemiae* was the first alchemical treatise translated into Latin (1144). See *A Testament of Alchemy*, trans. Lee Stavenhagen (Hanover, NH: University Press of New England, 1974), 45.

Note Well. Note Well. Note Well. Note Well.

If the said amalgam of lead or cinnabar be ground with common sulphur, and descend through a *cucurbit, there will be beyond doubt a noble arcanum. But mark, very often it is the final undertaking of the art!

Make the unguent from sulphur, mercury, arsenic, as you know. Concoct with the heat of the ashes for twenty-four hours. And let there be one part of mercury to two of sulphur and arsenic. Save the juice, for it is quicksilver made by gilded subterfuge. Grind black sand with sublimate, and calcine within two small vessels. Take four ounces of this calx, one pound of nitric salt, and just so much alvite. Mix in together, and distill with a bare flame, and you will have it. That black sand is the saturnine antimony of Artefius, and the *eudica of Morienus, and the dregs of vitriol. About this Zadith[45] said: "only one key to it exists, of a common root of no special value, and because in the operation it is cast forth to the ignorant, it is all the more worthless." And Sendivogius, that many cast forth what the philosophers love.[46]

B.   It should be noted, nonetheless, that if the quicksilver be from tin, then the first quicksilver is judged the second. About this tin the *Turba* said: Take ore, and lead for black dye, and tin for liquefaction. And elsewhere, the tincture however is not made from that black dye, but I have made known to you that it is the key.[47]

T. R. V. 1659.

---

[45] The Arabic alchemist Zadith Senior (Muhammad b. Umail al-Tamimi) was known as the author of the *Aurelia Occulta Philosophorum*. See the article on "Ibn Umayl" in *Encyclopaedia of Islam*, 3: 961–62. Jean Jacques Manget printed all three parts in his *Bibliotheca Chemica Curiosa*, 2 vols. (Geneva, 1702). The first part was a dialogue between Senior and a neophyte on the divine origins of alchemy; the second, a brief exposition of twelve figures; the final part, called *Senioris Antiquissimi Philosophi libellus* (Manget, *Bibliotheca*, 2: 216–35), offered a full exposition, at the beginning of which Zadith explained, "Sera & sera, infra seram, clavis ei una existit, vilis radicis, & id quod in operatione projicitur ignorando, minus est vilius" (Manget, *Bibliotheca*, 2: 218). Since this final part was not in Zetzner's *Theatrum Chemicum*, Vaughan probably used a ms. version.

[46] While this was a commonplace among alchemists, Vaughan may have in mind a passage from the Preface to the *Ænigma philosophicum ad filios veritatis*. See Michael Sendivogius, *A New Light of Alchymy*, trans. John French (London, 1650), 47–50.

[47] Vaughan probably had in mind a passage from the eleventh discourse of the *Turba Philosophorum* (though it is not an exact quotation) in *Theatrum Chemicum*, 5: 8; the fourteenth discourse described the color changes (5: 12–13). This anonymous tract probably may date from the ninth century and was widely available. See Martin Plessner, *Vorsokratische Philosophie und griechische Alchemie in arabisch-lateinischer Überlieferung: Studien zu Text und Inhalt der Turba philosophorum*, Boethius, 4 (Wiesbaden: Franz Steiner, 1975).

[fol. 26ᵛ]   Arcanum Nobile.

℞. dictum unguentum Compositum: tere cum Sulphure vulgari, et inter
duo vascula combure. Fiet autem spongiosum quid, et concavum. Iterùm
cum novo Sulphure combure, et repete, donec in calcem reducatur. Sal, inquit Basilius, ex hac calce Febres Tertianos, & quartanos abigit. Quicquid
sit, nam librum istum suspicor, calx saltem optima est, præsertim si sit ex
secundâ Compositione. Solve in urinâ Saturni, et sublima, et habebis rem
nobilem. Expertum est in diebus Conjugis meæ Charissimæ.

Laus vero sit Tibi, Deus meus,
misericors! Amen in Jesu Christo,
filio tuo dilecto, Animarum
fidelium Redemptore Unico!

T. R. V.

Non confundar in Æternum.[48]

[fol. 27ʳ]   Metallum Nobile.

Saturnum et Jovem Carceri include, et per Mercurium iterum libera. Libe-
ratos solo igne calcina, et in Corpus reducito, et habebis. Evigila, et excute,
subest enim Arcanum maximum.
                          T. R. V. 1659.°

---

[48] Psalm 31:1, 71:1.

A Noble Arcanum.

Take the said composite unguent; grind with common sulphur, and heat within two small vessels. A spongy and concave substance will be made. Heat again with new sulphur, and repeat until it is reduced to calx. Salt from this calx, says Basilius, drives away tertian and quartan fevers. Whatever it may be, for I suspect that book, it is at least the best calx, especially if it be from the second composition. Dissolve in the urine of Saturn, and sublime, and you will have a noble thing. This has been tested in the days of my dearest wife.

Praise indeed be to You, my merciful God!
Amen in Jesus Christ,
your beloved Son,
Only Redeemer of faithful souls!

T. R. V.

Let me never be confounded.

A Noble Metal.

Confine lead and sulphur in prison, and free them again by mercury. Calcine the freed ones with fire alone, and reduce again into a body, and you will have it. Watch carefully, and examine, for a very great arcanum is near at hand.

T. R. V. 1659.

NB.   Compositio Sericonis,   NB.
ad Ignem naturalem.

Calcina partem unam Draconis, cum Quinque, vel sex partibus Anatri. Salem ablue, et calcem Residuam sicca. ℞ huius calcis, et Sacchari præparati, sicut scis, partes æquales. Combure inter duo vascula, et congela in lapidem durum coloris flavi, aut citrini. Solve in Aceto distillato, vel in spiritu ex oleo Lombardi. Salem Solutum Sicca, et nudo igne distilla, & habebis.

T. R. V.
1659.

Turba dicit: Miscete ea æqualitèr, et assate Aurum cum iis. Intellige Aurum vivum, et sublimatum, vel calcinatum.

[fol. 27ᵛ]   Verus modus est
iste:

℞. Terram magnesiæ, vel calcem ex succo Lunariæ. reduc in Salem, quem contere, et congela cum sputo, et servo fugitivo. Compositum corpus solve in aquâ fœtidâ, et habebis.

T. R. V. 1659.°

Atque hæc sunt, Quæ inveni, in diebus Conjugis meæ Charissimæ, Quam iterum videre, et alloqui, in Cœlis suis sanctis, dabit Deus meus misericors.

Christe Jesu! Lux, & Vita mundi: Filius Dei: Filius, & Redemptor Hominis: trahe me post Te, Curremus! Amen!

Inquiunt T. R. V.
1659.°

Note Well. Composition of Red Lead
for natural Fire. Note Well.

Calcine one part of the dragon with five or six parts nitric salt. Wash away
the salt, and dry the residual calx. Take equal parts of this calx and prepared sugar, as you know. Heat within two small vessels, and congeal into
a hard stone, golden or yellow in color. Dissolve in distilled vinegar, or in
spirit from oil of Lombard. Dry the dissolved salt, and distill with a bare
flame, and you will have it.

T. R. V.
1659.

The *Turba* says: "Mix them equally, and *assate the gold with them."[49]
Understand it is living gold, and sublimated or calcinated.

That Way is
True:

Take earth of magnesia, or calx from the juice of lunaria. Reduce into salt,
which [you] grind and congeal with spittle and the *fugitive attendant.
Dissolve the composed body in fetid water, and you will have it.

T. R. V. 1659.

And indeed these are the things that I discovered and proved in the
days of my dearest wife, whom my merciful God will grant that I see again
and speak with in his holy heavens.

O Christ Jesus! Light and Life of the world: Son of God, Son and
Redeemer of Mankind: draw me after Thee, We shall run! Amen!

Thus say T. R. V.
1659.

---

[49] Almost an exact quotation from the seventeenth discourse of the *Turba Philosophorum*, in *Theatrum Chemicum*, 5: 15.

[fol. 28ʳ]   Dixit Rosinus:

Accipite sputum Lunæ, et Gummam ex magnesiâ et Lunâ, et in simul liquefacite: postquam vero liquefiunt, non oportet nos Rubra facere, sed Colores, et flores eorum extrahere jubent, puta, cum Aquâ nostrâ primâ &c. NB.

T. R. V. 1659.°

Lapis Arnoldi ex succo
Trium Herbarum.

℞ Arsenicum sublimatum, vel sputum eius: Tere cum Magnesiâ calcinatâ, solutâ, siccatâ, et extractâ sicut scis. Adde [mercurium] congelatum, ut sequitur.

Solve [mercurium] in A[quâ]F[orti] et abstrahe: digere in frigidâ distillatâ, et abstrahe, et sublima. Quod subsidet, solve in Aceto distillato, abstrahe, et sicca. Tunc conjunge cum Sulphure, et Arsenico, et fiet.

Laus vero sit tibi Domine, Deus
misericors!
Amen in filio tuo Dilecto
Jesu Christo!

T. R. V. 1659.

[fol. 28ᵛ blank]
[fol. 29ʳ blank]

Rosinus[50] said:

"Take the spittle of silver and gum from magnesia and silver, and liquefy them together; after they are truly liquefied, it is not proper for us to make red things but colors, and they order us to extract their flowers, for instance, with our first water, etc." Note Well.

T. R. V. 1659.

Arnold's Stone from the Juice of Three Herbs.[51]

Take sublimated arsenic, or its spittle. Grind with calcinated magnesia, dissolved, dried, and extracted, as you know. Add congealed mercury, as follows.

Dissolve mercury in aqua fortis and draw out; decoct it in cold distilled [water], and then draw out, and sublime. Because it will settle, dissolve in distilled vinegar, draw out, and dry. Then join with sulphur and arsenic, and it will be made.

Praise indeed be to thee, O Lord,
merciful God!
Amen in your beloved Son,
Jesus Christ!

T. R. V. 1659.

---

[50] While I have not identified this quotation, the name "Rosinus" can be found frequently in alchemical collections of the time, such as the *Rosarium Philosophorum*. According to alchemical mss in the Mellon Collection at Yale University and the Wellcome Institute in London, Rosinus was apparently an alchemical writer to whom are attributed works entitled *De lapide, Liber definitionum*, and some letters. On "Rosinus" being another name for Zosimus of Panopolis, see Marianne Marinovic-Vogg, "The 'Son of Heaven': The Middle Netherlands Translation of the Latin *Tabula Chemica*," in *Alchemy Revisited*, ed. Z. R. W. M. von Martels, Collection de travaux de l'académie internationale d'histoire des sciences, 33: 171–74 (Leiden: Brill, 1990).

[51] Because the process Vaughan described is plainly not an herbal extraction but rather a mineral compound, he may have in mind the discussion in Arnold's *Speculum Alchymiæ*, in *Theatrum Chemicum*, 4: 515–19, of the three stones, *sol, luna,* & *mercurius*.

[fol. 29ᵛ]   Scarabæus

Etiam pro opere minerali sic præparatur. Fige cum [aquâ forti] et pluviâ:
fixum solve, et sublima cum Aquâ vitæ. Vel solve priùs in Aceto, postea
in Aqua vitæ: vel in aquâ communi, et posteâ sublima.

NB. Sublimatum istud solve in oleo Aquilæ, et distilla in menstruum
admirandum.

Talcum operationem impedit, nam spiritu suo sulphureo, et calido
cæteros sales violentissimè explodit. Sic autem feci in diebus conjugis meæ
Charissimæ. Collam cum Alkali marino contrivi: Contritis Aquilæ partem
unam, hoc est, tertiam addidi, et cum oleo vitri distillavi. Vicem Collæ supplet Halinitrum, et ut puto, Sal fontarum.

[fol. 30ʳ]   Praxeos utriusque
                     Mineralis, et Metallicæ, Synopsis
                              Apertissima:

                                Accessit
                   Utriusque Mercurii, Animalis, et
                       Vulgaris, Philosophica
                              Congelatio.

                 Omnia probata, et inventa in Diebus
                     Conjugis meæ Charissimæ.
                          R. V. 1659.°

                        Menstruum minerale.

1°. Fit optimè cum Anatro dealbato per venenum suum proprium. 2°. Fit
cum Anatro, et Talco conjunctis, et depuratis. 3°. Fit cum Alkali marino,
et Halinitro areneso, adjecta Talci portiunculâ. Hæ sunt materiæ passivæ,
et Mercuriales: Sulphura vero Agentia, sunt oleum vitri, et Sputum **Draco-
nicum**. Chalybs enim in opere minerali valdè potens est; Sed et

                        Ex eius sputo.

Fixato, tertio menstruo operante, extrahitur oleum Sanguineum, et nobilissimum.

                        Soli Deo Gloria!
                             Amen!
                       T. R. V. 1659.°

        {* symbol for emphasis used}

Scarab

Is also prepared in this way for the mineral work. Fix with aqua fortis and rain water; dissolve what has been fixed, and sublime it with the aqua vitæ. Or dissolve first in vinegar, afterwards in the aqua vitæ, or in common water and afterwards sublime.

Note Well. Dissolve that sublimate in oil of sal ammoniac, and distill into an admirable menstruum.

Talc hinders the operation, for it explodes other salts most violently by its sulphurous and hot spirit. I have done so in the days of my dearest wife. I have ground colla together with sea alkali; to what has been ground together, I have added one part ground sal ammoniac, that is, a third part, and I have distilled it with vitriol. In place of colla saltpeter suffices, and as I think, salt from well water.

A Praxis and
Very Open Synopsis,
Both Mineral and Metallic:

[To Which] Is Added
The Philosophical Congelation
Of Mercury, Both Animated
and Common.

All proved and discovered in the days
of my dearest wife.
R. V. 1659.

Mineral Menstruum.

First, it is made best with nitric salt, whitened by its proper venom. Second, it is made with nitric salt and talc, conjoined and cleansed. Third, it is made with sea alkali and sandy saltpeter, with a little portion of talc thrown in. These are passive and mercurial materials. The agents are truly sulphurs, vitriol and spittle **of the dragons**. For chalybs is exceedingly potent in mineral work; and even from its spittle.

Once the third menstruum is fixed and working, a bloody and very noble oil is extracted.

Glory Be to God Alone!
Amen!
T. R. V. 1659.

[fol. 30ᵛ]   Mercurius quem scimus.

Succum Lunariæ evapora, ut Æs etiàm avolat. Tunc ℞ magnesiæ albæ partes duas, Lunæ vivæ partem unam. Misce sicut scis, et in menstruo minerali
solve, et sublima, et habebis.

Abbreviatio Menstrui
mineralis.

℞ Anatri dealbati, vel cum Talco conjuncti lib[ras] 2. Draconis per Resinam purgati uncias tres, olei vitri, quantum sufficit. Distilla, et fiet.

Draco enim per Resinam purgatus, valebit æquè ac sputum. Et
sic tam Tempori consules, quàm sumptibus.

[fol. 31ʳ]   Congelatio Mercurii
                                    Metallici.

Succum Lunariæ Quartâ vice evapora: ita tamen, ut Æs non avolet.
Evaporatum pondera, et cum matre suâ frigidâ, Ana incorpora. Coque in
igne primi gradus, qui talis est, ut lapis semper liquescat. Coque, inquam,
donec omnia vertantur in pulverem nigrum. Hunc sublima, et habebis.

Congelatio Mercurii
Animalis.

Anatron calcinatum tere cum Talco, vel cum Alkali marino. Trituram
funde in substantiam spissam, et nigerrimam. Succum eius extrahe per solu-
tionem. Extractum iterum funde, et habes fermentum minerale, quo omnis
Aqua congelari potest.

Hæc sunt, Quæ inveni,
In diebus Conjugis meæ Charissimæ: Quam iterum in cœlis videre, et alloqui, dabit Deus meus misericors.

Christe Jesu! Lux, & vita mundi: Filius Dei: Filius, & Redemptor
Hominis: Trahe me post Te, Curremus! Amen!

T. R. V.
As God decreed: so wee Agreed.

[fol. 31ᵛ blank]

A Mercury Which We Know.

Evaporate the juice of lunaria, so that the ore also flies away. Then take two parts white magnesia, one part quicksilver. Mix, as you know, and dissolve in a mineral menstruum, and sublime, and you will have it.

A Shortcut for the Mineral Menstruum.

Take two pounds of whitened nitric salt, or joined with talc, three ounces of the dragon purged by resin, and as much vitriol as suffices. Distill, and it will be made.

For the dragon purged by resin will be efficacious equally with spittle. And in this way you will have regard for time as well as expense.

The Congelation of Metallic Mercury.

Evaporate the juice of lunaria on the fourth turn—although in such a way that the ore does not fly away. Weigh what has evaporated, and incorporate an equal quantity with its cold mother. Concoct in a fire of the first grade, which is such that the stone always liquefies. Concoct it, I say, until all be turned into a black powder. Sublime this, and you will have it.

Congelation of Animated Mercury.

Grind calcinated nitric salt with talc, or with sea alkali. Melt what has been ground into a thick and very black substance. Extract its juice by solution. Melt again what has been extracted, and you have a mineral ferment, with which all water can be congealed.

These things are what I have discovered in the days of my dearest wife, whom my merciful God will grant that I see again and speak with in the heavens.

O Christ Jesus! Light and life of the world: Son of God: Son and Redeemer of Mankind: Draw me after Thee, We shall run! Amen!

T. R. V.
As God decreed so wee Agreed.

[fol. 32ʳ]   NB. NB. NB.

Paracelsus multa fabulatur de suo Corallato, quod sic ineptè nominavit, cum aliud non sit quam Mercurius præcipitatus, et oleo Tartari ablutus.

Sic vero Præstantiorem medicinam præparabis.

Mercurium præcipitatum, vel [aquâ forti] fixatum tere cum sublimato. Trituram sublima instar [mercurii] dulcis, ut vocant, &c. Potes et Mercurium crudum duobus istis **priùs sublimatis** admiscere, et omnia simul sublimare. Rumina super his, et diligentèr expende, quæ dixi.

Menstruum Universale.

Aquam ultimam de B[alneo] cohoba super Salem ex sphærâ solis, et fiet pro certo.

Menstruum particulare.

Oleum Lombardi distilla cum Corpore suo albo, et habebis. Laus Deo! Amen!

T. R. V. 1659.°

Note Well. Note Well. Note Well.

Paracelsus chatters much about his coralline, which he has thus ineptly named, when it is none other than mercury precipitated and cleansed in oil of tartar.[52]

In this Way in Truth You will prepare a more excellent medicine.

Grind mercury precipitated, or fixed with aqua fortis, with sublimate. Sublime what has been ground like sweet mercury,[53] as they call it, etc. You can blend crude mercury to those two **before they have sublimated**, and sublime altogether. Ruminate upon this, and diligently consider what I have said.

Universal Menstruum.

Cohobate the hottest water from the bath over salt from the sphere of the sun, and it will be made for certain.

A Particular Menstruum.

Distill oil of Lombard with its white body, and you will have it. Praise be to God! Amen!

T. R. V. 1659.

---

[52] A concentrated solution of potassium carbonate (K_2CO_3), which may have been what van Helmont called his *alkahest*; see Maurice P. Crosland, *Historical Studies in the Language of Chemistry* (Cambridge: Harvard University Press, 1962), 82.

[53] I.e., calomel, a remedy made popular by Oswald Croll's *Basilica Chymica* (Frankfurt, 1620).

[fol. 32ᵛ]   NB.
                                   NB.   NB.

NB.   ℞ Duos nigros ana: projice in [aquam fortem] depuratam, et agita cum
         Bacillo, donec nihil amplius agere potest: Tunc affunde [aquam fortem]
         communem, et agita in Lac album, quod in aliud vitrum effunde; et si quid
         remansit insolutum, iterum solve, addita nova [aquâ forti], et communi.
         Solutum rursùs agita, et effunde. Solutiones omnes coque in Cineribus,
         aperto vase, per horas 24. Aquam tinctam, et claram decaputa, et novo
         Retorto vitro⁵⁴ impositam distilla. Fæces vero unde Aquam decaputasti,
         sicca, et nudo igne distilla. Hæc est vera via, cum solis monte Tutiâ. Et sic
         habebis de sanguine Draconis.

                                   Quantum vis.
                                   T. R. V.

[fol. 33ʳ]   Spiritus sublimans omnem
                                   calcem metallicam, et sine
                                quo Aurum potabile nunquàm
                                       fieri potest.

         Magnesiam nigram cum Anatro calcinatam, et ablutam: vel crudam, et non
         calcinatam; vel in salem solutam, contere cum Croco. Trituram solve, et
         habebis. Si vero dictam Magnesiam, aut eius calcem, vel salem, cum sputo
         fixato conjungas, et solvas, habebis spiritum longè præstantiorem. **Idem**
NB.   **fiet si conjungatur cum Dracone crudo, et sanè Crudum cum crudo**
         optimum est. Ne, quæso, obliviscaris.

---

⁵⁴ Sic, for *vitreo*.

Note Well.
Note Well.   Note Well.

NB.   Take equal quantities of the two blacks; project into cleansed aqua fortis,
and agitate with a rod, until nothing more can be put in motion. Then
pour in common aqua fortis, and agitate into a white milk, which [you]
pour out into another glass; and if anything remains insoluble, dissolve
again, once new and common aqua fortis has been added. Agitate the solution anew, and pour out. Concoct all solutions with the heat of the
ashes, in an uncovered vessel, for twenty-four hours. Skim the top of the
tinged and clear water, and distill it in a new glass retort. Dry indeed the
dregs from which you have skimmed off the surface of the water, and
distill with a bare flame. This is the true way, with mountain of gold,
*tutia. And in this way you will have it concerning the blood of the
dragon.[55]

However much you wish.
T. R. V.

A Spirit subliming every
metallic calx and without
which potable Gold
can never be made.

With *crocus grind black magnesia calcinated with nitric salt and
cleansed, or crude uncalcinated magnesia, or magnesia dissolved into salt.
Dissolve what has been ground, and you will have it. If indeed you join
the said magnesia or its calx or salt with fixed spittle, and you dissolve it,
you will have a far more excellent spirit. **The same will be made if it be**
B.   **joined with the crude dragon, and to be sure crude is best with crude.
Do not, I pray, forget.**

---

[55] Though a variety of rhubarb is known as bloodwort or *sanguis draconis* (Gerard, *Herball*, 391), Vaughan meant something else.

Aqua mineralis,
ut puto.

Magnesiam nigram contere cum croco: Adde Anatri partem mediam, vel
sit Ana, si violentia non impedit: vel adde Talci portiunculam, et nudo igne
distilla. Vel calcinetur Magnesia priùs per se, postea cum Croco, et Anatro
de novo teratur, et distilletur.

T. R. V. 1659.°

Laus vero sit Tibi, Deus meus,
misericors!
Amen!

[fol. 33ᵛ blank]

[fol. 34ʳ]   Dixit Valentinus: ℞. rubeam
              Mercurii mineram instar Cinnabaris
              apparentem: item ℞. optimam Auri
              mineram, quam reperire potes.

Rubea mercurii minera, vel est Jecur Draconis cum solo tartaro præparatum, et fixum: Vel est Reguli Scoria cum nitro et Tartaro facta. ambæ
enim hæ mineræ rubeæ sunt, quin et fixæ, undè spiritum dare possunt,
agente Plutone. Quin et tartarum nitro adjectum Draconis spiritum eva-
porare nòn permittit. Experire, quid faciet nitrum prius calcinatum, si cum
novo Tartaro Draconi adjungatur.

Gloria Tibi, Deus meus,
misericors,
Qui unus, et Solus, Sciens
es, et Sapiens.

T. R. V.
1659.°

[fol. 34ᵛ blank]

Mineral water,
according to me.

Grind black magnesia with crocus; add a half part nitric salt, or it may be an equal quantity, if the fierceness hinders not; or add a little portion of talc, and distill with a bare flame. Or magnesia may first be calcinated by itself, then be ground with crocus and nitric salt anew, and distilled.

T. R. V. 1659.

Praise indeed be to Thee,
My merciful God!
Amen!

Valentine said: Take red ore of Mercury appearing like cinnabar; likewise take the best mineral of Gold, which you can find.[56]

The red ore of mercury is either the dragon's liver,[57] prepared and fixed with tartar alone, or the slag of *regulus made with nitre and tartar; for both these are red minerals, and furthermore both are fixed, from whence they can give the spirit, once the *Pluto acts in the matter. And furthermore it is not allowed for tartar cast into nitre to evaporate the dragon's spirit. Test what nitre first calcinated will do, if it is attached with new tartar to the dragon.

Glory to Thee,
my merciful God,
Who art one and only,
Knowing and Wise.

T. R. V.
1659.

---

[56] The properties of antimony were celebrated in the *Triumph-Wagen Antimonii* (1604), attributed to Basil Valentine in the 1624 edition. Since it could free gold from its impurities, antimony was believed to have similar effects on humans. Vaughan perhaps has in mind the procedure for removing the poison or "sulphur" from the antimony to make it a medicine. See *Basil Valentine His Triumphant Chariot of Antimony*, ed. L. G. Kelly, English Renaissance Hermeticism, 3 (New York: Garland, 1993).

[57] I.e., mercury.

[fol. 35ʳ]   Spiritus Mercurii.

Fiat Cinnabaris ex magnesiâ gryseâ, lividâ nec depuratâ. Teratur cum Regulo, vel Mercurio vitæ, vel cum stybio fuso absque Resinâ, vel cum resinâ, quod melius est, &c.

Vel.

Fige [mercurium] cum [aquâ forti]. Fixatum tere cum [plumbo] Philosophico &c. Præcipitatum est rubea Mercurii minera, de qua supra, et Basilio
Valentino. &c. NB.

Mercurius
dulcis, et fixus.

Congela Mercurium cum vapore [plumbi]. congelatum cum sublimato tere,
et eleva, donec figatur. Hæc est vera cura Lues Veneriæ: præsertim spiritus
eius distillatus ex Magnesiâ philosophicâ, cum [aquâ forti] et pluviâ.

Laus Deo, Amen dicunt

T. R. V. 1659.°

[fol. 35ᵛ blank]
[one blank, unnumbered leaf]

[fol. 36ʳ]   Liber Arcanorum T. R. V. 1659.

Aqua Regis.

Anatri part[em] 1. cum 2 vel 3ᵇᵘˢ Scarabæi, combure in mineram citrinam.
Hanc cum oleo vitri distilla, et habebis.

Anatri præparatio.

Digeratur in veneno proprio per dies 8, vel 12, vel 40: et fiet.

Spirit of Mercury.

Cinnabar may be made from grey, leaden, uncleansed magnesia. It may be ground with regulus or the mercury of life,[58] or with antimony fused without resin, or with resin, which is better, etc.

Or.

Fix sophic mercury with aqua fortis. Grind what has been fixed with philosophical lead, etc. The precipitate is the red ore of mercury, concerning which see above,[59] and Basil Valentine, etc. Note Well.

Mercury,
sweet and fixed.

Congeal mercury with vapor of lead. Grind what has been congealed with sublimate; rarefy until fixed. This is the true cure for venereal disease, especially its spirit distilled from philosophical magnesia with aqua fortis and rain water.

Praise be to God, Amen say

T. R. V. 1659.

The Book of Arcana of T. R. V. 1659.

Aqua Regia.

Heat one part nitric salt with two or three parts scarab into a yellow mineral. Distill this with vitriol, and you will have it.

Preparation of Nitric Salt.

It may be decocted in a proper venom for eight, twelve, or forty days, and it will be made.

---

[58] I.e., sophic mercury.
[59] I.e., fol. 34^r.

Acetum Salis.

Talcum, sal commune, et Halinitrum, tere cum crystallis Tartari. Trituram distilla cum oleo vitri, et habebis.

Aqua Draconis.

Anatron tere cum sputo; et cum oleo vitri, vel cum ipso vitro distilla, et fiet.

Aqua Mercurii.

Cinnabarin magnesiæ rufam tere cum vitro, et Anatro, et nudo igne distilla.

Præter hæc, Menstrua sunt nulla, hoc uno, et sequente, excepto.

[fol. 36ᵛ]   NB.

Aqua Scarabæi ad [Solem]
absque Corpore Anatri.

Fige Scarabæum cum [aquâ forti] et pluviâ. Fixatum cum oleo vitri distilla, et fiet.

Si Scarabæus fixus

Cum sputo fixato teratur, et utrumquè cum oleo vitri distilletur, fiet menstruum incomparabile.

NB.

Sputum crudum distillari potest cum Anatro & Talco. Item cum minerâ citrinâ ex Anatro, et Scarabæo.

T. R. V.

Quos Deus conjunxit, Quis
Separabit?

Vinegar of Salt.

Grind talc, common salt, and saltpeter with crystals of tartar. Distill what has been ground with vitriol, and you will have it.

Dragon's Water.

Grind nitric salt with spittle; and distill with vitriol, or with vitriol itself, and it will be made.

Water of Mercury.

Grind red cinnabar of magnesia with vitriol and nitric salt, and distill with a bare flame.

Beyond these menstrua there are none, except the one following.

Note Well.

Water of Scarab for Gold
without the Body of Nitric Salt.

Fix scarab with aqua fortis and rain water. Distill what has been fixed with vitriol, and it will be made.

If fixed Scarab

Be ground with fixed spittle, and both be distilled with vitriol, an incomparable menstruum will be made.

Crude spittle can be distilled with nitric salt and talc. Likewise with the yellow mineral from nitric salt and scarab.

T. R. V.

Whom God has joined, Who
Will separate?

[fol. 37^r]
NB.   Aqua Draconis absque Sputo.

Dracones nigros, et crudos interfice cum veneno Anatri. Interfectis **et effuso veneno**, pluviam affunde; ~~parumque veneni.~~ Digere per dies tres, et
abstractam ~~veneno, igne~~ **pluviam veneno priùs effuso conjunge, et igne**
forti distilla, et habebis. Hæc Draconum aqua a veneno separata, mira facit
super Rebis: Quin et super sputum fixatum: Item super Mercurium veneno
Anatri interfectum. probatum est.

                                    Sal fusibile.

Talcum, et Anatron calcinatum tere Ana, et cum Tartaro funde, et fiet.
iterum incorpora cum Scarabæo.

                                    Aqua secunda,

Fit cum Rebis, sive succo Lunariæ, sicut scis. Laus Deo, Amen!

                            T. R. V. 1659°

[fol. 37^v]   Ex sputo fixato, et per se
                        in menstruo soluto, fit oleum rubeum
                                    et mirabile.

Item ex saccharo magnesiæ, et Aquâ Batrachii, fit aqua solvens ad
[solem] calcinatum, et perlas &c.

                            Aqua Calcinativa
NB.   Raymundi.

Cinnabarin rubeam, et ponderosam ex Magnesiâ, tere cum vitriolo calcinato, et Anatro crudo, et nudo igne distilla.

Note Well.   Dragon's Water Without Spittle

Kill the black and crude dragons with a venom of nitric salt. Pour rain
water on those slain **and the venom already poured out;** ~~and a little venom.~~ Decoct for three days, and **join the rain water drawn out** ~~to the venom, by fire~~ to the venom already poured out, and distill **with a fierce fire,**
and you will have it. This dragons' water separated from the venom does
wonders upon the rebis; and furthermore upon fixed spittle. Likewise beyond sophic mercury slain with venom of nitric salt. It has been proved.

A meltable Salt.

Grind equal quantities of talc and calcinated nitric salt, and melt with tartar, and it will be made. Incorporate again with scarab.

A Second Water,

Is made with rebis, or the juice of lunaria, as you know. Praise be to God,
Amen!

T. R. V. 1659

From spittle fixed and dissolved by itself
in menstruum is made a red
and wondrous oil.

Likewise from sugar of magnesia and from water of borax, a dissolving water is made for calcinated gold and pearls, etc.

                        Calcinated Water
Note Well.   of Ramon Lull.

Grind red and heavy cinnabar from magnesia with calcinated vitriol and
crude nitric salt, and distill with a bare flame.

[fol. 38ʳ]   Tandem nota benè de Quatuor
                              menstruis Salinosis, et
                              Mineralibus.

Primum

Fit ex Anatro dealbato sicut scis, estque Elixir salis universalis, et Arcanum
Arcanorum.

Secundum

Fit ex Anatro crudo, non dealbato, mediantibus sputo, et oleo vitri, estque
venenum mercurii rubeum, figens, et solvens omnia.

Tertium fit

Ex sale citrino ex unâ parte Anatri, et tribus Scarabæi composito, et cocto:
vel ex Scarabæo cum [aquâ forti] et pluvia fixato, estque Balneum solis minerale.

Quartum

Fit ex Anatro crudo et Talco contritis, et cum sputo in oleum coactis: vel
fit ex istis simul calcinatis, et postea cum Scarabæo ad pondus commixtis,
et assatis, Quin et solutis.

Præter Hæc

Nulla sunt menstrua Salinosa: sed ex Duobus nigris crudis, vel ex sputo fixato, et cum Magnesiâ nigrâ soluto, fit Acetum nobile Metallicum.

A Final Note concerning the Four
Saline and Mineral
Menstrua.

The First

Is made from whitened nitric salt, as you know, and it is the universal
*elixir of salt, and the arcanum of arcana.

The Second

Is made from crude nitric salt, not whitened, after halving the spittle and
vitriol, and it is the red venom of mercury, fixing and dissolving every-
thing.

The Third

Is made from yellow salt, composed of one part nitric salt and three of
scarab, and concocted; or from scarab fixed with aqua fortis and rain
water, and it is a mineral bath of gold.

The Fourth

Is made from crude nitric salt and talc ground together and thickened with
spittle into an oil; or it is made from those calcinated together, and afterwards mixed with an equal weight of scarab, assated, and furthermore dissolved.

Besides These

There are no saline menstrua; but from two crude blacks, or from fixed
spittle that is dissolved with black magnesia, a noble metallic vinegar is
made.

[fol. 38ᵛ]   NB.

In Anatri venenum Talcum et Anatron ana projice. digere, distilla, et habebis rem mirabilem. Idem fiat cum Talco solo, vel cum sale communi: estque Arcanum maximum. Expertum in diebus Conjugis meæ dulcissimæ. T. R. V.

Soli Deo Gloria!

Amen!
1659.°

[fol. 39ʳ]   Aqua Sublimans.

~~Spiritum Talci & salis Com[munis] a Draconibus nigris expulsum, projeci super crystallos Tartari: et sublimatus est Tartarus in Glaciem Salinosam, volatilem, et [mercurialem] relicto in fundo sale fixo. Projice ergo [Aquam fortem] superdictos crystallos, et cohoba ad Temperamentum super novam mineram, interpositâ semper Trium dierum digestione, et habebis men-~~
NB.   ~~struum mirabile, & Efficacissimum.~~ **Idem fiat cum Talco, Halinitro, et ~~sale communi, cum Oleo vitri, vel cum Draconibus: vel cum oleo, et sputo.~~**

NB.   Idem fiet,

Si dicti crystalli terantur cum Talco,
Halinitro, et matrice marinâ; distillenturque
cum Oleo vitri.

Laus Deo!
Amen!
T. R. V. 1659.°

Note Well.

Into a venom of nitric salt project equal quantities of talc and nitric salt. Decoct, distill, and you will have a wondrous thing. The same may be made with talc alone, or with common salt; and it is a very great arcanum. Tested in the days of my sweetest wife. T. R. V.

Glory Be to God Alone!

Amen!
1659.

A Subliming Water.

I projected the spirit of talc and common salt expelled from the black dragons upon crystals of tartar; and the tartar was sublimated onto a glassy saline surface, volatile and mercurial, after the remaining salt was fixed in the bottom. Project therefore aqua fortis upon the crystals described above, and cohobate to a temperament beyond a new mineral, after three whole days have been set aside for decoction, and you will have a wondrous and efficacious menstruum. The same may be made with talc, saltpeter, and common salt, with vitriol or with the dragons; or with oil and spittle.

NB.

NB.   The same will be made,

If the said crystals be ground with talc and saltpeter, and in a saline *matrix; and they be distilled with vitriol.

Praise Be to God!
Amen!
T. R. V. 1659.

[fol. 39ᵛ]   NB. NB.

Vel fiat Athanor absque Craticulâ, cum fundo lateritio: sitque juxta fundum ostiolum per quod Cineres eximantur: et in summitate Turris sit fora-
men carbonibus intromittendis accommodatum, atque hac ratione cooper-
culum Turris semel impositum, et lutatum, deponere non erit necesse, estque modus satis Arcanus, et præstantissimus.

Laus tibi mitissime
Jesu! Amen, et
Amen!

[fol. 40ʳ blank]
[Here, in the middle of a gathering, Vaughan turned the notebook upside
down and began to enter his memoranda from the back of the book; thus
the writing is reversed or upside down.]

[fol. 40ᵛ]   Pulvis liquefactivus
                                         noster.

Teratur lacerta cum sale communi, sale nitro, et sulphure: Tunc funde in
gummi nigerrimum. nam hac via separabitur omnino a salibus, quod in
pulvere Paracelsi non evenit.

Gummi

hoc tere cum Sublimato, vel tere regulum cum sulphure prius fusum. Tunc
sublima, et habebis utriusque metalli flores: quos cum sale citrino commisce, et coque, ut docet Turba.

[fol. 41ʳ blank]

Note Well. Note Well.

If you like, let the *athanor be without a grate and with a brick bottom; and let there be a little door near to the bottom by which the ashes may be taken away; and at the summit of the tower let there be an opening suitable for letting charcoal pass within; and with this arrangement it will not be necessary to remove the cover of the tower once it is fitted and sealed with clay; and this is a fairly secret and most excellent way.

Praise Be to Thee
Most Mild Jesus!
Amen and Amen!

Our Liquefying Powder.

Let colcothar be ground with common salt, nitric salt, and sulphur. Then melt into a very black gum. For in this way it will be altogether separated from the salts, which does not happen in Paracelsus's powder.

Grind

This gum with sublimate, or grind regulus melted first with sulphur. Then sublime it, and you will have flowers of each metal, which [you] mix with yellow salt, and concoct, as the *Turba* teaches.[60]

---

[60] The twelfth discourse of the *Turba Philosophorum* discussed something similar, but called it a white salt not a yellow (*flos salis albi*), in *Theatrum Chemicum*, 5: 10–11.

[fol. 41ᵛ]   Idem Corpus

Nigrum de Duobus tere cum Talco, et sale marino: Trituram solve, et pro
certo habebis spiritum igneum omnia solventem.

　　　　Crysolithum purga injecta Resinâ, tunc funde, et Æri fuso
　　　　impone: Mixturam hanc funde cum Resinâ, et paratum
　　　　est.

T. R. V. 1662

Sapientiæ Cor, Constantia.

Laus Deo,

Amen!

[two blank, unnumbered leaves]

[fol. 42ʳ]   Dicit Sendivogius:

Aqua nostra elicitur duspliciter[61]: Suaviter, et cum violentiâ. Suaviter ex
floribus: violenter ex Croco, puta igne nudo. vel suaviter, si Compositum
solvatur in spiritu salis, &c.

NB. De RESINÂ.

Sicut metalla aperit, sic et salia:

Fluat ergo Sal marinum per Resinam, sic et Talcum, et nitrum.
Tunc solvantur, et distillentur cum oleo vitri.

---

[61] Sic, for *dupliciter*.

Grind the Same Black Body

From the two with talc and sea salt. Dissolve what has been ground, and for certain you will have a fiery spirit dissolving all things.

Purge *chrysolite with injected resin, then melt, and put in with molten ore. Melt this mixture with resin, and it is prepared.

T. R. V. 1662

The Heart of Wisdom, is Steadiness.

Praise Be to God,

Amen!

Sendivogius[62] Says:

Our water is drawn out in two ways: sweetly and with fierceness. Sweetly from flowers; fiercely from crocus, that is to say with a bare flame. Or sweetly, if what has been composed is dissolved in spirit of salt, etc.

Note Well. Concerning RESIN.

Even as it opens metals, so it does salts:

Let sea salt therefore flow through resin, and in this same way through both talc and nitre. Then let them be dissolved and distilled with vitriol.

---

[62] Vaughan may have in mind a passage from the *Enigma of the Sages* in *A New Light of Alchymy*, 54.

[fol. 42ᵛ]   Nota de Resinâ.

Totum opus primum abbreviat mirabiliter; nam æris corpus ita aperit, ita
solubile, et volatile facit, ut nihil supra. Æs sic præparatum cum crysolitho
terit Psellus, et per tres dies coquit, deinde solvit. &c. Et sic non opus erit
floribus, sed Ære nostro nigro per Resinam fuso.

                                    Quin et ipse

Crysolithus, absque Chalibe, optimè purgatur injectâ Resinâ, ut expertus
sum. et sic opus primum valdè abbreviatur.

                                  Sic vero longè

Brevius efficies. Utrumque sulphur per Resinam fluant in corpus nigerrimum: Corpus hoc tere cum Aquilâ, et assa per diem integrum; tunc solve,
et Aquila transibit in spiritum subtilissimum. Probatum est in Diebus
Animæ meæ suavissimæ R. V.

Note Concerning Resin.

The entire first work may be shortened wondrously, for the body of the ore so opens itself, makes itself so soluble and volatile, that nothing exceeds it. Psellus grinds the ore thus prepared with chrysolite, and concocts it for three days; afterwards he dissolves it, etc.[63] And in this way there is no need for flowers, but for our black ore poured through resin.

And furthermore Chrysolite Itself

Without chalybs may be best purged with injected resin, as I have proved, and in this way the first work may be exceedingly shortened.

In This Way in Truth

You will make it very much shorter. Let sulphur of both kinds flow through resin into a very black body. Grind this body with sal ammoniac, and assate for a whole day; then dissolve, and the sal ammoniac will turn into a very subtle spirit. It has been tested in the days of my sweetest soul, R. V.

---

[63] No process (see also fol. 43ʳ) involving chrysolite ground with ore can be found in the most likely source, *De lapidum virtutibus* of the Byzantine polymath Michael Psellus; hence, Vaughan may be using a manuscript. See Psellos, *Philosophica Minora*, ed. John Duffy and Dominic O'Meara, 2 vols. (Stuttgart and Leipzig: Teubner, 1989), 1: 116–19.

[fol. 43ʳ]   NB. de processu Pselli.

Dicit crysolithum cum Ære contritum, nigrum fieri instar Atramenti
scriptorii. quod eveniet, si Æs solâ resinâ fusum sit. si vero Resinæ nitrum
addatur, et **Sal commune,** ~~tartarum, ut in Paracelsi pulvere liquefactivo~~,
tunc Æs calcinabitur in gummi nigerrimum, quod commixitioni,[64] et assa-
tioni magis aptum erit.

Aliquid Secreti

In Æris nigredine latere, satis testantur verba Paracelsi, ubi de pulvere isto
liquefactivo agit.

Laus Deo,
Amen!

[fol. 43ᵛ]   Operatio cum Sale
                                        Nitro.

In initio, nullum argentum vivum vulgi valet: sed solum argentum vivum
n[ost]rum rubeum, cum floribus, vel Croco Ciliciæ conjunctum.

℞ plumbi æris **albi,** per Resinam fusi partem unam. Salis nitri partem
sesquialteram. Calcinentur igne fortissimo per horam integram. Calcem
solve, cohoba, et ultimo nudo igne distilla. Sic corpus Æris ascendet in
gummi album, et aureum, cum Magnesiâ tinctum. Gummi hoc cum [aquâ
forti] et frigidâ fige in terram flavam: ex qua extrahe sanguinem Leonis,
cum quo mirabilia facies in succo, et auro: nec-non in Nigro Æris plumbo
per Resinam fuso. Laus Deo, Amen!

[fol. 44ʳ blank]

---

[64] Sic, for *commixtioni.*

Note Well. Concerning the Process of Psellus.[65]

He says chrysolite ground with ore is made black like writer's ink, which will happen if ore be melted with resin alone. If nitre in fact is added to the resin, and **common salt** ~~and tartar as in the liquefying powder of Paracelsus~~, then the ore will be calcinated into the blackest gum, which will be more suitable for mixing and *assation.

Something Secret

On the black-dyed brick of the ore, the words of Paracelsus give evidence enough, where he deals with that liquefying powder.

Praise Be to God,
Amen!

Operation with
Nitric Salt.

In the beginning, no common quicksilver will be efficacious: except our red quicksilver alone joined with flowers or crocus from Cilicia.

Take one part **white** ore of lead, melted by resin. One and a half parts nitric salt. Let them be calcinated for a whole hour with a very fierce fire. Dissolve the calx, cohobate, and distill for the last time with a bare flame. In this way the body of the ore will ascend into a white and golden gum, tinged with magnesia. Fix this gum with cold aqua fortis into a golden earth, from which [you] extract the blood of the lion, with which you will make many wondrous things in juice and gold; and also in black lead of the ore melted by resin. Praise Be to God, Amen!

---

[65] No process involving chrysolite ground with ore can be found in Psellus's *De lapidum virtutibus*; hence, Vaughan may be using a manuscript.

[fol. 44ᵛ]   Via Brevis, et levis.

℞ [Antimonii], et auri nigri, ut ex mineris venit, ana partes æquales. Terantur cum limaturâ martis, et fundantur in Regulum.

℞ Regulum, et funde, et impone sulphuris Aquei 4.ᵗᵃᵐ partem. Tunc extrahe, et fiet.

~~Extractiones~~

~~Omnes evapora, et Magnesiam albam accipe, et cum Chalybe equalitèr funde. Jusis impone parum [sulphuris] aquei, ita ut teri possint. Trituram cum veneno albo calcina igne fortissimo.~~

Et sic

Non opus erit floribus, aut sputo, neque ip[s]o chalybe in operatione primâ.

Nam hac viâ omnia præparantur in simul, et fit Calx mirabilis in effectu, ut inquit Autor Rosarii minoris.

T. R. V. Laus Deo, Amen.

[fol. 45ʳ blank]

A Short and Easy Way.

Take equal parts antimony and black gold, as it came from the minerals. Let them be ground with iron filings and melted into regulus.

Take the regulus, and melt, and place in a quarter part aqueous sulphur. Then extract it, and it will be made.

~~Evaporate~~

~~All the extracts, and take white magnesia, and melt equally with chalybs. In the juice put in a little aqueous sulphur, so that they can be ground. Calcine what has been ground with a white venom with a very fierce fire.~~

And In This Way

There will be no need for flowers or spittle, nor for chalybs itself in the main operation.

For in this way all things are prepared together, and the calx is made wondrous in effect, as the author of the *Rosarium Minor* says.[66]

T. R. V. Praise Be to God, Amen.

---

[66] See chapter I.iii of the *Rosarium Minor*, in Gratarolo, *Vera Alchemia*, 1: 114 [in *Theatrum Chemicum*, 2: 409–10]. This treatise first appeared anonymously in 1541 and was called "lesser" to distinguish it from Arnald of Villanova's *Rosarium Philosophorum*.

[fol. 45ᵛ]   Sequitur Extractio

Humiditatis viscosæ, et spermaticæ, pro
Opere Secundo.

Magnesiam et Chalybem ana commisce: adde parum sulphuris aquei, sive
Resinæ argenteæ, puta partem [quartam]. Tunc extrahe, et fiet.

Laus Deo, Amen!

T. R. V. 1662.

August the 8th.

[fol. 46ʳ blank]

[fol. 46ᵛ]   Isti Duo

Ultimi modi expeditissimi sunt; Hac enim viâ acquiritur mercurii spiritus
nobilissimus, quin et gustu sapidissimus et amabilis: ut expertus sum in
Diebus Vitæ, Animæque meæ Suavissimæ, R. V.

Alia via

Nulla est, nisi magnesia excorietur cum Salibus, quod non convenit.

Laus Deo, Amen!

Si Tu, Jehovah, Deus meus, illuminaveris me: Lux fient Tenebræ meæ.[67]

[fol. 47ʳ blank]

---

[67] Vaughan uses this prayer to close *Anima Magica Abscondita* in *Works*, 137. It is based
on Psalm 18:28 and 2 Samuel 22:29.

Here Follows the Extraction

of the viscose and spermatic Humidity
for the Second Work.

Mix together equal quantities magnesia and chalybs; add a little aqueous
sulphur or silvery resin, that is to say a quarter part. Then extract it, and
it will be made.

Praise Be to God, Amen!

T. R. V. 1662.

August the 8th.

Those Two

Last methods are easy to perform. For by this way a very noble spirit of
mercury is acquired, and furthermore very lovely and savory to the taste;
as I have tested in the days of my sweetest life and soul, R. V.

There is No Other Way

Unless magnesia be made caustic with salts, which is not proper.

Praise Be to God, Amen!

If You, Jehovah, my God, have illuminated me, my darkness will be made
light.

[fol. 47ᵛ]   Viæ variæ, et veræ
                                             ad
                            Primam aquam metallicam.

                            Modus solennis est,

Ut succus calcinatus teratur cum Arsenico sublimato, vel cum pulvere albo
præcipitato.

                                  Item,

℞ Crocum Ciliciæ, cum flore Cirici, conjunctum cum succo vitis. &c.

                                  Item

Magnesiam albam funde cum Chalibe, amalgama, et calcina cum sublimato,

                                  Item

Liquefac lapidum lividum: liquefactum affunde stellæ nostræ nubibus suis
obductæ. Tunc calcina in pulverem nigrum, quem igne forti reduc in albe-
dinem. Item isti duo lapides fundi possunt cum [sulphure], et postea calcinari.

[fol. 48ʳ]   In processibus ex adverso

Scriptis notandum erit: Quod Argentum
vivum **rubrum** cum sulphure̶i̶b̶u̶s̶ **aqueo** mixtum
f̶i̶g̶i̶ ̶e̶t̶ calcinari debet assatione
levi f̶o̶r̶t̶i̶, antequàm solvatur: Atque
de his ulteriùs consule Salomonem
de Lapide minerali: et Nicolai
Flammelli Annotata Eruditissima.

[fol. 48ᵛ blank]
[fol. 49ʳ blank]

Various and True Ways
to the
First Metallic Water.

The accustomed method is,

That calcinated juice be ground with sublimated arsenic or with white precipitated powder.

Likewise

Take crocus from Cilicia with flower of Cirna,[68] joined with the juice of the vine, etc.

Likewise

Melt white magnesia with chalybs; amalgamate, and calcine it with sublimate.

Likewise

Liquefy the leaden stone; pour what has liquefied of our star hidden by its clouds. Then calcine it into a black powder, which [you] reduce with a fierce fire into a whiteness. Likewise those two stones can be melted with sulphur, and afterwards calcinated.

On the Processes Written Opposite

In addition to what has been written, it will be noted that **red** quicksilver mixed with **aqueous** sulphur ought to be ~~fixed and~~ calcinated by **easy,** ~~hard,~~ assation, before it be dissolved. And concerning these matters consult further Solomon *On the mineral stone*, and the very erudite annotations of Nicholas Flamel.[69]

---

[68] I.e., Czersk, Poland.
[69] For Flamel, see the bibliography.

[fol. 49ᵛ]   Caballa Metallorum.

Materiam nostram putrefac per dies 40: vel per 9 dies mediocriter intellectos, inquit Lullius in Codicillo. Autor vero Aureliæ Occultæ dicit per Octiduum. Tunc ex terrâ nostrâ Æthiopiæ extrahe spiritum vitæ, in quo solve succum mercurialem, &c.

Aliter.

Materiam nostram tere cum [sulphure] communi, et in Crucibulo combure. Tunc iterum tere, et coque in Arenâ per dies aliquot, tunc susblima.[70] Vel post Combustionem, statim solve in aquâ salis trium generum, &c.

Arcanum Resinarum.

℞. Dendrocollæ partem 1. Sulphuris mineralis partes 2, vel tres. Sublima, &c. Vice versâ, ℞ sulphuris mineralis part[em] 1. Dendrocollæ partes 2, vel 3. Sublima, et fiet.

Soli Deo Gloria! Amen!

T. R. V. 1661=2.

---

[70] Sic, for *sublima*.

Cabala of Metals.

Putrefy our material for forty days, or for nine days as commonly understood, says Lull in his *Codicillus*.[71] In truth the author of the *Aurelia
Occulta* says for eight days.[72] Then from our earth of Æthiopia extract the
spirit of life, in which [you] dissolve mercurial juice, etc.

By Another Way.

Grind our material with common sulphur, and heat in a crucible. Then
grind again, and concoct in the fire of sand for several days, then sublime.
Or after heating, dissolve immediately in three kinds of salt water, etc.

The Mystery of Resins.

Take one part *dendrocolla, two or three parts mineral sulphur. Sublime,
etc. Or vice versa, take one part mineral sulphur, two or three parts
dendrocolla. Sublime, and it will be made.

Glory to God Alone! Amen!

T. R. V. 1661=2.

---

[71] Pseudo-Lull, *Codicillus, seu vade mecum & Cantilena in quo fontes alchemicæ artis, ac
Philosophiæ reconditioris uberrimè traduntur*, chapter XXXiii, in Manget, *Bibliotheca Chemica
Curiosa*, 1: 890.

[72] Zadith, *Aurelia Occulta Philosophorum*, in *Theatrum Chemicum*, 4: 496 [Manget, *Bibliotheca Chemica Curiosa*, 2: 212]. In the opening paragraph of *Pars Altera*, the author boldly
declared that he will relate openly and exactly the secrets of this art, which other philosophers can only do in parables; moreover, that the work can be done without great cost and
labor, that few instruments are required, and that he can teach in twelve hours the operation that takes only eight days.

[fol. 50ʳ]   De Sale Nitro.

Digeritur in Veneno suo proprio per dies 8, vel 40: Tunc distillatur. Digestio vero fit igne suavi, et lentissimo, aliter non succedit.

T. R. V.

1661=2.

Spiritus salis.

℞ Alkali terrei, et marini partes æquales. adde parum salis gemmæ, cum Ammoniaco ad pondus Alkali. Solve, filtra, sicca. Tunc tere cum Dendrocollâ, et distilla. Omnia Experta in diebus conjugis meæ fidissimæ.

Sal Butleri.

℞. salis tartari, et gemmæ ana: tere, solve, sicca, sed prius funde. Vel ℞ salis naturæ calcinati, et salis Tartari ana &c.

Concerning Nitric Salt.

It is decocted in its own proper venom for eight days, or forty. Then it is distilled. Decoction in truth is accomplished with a sweet and very slow fire; it does not succeed by any other way.

T. R. V.
1661 = 2.

Spirit of Salt.

Take equal parts earthen and sea alkali; add a little rock salt with ammonia in a weight equal to the alkali. Dissolve, filter, dry. Then grind with dendrocolla, and distill. All this was tested in the days of my most faithful wife.

Butler's Salt.[73]

Take equal quantities of salt of tartar and rock salt; grind, dissolve, dry, but first melt. Or take equal quantities of nature's calcinated salt and salt of tartar, etc.

---

[73] The name Butler was associated with a stone possessed with miraculous curative powers. J. B. van Helmont related that an Irishman named Butler had cured someone of erysipelas "by dipping a little stone in a spoonful of milk of almonds." The cure worked almost immediately. See Lynn Thorndike, *A History of Magic and Experimental Science*, 8 vols. (New York: Columbia University Press, 1923–1958), 7: 225–26, 233–35.

[fol. 50^v]   De Salibus.

De Tartaro.

Ex illo cum Anatro calcinato extrahitur aqua vitæ, sicut scis. Aquam illam projice super salem tartari simplicem, Sed prius fundatur sal super magnesiam fusam, donec suæ puritatis signum appareat. Salem solutum digere, cohoba, circula, &c.

De Ammoniaco.

Parum valet, nisi prius figatur cum sale naturæ calcinato, et sic fixatum, Arcanum est. Crudum vero teratur cum sale petræ, et communi, et cum Draconibus nigris. Trituram solve cum [aquâ forti] et pluviâ, &c.

De Sale Naturæ.

Illud est nitrum nostrum. Teritur, et calcinatur cum [sulphure] vegetabili, idque bis, vel ter. Calcinatum super magnesiam funditur, &c.

De Sale gemmæ.

Tritum æqualiter cum Alkali marino, vel terreo, dat spiritum mirabilem cum Draconibus nigris, [aquâ forti], et pluviâ.

Iste spiritus Cremorem tartari sublimat in salem volatilem. Idem faciet forsan spiritus eius cum oleo vitri. Sal vero Tartari volatilis, si vinatur cum sale Tartari fixo, fiet inde res mirabilis.

[one blank, unnumbered leaf]
[fol. 51^r blank]

Concerning Salts.

Concerning Tartar.

From this [tartar] along with calcinated nitric salt is extracted the aqua vitæ, as you know. Project this water upon simple salt of tartar, but first let the salt be melted over molten magnesia, until the sign of its purity appear. Decoct the dissolved salt, cohobate, circulate, etc.

Concerning Ammonia.

It is of little use, unless first it be fixed with nature's calcinated salt, and fixed in this way it is an arcanum. Verily let the crude be ground with rock salt and common salt and with the black dragons. Dissolve what has been ground with aqua fortis and rain water, etc.

Concerning Salt of Nature.

This is our nitre. It is ground and calcinated with an animating sulphur, and this is done, twice or thrice. What has been calcinated is melted over magnesia, etc.

Concerning Rock Salt.

What has been ground yields a wondrous spirit equally with sea or earthen alkali with the black dragons, aqua fortis, and rain water.

That spirit sublimes *cream of tartar into a volatile salt. Its spirit will perhaps do the same with vitriol. Volatile salt of tartar in truth, if it becomes spirituous with fixed salt of tartar, will thence make a wondrous thing.

[fol. 51ᵛ]   Aquæ nobiles.

℞ utriusquè Salis terrei, et marini, sitque utrumque, commune, semilibram. Salis magnesiæ tantundem. distilla cum oleo vitri, et fiet.

Aliter.

℞ Talci, et Anatri partes æquales: sintque priùs soluta, et siccata. tere cum sale magnesiæ, et distilla ut supra, et habebis.

Aliter.

℞. Anatrum cum veneno suo dealbatum: tere cum Sale magnesiæ, et fiet.

Vel,

Corrigatur cum Scarabæo, vel cum Lombardo; Correctum tere cum Sale magnesiæ, et fiet.

NB. NB.

Sali terreo, et marino, adde parum Talci. Tunc adde Salem magnesiæ ad pondus omnium, et fiet.

Omnia Probata, Et experta in Diebus Conjugis meæ Charissimæ.
Laus Deo! Amen! T. R. V. 1659.

[fol. 52ʳ]   NB. NB.

Salia omnia, cuiuscunque generis sint, cum Draconibus immixta, transeunt in Butyrum spissum, et non in aquam, aut oleum tenue. Opus erit ergo mixturâ quadam salium, quæ fit, ut sequitur.

℞ Talci et Anatri solutorum partes æquales. Tere cum Draconibus nigris, et transibunt in oleum tenue.

Item, ℞

Talcum, Anatrum, Sal commune ana: Tere cum Draconibus: Trituram solve, et distilla. Hæc est via, si oleum vitri haberi non potest.

Noble Waters.

Take half a pound each of earthen and sea salt, and each may be common. And just as much salt of magnesia. Distill with vitriol, and it will be made.

By Another Way.

Take equal parts talc and nitric salt; and first let them be dissolved and dried. Grind with salt of magnesia, and distill as above, and you will have it.

By Another Way.

Take nitric salt whitened with its venom; grind with salt of magnesia, and it will be made.

Or,

Let it be corrected with scarab, or with Lombard; grind what has been corrected with salt of magnesia, and it will be made.

Note Well. Note Well.

Add a little talc to earthen and sea salt. Then add salt of magnesia in an amount equal to the weight of all other ingredients, and it will be made.

All proved, and tested in the days of my dearest wife.
Praise Be to God! Amen! T. R. V. 1659.

Note Well. Note Well.

All salts, whatever kind they may be, if mixed in with the dragons, turn into a thick butter and not into water or thin oil. There is need, therefore, for a certain mixture of salts, which is made as follows.

Take equal parts of dissolved talc and nitric salt. Grind with the black dragons, and they will turn into a thin oil.

Likewise, Take

Equal quantities of talc, nitric salt, and common salt. Grind with the dragons. Dissolve what has been ground, and distill. This is the way, if vitriol cannot be had.

[fol. 52ᵛ]   Ignis contra naturam.

Fac cinnabarin ex mercurio, et [sulphure] philosophico. Hunc tere, et
distilla cum Anatro crudo, et habebis.

                          Elixir Universale
                          ex Anatro solo.

Crudum funde, et projice in venenum suum proprium. digere in Cineribus
per dies 8, vel 12. Tunc distilla, cohoba, sublima, et habebis.

                          Lapis Animalis.
Fit sicut scis, estque Arcanum Arcanorum.

                          Ignis naturæ tenuis,
                          et sublimans.

Crocum tere cum sale facto per corrosivam ex magnesiâ nigrâ, et crudâ.
Trituram solve in [aquâ forti] et pluviâ. Digere per horas 24, et distilla, et
fiet pro certo.

Item ℞ crocum, et tere cum Anatro, et magnesia nigrâ, et nudo igne
distilla.

                     Gratiæ sint Deo Altissimo,
                     et filio suo Jesu Christo, Amen!
                     T. R. V. 1659.°

[fol. 53ʳ]   Sequitur vera Expositio
                     Ænigmatis Sendivogiani in Tractatu
                          suo de Sulphure.

Vidit in illo Nemore fontem Aquâ plenum, circa quem deambulabat sal
cum sulphure, inter se altercando, donec ultimò cœperunt pugnare, &c.

Unnatural Fire.

Make cinnabar from sophic mercury and philosophical sulphur. Grind this, and distill with crude nitric salt, and you will have it.

Universal Elixir
From Nitric Salt Alone.

Melt the crude, and project into its proper venom. Decoct with the heat of the ashes for eight or twelve days. Then distill, cohobate, sublime, and you will have it.

The Animated Stone.

It is made in the way you know, and it is the arcanum of arcana.

Nature's Thin
and Subliming Fire.

Grind crocus with salt made by a corrosive from black and crude magnesia. Dissolve what has been ground in aqua fortis and rain water. Decoct for twenty-four hours, and distill, and you will have it for certain.

Likewise take crocus and grind with nitric salt and black magnesia, and distill with a bare flame.

Thanks Be to the most High God
and to His Son Jesus Christ, Amen!
T. R. V. 1659.

Here Follows a True Exposition
of the Sendivogian *Enigma* in his
Tractatus de Sulphure.[74]

He saw in this grove a fountain full of water, around which salt walked about with sulphur, quarreling among themselves, until at last they began to fight, etc.

---

[74] The parable, *Ænigma philosophicum ad filios veritatis*, was added as an appendix to various works, including French's edition, *A New Light of Alchemy . . . To which is added a Treatise of Sulphur* (51–58). The *Enigma of the Sages* is a dialogue between an alchemist and the voice of "Sulphur" on the nature of true philosophical sulphur necessary for the great work.

Alius Ignis Naturæ.

Sputum fixatum cum Magnesiâ excoriatâ coctum, tere cum capite mortuo
Maris nostri: hoc est, cum sale fixo Batrachii. Trituram solve in aquâ
ultimâ eiusdem salis, et habebis. Potest et dicta Aqua, sine sale, (sal enim
non dat, nisi diù steterit,) digeri cum Sericone, et sic congelabitur, instar
NB.   [mercurii] vulgaris. Hoc est Arcanum Sendivogii, et coagulum Roris nostri,
non est nitrum vulgi, sed nitrum nostrum ex petrâ rubeâ: Magnesiam puta, in cuius ventre sal n[ost]rum Armoniacum occultatur, et congelatur.

[fol. 53ᵛ]   Ars tota: ut inventa est
                              in Diebus Conjugis meæ
                              Charissimæ R. V. 1659.°

Sine [aquâ forti] nihil fit in opere universali, quia mercurius sine isto
menstruo figi non potest. Sufficit vulgaris [aqua fortis], sed ex oleo vitri, &
Anatro crudo fit Aqua longè præstantior.

Oleum Salis.

fit ex Anatro per Lombardum correcto: Quin et ex sale marino, et Halinitro, cum tantillo Salis gemmei. Item ex sale marino, et Collâ piscium.
Item ℞ Gemmam, collam, salem marinam, et Anatron ana. distilla cum
oleo vitri, et habebis aquam nobilem. Vicem Collæ supplet Halinitrum. Experire etiàm quid Cremor tartari præstet, cum dictis salibus tritus, et distillatus. Item fige duas, aut tres partes Scarabæi cum unâ Anatri crudi. Fixum
distilla cum oleo vitri. Vel fige Scarabæum cum [aquâ forti], et pluviâ distillatâ. Tunc misce, &c.

Ignis naturæ.

Fit ex sputo Draconis fixato cum magnesiâ excoriatâ. Sed ecce modus bre-
vior, et præstantior! Extrahe salem magnesiæ cum Corrosivâ sicut scis: Extractum distilla cum oleo vitri, et habebis. Idem facere potes cum Mercurio
per Corrosivam fixato, Quin et cum sputo Draconis; sed oleum salis ex
sputo fixato, sanguinem extrahit purissimum.

[fol. 54ʳ blank]

Nature's Other Fire.

Grind spittle, fixed with caustic magnesia and concocted, with the residue of our sea, that is, with fixed salt of borax. Dissolve what has been ground in the last water of the same salt, and you will have it. And the said water, without salt (for salt yields not unless it has stood for a long time), can be decocted with red lead, and in this way it will be congealed, like common mercury. This is the arcanum of Sendivogius, and the cream of our dew, not common nitre, but our nitre from the red stone; for instance magnesia, in whose belly our sal ammoniac is hidden and congealed.

NB.

The Whole Art As It Was Discovered in the Days of my Dearest Wife R. V. 1659.

Without aqua fortis nothing is made in the universal work, because sophic mercury cannot be fixed without that menstruum. Common aqua fortis suffices, but from vitriol and crude nitric salt is made a far more excellent water.

Oil of Salt.

It is made from nitric salt corrected by Lombard, and furthermore from sea salt, and from saltpeter with a small bit of rock salt. Likewise from sea salt and the colla from fish. Likewise take equal quantities of rock salt, colla, sea salt, and nitric salt. Distill with vitriol, and you will have a notable water. Saltpeter [will] take the place of colla. Try also whether cream of tartar may excel, ground with the said salts, and distilled. Likewise fix two or three parts scarab with one of crude nitric salt. Distill what has been fixed with vitriol. Or fix scarab with aqua fortis and distilled rain water. Then mix, etc.

Nature's Fire.

It is made from spittle of the dragon fixed with caustic magnesia. But mark, there is a shorter and more excellent way! Extract salt of magnesia with a corrosive, as you know. Distill what has been extracted with vitriol, and you will have it. You can make the same thing with mercury fixed by a corrosive, and furthermore with spittle of the dragon; but oil of salt, fixed from spittle, extracts very pure blood.

[fol. 54ᵛ]   Febrifugum Nobile.

Somniabam me medicam quandam mixturam ex Anatro et Crystallis
Tartari intentasse. Tartarus vero apparuit instar Aluminis, puta in uno
magno frusto instar Rupis, aut glaciei. Tandem vero instar salis petræ, in
Chrystallos oblongos, sed nitro fragiliores, mutari videbatur. Hi crystalli
(ut interpretor) ex Commixtione minerarum oriebantur, cum Tartarus per
se in eiusmodi Rupem, aut crystallos figurari, aut terminari non possit.
Hoc mihi peccatori indignissimo, in solatium Ægrorum febricitantium,
monstrasse Deum, et impartivisse spero: Pro quo Misericordiæ suæ dono,
sit illi Laus Æterna,

In filio suo Jesu Christo
Animarum fidelium,
Redemptore Unico:
Amen, & Amen!
T. R. V.
1658.

[fol. 55ʳ]   NB. NB. NB. NB. NB.

Sal Naturæ, et Petra salis Raymundi, est nitrum ut è terrâ eruitur, ante
separationem, quam Nitrarii faciunt pro pulvere pyrio componendo. Istud
Nitrum, et parum, puta partem mediam Talci, cum oleo vitri distilla, et
habebis.

Idem fiat cum Alumine crudo,
et stybio per Resinam purgato.

Aqua Nobilis.

NB.   ℞. vitrioli & Aluminis ana: Calcinentur in simul. ℞ huius calcis lib[ram]
1. nitri vulgaris, et crudi lib[ram] 1. Azoc vitrei per Resinam purgati Quartam partem. Tere in simul, et nudo igne distilla. Nitrum corrigi potest
lento igne per Scarabæum. {*}

{* symbol for emphasis used}

A Notable Medicine to Reduce Fever.

I dreamed that I had intended to fashion a certain medicine mixed from nitric salt and crystals of tartar. The tartar truly appeared like alum, that is to say in one great piece like a rock or ice. At length truly it seemed to be changed into oblong crystals, like rock salt, but more fragile than nitre. These crystals (as I judge) arose from the commingling of minerals, when the tartar could not be shaped into a rock of this kind by itself or fixed into crystals. I hope that God has shown and shared this to me, a most unworthy sinner, in solace of those suffering fever. For which gift of His mercy, eternal praise be to Him,

In His Son Jesus Christ,
Only Redeemer of faithful souls,
Amen, and Amen!
T. R. V.
1658.

Note Well. Note Well. Note Well. Note Well. Note Well.

Nature's salt and Ramon Lull's rock salt is nitre as it is dug from the earth before separation, which the nitre-workers do for compounding philosophical sulphur powder. Distill that nitre, and a little talc, that is to say a half part, with vitriol, and you will have it.

The Same May Be Made with Crude Alum,
and Antimony Purged by Resin.

A Notable Water.

Take equal quantities of vitriol and alum. Let them be calcinated together. Take one pound of this calx, one pound of common and crude nitre, a quarter part *azoc purged by resin. Grind together, and distill with a bare flame. The nitre can be corrected with a slow fire by scarab. {*}

[fol. 55ᵛ]   NB. NB.

Fige Mercurium cum [aquâ forti]. Tunc fige sputum. Fixa contere in simul, et aliquantulum coque. Tunc contere cum sulphure magnesiæ, et solve: sic habebis spiritum mercurialem admirandum.

Laus Deo Optimo,
Maximo:
Uni, Soli, Summo, et
Sancto!
Amen! in suo, Quem misit
Jesu Christo!

Amen! et Amen!
T. R. V.
1658.

Quos Deus conjunxit, Quis separabit?

NB. NB. NB. Aqua Calcinativa NB. NB.
Raym: Lullii

℞.   Aluminis & vitrioli calcinatorum lib[ram] 1. nam vitriolum viride valet loco vitrioli Azoquei, in confectione Aquæ n[ostr]æ primæ. Cinnabaris, vel magnesiæ Cinnabarinæ lib[ram] 1. salis nitri lib[ram] 1. Distilla nudo igne, sed relicto spiraculo, et fiet.

T. R. V.

Note Well. Note Well.

Fix mercury with aqua fortis. Then fix the spittle. Grind together what has been fixed together, and concoct a little bit. Then grind together with sulphur of magnesia, and dissolve. In this way you will have a wondrous mercurial spirit.

Praise be to God,
Incomparably Good and Great:
The One, Only, Most High, and
Sacred!
Amen! in His Jesus Christ
Whom He Sent Himself!

Amen! and Amen!
T. R. V.
1658.

Whom God has joined, Who will separate?

Note Well. Note Well. Calcinated Water Note Well. Note Well.
of Ramon Lull

Take one pound of alum and calcinated vitriol, for green vitriol is efficacious in place of azoc in preparing our first water. Distill one pound of cinnabar, or cinnabarine magnesia, and one pound of salt of nitre, with a bare flame, but with a vent left open, and it will be made.
T. R. V.

[fol. 56ʳ]   Additio ad Coronidem.

Aqua composita, mineralis
et metallica.

Sputum fixatum tere cum Anatro per Lombardum correcto. Trituram cum
oleo vitri distilla, et habebis. Idem facito cum omnibus salibus supradictis,
et hoc est Arcanum maximum, cum Talco, et Anatro crudo.

Aqua metallica
Simplex.

Sputum fixatum, aut Mercurium fixatum, unumquodque per se, aut simul
trita, distilla cum oleo vitri, et habebis. Idem fiat cum Sale magnesiæ, et
mercurio fixato.

Alia aqua
metallica.

Sputum fixatum contere cum Sale Magesiæ: Trituram solve in Aquâ, vel
oleo Salis, et fiet pro certo.

[fol. 56ᵛ]   Coronis Aquarum mineralium.

In defectu Scarabæi, calcinetur lacerta cum Anatro crudo, et hæc erit rubea
Mercurii minera instar Cinnabaris apparens, ut dixit Valentinus. Teratur
cum magnesia nigrâ, vel cum eius Sale, solvanturque omnia in [aquâ forti]
et pluviâ rectificatâ. **Loco istius mineræ rubeæ sumatur. Fæx Reguli,
conteraturque cum Magnesiâ nigrâ, et cum novo nitro, &c.** Notandum
est, Quod hæc minera rubea in sublimatione non sputat, sed spiritum dat
subtilissimum, et ferventem, qui est Ignis Pontani, et Philosophiæ.

An Addition to the Conclusion.

A Metallic and Mineral
Compounded Water.

Grind a fixed spittle with nitric salt corrected by Lombard. Distill what has been ground with vitriol, and you will have it. Make the same with all the salts described above, and this is the greatest arcanum, with talc and crude nitric salt.

Simple
Metallic Water.

Grind fixed spittle, or fixed mercury, each one individually by itself, or together; distill with vitriol, and you will have it. The same may be made with salt of magnesia and fixed mercury.

Another
Metallic Water.

Grind a fixed spittle together with salt of magnesia. Dissolve what has been ground in water, or oil of salt, and it will be made for certain.

The Conclusion of Mineral Waters.

When lacking scarab, colcothar may be calcinated with crude nitric salt, and this will be the red ore of mercury appearing like cinnabar, as Valentinus said. It may be ground with black magnesia, or with its salt, and all may be dissolved in aqua fortis and rectified rain water. **In place of that red ore, the dregs of regulus may be supplied and ground together with black magnesia and with new nitre, etc.** It ought to be noted that this red ore does not spit out in sublimation, but yields a very subtle and boiling hot spirit, which is the fire of Pontanus and of philosophy.[75]

---

[75] The epistle of Joannes Pontanus (d. 1572) on the secret mineral fire necessary for the great work was first printed in Latin in 1600, *Epistola in qua de lapide quem Philosophorum vocant agitur*, and was frequently published during the seventeenth century. An English translation by Eirenæus Orandus was issued with an edition of Flamel's *Exposition of the Hieroglyphicall Figures* and *The Secret Book* of Artephius (London, 1624); and another in the *Cheiragogia Heliana* (London, 1659). See John Ferguson, *Bibliotheca Chemica*, 2nd ed. 2 vols. (London: Derek Verschoyle, 1954), 2: 212–13.

Atque hæc sunt,

Quæ in Mineralibus Secretissima inveni, in diebus Conjugis meæ Charissimæ: Quam iterum in Cœlis videre, & alloqui, dabit Deus meus misericors.

Christe Jesu! Lux & Vita Mundi: Filius Dei: Filius, et Redemptor Hominis: Trahe me post Te, Curremus! Amen!

T. R. V. 1658.

Quos Deus conjunxit, Quis separabit?

[fol. 57ʳ]   NB. NB. NB.

Tradunt Antiqui Scriptores, Nitrum fuisse rubei coloris, substantiæ raræ, et spongiæ instar, foraminosæ. Hanc vero nitri speciem perisse putant Neoterici. Est vero nitrum philosophicum, et Scarabæus, ut sequitur, fixatus.

Scarabæi fixi spiritus
admirandus.

℞ illius part[es] 2. Anatri part[em] 1. Combure in Crucibulo ad Colorem subrufum, eritque Saporis, instar salis communis. Si proportio talis sit, ut Scarabæus totus figatur, præstantior erit Operatio.

NB.
Tere, et distilla cum Oleo vitri, et habebis Balneum solis Efficacissimum. **Vel cum vitriolo & Alumine calcinatis, & Azoc vitreo per Resinam purgato. Idem fiat cum Anatro crudo.**

T. R. V. 1658.

Idem eveniet, si Scarabæus **solutus** cum Talco, et halinitro comburitur: Sed cum Anatro probatum est.

And Indeed These Are,

The most secret things in minerals which I have found in the days of my dearest wife, whom my merciful God will grant that I see again and speak with in the heavens.

O Christ Jesus! Light and Life of the world: Son of God: Son and Redeemer of Mankind: Draw me after Thee, We shall run! Amen!

T. R. V. 1658.

Whom God has joined, Who will separate?

Note Well. Note Well. Note Well.

Ancient writers tell us that nitre was of a red color, a rare substance, and like a sponge, full of holes. The moderns in truth suppose that this species has been lost. This in truth is philosophical nitre, and the scarab fixed, as follows.

A Wonderful Spirit of
Fixed Scarab.

Take two parts of this [i.e., scarab], one part nitric salt. Heat in a crucible to a color suffused with red, and it will taste like common salt. If the proportion be such that all the scarab be fixed, the operation will be more excellent.

Grind, and distill with vitriol, and you will have a very efficacious bath of gold. **Or with vitriol and alum of calcinate, and azoc purged by resin. The same may be made with crude nitric salt.**

T. R. V. 1658.

The same will happen if **dissolved** scarab is heated with talc and saltpeter; but it has been proved with nitric salt.

[fol. 57ᵛ]   Coronis Aquarum mineralium.

In defectu collæ, tere cum Talco Halinitrum, et salem marinum: si vero ista
compositio non valet, tunc cum Talco et Halinitro, vel cum talco et sale
marino, tere Anatrum cum Lombardo correctum: vel tere istud Anatrum
cum Talco, Halinitro, et sale marino, et distilla cum oleo vitri, et habebis.
Sintque omnium partes æquales.

Sine oleo vitri,

Tere Anatrum crudum cum Talco, Halinitro, et sale marino: vel sine sale
marino: Trituram cum Alumine, nudo igne distilla, et habebis aquam bonam pro opere incipiendo.

Hac Aquâ

Solve magnesiam contritam cum lacertâ calcinatâ cum Anatro per Scarabæum correcto. Idem fit cum [aquâ forti], et pluviâ rectificatâ. Quin et
cum Duobus nigris crudis, cum Talco, et Anatro crudo contritis.

In calcinatione

Corporum nullum sal valet præter Anatrum cum Scarabæo correctum: vel
spiritu suo venenoso dealbatum, et hoc est secretum maximum.

In opere hoc minerali

Sine Aquâ forti nihil unquam fit. Fit [aqua fortis] optima ex oleo vitri, &
Anatro crudo.

The Conclusion of Mineral Waters.

When lacking colla, grind saltpeter and sea salt with talc. If in truth that composition is not effective, then, with talc and saltpeter, or with talc and sea salt, grind nitric salt corrected with Lombard; or grind that nitric salt with talc, saltpeter, and sea salt, and distill with vitriol, and you will have it. **These should be in equal parts of each.**

Without vitriol,

Grind crude nitric salt with talc, saltpeter, and sea salt; or, without sea salt. Distill what has been ground with alum with a bare flame, and you will have a good water for beginning the work.

With This Water

Dissolve magnesia ground with colcothar calcinated with nitric salt corrected by scarab. The same is made with aqua fortis and rectified rain water. And furthermore with the two crude blacks ground with talc and crude nitric salt.

In the calcination

of the bodies no salt is efficacious besides nitric salt corrected with scarab, or whitened by its poisonous spirit, and this is the greatest secret.

In this mineral work

Nothing is ever made without aqua fortis. The best aqua fortis is made from vitriol and crude nitric salt.

[fol. 58ʳ] Modus singularis, quo sublim=
atum aut figatur, aut in
Aquam solvatur.

Includatur Matratio, aut sphæræ vitreæ colli longissimi, obtureturquè quàm optimè. Vitrum cum suo Sedili, Caldario, aut Ollæ ferreæ Aquâ plenæ immergatur. Fac ut Aqua bulliat per horas 12 igne violento. Tunc extrahe, et vide, si satis sit: sin aliter, repete donec fiat. Idem experiri potest cum Mercurio crudo currente: quin et cum salibus omnibus, et cum sulphure vulgari, Ambrâ, Mannâ, et Camphorâ, et saccharo. &c. NB. Eodem modo calcinari possunt crystalli et perlæ, absque lagenâ stanneâ.

[fol. 58ᵛ] Coronis Operis
mineralis.

Extrahe Succum Lunariæ, et evapora: Residuum pone in Terra sua ad debitum pondus. Tunc cum veneno albo tere, et calcina ad rubedinem. Rubeum hoc solve in Aquis mineralibus suprascriptis, et invenies.

Cinnabaris cruda, sine Ære, solvi potest, et sublimari, quin et in Aquam converti, estque Lullii menstruum ad Aurum potabile.

Lapis Animalis.

Magnesiam evaporatam pone ad pondus in Terrâ Veneris purissimâ. Adde Lunam ad pondus utriusque. Tunc putrefac, et habebis.

Laus vero sit Uni, Soli, et
Summo Deo! Amen in
Filio suo Jesu Christo! Amen
dicunt T. R. V. 1658.

A Singular Method by which sublimate
is fixed or dissolved into water.

Let a *matrass or glass spheres with a very long neck be inclosed, or sealed
as well as may be. A glass with its own seat may be immersed in a
cauldron or in the water of a full iron pot. Do this so that the water will
seethe for twelve hours with a fierce fire. Then extract it, and see if it be
enough; if not, repeat until it be made. The same can be proved with
crude, running mercury, and furthermore with all salts, and with common
sulphur, amber, *manna, and camphor and sugar, etc. Note Well. By the
same method crystals and pearls can be calcinated without a tin vessel.

The Conclusion of the
Mineral Work.

Extract and evaporate the juice of lunaria. Place the residue in its own
earth to the required weight. Then grind with a white venom, and calcine
to a redness. Dissolve this red matter in the mineral waters described
above, and you will discover it.

Crude cinnabar, without ore, can be dissolved and sublimed, and furthermore converted into water. This is Lull's menstruum for potable gold.

The Animated Stone.

Place evaporated magnesia in an equal weight of the very purest earth of
Venus. Add silver in an amount equal to the weight of each. Then putrefy,
and you will have it.

Praise indeed be to the One, Only and
Most High God! Amen in
His Son Jesus Christ! Amen
Say T. R. V. 1658.

[fol. 59ʳ]   NB. de opere minerali.

Factâ compositione Æris, et magnesiæ albæ, repurgatæ: pone intùs uncias
2, vel tres Mercurii crudi: ita tamen ut compositio tenax sit, et dura: si
enim flueret, aut emolliretur, periret opus omnino: adde ergo parum fumi
albi, scil[icet] part[em] 1, ut teri possit, et ut docet Morienus. Tunc cum veneno suo albo calcina. &c. Si Magnesia sit ex stanno, per se in [aquâm] dis-
tillabit, sine omni liquore solvente.

Laus Deo, Amen!

T. R. V. 1658.

NB. NB. NB. NB.

℞. rubeam [mercurii] mineram ex magnesia impurâ: teratur cum Ære, et nitro, et nudo igne distilletur. Hic est ignis contra naturam, et si fumus albus
abesset, esset Ignis verus naturalis.

[fol. 59ᵛ]   Atque hæc sunt,

Quæ in Mineralibus, et Salibus, secretissima inveni, in diebus Conjugis
meæ Charissimæ, Quam iterum in Cœlis videre, et Alloqui, dabit Deus
meus optimus et maximus. Restat nunc Lapis Animalis, in Cuius solutione,
et Calcinatione, Salia, et sublimatum, locum nòn habent: Cum totum hoc
fiat Aquâ suâ propriâ, currente, et Metallicâ, &c.

Benedictum sit nomen Dei,

Domini nostri, Sublimis, et Gloriosi:

Amen

In Filio suo, Jesu Christo! Qui

Contritæ omnis, et Humilis Animæ,

Salvator est Fidelis, et

Misericors.

Amen! & Amen!

T. R. V.

Christe Jesu! Lux, & Vita Mundi: Filius Dei: Filius, & Redemptor Hominis: Trahe me, Post Te: Curremus. Amen!

T. R. V. 1658.

Note Well. Concerning the mineral work.

After the ore and the restored white magnesia have been compounded, place two or three ounces of crude mercury within, so that the composition be firm and hard; for if it liquefied or softened, the work would be lost altogether. Add therefore a little white smoke, namely one part, so that it can be ground, as Morienus teaches. Then calcine with its white venom, etc. If the magnesia be from tin, it will distill by itself into water, without any sort of dissolving liquid.

Praise Be to God, Amen!
T. R. V. 1658.
Note Well. Note Well. Note Well. Note Well.

Take red ore of mercury from impure magnesia; let it be ground with ore, and nitre, and distilled with a bare flame. This is unnatural fire, and if the white smoke were absent, it would be true natural fire.

And Indeed These Are

Those most secret things that I found in minerals and salts in the days of my dearest wife, whom my incomparably good and great God will grant that I see again and speak with in the heavens. Now the animated stone remains, in whose solution and calcination the salts and the sublimate will not have a place, since this whole may be made with its proper water, running and metallic, etc.

Blessed be the name of God,
Our Lord, Sublime and Glorious,
Amen.
In His Son, Jesus Christ, Who,
of every Contrite and Humble Soul,
Is the Faithful and Merciful
Savior.
Amen! and Amen!
T. R. V.

O Christ Jesus! Light and Life of the world: Son of God: Son and Redeemer of Mankind: Draw me, after Thee. We shall run! Amen!
T. R. V. 1658.

[fol. 60ʳ]   Calcinatio Antimonii.

℞ illius libr[am] 1. salis petræ tantundem, cum unciâ unâ salis communis.
Tere in simul, et in patellâ combure, vel in Crucibulo, ut supra dixi de
Draconibus, subtitulo Secreti Occultissimi. Laus Deo, Amen!

T. R. V.
1658.

℞ Lithargyrii et Talci: vel magnesiæ nigræ et Talci: vel salis Crysolithi et
Talci partes æquales. distilla cum oleo vitri, et fiet. Valet etiam Sal Lithargyrii factum cum A[quâ]F[orti], sicut scis. Idem fieri potest cum solo Stybio, et hæc diligentèr annotabis.

T. R. V.
1658.

[fol. 60ᵛ]   De Mercurio, et sputo.

Figuntur cum [aquâ forti] et tunc solvi possunt in oleo Salis mineralis, et
compositi. Vel in Aquâ ex sale Crysolithi, et oleo vitri. Mercurius cum
[aquâ forti] fixus, et in Aceto solutus, si denuò cum oleo vitri distilletur,
dabit spiritum utilissimum. **Oleo vitri adde spiritum salis, in utràque
distillatione Crysolithi, et Mercurii fixati.**

De Anatro Solo.

Occiditur, et mitescit omninò digestione in spiritu suo venenoso, sicut scis.
Et sic habebis Acetum eius album, et subtilissimum: Quin et oleum rubens
instar Rubini. Secretum hoc nobilissimum est, quod inveni diebus Conjugis
meæ Charissimæ.

Calcination of Antimony.

Take one pound of this [antimony], just as much rock salt, with one ounce of common salt. Grind together, and heat in a dish, or in a crucible, as I said above concerning the dragons, under the title of Very Hidden Secrets.[76] Praise Be to God, Amen!

T. R. V.

1658.

Take equal parts litharge and talc, or black magnesia and talc, or chrysolite salt and talc. Distill with vitriol, and it will be made. Salt of litharge is also efficacious made with aqua fortis, as you know. The same can be made with stibium alone, and this you will note diligently.

T. R. V.

1658.

Concerning Mercury and Spittle.

They are fixed with aqua fortis and then can be dissolved in oil of mineral and compounded salt. Or in water from salt of chrysolite and vitriol. Mercury fixed with aqua fortis and dissolved in vinegar, if distilled once more with vitriol, will yield a very useful spirit. **Add spirit of salt to the vitriol, in both the distillation of chrysolite and of fixed mercury.**

Concerning Nitric Salt Alone.

It is struck down and becomes soft altogether in decoction in its poisonous spirit, as you know. And in this way you will have its white and very subtle vinegar, and furthermore a crimson oil like a ruby. This is a very noble secret, which I discovered in the days of my dearest wife.

---

[76] See fol. 62^r.

Compositio mira.

Stybium effusum, et fervens extingue frustulatìm in Mercurio bullienti: vel
congelatum tere cum stybio fuso, et inter duo Crucibula coque in Arenâ,
igne forti, ut in unum corpus coalescant. Hoc corpore sublimatum contere,
vel salem &c.

Acetum, et Aqua Vitæ R. L.

Nigrum nigrius nigro, Corpore suo albo commixtum distilla in Cineribus,
per se. vel solve illud in Aqua vitæ Tartarizatâ sicut scis, sitque Tartarum
optimum ex vino rubro, &c.

Laus Deo. Amen!

[fol. 61ʳ]   De oleo vitri, & Salibus.

Quando spiritus ex dictis salibus, et Oleo extraxisti, Caput mortuum contere cum Draconibus, et nudo igne distilla: sintque duæ partes Draconum,
ad unam Cap[itis] mortui. Sic totum oleum recuperabis, et longè præ-
stantiùs quam fuit primum, tam ad Alchemiam, quam ad Medicinam.

Talco, Aquilæ,

Et Draconibus affunde spiritum vitrioli vel eius oleum aquâ mixtum; digere, et distilla.

T. R. V. 1658.

Oleum vitri rectifica a Lithargyrio, et Antimonii Croco: sic habebis rem
nobilem ad medicinam. Vel rectificetur[77] a duobus draconibus nigris, et
crudis.

Vel a solo chalybe, et sublimato: sitque oleum Aquâ mixtum.

NB. NB.

---

[77] Sic, for *rectificietur*.

An Astonishing Composition.

Little bit by little bit extinguish in the bubbling mercury the seething stibium poured out; or grind what has congealed with molten stibium, and concoct between two crucibles in the fire of sand with a fierce fire, so that they may coalesce into one body. With this body grind the sublimate together, or the salt, etc.

Vinegar and the Aqua Vitæ of Ramon Lull.[78]

Distill with the heat of the ashes, by itself, a black blacker than black,[79] commingled with its white body. Or dissolve this in the aqua vitæ tartarized, as you know, and let it be the best tartar from red wine, etc.

Praise Be to God. Amen!

Concerning Vitriol and Salts.

When you have extracted the spirit from the said salts and oil, grind the residuum with the dragons, and distill with a bare flame; and let there be two parts dragon to one of the residuum. In this way you will recover all the oil, and it will be more excellent by far than it was at first, both for alchemy and for medicine.

Pour spirit of vitriol,

In talc, sal ammoniac, and the dragons, or pour its oil mixed with water; decoct and distill.

T. R. V. 1658.

Rectify the vitriol from litharge and crocus of antimony; in this way you will have an excellent medicament. Or it will be rectified from the two black and crude dragons.

Or from chalybs alone and sublimate, and let the oil be mixed with water.

Note Well. Note Well.

---

[78] Vaughan may have in mind one of the versions for a fortified *aqua calcinativa* described on fol. 14ʳ; see note 26.

[79] See fol. 20ʳ and note 35.

[fol. 61ᵛ]   Praxis operis mineralis.

℞ duo Nigra: Calcina cum Anatro per Scarabæum correcto, et ablue. Tunc sicca calcem, et contere cum Aquilâ, quæ fit, ut sequitur. ℞ Talci part[em] 1. Anatri part[es] 2. purga cum Scarabæo, sitque Scarabæus ad pondus Talci. Iste sal est Aquila.

Vel calcina cum Anatro crudo, sed cum Talco, Halinitro, et sale communi composito, et tunc non opus erit ablutione: sed statim solve in Aquâ forti, et pluviâ.

In Defectu [Aquæ fortis],

℞. Talci, Halinitri, salis petræ, de unoquoque semilibram: Aluminis crudi tantundem, vel libram unam. Distilla igne nudo, et habebis.

Operatio cum Oleo vitri.

Fit cum Talco; sale communi, et Collâ: Et in defectu Collæ, cum Halinitro. Item Aquila ut supra composita et Tartari Crystallus cum dicto oleo distillatus, dabit menstruum egregium.

De Scarabæo.

Sublimatur cum Aceto, et Aqua vitæ. Quin et cum Aceto, et Anatro transit in oleum acidissimum, quod Auri Balneum est.

Calcinatio Corporum
perfectorum.

Fit cum Mercurio crudo, et sublimato: adjecto Anatro crudo, vel correcto: et ita sol calcinatur. Et sic [mercurius] cum Magnesiâ philosophice sublimatur:

Quinta Essentia Salium.

Media est Illorum, et oleosa substantia. Extrahitur distillatione per Kyman, nec aliter fieri potest.

Praxis of the Mineral Work.

Take the two blacks. Calcine with nitric salt corrected by scarab, and wash away. Then dry the calx, and grind with sal ammoniac, which is made as follows. Take one part talc and two parts nitric salt; purge with scarab, and let the scarab be in an amount equal to the weight of talc. That salt is sal ammoniac.

Or calcine with crude nitric salt, but compounded with talc, saltpeter, and common salt, and then there will not be any need for washing; but dissolve immediately in aqua fortis and rain water.

When lacking Aqua fortis,

Take talc, saltpeter, rock salt, a half pound of each; [take] the same amount of crude alum, or one pound. Distill with a bare flame, and you will have it.

The Operation with Vitriol.

It is made with talc, common salt, and colla; and when lacking colla, with saltpeter. Likewise sal ammoniac, compounded as above, and crystal of tartar, distilled with the said oil, will yield an uncommon menstruum.

Concerning Scarab.

It is sublimed with vinegar and aqua vitæ. And, furthermore, with vinegar and nitric salt, it turns into a very acidic oil, which is a bath of gold.

Calcination of Perfect Bodies.

It is made with crude mercury and sublimate, after the crude nitric salts have been thrown in or corrected; and so gold is calcined. And in this way mercury with magnesia is sublimed philosophically.

The Quintessence of Salts.

It is the middle of these and an oily substance. It is drawn out by distillation through a cucurbit, nor can it be made by any other way.

[fol. 62ʳ]   Secretum mirabile, et occultissimum.

Dracones nostros Nigros cum Talco, et Aquilâ tere. Trituram in Crucibulo positam combure, et quam primùm incalescet, avolabit Aquila cum sputo, elevabitque sese supra massam in formâ liquidâ, & oleosâ: quæ statim indurabitur, et concrescet in Cinnabarin fixam, & nobilem. Repete operationem cum novis Avibus, donec Draco totalitèr ascendat. Tunc lava, et utere.

Magna sunt hæc, et mirabilia: Sunt et mihi gratissima, Quòd Te vivente, quòd Natibus tuis Comparata sunt, O Conjux[80] Charissima! Neque enim ista periclitari, tantùm passa es, sed renitentibus Amicis, hortabaris: adstitisti mihi sempèr, et annuisti
—Sydereo Læta Supercilio.

Hæc Ego in Tui gratiam recepi: Hæc Tecum in Dotem mihi dedit Deus.
T. R. V. 1658.

[fol. 62ᵛ]   Ex Libris Th: & Reb: Vaughan.
                                   1658.

                    Quos Deus conjunxit: Quis separabit?

                    As God decreed, So wee agreed.

                    In Te Domine speravi: non
                    Confundar in Æternum.[81]

                             T. R. V.
                              1658.

[fol. 63ʳ blank]

---

    [80] Sic, for Conjunx.
    [81] Psalm 31:1; 71:1. This prayer also forms the last response of the medieval hymn, "Te Deum," which was prescribed for daily use at Matins in the Book of Common Prayer.

A Wondrous and very Hidden Secret.

Grind our black dragons with talc and sal ammoniac. Heat in a crucible
what has been ground, and as soon as it grows warm, sal ammoniac will
fly off with the spittle and will rise itself up above the mass in a liquid and
oily form, which will immediately be hardened and clot into a fixed and
notable cinnabar. Repeat the operation with new birds until the dragon to-
tally ascends. Then wash and use.

Great are these things and wonderful. They are very pleasing to me, because they were prepared in your time, while you were living, oh dearest
wife! For you did not only suffer me to put those things to the trial, you
actually urged me to do so against the oppostion of friends: you stood by
me always and cheerfully nodded
        —your heavenly approval.

These I received thanks to you; these God gave me with you in a wedding
portion. T. R. V. 1658.

From the Books of Thomas and Rebecca Vaughan.
1658.

Whom God has joined, Who will separate?

As God decreed, so wee agreed.

In Thee, O Lord, have I trusted.
Let me never be confounded.

T. R. V.
1658.

[fol. 63ᵛ]   De Anatro solo.

Purgatur Anatron mirabiliter in spiritu suo venenoso: et sic habebis Acetum album, subtilissimum, cum oleo rubeo instar Carbonis igniti. Tene secretum hoc admirabile, inventum in diebus conjugis meæ Charissimæ.

De Scarabæo.

Sublimatur cum Aceto distillato, et Aquâ Vitæ, et cum Aceto, et Anatro distillatur in oleum Acidissimum, quod Auri Balneum est.

De Mercurio, et sputo.

Figuntur cum [aquâ forti], et postea solvuntur in oleo Salis Compositi. Corpora calcinantur cum sublimato, et sale, et sic servatur sublimatum, et crescit. Sic et [aurum] calcinatur.

Quinta Essentia

Salium extrahitur, et separatur per Kymam, sicut scis. &c.

[fol. 64ʳ blank]

Concerning Nitric Salt Alone.

Nitric salt is purged wondrously in its poisonous spirit; and in this way you will have a white vinegar, very subtle, with a red oil like ignited charcoal. Keep this admirable secret, discovered in the days of my dearest wife.

Concerning Scarab.

It is sublimated with distilled vinegar and aqua vitæ, and with vinegar and nitric salt is distilled into a very acidic oil, which is a bath of gold.

Concerning Mercury and Spittle.

They are fixed with aqua fortis, and afterwards are dissolved in oil of compounded salt. The bodies are calcinated with sublimate and salt, and in this way the sublimate is saved and it grows. And in this way gold is calcinated.

The Quintessence

Of salts is extracted and separated in a cucurbit, as you know, etc.

[fol. 64ᵛ]   Praxis Operis mineralis.

Pro isto incipiendo, sufficit Aq[ua] fort[is] et pluvia. Duo nigra vero calcinantur optimè cum Anatro per Scarabæum correcto. Tunc ablutæ calces
teruntur ad pondus cum Talco, et Anatro, et solvuntur o[mn]ia in A[quâ]
F[orti] supradictâ. ℞ Talci part[em] 1. Anatri part[es] 2. purga cum Scarabæo. Iste sal Aquila vocatur.

Alia Nigrorum
Calcinatio.

℞ Talci, Halinitri, salis communis: Halinitri puta, et salis communis partes
æquales: Talci vero quantum utriusque: Salis petræ quantum Talci. Terantur cum duobus nigris, et tenuiter sparsa calcinentur in patellâ. Ista Calx
~~Calx~~ solvi debet absque ulla ablutione.

In defectu vero [Aquæ fortis],

℞ Talci, Halinitri, salis petræ, de unoquoque libram mediam. Terantur in
simul cum librâ unâ Alumnis crudi, et nudo igne distilla. Addi potest sal
Commune.

Operatio cum oleo
vitri.

Fit cum Talco, sale communi, et collâ. Et in defectu collæ, cum Halinitro.
Quin et cum Talco, et Anatro per Scarabæum correcto.

Valet et Tartari Crystallus cum istis salibus commixtus.

                                                        T. R. V. 1658.

[fol. 65ʳ blank]

Praxis of the Mineral Work.

For beginning that work, aqua fortis and rain water suffices. The two *blacks indeed are calcinated best with nitric salt corrected by scarab. Then the washed calxes are ground with an equal weight of talc and nitric salt, and all are dissolved in the aqua fortis described above. Take one part talc, two parts nitric salt. Purge with scarab. That salt is called sal ammoniac.

Another Calcination of the Blacks.

Take talc, saltpeter, common salt. Take, that is to say, equal quantities saltpeter and common salt; take as much talc as of each, then as much rock salt as talc. Let them be ground with the two blacks, and let that be calcinated thinly spread out in a dish. That calx ought to be dissolved with any washing.

When Lacking Even Aqua fortis,

Take a half pound each of talc, saltpeter, and rock salt. Let them be ground together with one pound of crude alum, and distill with a bare flame. Common salt can be added.

The Operation With Vitriol.

It is made with talc, common salt, and colla. And when lacking colla, with saltpeter. And furthermore with talc and nitric salt corrected by scarab.

Crystal of tartar is also efficacious mixed with those salts.

T. R. V. 1658.

[fol. 65ᵛ]   Alius modus faciendi
                          primam [Aquam] mineralem.

Calcina stybium cum 4, 5 aut sex partibus nitri. Tunc ablue salem, et sicca.
Eodem nitro calcina compar eius nigrum. Ablue salem, et sicca. Tunc
utramque calcem conjunge, et aliquantulum combure. ℞. huius calcis
part[em] 1. Talci et Anatri correcti partem mediam: solvantur omnia in
A[quâ] F[orti] et pluviâ. digere, distilla, repete, et habebis.

                                    NB.

Stybium cum 5 partibus nitri calcinatum, et ablutum, iterum cum sui pondere de novo nitro combure, igne forti. Tunc ablue, et iterum per se combure, ita ut non fluat. Tunc solve in aquâ Talci, et Halinitri, sicut scis, et
habebis oleum eius verum.

                            T. R. V. 1658.
                          Deo summo, et soli
                          sit omnis Gloria:
                               Amen!

[fol. 66ʳ blank]

Another Way of Making the
First Mineral Water.

Calcine stibium with four, five, or six parts nitre. Then wash the salt, and dry. With this same nitre, calcine an equal amount of its black. Wash the salt, and dry. Then join each calx, and heat a little. Take one part of this calx, a half part talc and corrected nitric salt; let them all be dissolved in aqua fortis and rain water. Decoct, distill, repeat, and you will have it.

Note Well.

Take stibium, calcinated with five parts nitre and washed, and heat again with its own weight of new nitre with a fierce fire. Then wash and heat again by itself, so that it does not liquefy. Then dissolve in water of talc and saltpeter, as you know, and you will have its true oil.

T. R. V. 1658.
May All Glory Be
To God Alone and Most High
Amen!

[fol. 66ᵛ]   Nota bene.

Calcina stybium cum nitro, et Scarabæo. Calcem contere cum crysolitho
nigro, et Talco ad mediam partem crysolithi. Solvantur omnia in [aquâ
forti], et fiet.

                                        Nota bene.

Quando sublimatum cum stybio, vel Regulo conjungis, adde parum Scarabæi. Si vero Regulus ex pluribus, et mollibus metallis compositus sit, calcinabis illud cum Anatro per Scarabæum correcto. Quin et eodem Anatro
calcinari potest stybium, et regulus eius in medicamenta diaphoretica. Quin
NB.   et duo nigra calcinari possunt cum Anatro, Talco, et Scarabæo tritis, et
simul mixtis. postea solvuntur in Aquâ forti, atque ita tolli potest sumptus,
quem in Renovatione [aquæ fortis] expendi, aliter necesse est.

        Christe Jesu! Lux, et vita Mundi: Filius Dei: Filius, et Redemptor Ho-
minis: Trahe me post Te: Curremus! Amen!
                        T. R. V. 1658.

[fol. 67ʳ blank]

[fol. 67ᵛ]   De Calcinatione Corporum.

Purga Crysolithum per Resinam. Tunc contere cum mercurio crudo, et
sublimato. Adde salem et in Arenâ sublima. Sic optime calcinabitur, Quin
et sublimatum multiplicabis, et longè præstantius efficies.

                                  Calcinatio solis.

Candefactum, aut ignitum projice in [mercurium]. Tunc tere cum sublimato, et Anatro crudo, vel per Scarabæum correcto, et fiet.

Note Well.

Calcine stibium with nitre and scarab. Grind the calx together with black chrysolite and half as much talc as chrysolite. Let all be dissolved in aqua fortis, and it will be made.

Note Well.

When you join sublimate with stibium or regulus, add a little scarab. If indeed the regulus is compounded from many soft metals, you will calcine this with nitric salt corrected by scarab. And furthermore stibium can be calcinated with the same nitric salt, and its regulus into dia-phoretic medicaments. And furthermore the two blacks can be calcinated NB with nitric salt, talc, and scarab, ground and mixed together. Afterwards they are dissolved in aqua fortis, and so the expense can be avoided, which otherwise is necessary to incur in the renovation of aqua fortis.

O Christ Jesus! Light and life of the World: Son of God: Son and Re-deemer of Mankind: Draw me after Thee: We shall run! Amen!
T. R. V. 1658.

Concerning the Calcination of Bodies.

Purge chrysolite through resin. Then grind with crude mercury and subli-mate. Add salt and sublime in the fire of sand. In this way it will best be calcinated, and furthermore you will multiply the sublimate, and you will make it more excellent by far.

Calcination of Gold.

Project what has been made white or ignited into mercury. Then grind with sublimate and crude nitric salt, or corrected by scarab, and it will be made.

Compositio mira.

Stybium fusum projice in mortarium, et dum fervet, frustillatìm extingue in [mercurio] bullienti. Vel si hac viâ non succedet: fusum et tritum contere cum [mercurio] congelato. Tunc inter duo crucibula coque in Arenâ igne forti, ut ferè fundatur, et in unum corpus coalescat. Hoc corpore sublimatum contere, et distilla. &c.

Aliud Menstruum.

Salem crysolithi ut supra calcinati, tere, et distilla cum oleo vitri. Idem facito cum sputo fixato. T. R. V.

[fol. 68^r]   NB.

In Confectione Aquæ primæ mineralis cum [aquâ forti], sint tres partes stybii ad duas Crysolithi: vel sint utriusque partes æquales, quod expertus sum.

Fixatio stybii
in medicamentum efficacissimum.

Figitur totum, ut sequitur. ℞ illius partem unam: salis petræ partes 4. vel 5. terantur in simul, et igniantur in mortario. Si admoto igne, non flagrant, bene est: sin alitèr, adde plus salis petræ, et fiet.

In hac operatione

Sumptus facit sal petræ: ℞ ergo salis petræ et stybii partes æquales. Scarabæi partem sesquialteram respectu salis petræ. contere, et combure, et habebis.

An Astonishing Compound.

Project molten stibium into a mortar, and while it seethes, little bit by little bit extinguish it in bubbling mercury. Or, if it does not succeed by this method, grind what has been melted and ground with congealed mercury. Then heat between two crucibles in the fire of sand with a fierce fire, so that it is nearly all melted and coalesces into one body. With this body grind the sublimate, and distill, etc.

Another Menstruum.

Grind salt of chrysolite, calcinated as above, and distill with vitriol. Do it again with fixed spittle. T. R. V.

Note Well.

In preparation of the first mineral water with aqua fortis, let there be three parts stibium to two of chrysolite; or equal parts of each, which I have tested.

Fixing Stibium
into a very efficacious medicament.

The whole is fixed as follows. Take one part of this [stibium], four or five parts rock salt; let them be ground together and ignited in a mortar. If they do not burn when fire has been applied, it is well; if not, add more rock salt, and it will be made.

In this Operation

Rock salt creates the expense; therefore take equal parts rock salt and stibium, one and a half parts scarab with respect to the rock salt. Grind together, and heat, and you will have it.

[fol. 68ᵛ]   Ars vera, Quam concessit
                                mihi D. O. M. in Diebus
                                Conjugis meæ Charissimæ.
                                        1658.

Aqua Prima mineralis.

Tere Duos Nigros, ut ex mineris veniunt, sintque tres partes chrysolithi ad
duas stybii. Adde Anatrum et Talcum: sintque Anatri partes duæ, ad unam
Talci, si cum Scarabæo præparare velis. Solvantur omnia in [aquâ forti], et
pluviâ, et in Arenâ distillentur, et fiet. Aquâ[82] fortis Clavis est operis
universalis, secundum viam mineralem, nam sine istâ aquâ Draco, aut sputum eius figi non potest.

Hoc menstruo minerali,

solve sulphur Aquosum, vel succum Lunariæ, et habebis verum mercurium
philosophorum.

Sanguis Draconis
Simplex.

Fige sputum cum [aquâ forti]. tunc solve in aquâ Talci et Halinitri cum
oleo vitri, et habebis.

   Istis salibus adde crystallos Tartari, tunc distilla cum oleo supradicto, et
habebis menstruum nobile.

[fol. 69ʳ blank]

---

[82] Sic, for *aqua*.

The True Art, Which the Best and Greatest God
Granted Me in the Days
of my Dearest Wife.
1658.

The First Mineral Water.

Grind the two blacks, as they come from minerals, and let there be three parts chrysolite to two of stibium. Add nitric salt and talc, and let there be two parts nitric salt to one of talc, if you wish to prepare it with scarab. Let all be dissolved in aqua fortis and rain water and distilled in the fire of sand, and it will be made. Aqua fortis is the universal key to the work, following the mineral way, for without that water the dragon or its spittle cannot be fixed.

With this mineral menstruum,

dissolve aqueous sulphur or the juice of lunaria, and you will have the true mercury of the philosophers.

Simple
Blood of the Dragon.

Fix spittle with aqua fortis. Then dissolve in water of talc and saltpeter with vitriol, and you will have it.

To those salts add crystals of tartar, then distill with the above described oil, and you will have a notable menstruum.

[fol. 70ᵛ]   Pro Coronide:

Non celabo summum Artis divinæ Arcanum, quod mihi peccatori patefacere dignatus est Deus misericors. Post plures Dies, et Errores innumeros, tandem vivente Conjuge meâ dulcissimâ, incidi in Sequentem, et mirabilem mineram.

Crysolithum accepi, & cum igne contra naturam, despumando, repurgavi: sed hoc non sine periculo, et sumptibus; et in hac operatione vidi tres diversas substantias: unam nigram: alteram albam, et quantitate minimam: Tertiam vero Citrinam, et fœtidam.

Tandem vero sic operatus sum: Eundem lapidem cum resinâ purgavi: tunc per calcinationem in salem redegi fusibilem, citrinum, et porosum. Quin et per Arenam albam purgavi, et solo igne in calcem reduxi.

{*}   Tunc per supradictam resinam Typhonem correxi, et in favillas candidissimas sublimavi. quin et cum pulvere nostro albo stellato in sputum coegi. ℞ huius incinerati, aut in Gummi reducti part[em] 1. Salis citrini part[em] 1. trita simul misce, et coque donec nigres[c]ant, albescant, et rubescant, quod in . . .

[fol. 69ᵛ]
. . . una horâ naturali fiet. Hic est primus masculus noster: modo audi præparationem primæ suæ fœminæ.

Projice auripigmentum in Balneum suum proprium: et digere per dies 8: sic enim dealbabitur, absque virium suarum diminutione. In separatione Balnei invenies Acetum subtilissimum, in quo iterum illud solve, vel solve in Aceto vini. Tunc contere cum Sericone, et solvantur ambo in Aceto suo proprio, quod ex Balneo venenoso separasti.

Hæc est vera via, cum Solis monte Tutiâ.

T. R. V.
1658.

{* Typhon (ut opinor) per Resinam purgatus, transibit totus in sputum. Adde parum Scarabæi.}

For the Conclusion:

I will not hide the highest arcanum of the divine art, which merciful God deigned to disclose to me, a sinner. After many days and innumerable errors, finally when my sweetest wife was living, I fell upon the following wondrous mineral.

I took chrysolite and cleansed it again by skimming with a fire against nature; but this was not without danger and expense. And in this operation I saw three diverse substances: one black, the other white, and very little in quantity, but the third yellow and fetid.

Finally I worked in this way. I cleansed the same stone with resin; then by calcination I converted it to a meltable, yellow and porous salt. And furthermore I cleansed it with white sand, and reduced it to calx with fire alone.

Then I corrected the Typhon by the above described resin, and I sublimed it into very white embers. And furthermore with our white starry
*} powder I thickened it into spittle. Take one one part of this incinerated or reduced to a gum, one part yellow salt. Mix together what has been ground, and concoct until they blacken, whiten, and redden, which in
. . .

. . . one natural hour will happen. This is our first male; now hear the preparation of his first female.[83]

Project *orpiment into its proper bath, and decoct for eight days; for in this way it will be whitened without diminution of its powers. In the separation of the bath you will discover a very subtle vinegar, in which [you] dissolve this again, or dissolve it in vinegar from wine. Then grind with red lead, and let both be dissolved in its proper vinegar, which you have separated from the poisonous bath.

This is the true way, with the mountain of gold, tutia.

T. R. V.
1658.

{* Typhon (in my opinion) cleansed by resin will turn entirely into spittle. Add a little scarab.}

---

[83] The *primus masculus* was usually mercury; the *prima fœmina*, magnesia.

Quæ supra scripsi de salium compositione, et oleo vitri, verissima sunt, et valent.

Tandem notabis:

Quod Talcum, et Anatron conjuncta, et cum Duobus nigris crudis contrita, et in [aquâ forti] soluta, dabunt menstruum egregium, et hoc est verum sine mendacio, certum, & verissimum.

Te Deum Laudamus: Te Dominum
confitemur.
T. R. V.

[fol. 70ʳ blank]

[fol. 71ʳ]   De Eudica NB.

℞. illam crudam, nigram, et pulverulentam: Tere cum Anatro, et in crucibulo calcina. Tunc solve in spiritu Salium, et olei vitri. Potes in Calcinatione addere parum Scarabæi, ad minuendam acredinem, et violentiam. Sic absque omni labore, aut ulteriore fusione optatum assequi poteris.

Laus Tibi
Creator Altissime, et misericors!
Amen! & Amen!

T. R. V.
1658.

In confectione Eudicæ, ponite Plumbum cum Ære, donec spissum fiat, &c. Si vero absque Eudica operaturus es, tunc in Confectione tuâ, sint tres partes Plutonis ad unem Lacertæ, nam iste Pluto est Agens, sine quo nihil fit.

What I have written above concerning the compounding of salts and vitriol is very true and efficacious.

Finally you will note

That talc and nitric salt, joined together and ground with the two crude
blacks and dissolved in aqua fortis, will yield an uncommon menstruum,
and this is the truth without falsehood, certain and very true.

We Praise Thee, O God:
Thee We Acknowledge to Be the Lord.[84]
T. R. V.

Note Well Concerning Eudica.

Take this crude, black, and powdery [eudica]. Grind with nitric salt, and
calcine in a crucible. Then dissolve in spirit of salts and vitriol. You can
add a little scarab in calcination to diminish its pungency and fierceness. In
this way without any labor or further melting, you will be able to attain
what you wish.

Praise to Thee
Most Exalted and Merciful Creator!
Amen! and Amen!

T. R. V.
1658.

In the preparation of eudica, place lead with ore, until it be thick, etc. If
indeed you are about to work without eudica, then in your preparation let
there be three parts Pluto to one of colcothar, for that Pluto is the agent
without which nothing is made.

---

[84] This is the opening line of the "Te Deum." See note on fol. 62ᵛ.

[fol. 71ᵛ]   Aqua vitæ Vegetabilis.

Fit ex Tartaro minerali, sicut scis: vel ex Oleo Lombardi cum suo corpore commixto, et distillato.

Tartarum nostrum

Minerale figit o[mn]es spiritus sublimatos, et miranda facit cum Ammoniaco, Mercurio, et Arsenico.

{*}
Quinta Essentia
[Sulphuris] vulgaris.

Sublimatur in Retortâ cum Resinis: sitque Artifex accuratus, et diligens in proportionibus inveniendis, cum in his solis Arcanum delitescit. Inter Resinas præstat Pixode Burgundiâ, Cera Flava odorifera, et gummata omnis generis, sed præstant Suavia, et ponderosa.

Hydragogum excellens.

Radicis Jalop **Opoponacis**, et Cremoris Tartari, partes æquales commisce, et cum syrupo convenienti porrige in Jusculo tepido, vel in vino albo. &c.
NB.   Cremor imbibi potest cum spiritu vitrioli, aut cum spiritu ex spumâ Typhonis, sicut scis. Maximè valet in Hydropicis.

T. R. V. 1658.

In Te, Domine Jesu, speravi:
Nòn confundar in Æternum.[85]

{* symbol for *oleum* [∴] used}

---

[85] Psalm 31:1, 71:1, and the "Te Deum."

An Animating Aqua Vitæ.

It is made from mineral tartar, as you know, or from oil of Lombard mixed together with its body and distilled.

Our Mineral Tartar

Fixes all sublimated spirits and makes wondrous things with ammonia, mercury, and arsenic.

{*}

Quintessence
of Common Sulphur.

It is sublimed in a retort with resins, and let the worker be accurate and diligent in finding the proportions, since the arcanum lies hidden in these alone. Among resins golden, odorous wax is superior to Burgundy pitch, and so are gums of every kind, but especially the sweet and heavy varieties.

An Excellent Hydragogue.

Mix together equal parts jalap root, panax,[86] and cream of tartar, and with an appropriate syrup dilute in a tepid broth or in white wine, etc. The cream can be instilled with spirit of vitriol, or with spirit from the foam of Typhon, as you know. This is greatly efficacious for dropsical persons.

T. R. V. 1658.

In Thee, O Lord Jesus, have I trusted:
Let me never be confounded.

---

[86] Panax was widely used as a salve. Vaughan may have had in mind the variety known as Hercules all-heal or wound-wort, whose yellow gum was also called *opopanax* (see Gerard, *Herball*, 1003).

[fol. 72ʳ]   NB. NB.

Talci et Salis marini, vel communis partes æquales sumito: vel Talci et Halinitri: contere cum crystallis Tartari, et cum oleo vitri distilla. Idem facias
cum Talco, et Aquilâ per Scarabæum correctâ.

NB. De Eudicâ.

Ferri nostri, et Cupri partes sumito æquales: Adde Boritin ad pondus
utriusque: Tunc purga per Cribrum Ignis, cum, vel sine matre metallicâ.
NB.   Eudicam[87] vero antequam fundatur, tere cum Typhone crudo, & tùnc
funde, &c.

NB.

Spiritum vitrioli a Crystallis Tartari abstrahe aliquoties. Hoc spiritu cremorem imbibe: valet etiàm ad solutionem ambaræ, et Corallorum, &c. vel
Oleum vitri cum Crystallis distilla, et habebis spiritum Præstantiorem.

---

[87] Sic, for *eudica*.

Note Well. Note Well.

Take equal parts talc and sea salt, or common salt, or talc and saltpeter; grind together with crystals of tartar, and distill with vitriol. You may make the same with talc and sal ammoniac corrected by scarab.

Note Well. Concerning Eudica.

Take equal parts of our iron and copper. Add boritin[88] in an amount equal to the weight of each. Then purge through a sieve of fire, with or without a metallic matrix. Before the eudica is melted, grind with crude Typhon, then melt, etc.

'B.

Note Well.

Draw out spirit of vitriol from crystals of tartar several times. With this spirit instill the cream; it is efficacious also for dissolving amber and corals, etc. Or distill the vitriol with crystals, and you will have a more excellent spirit.

---

[88] Vaughan may have in mind here *borith*, Hebrew for a grassy plant, which yields an alkali used by fullers for cleansing (OED).

[fol. 72ᵛ]   Ars Tota, ut inventa est,
                                    in Diebus Conjugis meæ
                                    Charissimæ. T. R. V.
                                          1658.

De Aquâ prima philosophicâ.

℞ Eudicam sicut scis: teratur cum Talco, Anatro, et Alkali cum Collâ, si
adsit: sin alitèr, cum Alkali et Halinitro: vel cum Alterutro per se. Tunc
solve in Aquâ Talci, et Halinitri: vel in aquâ Crystallorum, et Aquilæ, sive
Anatri correcti cum Scarabæo. Vel in Aqua solius Anatri cum Lombardo
præparati: vel in aquâ ~~Aqua~~ Anatri sic præparati, et cum Talco, et Halinitro conjuncti: Vel in Aquâ maris duplicatâ cum Anatro et Talco contrita. Et o[mn]es hæ Aquæ distillari debent, et educi cum oleo vitri. Oleum
[sulphuris] etiam sic conjunctum dabit menstruum mirabile.

Gumma vero Sicca de Eudicâ,

imbibatur cum Mercurio, depureturque per Distillationem philosophicam,
sicut scis.

Aqua prima Alitèr.

Sputum Lacertæ contere cum terrâ fœtidâ citrinâ: vel cum calce magnesiæ
albæ: vel cum calce ex Corpore crudo et impuro, cum sulphure vulgari
præparato. &c.

NB. NB.

Stannum cum Magnesiâ conjunctum, aurum philosophicum educit instar
matris suæ, cuius vicem optimè supplet in Operatione primâ, et siccâ.
Laus Deo! Amen.

The Entire Art, as it was discovered,
in the days of my
dearest Wife. T. R. V.
1658.

Concerning the First Philosophical Water.

Take eudica, as you know; it may be ground with talc, nitric salt, and alkali, with colla if it is on hand; if not, with alkali and saltpeter, or with
one of the two by itself. Then dissolve in water of talc and saltpeter, or in
water of crystals and sal ammoniac, or nitric salt corrected with scarab. Or
in water of nitric salt alone prepared with Lombard; or in water of nitric
salt prepared in this way and joined with talc and saltpeter. Or in twice as
much sea water ground with nitric salt and talc. And all these waters ought
to be distilled and drawn up with vitriol. Oil of sulphur[89] also joined in
this way will yield a wondrous menstruum.

A Dry Gum Indeed from Eudica,

may be instilled with mercury and refined by philosophical distillation, as
you know.

The First Water By Another Method.

Grind spittle of colcothar together with fetid yellow earth; or with calx of
white magnesia; or with calx from a crude and impure body prepared with
common sulphur, etc.

Note Well. Note Well.

Tin joined with magnesia draws out philosophical gold like its mother,
whose place it takes very well in the first and dry operation. Praise be to
God! Amen.

---

[89] An oil containing dissolved sulphur and linseed oil or turpentine; see Wolfgang
Schneider, *Lexikon alchemistisch-pharmazeutischer Symbole* (Weinheim: Verlag Chemie, 1962),
82.

[fol. 73ʳ]   Præparatio Salis Duplicati.

℞ Talci part[em] 1. Anatri partem sesquialteram. Tere cum unâ parte Scarabæi, et projice in Crucibulum candens. Solve, filtra, sicca: et habes sal
philosophorum verum, præter quod non est aliud. adde halinitrum, vel sal

NB.   commune, si vis. Putrefiat in [aquâ forti] per Dies 12. Tunc in Aceto solvatur. Hæc est vera via, sed et Aliæ subsequantur.

                                  Præparatio Salis petræ.

Teratur cum mediâ parte [sulphuris], et candente ferro igniatur in Crucibulo. Tunc solve, sicca, et cum novo nitro copula, et funde, iterumque
solve. Eodem modo præparetur cum Scarabæo, et Lombardo, Sed solutio
eius semper cum Aceto fit, nec aliter.

         Præparatur etiam optimè cum fuligine ex Carbonibus subterraneis, sic
NB.   enim neutiquam stringit. NB. Et ita præparatum, purgatumque Compar
erit Talci, et Maris, et Collæ piscis. Quin et sui salis, et Talci, quod præ-
NB.   stare credo, Sed supra est veritas.

                             Laus Deo, Amen!
                             T. R. V. 1658.

[fol. 73ᵛ]   Ex Libris Th: & Reb: Vaughan.

                        As God decreed: so wee agreed.
                     Quos Deus conjunxit, Quis separabit?

                                    1658.

                   Christe Jesu! Lux, et Vita Mundi: Filius Dei:
                   Filius et Redemptor Hominis: Trahe me,
                        post Te: Curremus. Amen! T. R. V.

[fol. 74ʳ blank]

Preparation of a *Doubled Salt.

Take one part talc, one and a half parts nitric salt. Grind with one part scarab, and project it into a glowing crucible. Dissolve, filter, dry, and you will have the true salt of the philosophers, beyond which there is
NB. none other. Add saltpeter or common salt, if you wish. It may be putrefied in aqua fortis for twelve days, then dissolved in vinegar. This is the true way, but also others follow.

Preparation of Rock Salt.

It may be ground with a half part of sulphur and ignited with glowing iron in the crucible. Then dissolve, dry, and mate with new nitre, and melt, and dissolve again. By the same method it may be prepared with scarab and Lombard, but its solution is always made with vinegar, and not by any other way.

It is also prepared very well with soot from subterranean charcoal, for
B.   after this fashion it in no way binds. Note Well. Thus prepared and purged, it will be the equal to talc, colla maris or colla from fish, and
B.   furthermore the equal of its salt and talc, which I believe it excels, but above is the truth.

Praise be to God, Amen!
T. R. V.   1658.

From the Books of Thomas and Rebecca Vaughan.

As God decreed: so wee agreed.
Whom God has joined, Who will separate?

1658.

O Christ Jesus! Light and Life of the World: Son of God:
Son and Redeemer of Mankind: Draw me,
after Thee: We shall run! Amen! T. R. V.

[fol. 74ᵛ]   Vas secretum pro Calcinatione
                              Corallorum &c. philosophicâ.

Fiat lagena stannea longitudinis Cubitalis, cum operculo suo stanneo. Hæc
imponatur igni sicut scis, cum materialibus contritis, et fiet. Si iidem vasi
alembicus vitreus imponatur, potes eodem artificio ex floribus, herbis, et
gummis Aquas, et olea extrahere absque omni nidore, aut Combustione,
quod Arcanum est pulcherrimum. Hoc Artificium excogitavi in diebus
Conjugis meæ Charissimæ. T. R. V. 1658.

                         In te Domine, Speravi: non
                         Confundar in Æternum.⁹⁰
                                  Amen.
                             Domine Jesu!

[fol. 75ʳ blank]

[fol. 75ᵛ]   Oleum [Sulphuris].

Teratur cum Nitro calcinato. Tunc distilla nudo igne in frigidam, et habebis. Nitro adde parum Salis communis, sed **præstat Scarabæus**. Teratur
etiam cum styrace, et fiet. Scarabæus per se tritus cum Nitro calcinato,
dabit spiritum egregium. **Sit in calcinatione media pars Tartari ad unam
Nitri.**

                             De Oleo [Sulphuris].

Si Extractum cum salibus conjungatur, et distilletur, faciet mirabilia, et de
hoc experimento, non est ultra loquendum.

---

⁹⁰ Psalm 31:1, 71:1, and the last response of the "Te Deum."

A Secret Vessel for the Philosophical
Calcination of Corals, etc.

A tin vessel may be made a cubit long in length, with its lid also tin. This may be placed in fire, as you know, with ground materials, and it will be made. If a glass alembic be placed in this same vessel, you can extract with this same device waters and oils from flowers, herbs, and gums without any smell or combustion, which is a very beautiful mystery. This device I contrived in the days of my dearest Wife. T. R. V. 1658.

In thee, O Lord, I have trusted:
Let me never be confounded.
Amen.
O Lord Jesus!

Oil of Sulphur.

Let it be ground with calcinated nitre. Then distill with a bare flame into a cold matter, and you will have it. To the nitre add a little common salt, **but scarab is better**. It may be ground also with a resinous gum, and it will be made. Scarab by itself ground with calcinated nitre will yield an uncommon spirit. **In calcination a half part tartar may be used to one of nitre.**

Concerning Oil of Sulphur.

If the extract be joined with salts and distilled, it will make wondrous things; but concerning this experiment, nothing more must be said.

Idem oleum cum [Mercurio] conjunctum,

Si rite fiat, miranda operabitur, quod, non sine periculo, expertus sum in diebus conjugis meæ Charissimæ. Idem cum oleo communi conjunctum purgat illud, et rubescere facit instar sanguinis, si parum [aquæ fortis] addatur. Plura sunt, et utilissima quæ cum dicto oleo perfici possunt. Tu investiga, et gaudebis.

Laus vero sit Deo Misericordiarum:
Uni, Soli, Summo, et Vero!
Amen! inquiunt
T. R. V. 1658.

[fol. 76r blank]

[fol. 76v] SUCCUS SALIS.

Talcum, vel Aquam maris, cum calce vivâ nostrâ conjunge; Tùnc distilla Per Kymam, et habebis.

Pro Conclusione.

Notabis de salibus, quod Terrestria & sulphurea, cum Terrestribus & Sulphureis: Mercurialia vero, et Aquea, cum Mercurialibus & Aqueis conjungenda sunt: Ita ut Talcum sit Aquilæ compar: Colla vero, matricis suæ salsæ. Item Halinitrum Aquilæ, Talco correspondet, et cum illo conjunctum, longè plus spirituum effundit, quam matrix illa marina, et hoc expertus sum apud quendam Apothecarium Wappingensem, cum illic Halinitrum adduxissem, in diebus Conjugis meæ Charissimæ T. R. V. 1658.

NB.

NB.

Christe Jesu! Lux, & Vita Mundi: Filius Dei: Filius, et Redemptor Hominis: Trahe me, post Te: Curremus. Amen!

The Same Oil Joined with Mercury,

If it be made as it should be, will produce wondrous things, which I tested, not without danger, in the days of my dearest wife. The same joined with common oil may purge this and make it red like blood, if a little aqua fortis be added. There are many, very useful things which can be accomplished with the said oil. Investigate, and you will be happy.

Praise indeed be to the God of Mercies:
One, Only, Most High and True!
Amen! Thus say
T. R. V. 1658.

THE JUICE OF SALT.

Join talc, or sea water, with our live calx; then distill through a cucurbit, and you will have it.

In Conclusion.

You will note about salts that the earthly and sulphurous salts must be joined with earthly and sulphurous; mercurial and aqueous salts must be joined with mercurial and aqueous: So that the talc may be equal to the sal ammoniac, the colla truly to its saline matrix. Likewise the saltpeter corresponds to the sal ammoniac [and] talc, and joined with this pours out very much more spirit than that saline matrix, and this I tested at a certain Apothecary in Wapping, when I had brought saltpeter there in the days of my dearest wife. T. R. V. 1658.

B.

B.

O Christ Jesus! Light and Life of the World: Son of God: Son and Redeemer of Mankind: Draw me, after Thee: We shall run. Amen!

[fol. 77ʳ]   NB. quod subsequitur.

Talci, Halinitri, & Aquilæ correctæ, partes æquales sumito. Distilla cum oleo vitri, et habebis.

[fol. 77ᵛ]   Arcanum Vegetabile.

℞ utriusque Sulphuris partes æquales. ablue si vis: vel quod melius **est**, calcina cum Resinâ. Sic enim sal non stringet. Tunc solve in aquâ minerali, et fiet.

Aliud [Sulphuris]
Arcanum.

℞. illius partes duas. Resinæ partem unam. Tere in simul, et sublima. Idem fiet, si pars una Aquilæ cum tribus [sulphuris] comburetur. Tunc extrahe tincturam, et habebis.

Sputum Lacertæ.

℞. Veneni albi partem unam: Lacertæ splendidissimæ partem aliam. Scarabæi optimi partem quartam, vel Tertiam, vel mediam. Terantur in simul, et sublimentur.

NB.

Sputum extractum lava. Tunc cum terrâ fœtidâ conjunge, et coque in mineram philosophicam.

Laus Deo! Amen!
T. R. V. 1658.

[fol. 78ʳ blank]

Note Well What Follows Below.

Take equal parts talc, saltpeter, and corrected sal ammoniac. Distill with vitriol, and you will have it.

An Animating Arcanum.

Take equal parts of each sulphur. Wash if you wish, or what is better, calcine with resin. For in this way the salt will not bind. Then dissolve in mineral water, and it will be made.

Another Arcanum of Sulphur.

Take two parts of this [sulphur], one part resin. Grind together, and sublime. The same will be made, if one part sal ammoniac be heated with three of sulphur. Then extract the tincture, and you will have it.

Spittle of Colcothar.

Take <u>one part white venom, another part very splendid colcothar, a quarter, third, or half part of the best scarab. Let them be ground together, and sublimed.</u>

Note Well.

<u>Wash the extracted spittle.</u> Then <u>join with fetid earth, and concoct into a philosophical mineral</u>.

Praise be to God! Amen!
T. R. V. 1658.

[fol. 78ᵛ]   NB. Quod subsequitur.

Talcum per se, vel Aquilæ [correctæ] conjunctum, facile transit in oleum,
{*}   si teratur cum <u>Duobus Nigris crudis</u>. Quin et ex <u>istis Crudis per se, et sine</u>
<u>sale solutis, extrahitur spiritus Efficacissimus</u>.

NB. NB.

Sputum Draconis cum oleo vitri conjunctum, totumque <u>in [aquâ forti]</u>
<u>solutum,</u> dabit menstruum nobilissimum. Idem fieri potest cum <u>capite</u>
<u>rubeo reducto, solutoque</u>. Estque Arcanum maximum. Quin et cum <u>fumo</u>
<u>albo, per Aquilæ venenum combusto, fixatoque</u>. Atque hæc omnia, et sin-
gula diligentèr Annotabis.

T. R. V.

Gloria vero sit Summo, & Soli Deo.
Tibiquè
Mitissime Jesu!
Amen!

NB.   <u>In defectu Collæ Marinæ, distilla Talcum Aquilæ correctæ conjunctum:</u>
<u>Quin et cum crystallis, si vis. Distillatio fiat primò cum oleo vitri: pos-</u>
<u>tea cum Duobus Nigris.</u>

{* refers to note on fol. 79ʳ}

Note Well What Follows Below.

{*} Talc by itself, or joined with the [corrected] sal ammoniac, easily turns into oil, if it be ground with <u>the two crude blacks</u>. And furthermore, <u>a very efficacious spirit may be extracted from these crude ones by themselves, dissolved without salt.</u>

Note Well. Note Well.

Spittle of the dragon joined with vitriol and dissolved wholly in aqua fortis will yield a very notable menstruum. The same can be made with <u>the red residuum reduced and dissolved</u>. And this is the greatest arcanum. And furthermore with <u>a white fume, heated and fixed by venom of sal ammoniac.</u> And indeed you will diligently note each and every one of these things.

T. R. V.

Glory be to God, Only and Most High.
And to Thee
Most Mild Jesus!
Amen!

3. <u>When lacking colla marina, distill talc joined with corrected sal ammoniac, and furthermore with crystals, if you wish. Distillation may be made first with vitriol, afterwards with the two blacks.</u>

[fol. 79ʳ]   NB. NB. NB.

Hunc processum his verbis obduxit R. Lullius in Arte Intellectivâ: NI-
{*}   TRUM: SAL: SULPHUR: VAPOR. Quin et salem illum Naturæ, in Prac-
          ticâ magni Testamenti, PETRAM SALIS vocavit. Et hæc est Aqua, quæ fit
NB.   ex Quatuor Rebus immassatis.

Sufficit ergo in Primâ

Operatione nostrâ, Ignis contra Naturam, sive [aqua fortis]: modò tempe-
retur cum matre suâ frigidâ. In hac Aquâ solve Petram salis, sitque Aquila
correcta. Abstrahe demum, et congela. Tunc petram cum [sulphure] crudo
conjunge, et utrumque solve &c.

Si vero in Solo Sulphure

Operaturus es: sic procede. ℞. [aquam fortem] ut supra temperatam. Hac
Aquâ solve Crystallos Tartari, & Aquilam correctam Ana. Cohoba donec
satis sit, et fiet. Hæc aqua omnes sales sublimat.

T. R. V. 1658.

{* note for fol. 78ᵛ}

Note Well. Note Well. Note Well.

Ramon Lull hid this process [as described on fol. 78ᵛ] with these words
{*}   in *Ars Intellectiva*: NITRE, SALT, SULPHUR, VAPOR.[91] And furthermore he called this ROCK SALT in the *Practica* of his great *Testamentum* the "salt of nature."[92] And this is the water, which is made from
NB.   four things lumped together.

What Suffices therefore

In our first operation is unnatural fire, or aqua fortis; in this way it may be
tempered with its cold mother. In this water dissolve rock salt, and corrected sal ammoniac may be used. Draw this out at last, and congeal it.
Then join the rock with crude sulphur, and dissolve both, etc.

If indeed in Sulphur Alone

You are about to work, proceed in this way. Take aqua fortis[93] as tempered above. In this water dissolve equal quantities of crystals of tartar and
corrected sal ammoniac. Cohobate until it be enough, and it will be made.
This water sublimes all salts.

T. R. V. 1658.

---

[91] The whole of pseudo-Lull's short treatise, *Ars Intellectiva super Lapidem Philosophorum*, concerns the differences between the "material" or common forms of substances
needed for the great work and their philosophical ones. Printed in Guglielmo Gratarola,
Veræ Alchemiæ Artisque Metallicæ, citra Aenigmata, Doctrina, certusque modus, 2 parts in 1
vol. (Basel, 1561), see especially 2: 114.

[92] This salt was briefly discussed in the pseudo-Lull's *Practica* (in *Theatrum Chemicum*,
4: 137); as a fundamental principle, it is mentioned throughout.

[93] The usual symbol for nitric acid is here inverted.

[fol. 79ᵛ]   De Salibus: eorumque Præparatione.

De Aquilâ.

Præparatur optimè cum Scarabæo, vel solâ fusione: Tunc solvitur, et putrefit in Aceto distillato, vel in Balneo suo Æthereo, acuatoque &c.

Præparatur etiàm

In Sulphur philosophicum, quo unico medio, extrahitur Sal nostrum Armoniacum ex Aquâ sua ponticâ. Hoc etiam Sulphure sistuntur omnes spiritus minerales, et Corporei, quod summopere notandum est. Hæc vero præparatio fit cum sulphure vegetabili: si vero cum Lombardo præparatur, tunc facillimè transit in salem volatilem &c.

De Talco.

Optimè præparatur, si in oleum transeat cum Rege philosophico: idque per se, vel cum Aquilâ c[orrec]tâ conjunctum, quod posterius præstantius est.

De Collâ Maris.

Duplicari debet per Conjunctionem cum matre sua salsâ. Tunc omnes sales excellit &c.

Atque hæc sunt, quæ inveni in Diebus Conjugis meæ Charissimæ, quam iterum in Cœlis videre, et alloqui, dabit Deus meus misericors. Christe Jesu! Lux, & Vita Mundi: Filius Dei: Filius, et Redemptor Hominis, trahe me post Te, Curremus! Amen!

T. R. V. 1658.

[fol. 80ʳ blank]

Concerning Salts and their Preparation.

Concerning Sal Ammoniac.

It is prepared very well with scarab, or through melting alone. Then it is dissolved and made putrid in distilled vinegar, or strengthened in its ethereal bath, etc.

It May also Be Prepared

Into philosophical sulphur, by which unique means our sal ammoniac is extracted from its briny water. <u>By this sulphur all spirits, mineral and corporeal, are caused to stand, which must be emphatically noted.</u> This preparation indeed is made with animating sulphur; if indeed it is prepared with Lombard, then it very easily turns into a volatile salt, etc.

Concerning Talc.

It is best prepared, if it be turned into an oil with the philosophical king; and that by itself, or joined with corrected sal ammoniac, which afterwards is more excellent.

Concerning Colla Maris.

It ought to be doubled by conjunction with its salty mother. Then it excels all salts, etc.

And indeed this is what I have discovered in the days of my dearest wife, whom my merciful God will grant that I see again and speak with in the heavens. O Christ Jesus! Light and Life of the World: Son of God: Son and Redeemer of Mankind, draw me after Thee, We shall run! Amen!

T. R. V. 1658.

[fol. 80ᵛ]   Mercurius Philosophicus:
                              Sive [Aurum]⁹⁴ Vegetabile.

Hic est ille Mercurius, Quem scimus. Cum vero solis filius sit, rubificari debet, et solvi in Aquis suprascriptis. <u>Potest etiam Crudus solvi, et subli-mari</u>. vide Lull: in Codicillo.

                              Menstruum particulare,
                              ad Aurum vulgi.

℞ Aquilæ fusæ, et Scarabæi partes æquales. Solve in Aceto distillato, solu-tionem distilla, et fiet.

                              De plumbo quædam
                              Annotata.

Amalgamatum tere cum sublimato, et <u>in Crucibulo funde igne nudo,</u> &c.

NB.   Aliud Amalgamatum tere cum Sulphure: vel fuso Sulphuri impone, et coque in Cinnabararin.⁹⁵ Tunc funde in metallum nigrum, et fragile. Hoc cum sublimato iterum tere, et funde, vel si vis distilla, &c. **[Saturnus] &**

NB.   **[Jupiter] uniri possunt, et purgari per Kymam, aut Sextum Barbatum.**

                              De Aquis vegetabilibus.

Optima fit ex Tartaro, sicut scis: & Nigro nigrius nigro. Hæc cum Mannâ imprægnari potest, et Servari ad suos usus.

                              T. R. V.
                              1658.

[fol. 81ʳ blank]

---

⁹⁴ The English abbreviation "G." is used.
⁹⁵ Sic, for *Cinnabarin*.

Philosophical Mercury:
Or Animating Gold.

This is that sophic mercury, which we know. But since it is truly the son
of gold, it ought to be made red and dissolved in the waters described
above. The crude can also be dissolved and sublimed; see Lull's *Codicillus*.[96]

A Particular Menstruum,
for Common Gold.

Take equal parts melted sal ammoniac and scarab. Dissolve in distilled
vinegar, distill the solution, and it will be made.

Certain Annotations Concerning Lead.

Grind the amalgam with sublimate, and melt in a crucible with a bare
flame, etc. Grind another amalgam with sulphur, or put in with melted
sulphur, and concoct into cinnabar. Then melt into a fragile and black
metal. Grind this again with sublimate, and melt, or distill if you wish,
etc. **Lead and tin can be united and purged by a cucurbit or sextum
barbatum.**[97]

Concerning Animating Waters.

The best is made from tartar, as you know, and from a black blacker
than black. This can be impregnated with manna and be saved for its
uses.

T. R. V.
1658.

_____

[96] In chapter L of the *Codicillus* (Manget, *Bibliotheca Chemica Curiosa*, 1: 899–900),
pseudo-Lull discussed the sublimation of mercury and, in chapter LXXII (Manget, *Bibliotheca Chemica Curiosa*, 1: 910), the dissolution and rubification of mercury.

[97] Literally "six bearded"; apparently, an alchemical apparatus with six compartments.

[fol. 81ᵛ]   Ars tota, ut inventa est in Diebus
                              Conjugis meæ Charissimæ. T. R. V.
                              Quos Deus conjunxit, Quis separabit.

LAPIS ANIMALIS.

Succum Lunariæ evapora, ut Magnesiam albam invenias: Hanc cum Fratricidâ conjunge, iterumque libera, digestione lentâ. Fæces, sive stercus, aut
Fimum animalem in quo lapis latet, abjice: succum vero per dies suos putrefac: Tunc sublima, et habebis, Quod quæris. T. R. V. 1658.

Ignis Pontani.

Excorietur Magnesia cum Corrosivis: vel sicut scis. Si fiat, sicut scis: Tunc
igne solo calcinabis, et solves. Salem eius cum Fratricidâ contere, et coque:
sitque malignus iste spiritus mortificatus, et in pulverem reductus: Quod
sic efficies. ℞. Aquilam cum Scarabæo præparatam &c. Compositum hoc
solve, & putrefac in Aquis mineralibus subsequentibus.

Aqua prima Mineralis.

℞. Talci partes duas: Matricis marinæ sicut scis, partem unam: Aquilæ
crudæ partem mediam. Distilla, et fiet.

Aliter.

℞. Aquilæ per Scarabæum præparatæ partem unam: Crystallorum Tartari
partem aliam. Distilla, sicut scis, et habebis. Eandem Aquilam correctam
cum Talco distilla, et fiet.

Gratiæ sint Christo!
Amen T. R. V.

[fol. 82ʳ blank]

The Entire Art, as it was discovered
in the days of my dearest Wife. T. R. V.
Whom God has joined, Who will separate.

THE ANIMATED STONE.

Evaporate the juice of lunaria, so that you may discover white magnesia;
join this through fratricide, and free it again through slow decoction. Cast
out the dregs, or ordure or animated dung in which the stone lies hidden.[98] Putrefy the juice truly for several days; then sublime, and you will
have what you seek. T. R. V. 1658.

Fire of Pontanus.[99]

Let magnesia be made caustic with corrosives, or as you know. If it is
made your way, then you will calcine it with fire alone, and you will dissolve it. Grind its salt through fratricide, and concoct; and let that malign
spirit be mortified and reduced into a powder, which you effect in this
way. Take sal ammoniac prepared with scarab, etc. Dissolve this compound and putrefy in the following mineral waters.

The First Mineral Water.

Take two parts talc, one part marine matrix, as you know, one half part
crude sal ammoniac. Distill, and it will be made.

By Another Way.

Take one part sal ammoniac prepared by scarab, another part crystals of
tartar. Distill, as you know, and you will have it. Distill the same sal ammoniac corrected with talc, and it will be made.

Thanks be to Christ!
Amen. T. R. V.

---

[98] Decoction was sometimes attempted using horse-dung as the source of heat; see Dorn,
Chymical Dictionary, 316; and Vaughan's *Lumen de Lumine* in *Works*, 337.

[99] See note on *pontanus* on fol. 56ᵛ.

[fol. 82ᵛ]   Ex Libris Th: & Reb: Vaughan.

As God decreed; so wee agreed.
Septemb: 28 1651. [aurum]
April: 17.° [plumbum]
1658.

Christe Jesu! Lux, et Vita Mundi: Filius Dei:
Filius, et Redemptor Hominis: Trahe me
post Te: Curremus. Amen!

T. R. V.

Quos Deus conjunxit, Quis separabit?

[fol. 83ʳ blank]

[fol. 83ᵛ]   Aqua nobilis ad medicinam.

Crystallos, vel utrumque Tartarum ablutum distilla cum oleo vitri, et fiet.
Valet contra omnes obstructiones, ut in Hydrope, Calculo, et suffocatione
matricis. Solvit etiam omnes margaritas, et Corallos.

From the Books of Thomas and Rebecca Vaughan.

As God decreed; so wee agreed.
28 September 1651. gold [i.e., marriage]
17 April 1658. lead [i.e., death]

O Christ Jesus! Light and Life of the world, Son of God:
Son and Redeemer of Mankind: Draw me
after Thee: We shall run. Amen!

T. R. V.

Whom God has joined, Who will separate?

A Notable Water for Medicine.

With vitriol distill crystals, or each kind of washed tartar, and it will be made. It is efficacious against all obstructions, as for dropsy, kidney stone, and suffocation of the mother.[100] It also dissolves all pearls and corals.

---

[100] *Suffocatio hysterica* or *uterina* was the medical name for what was called hysteria. See Lear's exclamation: "O how this mother swells up toward my heart! *Hysterica passio*, down, thou climbing sorrow" (II.iv.56–57). See also, Edward Jorden's *A Briefe Discourse of a Disease called the Suffocation of the Mother* (London, 1603).

Aliter.

Crystallos, vel &c. contere ad pondus cum aquilâ per Scarabæum præparatâ, et distilla ut supra, & habebis aquam solventem, et omnes sales sublimantem, ut expertus sum in Diebus Conjugis meæ Charissimæ.

Cum iisdem Crystallis, contere Talcum et Alkali ana, et fiet.

T. R. V.

Christe Jesu! Lux et vita mundi:
Filius Dei: Filius, et Redemptor Hominis.
Trahe me post Te, Curremus.

Amen! 1658.

[fol. 84ʳ]   Aqua Calcinativa

Raymundi Lullii temperata ab igne
Contra naturam, quam describit
in Practicâ magni Testamenti.

℞. [aquæ fortis] optimæ lib[ram] 1. rectificetur[101] semèl, nec ultrà ab oleo vitri, quod expertus sum in Diebus Conjugis meæ Charissimæ. Modo ℞. Argentum vivum universale, sive Aquam ultimam de B[alneo] & misce cum dictâ [aquâ forti] rectificatâ, distillenturque in simul bis, vel tèr. His ita præparatis, ℞. Aquilam a Scarabæo combustam, sicut scis. Contere cum Chalybe nostro, ut supra præparato, et inter duo Crucibula in igne Cinerum, vel Arenæ, calcina. Calcem frigefactam exime, et solve per dies 2 in aquâ supradictâ: Tunc distilla, et repete cum novâ minerâ, donec satis sit. Hæc aqua solvit omnia Corpora, et Argentum vivum in liquorem ignis convertit.

T. R. V.
Quos Deus conjunxit,
Quis separabit?

1658.

---

[101] Sic, for *rectificietur*.

By Another Way.

Grind crystals, or [each kind of washed tartar], together with an equal weight of sal ammoniac prepared by scarab, and distill as above, and you will have a dissolving water for sublimating all salts, as I have tested in the days of my dearest wife.

With these same crystals, grind equal quantities talc and alkali, and it will be made.

T. R. V.

O Christ Jesus! Light and life of the world:
Son of God: Son and Redeemer of Mankind.
Draw me after Thee, We shall run.

Amen! 1658.

The Calcinated Water

of Ramon Lull Tempered by unnatural fire,
which he describes
in the *Practica* of the great *Testamentum*.[102]

Take one pound of the best aqua fortis. It will be rectified once, no more, by vitriol, which I tested in the days of my dearest wife. Now take universal quicksilver, or the hottest water from the bath and mix with the said rectified aqua fortis, and let them be distilled together twice or thrice. After these have been so prepared, take sal ammoniac heated by scarab, as you know. Grind together with our chalybs, as prepared above, and calcine between two crucibles in the heat of ashes or the fire of sand. Take away the chilled calx, and dissolve for two days in the water described above. Then distill, and repeat with a new mineral until it be enough. This water dissolves all bodies and converts quicksilver into liquid fire.

T. R. V.
Whom God has joined,
Who will separate?

1658.

---

[102] *Aqua calcinativa* was discussed in both chapters XIV and XV of the *Practica* (in *Theatrum Chemicum*, 4: 145–46). Vaughan followed the first formula.

[fol. 84ᵛ]   Sanguis Draconis, et Mercurii.

Draconem cum plutone conjunctum solve cum Oleo Aquilæ, et cohoba, donec totum transeat in oleum spissum. Hoc oleum cum Igne contra Naturam coagula, et fige. Fixum in oleo Aquilæ solve, solutum distilla, et habebis. Probatum est in Diebus Conjugis meæ dulcissimæ.

Aliter.

Sulphur nostrum cum Sublimato calcina. Calcem cum oleo Aquilæ solve, & cohoba in oleum spissum. Hoc oleum ut supra fige. Fixum in oleo Aquilæ, vel in oleo Salis Alkali, quod melius est, solve. Solutum distilla, et fiet.

Aliter.

Si dictum sanguinem absque igne contra naturam habere cupis, tunc necesse est, ut oleum istud spissum putrefacias per mensem philosophicum, et habebis. Sed ignis contra naturam abbreviat opus, estque Arcanum maximum, et mirabile.

T. R. V.
Christe Jesu! Lux, et Vita Mundi: Filius Dei:
Filius, et Redemptor Hominis: Trahe me post Te
Curremus. Amen!

Blood of the Dragon and Sophic Mercury.

Dissolve the dragon joined with Pluto with oil of sal ammoniac, and cohobate, until the whole turns into a thick oil. Coagulate this oil with unnatural fire, and fix. Dissolve what has been fixed in the oil of sal ammoniac,
distill the solution, and you will have it. It was proved in the days of my
sweetest wife.

By Another Way.

Calcine our sulphur with sublimate. Dissolve the calx with oil of sal ammoniac, and cohobate into a thick oil. Fix this oil as above. Dissolve what
has been fixed in oil of sal ammoniac, or in oil of salt alkali, which is better. Distill the solution, and it will be made.

By Another Way.

If you wish to have the said blood without unnatural fire, then it is necessary that you putrefy that thick oil for a philosophical month,[103] and
you will have it. But unnatural fire shortens the work, and this is the
greatest arcanum and wondrous.

T. R. V.

O Christ Jesus! Light and Life of the World: Son of God:
Son and Redeemer of Mankind: Draw me after Thee.
We shall run. Amen!

---

[103] A period of thirty or forty days, during which putrefaction takes place; see William
Johnson, *Lexicon Chymicum*, 2nd ed. (London, 1657), 140.

[fol. 85ʳ]   NB. NB.

℞. Utriusque Tartari, Albi, et Rubri, partes æquales. Tere in simul, et
misce &c., et calcina, sicut scis. Si calcem hanc conjungas cum calce nigrâ
Sacchari, & ambæ solvantur in aquâ vitæ, habebis spiritum incompara-
bilem. Non dormias hic, sed vigila, et retine quæ scripsi: hic enim latet Arcanum Admirabile.

T. R. V. 1658.
Quos Deus conjunxit, Quis separabit?

Sitivit Anima mea ad Deum Ælohim:
ad Deum El vivum: Quando-nam veniam,
et visitabo faciem Dei Ælohim!

Si Tu Jehovah, Deus meus, Illuminaveris me:
Lux fient Tenebræ meæ.

Note Well. Note Well.

Take equal parts of tartar, white and red. Grind together, and mix, etc., then calcine, as you know. If you join this calx with the black calx of sugar, and both are dissolved in aqua vitæ, you will have an incomparable spirit. Do not sleep here, but be vigilant, and keep what I have written, for here lies hidden a wonderful arcanum.

T. R. V. 1658.
Whom God has joined, Who will separate?

My Soul has thirsted for God, my God:
for God, the living God: When shall I come,
and visit the face of God, my God?[104]

If You Jehovah, my God, have Illuminated me:
My Darkness will be made Light.

---

[104] Psalm 42:3. See note on fol. 2ᵛ.

[fol. 86ʳ]   NB. NB. NB.

When my deare wife and I lived at the Pinner of Wakefield, I remember I melted downe æquall parts of Talc and ye Eagle [sal ammoniac], with Brimstone, repeating the Fusion Twice: And after that, going to draw spirit of Salt with Oyle of Glass,[105] I chanced (as I think) to mingle some Bay-salt, or that of Colla maris, with the fomer Composition, and I had an Oyle with which I did miracles. But assaying to make more of it, I never could effect it, having forgott the Composition, but now I am confident the Eagle was in it, for I ever remembred the maner of the first fume, yᵗ came out, and could never see the like againe, but when I worked on yᵉ Eagle, though I never afterwards ...

[fol. 85ᵛ]

... worked on her præpared, as att that time. I know allso by experience, that Talc and Baysalt together will yeeld 6 times more spirit, then either of both will yeeld by it self. And that passage of Rhasis confirmes mee, where hee mentions Aqua salis trium generum:[106] But above all that one word of Lullie, namely Petra Salis, and especially that enumeration of Materials, which hee makes in his Ars Intellectiva, Nitrum, Sal, Sulphur, vapor, then which nothing could have been sayd more expressly.[107] And yet I doubt, I shall bee much troubled, before I finde, what I have lost, soe little difference there is, betweene Forgettfullnes, and Ignorance.

T. R. V. 1658.

Quos Deus conjunxit,
Quis separabit?

[Whom God has joined,
Who will separate?]

---

[105] *Oyle of Glass* is Vaughan's translation of *oleum vitri*, which I have elsewhere translated as vitriol.

[106] Vaughan may have in mind a very short treatise, "Præparatio salis Armoniaci secundum Rasim," printed in the *Theatrum Chemicum*, 3: 177–80, that discussed making solutions of various salts. Such discussions of salts abounded in alchemical literature. See, e.g., Arnold's *Speculum*, 5: 515.

[107] See note on fol. 79ʳ.

[fol. 86ᵛ]   Cum eadem Aquilâ,

Chalybs ex quatuor corporibus calcinatur, et solvitur. Vel Chalybs iste
conteri potest cum Talco, et sale marino, et solvi, et fiet.

NB.

        Talcum & sal marinum idem operantur, quod colla maris, imò
præstant, modo rite copulentur, ut expertus sum in diebus Conjugis meæ
Charissimæ. Cum chalybe sint utriusque partes æquales: Cum oleo verò
pars una Talci, ad tres Salis.

T. R. V. 1658.

Quos Deus conjunxit, Quis separabit?

Christe Jesu!

Lux, et Vita Mundi: Filius Dei: Filius, et Redemptor
Hominis: Trahe me post Te, Curremus.

Amen!

NB. NB.

Aquilam cum Scarabæo præparatam solve in Aceto, distillato, et subli-
mabitur. Hoc Arcanum ex sacrâ Scripturâ edocuit me Conjux charissima,
quod verum esse in Aquilâ simplicitèr fusâ, expertus sum.

Talcum

Eodem modo præparatum solve etiam in Aceto, & fiet.

T. R. V.

With this same Sal Ammoniac,

Chalybs is calcinated from four bodies and dissolved. Or that chalybs can be ground together with talc and sea salt, and dissolved, and it will be made.

Talc and sea salt work the same as colla maris, yea rather they are superior if mated together rightly, as I proved in the days of my dearest **JB.** wife. With chalybs let there be equal parts of each; with oil though, one part talc to three of salt.

T. R. V. 1658.

Whom God has joined, Who will separate?

O Christ Jesus!
Light and Life of the World: Son of God: Son and Redeemer
of Mankind: Draw me after Thee, We shall run.

Amen!

Note Well. Note Well.

Dissolve sal ammoniac prepared with scarab in distilled vinegar, and it will be sublimed. This arcanum my dearest wife taught me from holy Scripture—which I have proved to be true in sal ammoniac simply liquefied.

Dissolve

Talcum prepared by this same way also in vinegar, and it will be made.

T. R. V.

[fol. 87ʳ]   Arcanum Nobile,
                         Inventum in Diebus Conjugis meæ
                                      Charissimæ.

℞ Stybii part[em] 1 cum dimidio. Lithargyrii part[es] 2. funde cum [sul-
phure] et fiet. Loco Lithargyrii, utere magnesiâ crudâ, et fiet.

    Corpus hoc contere cum Aquilâ per Scarabæum præparatâ, et calcina
inter duo Crucibula. Calcem solve in aquâ ex oleo vitri, & nitro combusto
cum S[ublimato] sicut scis.

NB.   Idem Corpus contere cum Sublimato, et calcina inter duo Crucibula,
tunc solve in aquâ minerali, et fiet pro Certo: Vel in [aquâ forti] ab oleo
vitri rectificatâ. Vide Lullium in Test: Ultº.

                                    Aqua Mineralis.

    Fit ex oleo vitri & nitro cum S[ublimato] præparato. vel Sume Talci
NB.   part[em] 1. Salis marini, vel communis partes 3. tere, et distilla cum oleo
vitri, et habebis. Vel ℞. aquilam cum Scarabæo præparatam, et distilla cum
oleo vitri. NB.

                                          NB.
NB.   Aquila fœtida magnesiæ haberi non potest, nisi Magnesia priùs excorietur
cum Aquâ forti. &c.

NB.   Chalybs optimè calcinatur cum Aquilâ per Scarabæum præparatâ,
Tunc conjungitur, &c.

A Notable Arcanum,
Discovered in the Days
of my Dearest Wife.

Take one and a half parts stibium, two parts litharge. Melt with sulphur
and it will be made. In place of litharge, use crude magnesia, and it will
be made.

Grind this body together with sal ammoniac prepared with scarab,
and calcine between two crucibles. Dissolve the calx in water from vitriol
and nitre heated with sublimate, as you know.

NB.   Grind this same body together with sublimate, and calcine between
two crucibles, then dissolve in mineral water, and it will be made for certain; or in aqua fortis rectified from vitriol. See Lull's last *Testamentum*.[108]

Mineral Water.

NB. Is made from vitriol and nitre prepared with sublimate; or take one part
talc, three parts sea salt or common salt. Grind and distill with vitriol,
and you will have it. Or take sal ammoniac prepared with scarab, and
distill with vitriol. Note Well.

Note Well.

B. A fetid sal ammoniac of magnesia cannot be obtained, unless the magnesia is first made caustic with aqua fortis, etc.

B. Chalybs is calcinated very well with sal ammoniac prepared by scarab,
then joined together, etc.

---

[108] I have not been able to locate this reference.

[fol. 87ᵛ]

Lapis Animalis fit sicut scis, et putrescit per se, absque Sale: Si vero calcinetur, tunc solvi potest in Aquâ vegetabili, et fient mirabilia in medicinâ
Corporis humani.

Hæc omnia, cum sale dulci Argillæ, et oleo eius Acido, inveni in diebus
conjugis meæ charissimæ, quam iterum in Cœlis videre, et Alloqui, dabit
Deus meus misericors. Amen & Amen.

Christe Jesu!
Lux, et vita mundi: Filius Dei: Filius, et Redemptor Hominis! Trahe me
post te, Curremus.

Quos Deus conjunxit,
Quis separabit?
T. R. V. 1658.

Note yᵉ following aqua vitæ, which I found, when I liued with my
deare Wife, att yᵉ pinner of wakefield.

NB.

℞. [sulphur] nostrum vegetabile: solve in succo uvarum nostrarum, et
digere in Alembico cæco. Tunc distilla, et ascendet Æther philosophicus,
absque aquâ vitæ vulgari, aut spiritu vini. Repete cum novâ minerâ,
donèc satis habeas. Laus sit Deo! Amen!
T. R. V. 1658.

The animated stone is made, as you know, and it putrefies by itself without salt. If indeed it be calcinated, then it can be dissolved in an animating water, and wondrous things will be made as medicine for the human body.

All these, with the sweet salt of argil and its acidic oil, I discovered in the days of my dearest wife, whom my merciful God will grant that I see again and speak with in heaven. Amen and Amen.

O Christ Jesus!
Light and life of the world: Son of God: Son and Redeemer of Mankind!
Draw me after Thee, We shall run!

Whom God has joined,
Who will separate?
T. R. V. 1658.

[Note yᵉ following aqua vitæ, which I found, when I liued with my deare Wife, att yᵉ pinner of Wakefield.]

B.

Take our animating sulphur; dissolve in the juice of our grapes, and decoct in a blind alembic. Then distill, and philosophical ether will ascend, without common aqua vitæ or spirit of wine. Repeat with a new mineral, until you have enough. Praise be to God! Amen!
T. R. V. 1658.

[fol. 88ʳ]   Medicina universalis.

Fit ex [sulphure] vegetabili, et Aquâ nostrâ ponticâ: Ex quâ (inquit D'Espagnet) cum Masculo suo copulatâ, qui &c.

T. R. V.

Extractio Salis nostri Ammoniaci
ex aquâ nostrâ ponticâ.

Præpara sulphur nostrum vegetabile, sicut scis, quod supra etiam docui: et rejectâ fæce terrestri, iterum calcina. Calcinatum pone in Succo uvarum nostrarum, vel in aquâ ponticâ Animali. digere per horas 24. Tunc abstrahe phlegma, et videbis, quod optas. Probatum est in diebus Animæ meæ R. V. Tunc enim feci, et salem nostrum in aquâ suâ instar graminis crescere vidi, quin et pelliculâ clausum & circumductum inveni, ut fœtus nascitur in membranâ. Tunc abstracto phlegmate distillavi, & transivit in oleum, vel potius Succum clarissimum, et Balsamicum. Hoc est verum naturæ menstruum, et ignis non Corrosivus, quo omnia corpora, modo prius calcinentur, in primum Ens reduci possunt, et in medicinam Balsamicam, Cardiacam, et Confortativam.

T. R. V.

Universal Medicine.

Is made from animating sulphur and our briny water. From which (says D'Espagnet) mated with its masculus, ... etc.[109]

T. R. V.

Extraction of Our Sal Ammoniac
from our briny water.

Prepare our animating sulphur, as you know, which I have also taught you above; and after the earthly dregs have been rejected, calcine again. Place what has been calcinated in the juice of our wine, or in animated, briny water. Decoct for twenty-four hours. Then draw out the phlegm, and you will see what you wish for. It was proved in the days of my soul, R. V. For then I made it, and I saw that our salt grew in its water like grass, and furthermore I discovered something enclosed and concealed in the skin, as the fetus is born in the membrane. Then after the phlegm was drawn off, I distilled it, and it turned into oil or rather a very clear and balsamic juice. This is the true menstruum of nature, the non-corrosive fire, by which all bodies, if first calcinated in this way, can be reduced to the first being, and to a balsamic, hearty and comforting medicine.

T. R. V.

---

[109] Jean d'Espagnet, *Enchiridion Physicæ Restitutæ* was first issued at Paris in 1608; it was first translated by Elias Ashmole as *The Summary of Physics Recovered* (London, 1651). d'Espagnet discussed the great work using the florid metaphors characteristic of early alchemy: i.e., as the copulation of Sol and Luna, or light and water to produce Philosopher's earth (as at the Creation), whereas Vaughan usually refers to sulphur and mercury.

[fol. 88ᵛ]   Ars tota.

Nullum sal valet præter nitrum, Colla maris exceptâ. Si vero Colla desit,
NB.   utere sale gemmæ, qui cum Chalybe ex Ære, et duobus plumbis, facile in
oleum transit.

Chalybs sic fit.

Frustula æris candefac in Crucibulo, candefactis stybium injice, donec
omnia fluant. Tunc impone fratris pari pondere, et fiet.

Nitrum quatuor modis
præparatur.

Vel cum Aquâ forti, sicut scis, estque via nobilis. vel cum Scarabæo sublimato: vel cum saccharo, et oleo vitri, estque compendium optimum. Vel
cum sulphure vegetabili, sitque sulphuris pondus duplum, ad unum Nitri,
et hoc est Arcanum in Medicinâ.

Aliud Arcanum in
medicinâ.

Nitri pondus unum, cum duplo Sacchari projice in Crucibulum candens.
Tunc procede ut in Arcano suprascripto. Eodem modo procedere potes
NB.   cum [sulphure] communi, vel cum quacunque re sulphureâ, et combus-
tibili.

                         Extractio Tincturarum
             NB.   ex Rhabarbaro, Opio, et   {*}NB.
                         Scammoneâ &c.

Aquæ distillatæ, et olei vitri partes æquales commisce. tunc impone materiam, et digere, donec aqua tingatur. Aquæ Tinctæ infunde spiritum vini,
et abtrahet Tincturam ad se, &c.

       {* NB. Si cum nitro comburantur ad debitum pondus, tunc cum solâ
       aquâ vitæ extrahi potest Tinctura.¹¹⁰}

                         T. R. V.

---

¹¹⁰ Vaughan's marginal note.

The Entire Art.

NB. No salt is more efficacious than nitre, colla maris excepted. If indeed colla be lacking, use rock salt, which, with chalybs from ore and the two leads, easily turns into oil.

Chalybs Is Made in This Way.

Make a bit of ore very hot in a crucible; throw stibium in what has been made hot until all be fluid. Then place an equal weight of each *brother, and it will be made.

Nitre Is Prepared
in Four Ways.

Either with aqua fortis, as you know, and this is the known way. Or with sublimated scarab, or with sugar and vitriol, and this is the shortest way. Or with animating sulphur—and let it be a double weight of sulphur to one of nitre—and this is an arcanum in medicine.

Another Arcanum
in Medicine.

Project one weight of nitre with a double weight of sugar into a glowing crucible. Then proceed as in the arcanum described above. You can pro-
B. ceed in this same manner with common sulphur, or with any combustible and sulphurous thing whatsoever.

	Extraction of Tinctures	
Note Well.	from Rhubarb, Opium	{*} Note Well.
	and Scammony, etc.	

Mix together equal parts of distilled water and vitriol. Then put in the matter and decoct, until the water is tinged. Pour spirit of wine into the tinged water, and it will draw the tincture to itself, etc.

{* If they are heated with the required weight of nitre, then the tinctures can be extracted with the aqua vitæ alone.}

T. R. V.

NB: Quæ

Sequuntur.

1658.

Deo duce: comite Naturâ.

T. R. V.

Quære quid sit Holosachne, nam in officinis sperma ceti dicitur, sed falsò:
est coloris russi, et malè olet, et non solvitur in Aquâ. Credo quod multum in se habet salis volatilis &c.

Note Well:

What follows.[111]

1658.

With God as leader, with Nature as attendant.

T. R. V.

Seek what Holosachne[112] may be, for in the workshops it is said to be whale sperm but falsely. It is red in color and smells badly, and it is not dissolved in water. I believe that it has much volatile salt in itself, etc.

---

[111] Special emphasis was called to this material by the large *Note Bene* (measuring some 4 cm high).

[112] *Sachnos* is a Galenic word meaning "tender"; literally, then it means something "completely tender," but Vaughan seems to refer to a more specific substance that I have been unable to identify.

[fol. 89ᵛ]

The Dreame I writt on the fore-going page [i.e., on fol. 90ʳ], is not to bee neglected: for my deare wife a few nights before, appeared to mee in my Sleepe, and fore-told mee the Death of my deare Father, and since it is really come to passe, for hee is dead, and gone to my mercifull god, as I have been informed this very day by letters come to my neece, from the Countrey. It concernes mee therefore to præpare my self, and to make a right use of this Warning, which I received from my mercifull and most loving God, who useth not to deale such mercies to all men: and who was pleased to impart it to mee by my deare Wife, to assure mee shee was a Saint in his Holy Heavens, being thus imployed for an Angell, and a messenger of the god of of my Salvation: To him bee all prayse and glorie ascribed in Jesus Christ for ever.

Amen! T. R. V.

[fol. 90ʳ]

On the 28 of August, being Saturday morning, after daylight, god Almightie was pleased to reveale unto mee, after a wonderfull maner, the most blessed Estate of my deare Wife, partly by her self, and partly by his owne Holy spirit, in an Express discourse, which opened unto mee the meaning of those mysterious words of Sᵗ. Paul: For wee know, That if our Earthly house of this Tabernacle &c.

Bless the Lord, O my Soule! and all that is within mee, bless his holy Name![113]

T. R. V.

Quos Deus Conjunxit,
Quis separabit?

1658.

---

[113] Psalm 103:1.

[fol. 90ᵛ]

*}   On the 13 of June, I dreamed that one appeared to mee, and purged
her self from the scandalous Contents of certaine letters, which were put
into my hands by a certaine false friend. Then shee told mee, that her
father had informed her, that shee should dye againe about a Quarter of
**}   a yeare from that time shee appeared to mee: which is just the 14 of
September next, and on the 28 of the same moenth wee were maried. It
may bee, my mercifull god hath given mee this notice of the Time of my
Dissolution by one that is soe deare unto mee, whose person representing
mine, signified my death, not hers, for shee can dye noe more. Great is
the Love, and goodnes of my god, and most happy shall I bee in this
Interpretation, If I may meete her againe so soone, and beginn the
Heavenly and Æternall life with her, in the very same moenth, wherein
wee began the Earthly: which I beseech my good god to grant us for his
Deare Son, and our Saviour's sake, Christ Jesus. Amen!

Written on the 14ᵗʰ. of June,
the day after I dreamed it.
1658.

{* This happened on a Sunday night towards the Day-Break, and indeed I
think, it was morning light.}
{** symbol for emphasis in margin}

[fol. 91ʳ]   NB. NB.

T. R. V.

Aqua Sanitatis vera.

℞. Aquam ultimam de B[alneo] rectificatam ab Oleo vitri. Tunc ℞. Succum Lunariæ, et evaporatâ omni humiditate, calcina igne solo. Calcem solve, et putrefac in Aquâ de B[alneo]. Distilla, cohoba, et in hac aquâ solve Aurum, et fiet pro Certo.

Sola etiam Aqua de B[alneo] ab oleo vitri rectificata solvit Corallos, et Margaritas &c.

Aqua Mineralis.

Aquilam Albam, sive salem nostrum Ammoniacum extractum ab Aquâ siccâ sicut scis, contere cum Corpore nigro. {*} Trituram inspissa cum Aqua communi, & distilla, et fiet.

Idem faciet Regulus factus ex [antimonio,] [cupro,] [plumbo,] [stanno,] ut expertus sum in Diebus Conjugis meæ Dulcissimæ.

{* Si corpus nigrum prius calcinetur cum sublimato, melius erit.}

[fol. 92ʳ]   NB.

Salem plumbi absque Corrosivâ, sic facies: Lithargyrio minutissimè trito affunde Aquam communem ferventem, et agita cum Bacillo, donec tota albescat. Sine ut aliquantulum resideat, tunc effunde: Lithargyrio novam Aquam impone, iterumque agita, et Effunde: Et toties repete, donec tota plumbi substantia exeat cum Aquâ instar farinæ albissimæ. Aquam vero stare sinito, donec farina resideat & instar Cerusæ fundum petat. Tunc effunde aquam, & farinam exicca, siccatamque solve in Aceto distillato, et digere: vel si vis, solve in Corrosivâ debili, mixtâ cum aquâ pluvia, vel communi.

Note Well. Note Well.

T. R. V.

The True Water of Health.

Take the hottest water from the bath rectified by vitriol. Then take juice of lunaria, and after any moistness has been evaporated, calcine with fire alone. Dissolve the calx, and putrefy in water from the bath. Distill, cohobate, and dissolve gold in this water, and it will be made for certain.

By itself water from the bath rectified by vitriol dissolves corals and pearls, etc.

Mineral Water.

Grind together white sal ammoniac, or our sal ammoniac extracted from dry water, as you know, with the black body. {*} Thicken what has been ground with common water, and distill, and it will be made.

Regulus, made from antimony, copper, lead, and tin, will do the same thing, as I tested in the days of my sweetest wife.

{* If the black body is first calcinated with sublimate, it will be better.}

Note Well.

You may make salt of lead without a corrosive in this way. Pour boiling hot, ordinary water in litharge ground in very small pieces, and agitate with a rod until it all whitens. Without even a little of it remaining, then pour it out. Put new water in the litharge, and agitate again, and pour it out. And repeat often until the entire substance of the lead passes with the water like very white powder. Let the water stand indeed, until the powder remains and falls to the bottom like white lead. Then pour out the water, and dry the powder, and dissolve what has been dried in distilled vinegar, and decoct; or if you wish, dissolve in a weak corrosive, mixed with rain water, or ordinary water.

[fol. 92ᵛ]   NB. de Mercurio vulgi.

Calcinatum et fixum in [aquâ forti], solve in Aceto distillato. solutum sicca, et tere cum Croco Antimonii. Trituram solve in [aquâ forti] et pluviâ distillatâ; vel absque solutione Trituram solam, et siccam distilla.

Calcinatum porro, et in Aceto solutum, siccatumquè contere cum Regulo ex Marte et venere nigri obscuri coloris: vel cum chalybe ex duobus plumbis, et distilla primo trituram siccam, vel si vis solve, et postea distilla.

Calcinatum etiam cum [aquâ forti], tere cum sulphure communi, et combure; Combustum in Aceto solve, &c.

Turbith ex oleo vitrioli et mercurio, combure cum sulphure; combustum in aquâ vitæ solve, vel in Aceto distillato, et postea in spiritu vini, &c.

Plumbum nigrum pictorum miram in se Tincturam habet. Candescat ergo sæpius in igne, et toties mergatur in [aquâ forti] optimâ, donec ultimo rubescat instar Rosæ. Tunc extrahe Colorem eius cum spiritu vini acuato cum Oleo vitri, et fiet.

Talem quoque Tincturam habit Argilla, cum Sale dulci magnæ virtutis. Maceretur ergo per ...

[fol. 91ᵛ]
... Noctem in aquâ communi, ut docuit me Conjux charissima. demum exiccetur in pulverem, qui in Aceto solutus præparetur cum Agitabulo. Tunc digeratur, donec Acetum coloretur: coloratum effunde, et filtra, et sicca in salem; quem solve in Aquâ ultimâ de B[alneo] ab oleo vitri rectificatâ. Solutionem cohoba, et habebis Rem nobilem, et in medicinâ satìs efficacem.

Sal plumbi etiam si solvatur in aquâ illa ultimâ de B: spiritum suum facillime exhalat: præsertim vero si cum Plutone conjungatur. Extrahe ergo salem eius absque corrosivâ: Extractum contere cum plutone crudo, vel per Resinam et Tartarum purgato, vel per Resinam solam. Tunc digere, et cohoba patientèr, et habebis pro certo. Salem Argillæ quoque contere cum plutone, et fiet.

T. R. V. Quos Deus conjunxit,
nec Mors quidèm separabit.

Amen Domine Jesu!

1658.

Note Well Concerning Common Mercury.

In distilled vinegar dissolve [mercury] that has been calcinated and fixed in aqua fortis. Dry the solution, and grind with crocus of antimony. Dissolve what has been ground in aqua fortis and in distilled rain water; or distill without the solution what has been ground alone and dried.

And next grind together what has been calcinated and dissolved in vinegar and dried with regulus from iron and copper of a dark color; or grind it together with chalybs from the two leads, and distill first what has been ground and dried, or if you wish, dissolve, and afterwards distill.

With common sulphur grind also what has been calcinated with aqua fortis, and heat; dissolve what has been heated in vinegar, etc.

With sulphur heat *turpeth from vitriol and mercury; dissolve what has been heated in aqua vitæ, or in distilled vinegar, and afterwards in spirit of wine, etc.

Painters' black lead possesses a wonderful tincture in itself. It may often glow therefore in fire, and be merged many times in the best aqua fortis, until at last it reddens like a rose. Then extract its color with spirit of wine strengthened with vitriol, and it will be made.

Potter's clay possesses such a tincture too, with a sweet salt of great virtue. It may be softened therefore . . .

. . . for a night in common water, as my dearest wife taught me. Finally let it be dried into a powder, which dissolved in vinegar may be prepared with agitation. Then let it be decocted until the vinegar be colored; pour this out, and filter and dry into a salt, which [you] dissolve in the hottest water from the bath rectified by vitriol. Cohobate the solution, and you will have a notable thing, efficacious in medicine.

Salt of lead also if dissolved in this hottest water from the bath breathes out its spirit very easily—especially so if joined with Pluto. Extract its salt, therefore, without a corrosive. Grind together the extract with crude Pluto, or purged by resin and tartar, or by resin alone. Then decoct, and cohobate patiently, and you will have it for certain. Grind salt of argil too with Pluto, and it will be made.

T. R. V. Whom God has joined,
not even Death will separate.

Amen Lord Jesus!

1658.

[fol. 93ʳ]   NB.

Si Corpori nigro infra-scripto affundatur [aqua fortis] & pluvia, solvitur
instar Lithargyrii, dabitque salem philosophicum, absque ullo labore, aut
sumptibus. probatum in diebus Animæ meæ R. V.

NB. de Mercurio Sublimato.

Corpus nigrum evaporabile valde, inventum in diebus
Conjugis meæ dulcissimæ, contere cum sublimato,
et distillabitur in spiritum Butyro Antimonii
similem, sed longe Efficaciorem. Corpus quoque
ipsum forsan calcinabitur, quod Arcanum est
stupendum. Si vero corpori isti cum sublimato
addatur sal nostrum Ammoniacum, vel illud
vulgi, erit Res valdè Arcana, et ut conjector,
initium Artis philosophicæ.

  Sal etiam nostrum Ammoniacum per se
cum isto corpore distillari potest. Si vero corpus
prius calcinetur, facilior erit Operatio.

Note Well.

If aqua fortis and rain water are poured on the black body described below, it is dissolved like litharge, and yields a philosophical salt, without any labor or expense. Proved in the days of my soul R. V.

Note Well Concerning Sublimated Mercury.

The black body is highly capable of evaporation, as discovered in the days of my sweetest wife; grind it together with sublimate, and it will be distilled into a spirit similar to butter of antimony[114] but far more efficacious. The body itself too perchance will be calcinated, which is a stunning arcanum. If indeed to that body with the sublimate our sal ammoniac be added, or common sal ammoniac, it will be a greatly mysterious matter, and as I conjecture, the beginning of the philosophical art.

Our sal ammoniac also by itself can be distilled with that body. If indeed the body first be calcinated, the operation will be easier.

---

[114] Antimony chloride ($SbCl_3$), so named because of its consistency; see Crosland, *Language of Chemistry*, 74.

[fol. 93ᵛ]   Aqua vitæ mirabilis.

Tartarum crudum ablutum, vel crystallos eius calcina cum nitro. Calcem solve in aquâ vitæ, et invenies duos diversos liquores, quorum unus rubei coloris est, ~~XXXXXXX~~[115] et Ælterum super-natat, de quo etiam meminit Riplæus, Capite de Lapide vegetabili. liquor iste Rubeus admodum dulcis est, Sed majori in copia reperitur, si Tartarum comburatur cum duobus Salibus, et hic est ille Tartarus, qui nigrior est quam Tartarus de nigris uvis Cataloniæ. Solvatur ergo in Aquâ vitæ, & liquor rubeus super-natans per se distilletur. Ascendet primo oleum clarum, et spissum, estque aqua vitæ mira; hanc per se recipies antequàm ascendat phlegma, quam serva diligentèr, est enim res Arcana, et magnarum multarumque facultatum.

                                  Si vero ab Oleo

vitri rectificatur, menstruum erit potentissimum, sicut et Aqua ultima de B[alneo]. Si vero conjungatur cum oleo vitri philosophici, & sæpius ab eo distilletur, convertetur tota in gummi, sive glaciem claram instar unionis, de quâ vide Lullium, &c.

[fol. 94ʳ blank]

_____

[115] A word was heavily marked out here and et Ælterum was added above the line with a caret.

A Wondrous Aqua vitæ.

With nitre, calcine crude, washed tartar or its crystals. Dissolve the calx in aqua vitæ, and you will discover two diverse liquids, one of whose color is red and floats above **the other,** concerning which Ripley makes mention in his chapter on the animating stone.[116] That red liquid is quite sweet, but it is found in greater supply, if tartar be heated with the two salts, and this is the one tartar that is blacker than tartar from the black grapes of Catalonia. Let it therefore be dissolved in the aqua vitæ, and the red liquid floating above by itself be distilled. At first a clear, thick oil will ascend, and it is a wonderful aqua vitæ; you will take this by itself before the phlegm may ascend, which [you] diligently save, for it is a mysterious thing and a thing of great and numerous properties.

If indeed it be rectified by vitriol,

the menstruum will be very potent, as the hottest water from the bath. If it be joined indeed with philosophical vitriol and distilled more often by it, the whole will be converted to gum or a clear crystal like a pearl,[117] about which see Lull, etc.

---

[116] In *The Compound of Alchymy, or the ancient hidden Art of Alchemie,* Sir George Ripley describes the male and female principles, sulphur and mercury, that have separated during putrefaction (the fifth gate) as "the Red man and hys whyte Wyfe." See Ashmole's text in *Theatrum Chemicum Britannicum,* 154.

[117] "*Uniones* are pretious Pearls, or Gems" (Dorn, *Chymical Dictionary,* 350).

[fol. 94ᵛ]   Arcana quædam particularia
                               ad Rem medicam facientia,
                               inventa et experta in Diebus
                               Conjugis meæ Dulcissimæ.

1. Spiritus Terebinthinæ verus.

Communem illum, et venalem recipe, et rectifica super nitrum fusum. repete bis vel ter, nitrum semper renovando, & habebis spiritum Nobilem.
Si vero iterum ab oleo vitri rectificetur,[118] menstruum erit mirabile ad
extrahendas vegetabilium Tincturas, & pro solvendis salibus metallicis
quibuscunque.

Farina sulphuris.

Olei Terebinthinæ vulgaris, et olei vitri, partes æquales sumito. funde super
flores sulphuris: distilla, et habebis.

Secretum Nigrum.

Argentum vivum crudum, vel odore plumbi coagulatum bulliat in Crucibulo. Bullienti affunde stybium fusum guttatim et cautè, ne nimis incale-
scant. Habebis metallum acidum, et igneum, quo sublimatum in aquam
transit. Si vero simplex antimonium crudum cum sublimato teratur, et igne
moderato coquatur, dulcescit instar sacchari.

[fol. 95ʳ blank]

---

[118] Sic, for *rectificietur*.

Certain Particular Arcana
for making medicine,
discovered and tested in the days
of my sweetest Wife.

1. True Spirit of Turpentine.

Take this common kind that is purchasable, and rectify upon molten nitre. Repeat twice or thrice, always renewing the nitre, and you will have a notable spirit. If indeed it will be rectified again by vitriol, it will be a marvelous menstruum for extracting the tinctures of animating things and for dissolving all metallic salts whatsoever.

Powder of Sulphur.

Take equal parts oil of common turpentine and vitriol. Melt over flowers of sulphur; distill, and you will have it.

A Black Secret.

Let crude quicksilver or coagulate with the odor of lead boil in a crucible. Pour molten stibium in the boiling mixture, drop by drop and cautiously, lest it become too hot. You will have an acidic and fiery metal, with which sublimate will turn into water. If indeed simple, crude antimony be ground with sublimate and concocted with a moderate flame, it will sweeten like sugar.

[fol. 95ᵛ]   NB. NB. NB.

Si Anatron solum, vel Anatron et Talcum cum Stybio vegetabili præparatum, imponantur Aquæ nostræ, credo, Quod plus Aeris habebis. Hoc est
Secretum eximium, utere ergo ad Dei gloriam, et invenies.

Hæc Ego hic scripsi in Memoriam
Charissimæ Conjugis:
Quam aliquando in Cœlis videre, dabit
Deus Misericordiarum.

Amen Domine Jesu! Qui
Judex Nobis venturus es!

Sed Salvator cùm sis,
Condemnare nescis

T. R. V. 1658.

Lapis Animalis absque Salibus
aut Sublimato.

Succum Lunariæ putrefac per dies 40, donec vertatur in Terram nigram.
Hanc cum sulphure suo commisce, & sublima in Tabernaculis, sic habebis
[mercurium] philosophicum, & Aquam siccam non madefacientem.

Note Well. Note Well. Note Well.

If nitric salt alone, or nitric salt and talc prepared with an animating stibium, be put in our water, I believe that you will have more ore. This is an extraordinary secret; use therefore to the glory of God, and you will discover it.

This I wrote here in Memory
of my Dearest Wife:
Whom the God of Mercies will grant
that I see sometime in heaven.

Amen Lord Jesus! Who will
come to be Our Judge!

But since you are the savior,
You do not know how to condemn

T. R. V. 1658.

The Animated Stone without Salts
or Sublimate.

Putrefy the juice of lunaria for forty days, until it be turned into black earth. Mix this together with its sulphur and sublime in a tabernacle; in this way you will have sophic mercury and dry water that wets not.[119]

---

[119] On the water that wets not, see Sendivogius's *A New Light of Alchymy*, 39–46, and Vaughan's *Lumen de Lumine* and *Euphrates* (*Works*, 331, 546). See also Zbigniew Szydło, *Water Which Does Not Wet Hands: The Alchemy of Michael Sendivogius* (Warsaw: Polish Academy of Sciences, 1994).

[fol. 96ʳ]   Plumbum rubeum Philosophorum.

℞ succum Lunariæ, et evaporatâ humiditate, Terram eius conjunge ad pondus cum Ære nostro. Tunc calcina cum sublimato inter duo Crucibula, et combure Calcem igne forti donec rubescat instar Rosæ.

Alia Confectio
[Saturni] rubei.

Fluat Saturnus per Resinam: Tunc sublimetur in Florem subtilem, et levissimum. Hunc contere, et coque cum Magnesiâ per Corrosivam excoriatâ, et fiet.

Florum vero Omnium

Abbreviatio fit cum Corpore nigro, sive stybio philosophico sicut scis. Hoc enim corpus facillimè calcinatur, & facillimè solvitur, cum Aquâ Talci Hispanici factâ sicut scis, cum oleo vitri, et Rore Animali de B[alneo].

Laus Deo, Amen! T. R. V.

Red Lead of the Philosophers.[120]

Take juice of lunaria, and after the moistness has been evaporated, join its earth with an equal weight of our ore. Then calcine with sublimate between two crucibles, and heat the calx with a fierce fire until it reddens like a rose.

Another Preparation of
Red Lead.

Let lead flow through resin. Then let it be sublimed into a subtle and very light flower. Grind this together, and concoct with magnesia made caustic by a corrosive, and it will be made.

Of All Flowers Indeed

A diminution is made with the black body, or philosophical stibium, as you know. For this body is very easily calcinated and very easily dissolved, with water made of Spanish talc, as you know, with vitriol, and animated dew from the bath.

Praise be to God. Amen! T. R. V.

---

[120] According to Dorn, *Chymical Dictionary*, 341, "*Plumbum Philosophorum* is that which is extracted out of Antimony"; hence, Vaughan's formula for producing it with *lunaria* is novel.

[fol. 96ᵛ]   NB. NB.

Corpus nigrum ex Lithargyrio, & stybio sicut scis, contere cum duobus
salibus præparatis: Trituram solve in Aquâ Regis, cohoba, et fiet. Præstat
[aquâ forti] cum Rore mixta, et distillata.
Laus Deo. Amen!

Sal Ammoniacum vegetabile.

℞. Aeris congelati & salsi Mineram optimam: projice illius partem .1. super
partes duas Aquæ nostræ Ponticæ; et statim ascendet Aquila, et egredietur
ex mari nostro instar Butyri, aut olei albissimi. Collige illud: est enim
Cortex, et spuma maris, et Aqua nostra Rha-pontica, et Mercurius ~~ponticus~~
philosophicus, Cuius extractionem solus deus revelare debet, qui novit Ho-
minum corda &c.

Sit ergo soli deo Laus,
et Gloria. Amen!

T. R. V.

1658.

NB.   NB.

℞. vitrioli calcinati lib[ram] 1. salis Lunariæ lib[ram] mediam. Stybii per
Resinam purgati lib[ram] mediam. Tere in simul, et nudo igne distilla.

[fol. 97ʳ blank]

Note Well. Note Well.

Grind together the black body with the two prepared salts from litharge and stibium, as you know. Dissolve what has been ground in aqua regia, cohobate, and it will be made. It is superior to aqua fortis mixed with dew and distilled.

Praise be to God. Amen!

Animating Sal Ammoniac.

Take the best mineral of congealed and salty ore. Project one part of this upon two parts of our briny water, and immediately sal ammoniac will ascend and go forth from our sea like butter or very white oil. Collect this, for it is both the rind and foam of the sea,[121] our rha-pontic water,[122] and the sophic mercury, whose extraction God alone ought to reveal, He who knows the hearts of men, etc.

Thus Praise and Glory be
to God Alone. Amen!

T. R. V.

1658.

Note Well.   Note Well.

Take one pound of calcinated vitriol, a half pound of salt of lunaria, and a half pound of stibium purged by resin. Grind together, and distill with a bare flame.

---

[121] "*Cortex maris* is the Vinegar of the Philosophers" (Dorn, *Chymical Dictionary*, 322).

[122] *Rha ponticum* or *rheum rhaponticum* is a variety of rhubarb from the region beyond the Bosphorus that Dioscorides and Galen valued for its "dry and thinne essence containing in it selfe a purging force and qualitie to open obstructions, but helped and made more facile by the subtil and airious parts" (Gerard, *Herball*, 392–96). See also Pliny, *Natural History*, XXVII.cv.

[fol. 97ᵛ]   Salium duorum præparatio.

Funde Anatron, inter duo Crucibula lutata, per horas sex, aut Circitèr. Tunc solve in Aceto, filtra, sicca, et paratum est. Hæc est Aqua Rebecca.

Talcum similiter funde igne fortissimo: Tunc in Aceto solve, &c. et paratum est.

Quæ in priori libro scripsimus,

De præparatione Anatri cum [aquâ forti], et Ammoniaco, verissima sunt, et nullo modo contemnenda. Item quæ scripsimus de Collâ maris.

Item Quod

De stanno diximus, et purgatione eius absque servo fugitivo, Arcanum est altissimum. Sic ergo purgatum calcina solo igne: vel tere cum sublimato, et fiet.

Succus Lunariæ

Etiam, Aquilâ priùs evaporatâ, solo igne calcinari potest: & super istam calcem figi potest Aqua permanens, absque Ære, si vera sunt, quæ Arnoldus in suo Testamento docet, aut saltem docere videtur.

Laus Deo. Amen! T. V. R. 1658.

Preparation of the two Salts.

Melt nitric salt between two crucibles sealed with clay for six hours or thereabouts. Then dissolve it in vinegar, filter, dry, and it is prepared. This is Aqua Rebecca.

Melt the talc similarly in very fierce fire. Then dissolve it in vinegar, etc., and it is prepared.

What we have written in this book previously

about the preparation of nitric salt with aqua fortis and sal ammoniac is very true, and ought in no way to be condemned. Likewise what we have written about colla maris.

Likewise What

We said about tin and its purgation without the fugitive attendant. That is a most high arcanum. In this way therefore calcine with fire alone what has been purged; or grind it with sublimate, and it will be made.

The Juice of Lunaria

Can also be calcinated with fire alone, after the sal ammoniac has been evaporated; and a permanent water[123] can be fixed upon that calx, without ore, if those things are true, which Arnold teaches in his *Testamentum*, or at least seems to teach.[124]

Praise be to God. Amen! T. V. R. 1658.

---

[123] "*Aqua permanens* is that which is made of two most perfect metalline bodies by a Philosophical solution" (Dorn, *Chymical Dictionary*, 309).

[124] Vaughan may have in mind the very brief *Libellus qui Testamentum Arnaldi à Villa Nova Inscribitur*, in *Theatrum Chemicum*, 1: 28, which described how the "Lapis Philosophorum de terra scaturiens in igne perficitur seu exaltatur." But it is far more likely he had the *Testamentum* of the pseudo-Lull in mind: either the *Theorica*, chapter IX (*Theatrum Chemicum*, 4: 18), or the *Practica*, chapter XV (4: 146).

[fol. 98ʳ]   NB. De Succo Lunariæ.

In calcinatione succi, si mercurius crudus abundat, fit calx fusibilis instar
Ceræ, et totus Mercurius figitur.

Si vero parum Mercurii insit, fit calx sicca Cinerei coloris, nec fusibilis.
Et hæc qualitas forsan etiam a Marte provenit. Succus ergo non nisi moderato, et lentissimo igne prolici debet.

Experire etiàm, quod sequitur.

Sint partes duæ magnetis ad unam ferri, vel magnetis pars una cum Se-
misse, & fiet calx valdè fusibilis.

[fol. 98ᵛ]   ARS TOTA

Ut in Diebus Conjugis meæ Charissimæ inventa
est, breviter et dilucidè repetita.

Aqua prima
mineralis.

Salem duplicatum fusum, in Corrosivâ vel Aceto solutum, siccatumque
contere cum pari pondere salis Lunariæ. Contritum distilla cum oleo vitri,
et fiet.

Aqua 2ᵈᵃ.

Salem Lunariæ cum Chalybe, vel [stanno] per Resinam purgato contere, &
assa in calcem. Calcem cum sale duplicato tere, et solve in aquâ primâ, et
fiet. Loco Aquæ primæ sufficit [aqua fortis] ab oleo vitri distillata, et cum
Aquâ Roris temperata, repetitis Rectificationibus.

Note Well Concerning the Juice of Lunaria.

In the calcination of the juice, if crude mercury overflows, a calx meltable like wax is made, and all the mercury is fixed.

If only a little mercury be in it, a calx is made that is dry, the color of ashes, and not meltable. And this quality perchance also was produced by the iron. The juice therefore ought not to be drawn unless with a moderate fire and very slowly.

Prove also what follows.

Let there be two parts loadstone to one of iron, or one part loadstone with a half, and the calx will be made exceedingly meltable.

THE ENTIRE ART

As it was discovered in the Days of my Dearest Wife
briefly and clearly repeated.

The First Mineral Water.

Grind melted, doubled salt, dissolved in a corrosive or vinegar and dried, together with an equal weight of salt of lunaria. Distill what has been ground with vitriol, and it will be made.

The Second Water.

Grind salt of lunaria together with chalybs, or tin purged by resin, and assate into calx. Grind the calx with doubled salt, and dissolve in the first water, and it will be made. In place of the first water, aqua fortis, distilled by vitriol and tempered with water from a *balneum roris*, suffices for repeated rectifications.

Aqua Tertia.

Succum Lunariæ calcinatum contere cum Ære philosophico; Putrefac, et coque in Terram rubeam. Hanc solve, et cohoba in Aquâ Secundâ, et habebis. Hæc Compositio per se stillari potest, absque aquâ minerali, ad medicinam.

Laus vero sit Deo Nostro Sublimi,
et glorioso, in suo Quem misit,
Jesu Christo!

Amen & Amen, dicunt T. V. R. 1658.

[fol. 99ʳ]   NB. Quæ sequuntur
in adversâ paginâ.

Ex libris Th: et Reb: Vaughan. 1658.

Cupio dissolvi, et esse cum
Christo!

NB. de proportionibus.

In opere 2ᵈᵒ debent esse partes Æquales Martis et Magnesiæ, et hoc ex Turbâ palet in Confectione plumbi rubei.

In opere vero primo, et Aceti præparatione, debent esse stanni, vel Saturni purgati partes tres, ad unam Magnesiæ, quo facilius in Aquam transeat.

The Third Water.

Grind the calcinated juice of lunaria together with philosophical ore; putrefy, and cococt into a red earth. Dissolve this, and cohobate in the second water, and you will have it. This composition can be distilled by itself, without mineral water, into a medicine.

But praise be to Our Sublime and glorious God,
in His Jesus Christ
He Sent Himself!

Amen and Amen, say T. V. R. 1658.

Note Well What follows
in the opposite page.[125]

From the Books of Thomas and Rebecca Vaughan. 1658.

I wish to be dissolved, and to be with
Christ![126]

Note Well Concerning Proportions.

In the second work there ought to be equal parts iron and magnesia, and this may be supported from the *Turba* on the preparation of red lead.[127]

But in the first work, and in the preparation of vinegar, there ought to be three parts tin or purged lead to one of magnesia, by which it may turn more easily into water.

---

[125] I.e., fol. 98ᵛ.

[126] Philippians 1:23.

[127] See the twelfth discourse of the *Turba Philosophorum*, in *Theatrum Chemicum*, 5: 10–11; the seventeenth discussed red lead produced by ore and lead mixed equally (5: 15).

[fol. 99ᵛ]   Aqua Salis Nitri.

Nitrum fusum projice in Acetum distillatum. Abstrahe Acetum in fine igne fortissimo. Nitrum iterum solve, filtra, sicca, et cum Oleo vitri distilla. Hæc Aqua multum valet, et uti potest loco Aquæ fortis, quam supra descripsimus, præstat enim longè. Si Nitro Sal Lunariæ addatur, mirum quid fiet.

Nullum aliud Sal cum oleo vitri distillatum
valet: Atque hic Disquisitionis
nostræ finis esto!

Scias tamen quod sal petræ philosophorum, sal duplicatum est ex Talco Hispanico, et Anatron. Salem ergo Lunariæ per Corrosivam extractum, nec perfectè siccatum, contere cum chalybe, vel cum [stanno] per Resinam purgato. tunc assa, et tere cum sale duplato, et solve &c.

Cupio dissolvi, & esse cum Christo.

TR. V. —58.

In aqua suprascriptâ, vel in hac, quæ sequitur, ℞ salis dupl[ic]ati partem .1. salis Lunariæ partem .1. olei vitri partes 2. Distillentur igne fortissimo, et fiet.

Quodlibet sal per se præparetur,
vel in simul, et habebis,
cum [aquâ forti].

[fol. 100ʳ blank]

Water of Nitric Salt.

Project nitre melted in distilled vinegar. Draw out the vinegar in the end with a very fierce fire. Dissolve the nitre again, filter, dry, and distill with vitriol. This water is very efficacious, and can be used in place of aqua fortis, which we have described above, for it is greatly superior to it. If salt of lunaria be added to the nitre, an astonishing thing will be made.

No Other Salt Distilled with Vitriol
Is Efficacious. And This Shall Be
The End of Our Disquisition!

May you know nonetheless that rock salt of the philosophers is salt doubled from Spanish talc and nitric salt. Grind, therefore, the salt of lunaria, extracted by a corrosive and not perfectly dried, together with chalybs or with tin purged by resin. Then assate, and grind with doubled salt, and dissolve, etc.

I wish to be dissolved, and to be with Christ.

TR. V. 1658.

In the water described above, or in this which follows, take one part doubled salt, one part salt of lunaria, two parts vitriol. Let them be distilled with a very fierce fire, and it will be made.

Any salt may be prepared by itself,
or together with aqua fortis,
and you will have it.

[fol. 100ᵛ]   Ignis contra Naturam.

Succum Lunariæ calcinatum cum utroque vitriolo viridi et Azoqueo
contere: Adde Nitrum cum Aceto præparatum, et nudo igne
distilla, et habebis.

Eundem Succum cum Chalybe per Nitrum præparatum calcinato, contere, et solve in Aquis mineralibus, et fiet.

Hæc omnia inveni in Diebus Uxoris meæ Charissimæ: de Quâ dicere possum, quod de Sapientiâ suâ dixit Solomon: Venerunt mihi
paritèr cum Eâ, Omnia Bona, &c.

                                    T. V. R.
        Te sequar,   Ultima Vitæ Dies,
        et fruar.   Æternitatis prima est.

                                    Amen!

Pro Corollario sic facimus: ℞ Talci Hispanici libram .1.[,] Croci nostri libram .1[,] salis Lunariæ per Corrosivam extractæ, libram mediam. Terantur
in simul, & inspissentur cum Aquâ Roris, vel de B[alneo]. Tunc distilla igne nudo, & fiet. Talcum vero prius solutum, et siccatum esse debet.

                                Tandem notabis:

Quod si ex solâ Lunariâ oleum velis: Tunc sint duæ partes Croci, ad unam
Lunariæ, et invenies.

[fol. 101ʳ blank]

Unnatural Fire.

Mix the calcinated juice of lunaria together with both green and mercurial vitriol. Add nitre prepared with vinegar, and distill with a bare flame, and you will have it.

Mix this same juice prepared by nitre together with calcinated chalybs, and dissolve in mineral waters, and it will be made.

All these things I discovered in the days of my dearest wife about whom I can say, what Solomon said about his wisdom, all good things came to me in like manner through her, etc.

T. V. R.
Thee I will follow, and delight in.
The final day of life is the first of eternity.

Amen!

For a corollary we make it in this way. Take one pound of Spanish talc, one pound of our crocus, half pound salt of lunaria extracted by a corrosive. Let them be ground together, and thickened with water from a *balneum roris* or *balneum Mariæ*. Then distill with a barc flame, and it will be made. The talc ought to be first dissolved and dried.

Finally you will note

That if you wish oil from lunaria alone, then let there be two parts of crocus to one of lunaria, and you will discover it.

[fol. 101ᵛ]   Nota de Mercurio vulgi.

NB.   <u>Figatur cum Aquâ forti: Fixum calcina cum sulphure communi: Calcina-</u>
<u>tum solve in Aceto distillato, et fiet.</u> In calcinatione tamen cautus esto, in
sulphure proportionando, ne excedat, vel æquet Mercurium; sic enim
Mercurius destrueretur, et in Calcem abiret Inanimam, levem prorsùs et
insipidam.

                              Aqua Rebecca:

Quam sic voco, Quoniam hanc ex Sacrâ Scripturâ ostendebat mihi Conjux[128] mea Charissima. Ostendebat (inquam) nec unquàm alitèr invenissem: præparatur autem sic.

{*}   Aerem congelatum, et siccum, ignitum, et liquidum projice in Aerem Acetosum: Projice (inquam) Aerem Siccum, Quem Terra produxit, in Aerem
Humidum, Quem Sol produxit in vase vivo, et mortuo. Digere per horas
24. Tunc distilla; & distillabitur Aer Acetosus in formâ Olei Clarissimi,
cum Guttis rotundis, et Mercurialibus. Cohoba, donec satis sit, et in hac
Aquâ solve [mercurii] sublimatum, vel ut supra Calcinatum, et fiet pro
Certo. Hæc Aqua nobile Arcanum est tam ad Medicinam, quam ad Alchemiam. Laus Deo, Amen!

            {* Note on fol. 102ᵛ refers to this *aerem congelatum.*}

        [Aerem siccum combure inter duo Crucibula, per horas
        sex, aut ultra. Tunc frigescat. Frigefactum tere, & putrefac
        per dies 8 in Aere humido Acetoso, & fiet:[129]]

---

        [128] Sic, for *conjunx.*
        [129] This note refers to the formula on the leaf opposite (fol. 102ᵛ). The Latin text was
evidently already on this page, for the entry on the dream was fitted in around the note on
Aqua Rebecca.

Note Concerning Common Mercury.

NB. It is fixed with aqua fortis. Calcine what has been fixed with common sulphur. Dissolve what has been calcinated in distilled vinegar, and it will be made. During calcination nonetheless be cautious in proportioning the sulphur, lest it exceed or equal the mercury; for in this way the mercury will be destroyed and changed into a lifeless calx, absolutely light and insipid.

Aqua Rebecca:

Which I call thus, since my dearest wife showed me this from holy Scripture. She showed me (I say) nor would I have ever found it by another way. And it is prepared thus.

*} Project air, that is congealed, and dried, ignited, and liquid into a sour air. Project (I say) a dry air, which the earth has produced, into a moist air, which the sun has produced in a live and dead vessel. Decoct for twenty-four hours. Then distill; and sour air will be distilled in the form of a very clear oil, with round and mercurial drops. Cohobate until it be enough, and dissolve sublimate of mercury in this water, or sublimate of mercury calcinated as above, and it will be made for certain. This water is a very notable arcanum for medicine just as for alchemy. Praise be to God, Amen!

[fol. 102ʳ]

{* Heat dry air between two crucibles for six hours or more. Then let it cool. Grind what has cooled, and putrefy for eight days in a moist, sour air, and it will be made.}

[fol. 102ᵛ]   Aqua merè Mineralis:
                                              sive
                                   Præparatio Aquæ fortis
                                           ad Opus.

Rectificetur[130] ab oleo vitri: Rectificatam projice super Tria Salia, Gemmeum puta, Marinum, et Ammoniacum, et cohoba donec satìs sit.

                                        Nota de Duobus
                                            Salibus.

Funde Nitrum, & in alio Crucibulo funde salem marinum: quem liquefactum projice super nitrum fusum, et Quod ascendit, collige, et serva.

                                       Inter omnia salia

Maximè valet Colla Maris, Quam si nosti, nullo alio Sale, & nullâ præparatione opus **est**, ut expertus sum in Diebus Charissimæ Conjugis, et vitæ meæ suavissimæ R. V. Hanc ergo investiga, et cela, est enim Arabum Alkali, & philosophorum Sal commune, et Aqua Marina Acerrima &c.

                                       Laus Deo! Amen!

---

[130] Sic, for *rectificietur*.

A Mineral Water without Mixture: or
Preparation of Aqua fortis for the Work.

It will be rectified by vitriol. Project what has been rectified upon three salts, that is to say rock salt, sea salt, and sal ammoniac, and cohobate until it be enough.

Note about Two Salts.

Melt nitre, and in another crucible melt sea salt. Project what has liquefied upon melted nitre, and collect what ascends, and save.

Among all salts

Colla maris is most efficacious, which if you have learned, there is need for no other salt and no other preparation, as I tested in the days of my dearest wife, and my sweetest life R. V. Investigate this, therefore, and keep it secret, for it is the alkali of the Arabs, and common salt of the philosophers, and a very pungent sea water, etc.

Praise be to God! Amen!

[fol. 103ʳ]   April the 9th die [Sabbat]ⁱ —59.

I went to Bed after prayers, and hearty teares, and had this dreame towards
Day=Breake. I dreamed I was in some obscure, large house, where there
was a tumultuous rayling people, amongst whom I knew not any, but my
Brother H. [&] my deare wife was there with mee, but having conceived
som discontent at their disorder, I quitted the place, and went out leaving
my deare wife behind mee. As I went out, I consydered with my self, and
called to **at least seeming** mind som small unkindnesses I had used towards my deare wife in her life time, and the remembrance of them being
odious to mee, I wondered with my self, that I should leave her behind
mee and neglect her companie, having now the opportunitie to converse
with her after death. These were my Thoughts: whereupon I turn'd in, and
taking her along with mee, there followed us a certaine person, with
whom I had in former times revell'd away many yeares in drinking. I had
in my hand a very long cane, and at last wee came to a Churchyard, and
it was the Brightest day-light, that ever I beheld: when wee were about the
middle of the Church-yard, I struck upon the ground with my Cane at the
full length, and it gave a most shrill reverberating Eccho. I turned back to
looke upon my Wife, and shee appeared to mee in greene silks down to
the ground, and much taller, and slenderer then shee was in her life time,
but in her face there was so much glorie, and beautie, that noe Angell in
Heaven can have more. Shee told mee the noyse of the cane had frighted
her a little, but **saying soe**, she smiled upon mee, and looked most divine-
ly. Upon this I looked up to Heaven, and having quite forgott my first
Apprehension, which was true, . . .

[fol. 102ʳ]
namely that shee appeared thus to mee after her death, I was much troubled in mind least I should dye before her, and this I feared upon a spirituall
Accompt, least after my death shee might be tempted to doe amiss, and to
live otherwise then she did at present. Whiles I was thus troubled, the
Cane that was in my hand, suddainly broke in two, and when it was brok-
en, it appeared noe more like a Cane, but was a brittle, weake reede.[131]
This did put mee in mind of her death againe, and soe did put mee out of
my feare, and the doubts I conceived, if I dyed before her. When the Reede
was broken, shee came close to mee, and I gave her the longer half of the

---

[131] Davies, *Henry Vaughan*, 67, points out the cane "perhaps symbolises the power and
authority of the Hermetic magus" which turns into an impotent, brittle reed.

reed, and the furthest end, and the shortest I kept for my self: but looking on the broken end of it, & finding it ragged, and somthing uneven, shee gave mee a knife to polish it, which I did. Then wee passed both out of the Churchyard, and turning to the gentleman that followed mee, I asked him if hee would goe along with us, but he utterly refused, and the truth is, hee still follows the world too much. Then I turn'd to my deare wife, to goe along with her, and having soe done, I awaked.

By this dreame, and the shortest part of the Reed left in my hand, I guess, I shall not live soe long after her, as I have lived with her.

Praysed bee my God!

Amen!

[fol. 103ᵛ]   Aliud Arcanum nobile.

Jovem cum Marte commisce, iterumque liberetur, sicut scis. liberatum cum chalybe nitrato rursùs incarcera, **sed priùs** tere, calcina. Calcem vero per se, vel cum gemmâ mixtam solve in aquâ minerali, et cohoba. Hoc opus facilè fit, et sine sumptu, Quia [stannum] purgari potest, absque Servo fugitivo, quod in Magnesiâ non evenit, estque Arcanum nobile. Operare ergo (inquit philosophus) cum stanno, donec dives sis, &c. Salem Lunariæ per Corrosivam extractum, contere cum Croco, et sublimato: Tunc solve, &c.

Sic vos, non vobis, vellera fertis Oves.

Sitivit Anima mea, ad Deum Ælohim, ad Deum El vivum: Quando-nàm, veniam, et visitabo faciem Dei Ælohim!

T. V. R.

Consumptus, malè, debilisque vivo,
plusquàm Dimidium mei recessit.

usquè quò Domine!

Another Notable Arcanum.

Mix sulphur together with iron, and let it be released again, as you know. Incarcerate again what has been released with chalybs mixed with nitre, but first grind and calcine. In mineral water dissolve the calx indeed by itself, or mixed with rock [salt], and cohobate. This work is easily done and without expense, because tin can be purged, and without the fugitive attendant, which does not happen in magnesia, and this is a notable arcanum. Work therefore (said the philosopher) with tin, until you are rich, etc. Grind the salt of lunaria extracted by a corrosive together with crocus and sublimate. Then dissolve, etc.

So, sheep, you bear the fleeces, but not for your own benefit.[132]

My Soul has thirsted for God, my God, for God, the living God. When shall I come and visit the face of God, my God![133]

T. V. R.

Withered away and weak, I live unhappily,
More than half of me separated.

How long, O Lord![134]

---

[132] This saying—which often begins "Hos ego versiculos feci ..."—has a long tradition stretching from Virgil to numerous medieval authors. See *Proverbia Sententiaeque Latinitatis Medii Aevi: Lateinische Sprichwörter und Sentenzen des Mittelalters in alphabetische Ordnung*, ed. Hans Walther, 6 vols. (Göttingen: Vandenhoeck & Ruprecht, 1963–1969), 4: 1043. It also takes other forms: e.g., "... sic vos, non vobis fertis aratra, boves."

[133] Psalm 42:3.

[134] Psalm 13:1.

[fol. 104ʳ]   1659.° April 8.ᵗʰ die [Veneris]

In yᵉ Evening I was surprised with a suddaine Heavines of spirit, but
without any manifest Cause whatsoever: but I thank god, a great Tender-
nes of Heart came along with it: soe that I prayed most earnestly with
abundance of teares, and sorow for sinn. I fervently sollicited my gratious
god for his pardon to my self, and my most deare Wife: and besought
him to bring us together againe in his Heavenly kingdom, and that hee
would shew mee his mercie, and answer my prayers by such meanes, and
in such a way as might quicken my spirit, that I might serve him cheere-
fully, and with Joy prayse his name.

I went that night to bed after earnest prayers, and teares, and towards the Day-Breake, or just upon it, I had this following dreame. I
thought, that I was againe newly maried to my deare Wife, and brought
her along with mee to shew her to some of my friends, which I did in
these words. Heere is a wife, which I have not chosen of my self, but my
father did choose her for mee, and asked mee, if I would not marry her,
for shee was a beautifull Wife. Hee had no sooner shewed her to mee,
but I was extremely in love with her, and I married her presently. When
I had thus sayd, I thought, wee were both left alone, and calling her to
mee, I tooke her into my Armes, and shee presently embraced mee, and
kissed mee: nor had I in all this vision any sinnfull desyre, but such a
Love to her, as I had to her very Soule in my prayers, to which this
Dreame was an Answer. Hereupon I awaked presently, with exceeding
great inward Joy. Blessed bee my God, Amen.

{* This was not true of our temporall mariage, nor of our natural
parents, and therefore it signifies som greater mercie.¹³⁵}

[fol. 105ʳ]   1658.

The moenth, and the Day I have forgott: but having prayed earnestly for
Remission of Sinnes, I went to bed: and dreamed, That I lay full of sores
in my feete, and cloathed in certaine Rags, under the shelter of the great
Oake, which growes before the Court yard of my fathers house **and it
rain'd round about mee.** My feet that were sore with Boyles, and cor-
rupt matter, troubled mee extremely, soe that being not able to stand up,

---

¹³⁵ Vaughan's marginal note. No doubt he has in mind the meeting of Rebekah and
Isaac (Genesis 24:14): "let the same be she that thou hast appointed for thy servant Isaac."
I wish to thank Elenor Cook for making this connection.

I was layd all along. I dreamed that my father, & my Brother W. who
were both dead, came unto mee, and my father sucked the Corruption out
of my feete, soe that I was presently well, and stood up with great Joy, and
looking on my feete, they appeared very white and cleane, and the sores
were quite Gone!

Blessed bee my good God!
Amen!

[fol. 105ᵛ]
To the End wee might live well, and exercise our Charitie, which was
wanting in neither of us, to our power: I employ'd my self all her life time
in the Acquisition of some naturall secrets, to which I had been disposed
from my youth up: and what I now write, and know of them practically,
I attained to in her Dayes, not before in very trueth, nor after: but during
the time wee lived together att the Pinner of Wakefield, and though I
brought them not to perfection in those deare Dayes, yet were the Gates
opened to mee then, and what I have done since, is but the effect of those
principles. I found them not by my owne witt, or labour, but by gods
blessing, and the Incouragement I received from a most loving, obedient
Wife, whome I beseech God to reward in Heaven, for all the Happines and
Content shee affoorded mee. I shall lay them downe heere in their order,
protesting earnestly, and with a good Conscience, that they are the very
trueth, and heere I leave them for his Use, and Benefit, to whome god in
his providence shall direct them.

The Præparation of Salt Nitre.

Melt it downe in a Crucible, then powre it into a strong rectified [aqua
fortis]. Digest all in a soft heate in sand, in a Blinde glass for 8 dayes. Then
draw of, and first there will rise a most subtil white spirit in great Quantitie: after which there will come an oyle distilling in lines like to spirit of
wine, and of such a splendor, that it will reflect upon the walls of the
Roome like fire. In . . .

[fol. 104ᵛ]
The bottom there will remaine a salt, that will not take up in water, it is
soe fatt and oylie. Dissolve it therefore in the first subtil spirit, or in common vinegar rectified, and it will sublime into Salt Ammoniac philosophicall. But the true salt Ammoniac is our Citrine Salt.

Another preparation of Nitre.

Beate it to powder, then add to it an æquall Quantitie of common Salt Ammoniac sublimed. Put this mixture in a Crucible in a wind-furnace, and vapour away the Salt Ammoniac. The remaining nitre you shall dissolve in common vinegar distilled, together with the Excoriation, or philosophicall sublimation of the red Magnesia by Corrosives, I found, while wee lodged att Mr Coalemans in Holborne, before wee came to live att the Pinner of Wakefield.

[fol. 104ᵛ]   The Practice upon Metalls.

Succum Lunariæ calcina: Calcinatum cum Ære philosophico conjunge, et distilla in spiritum Mercurialem.

Aliter.

Succum absque Calcinatione per se putrefac per suum mensem, sitque ignis intensus, ut nosti. Tunc distilla, & fiet.

Aqua mineralis.

Calcina Chalybem cum nitro: Calcem cum Sale philosophico conjunge, solve, cohoba, et habebis.

The Practice upon Metalls.

Calcine the juice of lunaria. Join what has been calcinated with philosophical ore, and distill into a mercurial spirit.

By Another Way.

Putrefy the juice without calcination by itself for its month, and let the fire be intense, as you have learned. Then distill, and it will be made.

Mineral Water.

Calcine chalybs with nitre. Join the calx with philosophical salt, dissolve, cohobate, and you will have it.

[fol. 106ʳ]   Amos. cap: 5 ver. 8.

> Seek him, that maketh the Seven starrs, and Orion: and
> turneth the shadow of Death into the Morning, and mak-
> eth the Day dark with Night: That calleth for the waters
> of the Sea, and powreth them out upon the face of the
> Earth: The Lord is his Name.

[fol. 106ᵛ]

My most deare wife sickened on Friday in the Evening, being the 16 of April, and dyed the Saturday following in the Evening, being the 17. And was buried on yᵉ 26 of the Same Moenth, being a Monday in the Afternoone, att Mappersall in Bedfordshire. 1658. Wee were maried in the yeare 1651, by a minister whose name I have forgott, on yᵉ 28 of September.

God, of his infinite, and sure Mercies in Christ Jesus, bring us together againe in Heaven, whither shee is gone before mee, and with her my Heart, and my Faith not to bee broken, and this thou knowest o my God! Amen!

Left at M^{ris.} Highgates.

1. One flatt Trunk of my deare wifes, with her mayden Name upon it.

2. Another Cabinet Trunk of my deare wifes in which is her small pocket Bible, and her mayden Bible I have by mee.

3. One greate wodden Box of my deare wifes, in which is all her best Apparell, and in that is her greate Bible, with her practice of pietie, and her other Bookes of Devotion.

4. Another wodden Box with pillowes in it, and a sweet Basket of my deare wifes.

5. One large Trunk of my deare wifes, with my name upon it, in which are the Silver spoones. And in the Drawers are two small Boxes, one with a lock of my deare Wifes hayre, made up with her owne Hands; and another with severall small Locks in it.

6. One pare of grate Irons with Brass-knobs, and a single pare with Brass-Knobs. a fire-shovell, Tongs and Bellowes: my deare Wifes litle chaire, a round Table, Joynt stoole, and Close-stoole, with a great glass full of eye-water, made att the Pinner of Wakefield, by my deare wife, and my sister Vaughan, who are both now with god.

[fol. 107ʳ]   NB. NB. NB. 1658.

On Friday the 16 of July, I my self sickened att Wapping, and that night I dreamed, I was pursued by a stone = horse, as my deare wife dreamed, before shee sickened. and I was grieveously troubled all night with a suffocation att the Heart, which continued all next day most violently, and still it remaines, but with some little Remission. On the Saturday following being the 17 of July, I could not, for som secret Instinct of spirit, stay any longer at Wapping, but came that very night to Sʳ· John Underhill,[136] and the Sunday following after night, I understood that Mʳ· Highgate was dead, as my Heart gave mee att Wapping, a few dayes before. The will of my god bee done: Amen, and Amen!

That night I came to Sʳ· John, I dreamed, I had lent 20.1. pounds to my Cousin J. Waldebeoff, and that his mother had stole the money, and I was like to loose it. But my Cousin advised mee to give out, I had received it, and hee would secure it for mee. I pray god, my deare wifes Things doe not miscarrie!

---

[136] One of the many knights created by the Stuarts, John Underhill was entered among the Knights Bachelor on 22 July 1626 at Oatlands (a castle built in north Surrey by Henry VIII, extended by Inigo Jones, destroyed by Cromwell). See Shaw, *The Knights of England*, 2: 191.

[fol. 107ᵛ]   Edward Reynolds
                                     His booke

                              Ex libris Th: et Reb: Vaughan.

                              Deo duce: comite Naturâ.

[fol. 108ʳ blank]

[fol. 108ᵛ]   Balsamus [Sulphuris] Rulandinus.

℞. florem [sulphuris] unc[iam] 1. Camphoræ scrup[ulos] 2. Olei Amygda-
larum dulcium unc[ias] 4. coque in Cineribus, donec [sulphur] liquescat.

                       Emplastrum Diasulphuris.

℞ Balsami supradicti unc[ias] 3[,] Ceræ unc[ias] 8[,] Colophoniæ scrup[ulos]
3[,] Myrrhæ ad pondus o[mn]ium. Ceræ, Colophoniæ, Balsamoque lique-
factis inspergatur myrrha subtillissime trita, igneque lento, et spatula agi-
tentur, donec bene mixta fuerint, quod fiet post horæ quadrantem.

                         Miranda faciunt

In ulceribus, vulneribus, et fistulis, et contra gangrænam valent.

Edward Reynolds
His booke

From the Books of Thomas and Rebecca Vaughan.

With God as leader, with Nature as attendant.

Ruland's Balsam of Sulphur.[137]

Take one ounce of sulphur, two scruples[138] of camphor, four ounces oil of sweet almonds. Concoct with the heat of the ashes until the sulphur becomes liquid.

Plaster of Diasulphur.

Take three ounces of the balsam described above, eight ounces of wax, three scruples of colophony,[139] [and] myrrh in an amount equal to the weight of all other ingredients. Grind the myrrh very finely, and let it be sprinkled in the wax, colophony, and balsam liquefied with a slow fire; and let them be agitated with a spatula, until they have been well mixed, which will be done after a quarter of an hour.

They do wondrous things

On ulcers, wounds, and fistulas, and are efficacious against gangrene.

---

[137] This page was written in a different hand, perhaps that of the Edward Reynolds who owned the book briefly.

[138] Unit of apothecary weight. Twenty-four scruples made an ounce; it was also reckoned as twenty grains.

[139] A liquid resin that is dried and pulverized to make a very dry rosin; see Gerard, *Herball*, 1361.

[flyleaf]   108. folios.

Examined after Re-binding by JB.
Sept. 1961.[140]

---

[140] Librarian's note.

GLOSSARY

Unfamiliar words that are used more than once are glossed below. If a word is used only once or appears in only a single entry, the gloss is given as a footnote to the text. The Vaughans used symbols throughout the notebook for the celestial analogues of the seven prime metals, which I have translated as follows:

gold	=	Sol	=	*aurum*
silver	=	Luna	=	*argentum*
iron	=	Mars	=	*ferrum*
mercury	=	Mercury	=	*mercurius*
tin	=	Jupiter	=	*stannum*
copper	=	Venus	=	*cuprum*
lead	=	Saturn	=	*plumbum*

adrop: "denotes either that precise matter, as lead, out of which the mercury is to be extracted for the philosopher's stone; or it denotes the philosopher's stone itself" (OED).

æs: a term without a fixed meaning. Pliny used it to refer to any alloy whose main constituent was copper—i.e., bronze, brass, etc. (Crosland, *Language of Chemistry*, 104–50). Since Vaughan seems to have various metals in mind, I have translated it as *ore*.

air: Following d'Espagnet and others, Vaughan believed that air was a medium through which celestial powers are conveyed (i.e., not simply the atmosphere we breathe). *Spiritus mundi* extends itself through the regions of the air. To this notion was added the concept of "magnetism." Much research was done on the different kinds of moisture or vapor in the air, especially dew and rain water.

alkali: term originally used for the ashes of plants from which sodium or potassium carbonate (K_2CO_3), i.e., potash, had been leached. Pliny described how these "mild" alkalis were made "caustic" by treating them with lime to make soaps. The ashes of sea plants yielded a harder soap than land plants (*Britannica* 1: 636). In *Lumen de Lumine* (*Works*, 326–27), Vaughan wrote that the "the *secret Candle of God*" was purest and most abundant in *sal alkali*, or *Halicali*. "This *substance* is the *Catholick Receptacle* of *spirits*, it is *blessed* and *impregnated* with *Light* from *above*, and was therefore *styl'd* by the *Magicians, Domus signata, plena Luminis et Divinitatis* [a house shut up, full of light and divinity]."

alum: a mineral salt, aluminum potassium sulphate ($AlK[SO_4]_2 \cdot 12H_2O$), noted for its astringent properties. When alum was calcined or heated, it yielded sulphuric acid (H_2SO_4) and aluminum oxide (Al_2O_3).

alvite: "a reddish-brown mineral, a complex hydrous silicate" (OED).

amalgam: an alloy of mercury with some other metal.

animated: synonym for *sophic*, as in *sophic mercury*, q.v.

antimony: a semi-metal, now more commonly known as the mineral stibnite or antimony sulfide (Sb_2S_3). Since it could free gold from its impurities when heated, it seemed reasonable that antimony be able to purge impurities and illness from the body. When heated with iron filings and a fluxing agent, then cooled, crystals of antimony will form throughout that appear on the top surface as a star. The so-called *regulus* referred to metallic antimony, while the *regulus stellatus* was the star itself (Dobbs, *Foundations*, 146–48). Paracelsus called it the red lion, others the wolf because it devoured all metals but gold. It was used medicinally to make cicatrices, as a purgative, and for various other purposes (*Pharmacopœia Londinensis*, 319–48).

aqua fortis: literally, "strong water" in Latin; mainly nitric acid (HNO_3), used as a corrosive agent. Since the time of Geber, it was produced through the dry distillation of saltpeter with vitriol and alum.

aqua regia: literally, "royal water" in Latin; a mixture of hydrochloric acid and nitric acid; this corrosive agent was believed to be capable of dissolving gold into small particles.

aqua vitæ: alcohol concentrated by distillation, often distilled wine; also known as *burning water* or the *water of life*. "It beareth the syrname of life, because that it serveth to preserve and prolong the life of man" (Gerard, *Herball*, 882). Because of its clear blue flame and potency, it was regarded as the ultimate remedy against corruption.

aquila: see *eagle* and *sal ammoniac*.

arcanum: Paracelsus introduced this term to denote a medicine whose secret "virtue" allowed it to act directly as opposed to Galenic medicines that balanced or tempered the elements. Paracelsus believed that each of the four elements contained a fifth, the quintessence, an ethereal substance that constitutes its "virtue" and acts as the vehicle for the special powers in herbs or iatrochemical medicines. Vaughan also used the term more generally: "*Trueth* is the *Arcanum*, the *Mystery and Essence* of all things" (*Anima Magica Abscondita* in *Works*, 122).

assation: roasting or incinerating a substance in a glass vessel to desiccate it.

astrum: the seed of a metal or disease. Peter Severinus thought that elements contained *astra* or forces that joined with chemical principles to
form *semina* which then grew (Debus, *Chemical Philosophy*, 1: 130).

athanor: a digesting furnace in which constant heat is maintained by
means of a tower that provided a self-feeding supply of charcoal
(OED); also known as a *reverberatory* (Dorn, *Chymical Dictionary*, 312).

azoc: another name for latten or laton, i.e., copper tinged into a golden
color with calamine (Johnson 31). Others used *azoc* for the stone itself:
"Azoch est Lapis Philosophorum: & Philosophi ipsum multis nomini-
bus nominaverunt" (*Speculum Alchymiæ*, 4: 523).

azoth: "Quick-silver extracted out of any body, and it is properly called
the Mercury of the body, but in *Paracelsus* it is the universal Medicine
of things" (Dorn, *Chymical Dictionary*, 313); Paracelsus was said to
carry a white powder in a case inside the pommel of his sword which
bore the inscription "Azoth" (Paracelsus, 248). Vaughan also used it as
a synonym for *prima materia* (*Magia Adamica* in *Works*, 200).

balneum Mariæ: a warm water bath, named for its inventor, the legendary
Maria the Jewess or Maria Prophetissa; a *balneum roris* "is a furnace in
which the distillatory vase is suspended only over the steam of water,
in such a way that the waters do not touch the body" (Ruland, *Lexicon*, 69). Such water baths were used to control the heat coming from
a furnace.

bezoar: "calculus or concretion found in the stomach or intestines of some
animals, chiefly ruminants" (OED); valued as an antidote to poison, it
was among the most expensive drugs of the seventeenth century.

black: Black was the sign of putrefaction, the first stage in the great work,
which was signified by various degrees of blackness; white was the second stage, followed by red. On fol. 20^r (and elsewhere), Vaughan used
the phrase *nigrum nigrius nigro* to suggest total putrefaction. See also
dragon.

brothers, two or *fratres duo*: see *dragon*.

Burgundy pitch: resin from a Norway spruce, used in medicine as a stimu-
lating plaster. "It is hot and dry, Attractive, Anodyne, and Vulnerary:
applyed to the Temples it helps the Tooth-ach, to the nape of the
Neck, it draws Rheums from thence" (*Pharmacopœia Londinensis*, 170).

calcination: heating a solid substance at a high temperature to reduce it to
a *calx* or fine powder.

calx: usually "lime," in Latin but by Vaughan's time a specialist's term:
"A term of the alchemists and early chemists for a powder or friable
substance produced by thoroughly burning or roasting ('calcining') a
mineral or metal, so as to consume or drive off all its volatile parts, as
lime is burned in a kiln" (OED).

chalybs: literally, "steel" in Latin; it was considered a magnet that drew *sperm*, q.v., from gold and other metals by Sendivogius (*New Light of Alchymy*, 26–28, 41–42); he also spoke of it as the one metal having the power to consume all others.

chemical wedding: The union of alchemical substances was likened to a wedding of the principles of mercury or Luna (the feminine) and sulphur or Sol (the masculine). Successive stages of the great work refined this union, the most common emblem of which was the copulating lovers in an alchemical bath or grave—i.e., new generation through death (Abraham, *Alchemical Imagery*, 35–37).

chrysolite: literally, "golden stone" in Greek; a transparent green gem, noted for its hardness and density.

chymia: "the art of separating pure from impure, and of making essences" (Dorn, *Chymical Dictionary*, 319). The essence of the great work was *solve et coagula*, the process of dissolving a solid into a fluid (known as a *spirit*, q.v.) and then fixing or coagulating the fluid into a dry solid in order to refine it. Usually this process was repeated frequently.

cinnabar: the chief ore of mercury, mercuric sulphide (HgS), processed in a furnace; also called *minium*. As a red pigment, cinnabar had sacred associations to the Romans, for it was used to paint the face of the statue of Jupiter as well as the bodies of worshippers. Because cinnabar was often found in silver mines, chemists hoped to extract gold by heating this reddish sand (Pliny, *Natural History*, XXXIII.xxxvi–xxxvii).

cohobation: repeated distillation "by pouring a liquid back again and again upon the matter from which it has been distilled" (OED).

colcothar (or *lacerta*, literally, "lizard" in Latin): a brownish-red iron oxide (Fe_2O_3), often used as a pigment. Dorn, *Chymical Dictionary*, 320, said that it was "calcined Vitriol"—i.e., the end product of heating sulphuric acid.

colla maris: glue or size, from the Greek κόλλα. This glutinous substance was made from the skin of certain fish and from oxen and cows; it was used for strengthening glass or stoneware and for preparing surfaces for painting (Rufinus, *Herbal*, 104–5). The Vaughans considered it a salt (see fol. 88^v).

cream of tartar: a purified and crystallized form of tartar, potassium bitartrate ($KHC_4H_4O_6$), used in medicines.

crocus: saffron (*crocus sativus*) was valued for its medicinal properties (Gerard, *Herball*, 152–54); by extension this term was applied to any yellow pigment or dark red powder obtained from metals by calcination—e.g., *crocus martis* is ferric oxide (Fe_2O_3) or rust, used to provoke urine (*Pharmacopœia Londinensis*, 287).

cucurbit: a vessel named for its resemblance to a common gourd, "shaped for the most part like an inverted cone" (Ruland, *Lexicon*, 120).

decoction or *digestion*: separation of pure from impure substances through a gentle heat, which was analogous to the process by which food was broken down in the stomach.

dendrocolla: some kind of resin or κόμμι, perhaps from trees as its root suggests. Du Cange (*Glossarium graecitatis* 277) defines δενδρόκολλα as a gum or brine (βρύον). See, e.g., fol. 49ᵛ.

distillation: heating a substance to convert it into a vapor, then cooling it to extract its essence by condensation to refine it.

draco or *dragon* (or *serpens*): a complex alchemical symbol. During the great work, the alchemist dissolved the matter (usually a metal) into the *prima materia*, q.v., which Vaughan called "the *Sperm*, or *First matter* of the *Great World*" (Vaughan, *Lumen de Lumine* in *Works*, 329). This process reduced matter to a union of its fundamental principles, symbolized as *dragons*. "Winged and wingless serpents or dragons symbolise the volatile and fixed principles (mercury and sulphur) respectively; three serpents, the three principles (mercury, sulphur, salt); and a serpent nailed to a cross, the fixation of the volatile" (Read, *Prelude to Chemistry*, 107). The flying dragon was thus a symbol for the vital, animating agent; its father and mother were philosophical sulphur and mercury. Ruland, *Lexicon*, 128, wrote that "DRACO is Mercury, also the Black Raven, or the Black on the Floor. It devours the tail, drinks the mercury. It is called Salt and Sulphur of the Dragons. It is the Earth from the body of the Sun. It is killed when it loses the soul [*i.e.* the earth is killed], and rises again when the soul returns. The Dragon devours the mercury, like a poison, and dies; again drinks it and is made living." The *two dragons* or *two brothers* were thus forms of the principles of mercury and sulphur, as, for example corrosive mercury sublimate and antimony (Le Fèvre, *Compleat Body of Chymistry*, 1: 91). See *chemical wedding*.

eagle or *aquila*: symbol for the volatile principle; also commonly used to denote *sal ammoniac*, q.v., "by reason of its lightness in sublimation" (Dorn, *Chymical Dictionary*, 309), but refers as well to any acidic *spirit* from a metal. Newton, e.g., conducted experiments to make the eagle of Venus, i.e., copper, and that of Jupiter, i.e., tin (Dobbs, *Foundations*, 173–74). *Aquila volans* also symbolized *mercury* volatilized.

earth: While others used this term for a variety of minerals—and Dioscorides devoted many chapters of *De materia medica* to their medicinal uses—Vaughan wrote: "By *Earth*, I understand not this impure fæculent *body*, on which we *tread*, but a more simple pure *element*, namely the *naturall centrall salt Nitre*. This *salt* is fixed or permanent in the *Fire*, and it is the *sulphur* of *Nature*, by which she retains and congeales her *Mercurie*" (*Euphrates* in *Works*, 538).

elixir: one of the many names for the fabled agent of alchemical transmutation that would bring imperfect bodies to perfection. Since red was thought to be an intense yellow, "The red elixir makes substances yellow infinitely and transmutes all metals into purest gold" (Roger Bacon's *Speculum Alchemiæ*, in *Bibliotheca Chemica Curiosa*, 1: 616).

eudica: "a glaze, or the dregs or impurity of glass," obtained from vitreous minerals and used to prevent other substances from being consumed too quickly by fire (Morienus, *Testament of Alchemy*, 45, 37).

feathers of the dragon: In successive stages of the *chemical wedding*, q.v., the generation of the *philosopher's stone* is sometimes depicted emblematically as hatching a chick and its dissolution in the waters of the alembic as consuming its feathers (Abraham, *Alchemical Imagery*, 73–74).

fire: Ruland, *Lexicon*, 180, distinguished among four grades of fire. The first was called "heat of the tepid bath," which the Vaughans referred to as water of the *balneum Mariæ*. The second grade, called "heat of the ashes," was fiercer; it was produced by a fire kindled under a pan of ashes or cinders. The third, called "fire of sand," was compared to boiling sand or iron filings. The fourth grade, the fiercest, was produced from coals and a bellows. See Vaughan's *Magica Adamica* in *Works*, 221–23, for a discussion of the various grades.

fire unnatural or *ignis contra naturam*: a secret fire thought to be located "within" a substance that the alchemist had to activate. Ripley stated that the "Fyre against Nature must doe thy bodyes wo;/ That ys our *Dragon* as I thee tell,/ Fersely brennyng as Fyre of Hell" (in *Theatrum Chemicum Britannicum*, 142). See also Vaughan's *Euphrates* in *Works*, 542.

fixation: repeatedly heating a substance to reduce its volatility; "making that which flies in the fire to endure the fire" (Dorn, *Chymical Dictionary*, 326).

flores or *flowers*: Libavius defined flowers as a spiritous substance extracted by sublimation—i.e., the volatile oxides of zinc, phosphorus, sulphur, etc. (Crosland, *Language of Chemistry*, 74).

fugitive attendant: another name for *sophic mercury*, since the volatility of this principle made it susceptible to sudden transformation.

iatrochemistry: from the Greek *iatros* for "physician," it refers to the "chemical medicine" advocated by Paracelsus.

jalap or *turpeth* or *turbith*: a cathartic drug prepared from jalap root or from the turpeth root; *turpeth mineral* is a yellow, crystalline powder, mercury sulphate ($HgSO_4$), produced from mercury and sulphuric acid, used for medicinal purposes in the seventeenth century (Schneider, *Lexikon*, 91); "*Turbith minerale* is Mercury precipitated into a sweetness without any corrosive" (Dorn, *Chymical Dictionary*, 348).

Juno: synonym for *sophic mercury*; see Vaughan's *Anthroposophia Theomagica* in *Works*, 69.

lac virginis: literally, "virgin's milk" in Latin. Vaughan used this term for the *prima materia*, which he also called "*cælum terræ* and *terra cæli*" (*Magia Adamica* in *Works*, 199, 203); hence it was synonymous with mercurial water, sophic water, mercury of the philosophers, etc. (Ruland, *Lexicon*, 188). This term also referred to a suspension of basic lead carbonate, in which metals were dissolved (Crosland, *Language of Chemistry*, 71).

lead: lead was thought to be the oldest metal because of its association with Saturn. The most common mineral of lead is *minim* (q.v.). In addition to elemental lead, its common compounds are white lead, or lead carbonate ($PbCO_3$); sublimed white lead ($PbSO_4$); red lead (Pb_3O_4) (*Handbook of Chemistry and Physics*, 4–16). Lead compounds had medicinal value: e.g., sugar of lead was used as an anodyne for pain (*Pharmacopœia Londinensis*, 294–97).

litharge: literally, "silver stone" in Greek, though in actuality it is the yellow or reddish oxide of lead. It was thought an "Excrement arising from the refining of Silver or Gold with Lead" and had medicinal uses when prepared as an oil or balsam (*Pharmacopœia Londinensis*, 354).

Lombard: Vaughan used this substance as an oil and an extract (*succus Lombardi*). While Ruland, Dorn, and Gerard list many chemical and herbal oils, Vaughan's oft-used *oleum Lombardi* is nowhere mentioned. According to Latham, *Revised Medieval Latin Word-List*, 382, *pulvis Lombardus* or *pudurlumbartus* (ca. 1372) was a spice. Possibly it was associated with the *Margarita Preciosa* of Petrus Bonus, who hailed from Lombardy.

lunaria or *moonwart*: "Small Moonewoort is singular to heale greene and fresh wounds: it staieth the bloudy flix. It hath beene vsed among the Alchymistes and witches to doe wonders withall, who say, that it will loose lockes, and make them to fall from the feet of horses that grase where it doth grow, and hath beene called of them *Martagon*" (Gerard, *Herball*, 407). Also considered to be the "Sulphur of Nature" (Dorn, *Chymical Dictionary*, 334); and Vaughan referred to *sophic mercury* as "Lullies Lunaria" in *Lumen de Lumine* in *Works*, 345.

magnesia: "a stone, shining like silver, perhaps talc" that was reputed to be one of the ingredients of the philosophers' stone (OED). Following Sendivogius, *New Light of Alchymy*, 41–42, Vaughan also considered it an "aliment" for the *sperm* that ascends from within the earth in the spring and summer for the generation of the vegetable kingdom; see *Euphrates* in *Works*, 530–31. Crosland, *Language of Chemistry*, 25–26, explains that "In a technical sense it was usually the black oxide of manganese or iron, but in an alchemical context it was often used to denote the black prime matter sometimes represented as 'lead'."

manna: also known as dew-grass or *gramen mannæ*, used as a mild purgative and in poultices (Gerard, *Herball*, 27–28).

matrass: "A glass vessel with a round or oval body and a long neck, used by chemists for digesting and distilling" (OED).

matrix: a material "womb" of immature matter into which a masculine *sperm* was injected to induce the process of generation to produce gold—a basic principle for Sendivogius. See the "Epilogue" to *New Light of Alchymy*, 39–46.

menstruum: "that from which all metals are derived" (Ruland, *Lexicon*, 228). Normally Vaughan used this term to refer to *sophic mercury*, q.v., but it could be any solvent that would reduce a substance to the *prima materia*, q.v.

mercury: common or "vulgar" *mercury* (Hg); see also *sophic mercury*.

minium or *minim* or *sericon*: usually red lead, a bright-red powder used in paints, glass, etc. (Pb_3O_4). The Romans, according to Pliny, *Natural History*, XXXIII.xxxvi, referred to cinnabar (HgS) and *minium* interchangeably, though erroneously. Vaughan's phrase *rubea mercurii minera* is translated as "red ore of lead," i.e., cinnabar.

nitre or *saltpeter*: potassium nitrate (KNO_3). I have assumed throughout that the Vaughans used *nitrum* and *halinitrum* as synonyms. Ruland, *Lexicon*, 238–39, listed six species of nitre, all mined in different locales.

oleum: "oil" in Latin; it referred to an extract that could serve as a mediating or uniting agent, prepared by distillation or secretion.

orpiment or *auripigmentum*: literally, "gold pigment" in Latin; arsenic trisulphide (As_2S_3). Since it glittered, some alchemists thought it contained gold.

our: the possessive adjective was often used to differentiate what resulted from the alchemist's operation upon a substance from the common or "vulgar" form it first took; e.g., Vaughan refers to "our briny sulphur" (fol. 3^v) to distinguish it from common sulphur. The adjective *sophic* was also used in this same way.

philosopher's stone: the elusive goal of the great work, referred to in a highly enigmatic way, e.g., as a stone and not a stone. The *elixir* was generally regarded as its liquid form. The stone was sometimes depicted emblematically as the *philosophical child*, generated through the *chemical wedding*, q.v.

phlegm: a watery, often odorless and tasteless product of distillation, which appears either before and after its corresponding *spirit*. For example, the distillation of wine was thought to produce a vaporous, volatile *spiritus vini* along with *phlegm* materially in the water (Schneider, *Lexikon*, 83).

Pluto: As is indicated by the subtitle of Glauber's *Kurtze Erklärung, über die höllische Göttin Proserpinam, Plutonis Haussfrawen, was die philosophische Poeten, als Ovidius, Virgilius, und andere dadurch verstanden haben; und wie durch Hülff dieser Proserpinae die Seelen der abgestorbenen metallischen Leibern ausz der chimischen Höllen, in den philosophischen*

Himmel geführet werden, Pluto represented the chemical "hell" to which the dead "bodies" of metals were confined so that their "souls" could be led to the philosophical "heaven." According to Porta, *Natural Magick* (I,iv, 6), it was a synonym for elemental *earth*.

pontic water: another term for *sophic mercury* or *prima materia*, q.v., the bitterness of whose initial state, due to its impurity as an imperfect body, was likened to the salt of the sea. From this *aqua pontica*, according to Sendivogius, *New Light of Alchemy*, 41–42, metals were extracted by "magnetic" *chalybs*, q.v.

prima materia: In the chain of being, the middle nature between the "Subternaturall Darknesse" and the "supernaturall Fire" is formed by the *prima materia* (called *sperm* or *aqua prima* and by the Greek ὕλη or χάος): "These *Middle Natures* came out of a certaine *water*, which was the *Sperm*, or *First matter* of the *Great World*" (Vaughan, *Lumen de Lumine* in *Works*, 329). Elsewhere Vaughan states that this "*seed* then, or *first matter* is a certain *limositie* extracted from these foure [earth, water, air and fire], for every one of them contributes from its very *Center*, a thin *slimie substance*, and of their several *slimes* nature makes the *sperme* by an ineffable *union* and *mixture*" (Vaughan, *Aula Lucis* in *Works*, 461).

projection: the final process of "throwing" the stone on the molten metal to be transmuted.

putrefaction: the decomposition or disintegration of a substance, usually by chemical means, into "chaos." The analogy with contemporary theories of sexual generation is helpful: conception was thought to involve the decay and resolution of the male sperm and the female menstrual blood before a "vegetative" spirit animated the undifferentiated mass, much as the Holy Spirit had hovered over the waters of the deep at the creation. Cf. John 12:24: "Except a corn of wheat fall into the ground and die, it abideth alone: but if it die, it bringeth forth much fruit."

rebis: literally, *re bis* or "two-thing" in Latin: man and wife, or body and spirit, i.e., the stable union of the principles of mercury (the feminine) and sulphur (the masculine) that was often represented as copulating lovers or the hermaphrodite with a red (masculine) and white (feminine) half. Flamel, e.g., used the term to refer to the conjoined bodies of mercury and sulphur after putrefaction. It could also refer to the excrement of the bowels (Dorn, *Chymical Dictionary*, 343; Johnson, *Lexicon Chymicum*, 172).

regulus: "the purest metalline part of any Metal, or the purest part of a Mineral, the feces being separated" (Dorn, *Chymical Dictionary*, 343).

rubea mercurii minera: see *minium*.

sal ammoniac or *sal armoniacum*: ammonium chloride (NH_4Cl), used in washing or purifying processes. Ammonium chloride is unstable; when heated, two gases are formed: ammonia (NH_3) and hydrogen chloride (HCl). See also *eagle*.

salt: according to Paracelsus, one of the three fundamental principles. At this time any solid that was soluble in water was considered a salt; hence, there were neutral salts and also acids and alkalis. In their work, the Vaughans used various salts, including sodium chloride and borax. Natural mineral salts were widely used as medicaments. See the extensive list in *Pharmacopœia Londinensis*, 355–86.

salt doubled or *sal duplicatum*: potassium sulphate (K_2SO_4), a salt made of two constituents, i.e., "doubled."

salt of lead: lead acetate or *Salt of Saturn* ($Pb[C_2H_3O_2]_2 \cdot 3H_2O$). Though sometimes called "sugar of lead" because of its taste, lead acetate was classed as a fixed "salt" or extract of lead; it was used as an anodyne for pain and for ulcers.

scarabæus: While the Vaughans considered this a salt, it apparently was a powder or resin produced from the beetle. "1. It is used against pains and Contractions of the Nerves, and as an Amulet it is used against Quartans. 2. *An Oyl by infusion* dropt into the Ears, eases their pain. 3. The powder of the Ball-footed Beetle, is good against the falling out of the Eyes of the Fundament" (*Pharmacopœia Londinensis*, 263). In Egypt the scarab beetle was valued as an amulet signifying eternal life, because it was believed to be self-begotten, or born only of a father. In Egyptian art the winged scarab figured the vivifying soul. Since the dung beetle collected faeces to roll into a ball in which to lay its eggs, it also offered a natural parallel to alchemical death and rebirth—the *nigredo*. See Horapollo, *Hieroglyphics*, I.10.

sophic mercury or *Mercurius*: common mercury that has been refined; also a complex alchemical symbol for the universal agent of transmutation and the substance from which all metals were created, usually described as a water: e.g., Sendivogius's "water which does not wet hands" (Szydło, *Water*, 93–155). Natural philosophers believed that the seeds of metals were nurtured in an aliment in the earth just as a human fetus grew. Alchemists sought to replicate in the alembic what was accomplished naturally by a form of mercury generated within the bowels of the earth. Acquiring or producing *sophic mercury* was thus the necessary first step in the great work. Common synonyms were *azoc*, *draco volans*, *Juno*. In its exalted or philosophical form, it was considered one of the *tria prima*, q.v., or essential principles in the creation and generation of matter. As *Mercurius à naturâ coagulatus*, it was a solid metal; "*Mercurius Crystallinus* is that which by often sublimations is brought into a clearness like Crystal"; "*Mercurius Crudus* is that which is not yet separated from its Mine [i.e., mineral]"; "*Mercurius metallorum præ-*

cipitatus is Mercury extracted out of Metals, and precipitated" (Dorn, *Chymical Dictionary*, 336–37). Mercury "washed" with vinegar to purge it of its "filth" was used for venereal disease; and other mercury compounds had medicinal purposes (*Pharmacopœia Londinensis*, 298–319).

sperm or *seed*: see *prima materia*.

spirit or *spiritus*: "A Solvent Water produced from a simple and acrid substance, having the nature of a fiery breath, which is the chief part, though it is combined with a gaseous substance. It acquires an aqueous consistence, and possesses a specific virtue" (Ruland, *Lexicon*, 298). The most important were the spirits of mercury, sulphur, *sal ammoniac*, and orpiment. In connection with each *spiritus* was often a corresponding *phlegm* or material substrate.

spittle of the dragon or *sputum Lunæ*: most likely, a synonym for *prima materia*, q.v. Saliva was thought to have special curative powers; e.g., Christ's healing the blind man (John 9:6). Spittle was also a common diagnostic by physicians, who examined visually a patient's urine, stools, vomit, and spittle.

sublimate: usually sublimate of mercury, i.e., mercurous chloride (Hg_2Cl_2).

sublimation: vaporization without passing through a liquid state; technique for purifying a solid by converting it to a vapor.

sulphur: one of the principles of metals; see *tria prima*.

talc: occurring most often as soapstone, magnesium silicate ($Mg_3Si_4O_{10}[OH]_2$) was used for carving and as a dusting powder; hence, the Vaughans may have valued its binding properties.

tartar: potassium hydrogen tartrate [$KH(C_2H_2O_3)$] or ($KHC_4H_4O_6$)]; "a hard saltish dreg that sticks to the sides of Wine vessels" (Dorn, *Chymical Dictionary*, 347). When dried, this hard crust was pulverized and used for its binding properties. The burnt lees of wine were called *tartarum calcinatum*, which could be resolved into a liquid inside a stoppered glass vessell called the oil of tartar that had a caustic quality (Gerard, *Herball*, 883).

tincture: "that which tingeth any body with its color" (Dorn, *Chymical Dictionary*, 348).

tria prima: The Arab alchemist Jabir ibn Hayyan (known as Geber) first advanced the theory that all metals were made of mercury and sulphur. Paracelsus later added a third principle, salt, and argued that these were analogous to the trinity involved in the creation of the cosmos. Basil Valentine asserted that fire separated bodies into three fundamental principles, water, oil and salt. Mercury was sharp, fusible, subtle, and volatile (spirit). Sulphur was moist, sweet, oily, had a nourishing fire and natural heat (soul). Salt was dry, saltish, earthy, and endowed with qualities of dissolving, cleansing, congealing, etc. (Debus, *Chemical Philosophy*, 1: 162–63).

turpentine: the resin harvested from the branches of the turpentine tree has an astringent or binding quality; the volatile oil distilled from the resin was also useful in medicines (Gerard, *Herball*, 1433–35).

turpeth: see *jalap*.

tutia or *tutty*: crude oxide of zinc (ZnO), often deposited in furnace outlets; it was considered a lesser *spiritus*. It was used to dry out wounds or ulcers; also for fluxes in the eyes (*Pharmacopœia Londinensis*, 355).

Typhon: synonym for the great dragon. Maier (citing the Pseudo-Lull's *Testamentum* in his *Arcana arcanissima*, 204–5) explained that Isis, the feminine transformative substance, was the *prima materia*, while the corresponding masculine substance was red sulphur, the *vir* or *servus rubeus*, whose redness related him to Typhon. Killing Typhon, the brother of Osiris, meant recovering the constituent properties of the elements.

urine of Saturn: While Vaughan takes this as a synonym for *æther* in *Lumen de Lumine* (*Works*, 348, citing Sendivogius, 139), it also referred to an ammonium salt that was sublimated from putrid urine through a dry distillation and used as a potent solvent (Schneider, *Lexikon*, 87).

vegetabilis: Because of the supposed analogy between the "growth" of metals within the earth and that of plants, this term, which I have translated as "animating," was used frequently by alchemists.

venom: name for the transformative waters of *sophic mercury* that dissolved or "killed" the matter during the first phase of the great work. Similarly, disease to the iatrochemist was considered to be related to localized malfunctions of the body that could be treated homeopathically, i.e., *similia cum similibus* (in contrast to the Galenic theory of disease as humoral imbalance). The Greek φάρμακον meant both drug and poison.

vinegar or *acetum*: the vinegar of the philosophers was reputedly a solvent with powers greater than simple acetic acid; thus, it may have been a fortified mineral acid.

vitriol or *oleum vitri*: a sulphate, usually of iron ($FeSO_4 \cdot 7H_2O$) or copper ($CuSO_4 \cdot 5H_2O$), that formed a concentrated sulphuric acid; so named because of its glassy appearance.

BIBLIOGRAPHY

PRIMARY SOURCES

Albertus Magnus. *The Book of Secrets*. Ed. Michael R. Best and Frank H. Brightman. Oxford: Oxford University Press, 1973.

Archer, Rebekah. Will (1685). Bedfordshire Record Office, ABP/w 1685/90.

Archer, Thomas. Will (1630). Bedfordshire Record Office, ABP/w 1630/129.

Artephius, *Liber Secretus*, trans. Eirenæus Orandus. In Nicolas Flamel, *Exposition of the Hieroglyphicall Figures*. London, 1624.

Ashmole, Elias. *Elias Ashmole (1617–1692): His Autobiographical and Historical Notes, His Correspondence, and Other Contemporary Sources Relating to his Work*. Ed. C. H. Josten. 5 vols. Oxford: Clarendon Press, 1966.

———. *Theatrum Chemicum Britannicum. Containing Severall Poeticall Pieces of our Famous English Philosophers*. London, 1652.

Aubrey, John. *Aubrey's Brief Lives*. Ed. O. L. Dick. London: Martin Secker, 1949; Penguin, 1972.

Baker, George. *The Composition or Making of the Most Excellent and Pretious Oil called Oleum Magistrale*. London, 1574.

Beguin, Jean. *Tyrocinium Chymicum: or, Chymical Essays Acquired from the Fountain of Nature, and Manual Experience*. Trans. Richard Russell. London, 1669.

Bibliotheca Chemica Curiosa, seu Rerum ad Alchemiam pertinentium Thesaurus Instructissimus. Ed. Jean Jacques Manget. 2 vols. Geneva, 1702.

Bonus, Petrus. *Magistri Petri Boni Lombardi Ferrariensis physici & chemici excellentissimi. Introductio in artem chemiæ integra ... Margarita Preciosa*. Montbéliard, 1602.

Brunschwig, Hieronymus. *The Vertuose Boke of Distyllacyon of the Waters of All Maner of Herbes*. London, 1527.

Bulleyn, Willyam. *Bulleins Bulwarke of Defence against all Sicknes, Sornes, and Wounds*. London, 1562.

Butler, Samuel. *Characters*. Ed. Charles W. Daves. Cleveland and London: Press of Case Western Reserve University, 1970.

——. *Hudibras*. Ed. John Wilders. Oxford: Clarendon Press, 1967.

Cooper, Thomas. *Thesaurus Linguæ Romanæ & Britannicæ*. 2 vols. London, 1565.

Dorn, Gerhard. *A Chymical Dictionary: Explaining Hard Places and Words Met withal in the Writings of Paracelsus and Other Obscure Authors*. Published with Sendivogius's *A New Light of Alchemy*. Trans. John French. 2nd ed. London, 1674.

Duchesne, Joseph (Quercetanus). *The Practise of Chymicall and Hermetical Physicke*. London, 1605.

d'Espagnet, Jean. *Enchiridion Physicæ Restitutæ*. Paris, 1608.

——. *Enchyridion Phisicæ Restitutæ: or, The Summary of Physics Recovered (1651)*. Ed. Thomas S. Willard. English Renaissance Hermeticism, 1. New York: Garland, 1999.

——. *The Summary of Physics Recovered*. Trans. Elias Ashmole. London, 1651.

Flamel, Nicolas. *His Exposition of the Hieroglyphicall Figures (1624)*. Ed. Laurinda Dixon. English Renaissance Hermeticism, 2. New York: Garland, 1994.

Gerard, John. *The Herball or Generall Historie of Plants*. Rev. and ed. Thomas Johnson. London, 1633.

Gesner, Conrad. *The Newe Iewell of Health*. Trans. George Baker. London, 1576.

Glauber, Johann. *Kurtze Erklärung, über die höllische Göttin Proserpinam, Plutonis Haussfrawen, was die philosophische Poeten, als Ovidius, Virgilius, und andere dadurch verstanden haben; und wie durch Hülff dieser Proserpinae die Seelen der abgestorbenen metallischen Leibern ausz der chimischen Höllen, in den philosophischen Himmel geführet werden*. Amsterdam, 1667.

Gratarola, Guglielmo. *Veræ Alchemiæ Artisque Metallicæ, citra Aenigmata, Doctrina, certusque modus*, 2 parts in 1 vol. Basel, 1561.

Hartlib, Samuel. *Ephemerides*, Sheffield University Library MS, Hartlib.

Henshaw, Thomas. British Library MS, Sloane 243, Register Book of the Royal Society: Nr. 18: "The History of the Making of Salt Peeter. By M^r. Henshaw" (fols. 43^v–48^r); "The Manner of making Salt Peeter" (fols. 48^v–51^r); "To Refine Saltpeeter" (fols. 51^v–53^r); "The History of making Gunpowder" (fols. 53^v–57^r).

——. Letter, Halophilus to Sir Robert Paston at Oxnead, 5 November 1663, Norfolk Record Office, Bradfer-Lawrence MS, 1c/1.

——. Letter to Sir John Clayton at Oxnead, 29 August 1671. Norfolk Record Office MS, Bradfer-Lawrence, 1c/1.

Henshaw, Thomas, barrister. *A Vindication of Thomas Henshaw Esquire, Sometimes Major in the French King's Service ... concerning a pretended Plott for which J. Gerharde, Esquire and Peter Vowell, Gent., were mur-*

thered on the 10th of August, 1654. London, 1654.

Horapollo. *The Hieroglyphics of Horapollo*. Trans. and ed. George Boas. Princeton: Princeton University Press, 1993.

Johnson, William. *Lexicon Chymicum: cum Obscuriorum verborum, et rerum hermeticarum, tum phrasium Paracelsicarum, in scriptis eius*. 2nd ed. London, 1657.

Jorden, Edward. *A Briefe Discourse of a Disease Called the Suffocation of the Mother Written uppon Occasion Which Hath Beene of Late Taken Thereby to Suspect Possession of an Evill Spirit or Some Such Like Supernatural Power; Wherein Is Declared That Diverse Strange Actions and Passions of the Body of Man ... Have Their True Naturall Causes and Do Accompanie This Disease*. London, 1603.

Le Fèvre, Nicolas. *A Compleat Body of Chymistry*. 2nd ed. 2 vols. in 1. London, 1670.

——. *Discourse upon Sir Walter Rawleigh's Great Cordial*. Trans. Peter Belon. London, 1664.

Maier, Michael. *Arcana arcanissima, hoc est Hieroglyphica ægyptio-græca*. London, 1614.

Morienus. *A Testament of Alchemy: Being The Revelations of Morienus, Ancient Adept and Hermit of Jerusalem to Khalid Ibn Yazid Ibn Mu'awiyya, King of the Arabs*. Ed. and trans. Lee Stavenhagen. Hanover, NH: University Press of New England, 1974.

Paracelsus. *Selected Writings*. Ed. Jolande Jacobi. 2nd ed. Bollingen Series, 28. Princeton: Princeton University Press, 1958.

Pharmacopœia Londinensis. Or, the New London Dispensatory. Ed. William Salmon. 6 books in 1 vol. London, 1685.

Pliny. *Natural History*. Trans. H. Rackham, W. H. S. Jones, and D. E. Eichholz. 10 vols. Cambridge, MA and London: Heinemann, 1949–1971.

Plot, Dr. Robert. British Library MS, Sloane 3646, fols. 77–81.

Porta, Giambattista della. *Natural Magick ... in Twenty Books: Wherein Are Set Forth All the Riches and Delights of the Natural Sciences*. London, 1658.

Psellos. *Philosophica Minora*. Ed. John Duffy and Dominic O'Meara, 2 vols. Stuttgart and Leipzig: Teubner, 1989. 1: 116–19.

Pseudo-Geber. *The "Summa Perfectionis" of Pseudo-Geber: A Critical Edition, Translation and Study*. Ed. and trans. William R. Newman. Leiden: Brill, 1991.

Pseudo-Lull. *Testamentum Magistri Raymundi Lulli, & primùm de Theorica & Practica Magistri Raymundi Lulli super Lapide Philosophico*. In *Theatrum Chemicum*, 4: 1–170.

——. *Philosophical Experiments of that Famous Philosopher Raymund Lully*. Trans. Robert Turner. London, 1657.

Ripley, Sir George. *The Compound of Alchymy, or the ancient hidden Art of*

Alchemie. London, 1591. Also in *Theatrum Chemicum Britannicum*, 107–93.

Rufinus. *The Herbal of Rufinus*. Ed. Lynn Thorndike. Chicago: University of Chicago Press, 1946.

Ruland, Martin, *A Lexicon of Alchemy*. Ed. and trans. A. E. Waite. London: 1893; rpt. Kila, MT: Kessinger, 1991.

Sendivogius, Michael. *A New Light of Alchymy . . . To which is added a Treatise of Sulphur*. Trans. John French. London, 1650.

Speculum Alchymiæ. Attributed to Arnald of Villanova. In *Theatrum Chemicum*, 4: 515–41.

Stow, John. *A Survey of the Cities of London and Westminster*. Ed. John Strype. 6 vols. London, 1720.

Turba Philosophorum (ca. 12th c.). In *Theatrum Chemicum*, 5: 1–52.

Theatrum chemicum, præcipuos selectorum auctorum tractatus de chemiæ et lapidis philosophici antiquitate, veritate, iure et operationibus. Ed. Lazarus Zetzner. 6 vols. Strasbourg, 1659–1661. [Vols. 1–4 were first published between 1602 and 1622, then reissued in 1659 with vols. 5 and 6.]

Valentine, Basil. *Basil Valentine His Triumphant Chariot of Antimony*. Ed. L. G. Kelly. English Renaissance Hermeticism, 3. New York: Garland, 1993.

——. *Triumph-Wagen Antimonii*. Nuremberg?, 1604.

Vaughan, Henry. *The Complete Poems*. Ed. Alan Rudrum. New Haven: Yale University Press, 1981.

——. *The Works of Henry Vaughan*. Ed. L. C. Martin. 2nd ed. Oxford: Clarendon Press, 1957.

Vaughan, Thomas. *The Fame and Confession of the Fraternity of R.C., Commonly, of the Rosie Cross. With a Præface annexed thereto, and a short Declaration of their Physicall Work*. London, 1652.

——. *The Works of Thomas Vaughan*. Ed. Alan Rudrum. Oxford: Clarendon Press, 1984.

Walker, John. *An Attempt Towards Recovering an Account of the Numbers and Sufferings of the Clergy of the Church of England*. 2 vols. London, 1714.

Wood, Anthony à. *Athenæ Oxonienses*. Ed. P. Bliss. 3rd ed. 4 vols. New York and London: Johnson, 1967. Facsimile rpt. of London, 1817.

Zadith Senior (Zadith bin Hamuel). *Aurelia Occulta Philosophorum*. Manget printed all three parts in his *Bibliotheca Chemica Curiosa*, 2: 198–212, 212–16, 216–35.

SECONDARY SOURCES

Abraham, Lyndy. *A Dictionary of Alchemical Imagery*. Cambridge: Cambridge University Press, 1998.

Allen, Brigid. "Henry Vaughan at Oxford." *Jesus College Record* (1997/1998): 23–27.

———. "The Vaughans at Jesus College, Oxford, 1638–48." *Scintilla* 4 (2000): 68–78.

Allen, Don Cameron. *Mysteriously Meant: The Rediscovery of Pagan Symbolism and Allegorical Interpretation in the Renaissance.* Baltimore: Johns Hopkins University Press, 1970.

Archer, J. H. L. *Memorials of the Families of the Surname of Archer.* London, 1861.

Berthelot, Marcellin. *Collection des anciens alchimistes grecs.* 3 vols. Paris, 1887–1888.

Boyd, Percival, ed. *Roll of the Drapers' Company of London: Collected from the Company's Records and Other Sources.* Croydon: Gordon, 1934.

Brann, Noel L. "The Conflict between Reason and Magic in Seventeenth-Century England: A Case Study of the Vaughan-More Debate." *Huntington Library Quarterly* 43 (1980): 103–26.

Burnham, Frederic B. "The More-Vaughan Controversy: The Revolt Against Philosophical Enthusiasm." *Journal of the History of Ideas* 35 (1974): 33–49.

Cameron, H. Charles. *A History of the Worshipful Society of Apothecaries of London, Volume I: 1617–1815.* Rev. ed. London: Wellcome Historical Medical Museum, 1963.

Chambers, E. K., ed. *Poems of Henry Vaughan, Silurist.* 2 vols. London: Routledge, 1896.

Chambers, V. H. *Old Meppershall, A Parish History.* Meppershall: privately printed, 1979.

Chester, Joseph Lemuel, ed. *Allegations for Marriage Licenses Issued by the Bishop of London.* Harleian Society, vol. 26. London, 1887.

———. *The Reiester Booke of Saynte De'nis Backchurch Parish.* Harleian Society, 3. London, 1878.

Clucas, Stephen. "The Correspondence of a XVII-Century 'Chymicall Gentleman': Sir Cheney Culpepper and the Chemical Interests of the Hartlib Circle." *Ambix* 40 (1993): 147–70.

Cook, Harold J. "The Society of Chymical Physicians, the New Philosophy, and the Restoration Court." *Bulletin of the History of Medicine* 61 (1987): 61–77.

CRC Handbook of Chemistry and Physics. Ed. David R. Lide. 74th ed. Boca Raton, FL: CRC Press, 1993–1994.

Crosland, Maurice P. *Historical Studies in the Language of Chemistry.* Cambridge: Harvard University Press, 1962.

Davies, Stevie. *Henry Vaughan.* Bridgend, Wales: Seren (Poetry Wales Press), 1995.

Debus, Allen G. *The Chemical Philosophy: Paracelsian Science and Medicine in the Sixteenth and Seventeenth Centuries.* 2 vols. New York: Science History Publications, 1977.

———. *The English Paracelsians.* New York: Franklin Watts, 1966.

———. *The French Paracelsians: The Chemical Challenge to Medical and Scientific Tradition in Early Modern France.* Cambridge: Cambridge University Press, 1991.

Dickson, Donald R. "The Alchemistical Wife: The Identity of Thomas Vaughan's 'Rebecca'." *The Seventeenth Century* 13 (1998): 34–46.

———. *The Fountain of Living Waters: The Typology of the Waters of Life in Herbert, Vaughan, and Traherne.* Columbia: University of Missouri Press, 1987.

———. *The Tessera of Antilia: Secret Societies and Utopian Brotherhoods in Early Modern Europe.* Leiden: Brill, 1998.

———. "Thomas Henshaw, Sir Robert Paston and the Red Elixir: An Early Collaboration Between Fellows of the Royal Society." *Notes and Records of the Royal Society* 51 (1997): 57–76.

———. "Thomas Vaughan." In *Dictionary of Literary Biography*, Volume 131: 310–17. *Seventeenth-Century British Non-Dramatic Poets*, ed. M. Thomas Hester. Detroit: Gale, 1993.

Dobbs, Betty Jo Teeter. *The Foundations of Newton's Alchemy: or "The Hunting of the Greene Lyon."* Cambridge: Cambridge University Press, 1975.

———. *The Janus Faces of Genius: The Role of Alchemy in Newton's Thought.* Cambridge: Cambridge University Press, 1991.

Du Cange. Charles du Fresne. *Glossarium ad scriptores mediae et infimae latinitatis.* 10 vols. 1678. Graz: Akademische Druck, 1954. Rpt. of Paris, 1883–1887.

Du Cange. Charles du Fresne. *Glossarium ad scriptores mediae et infimae graecitatis.* Paris, 1688.

Emmison, F. G., ed. *Bedfordshire Parish Registers: Ampthill.* Vol. 17. Bedford: County Records Committee, 1938.

———, ed. *Bedfordshire Parish Registers: Meppershall.* Vol. 38. Bedford: County Records Committee, 1948.

Encyclopaedia of Islam. New ed. 9 vols. to date. Leiden: Brill, 1960– .

Encyclopædia Britannica. 24 vols. Chicago: William Benton, 1964.

Ferguson, John. *Bibliotheca Chemica: A Bibliography of Books on Alchemy, Chemistry and Pharmaceutics.* 2nd ed. 2 vols. London: Derek Verschoyle, 1954.

———. "Some English Alchemical Books." *Journal of the Alchemical Society* 2 (1913): 2–16.

Foster, C. W. "Institutions to Ecclesiastical Benefices in the County of Bedford, 1535–1660." *Publications of the Bedfordshire Historical Record Society* 8 (1924): 133–64.

Foster, Joseph, ed. *Alumni Oxonienses: The Members of the University of Oxford, 1500–1714.* 4 vols. Oxford, 1891–1892.

———. *London Marriage Licenses, 1521–1869.* London, 1887.

Gettings, Fred. *Dictionary of Occult, Hermetic and Alchemical Sigils.* London: Routledge & Kegan Paul, 1981.

Glare, G. W., ed. *Oxford Latin Dictionary.* Oxford: Clarendon Press, 1996.

Guinsberg, Arlene Miller. "Henry More, Thomas Vaughan and the Late Renaissance Magical Tradition." *Ambix* 27 (1980): 36–58.

Hill, W. Speed. "Editing Nondramatic Texts of the English Renaissance: A Field Guide with Illustrations." In *New Ways of Looking at Old Texts: Papers of the Renaissance English Text Society, 1985–1991,* ed. W. Speed Hill. MRTS, 107: 1–24. Binghamton, NY: Medieval & Renaissance Texts & Studies, 1993.

Hoppen, K. Theodore. "The Nature of the Early Royal Society." *British Journal for the History of Science* 9 (1976): 243-46.

Howlett, D. R. et al., *Dictionary of Medieval Latin from British Sources.* Oxford: Oxford University Press, 1997.

Hunter, Michael. "How to Edit a Seventeenth-Century Manuscript: Principles and Practice." *The Seventeenth Century* 10 (1995): 277–310.

———, ed. *Robert Boyle Reconsidered.* Cambridge: Cambridge University Press, 1994.

Huntley, Frank Livingstone. *Sir Thomas Browne: A Biographical and Critical Study.* Ann Arbor: University of Michigan Press, 1962.

Hutchinson, F. E. *Henry Vaughan: A Life and Interpretation.* Oxford: Clarendon Press, 1947.

Hutton, Ronald. *Charles II: King of England, Scotland, and Ireland.* Oxford: Oxford University Press, 1989.

Johnson, A. H. *The History of the Worshipful Company of Drapers of London.* 5 vols. Oxford: Oxford University Press, 1922.

Laslett, Peter. *The World We Have Lost: Further Explored.* 3rd ed. New York: Scribner, 1984.

Latham, R. E. *Revised Medieval Latin Word-List from British and Irish Sources.* London: The British Academy, 1965.

Lewis, Charlton T. and Charles Short. *A Latin Dictionary.* Oxford: Clarendon Press, 1879.

Linden, Stanton J. *Darke Hierogliphicks: Alchemy in English Literature from Chaucer to the Restoration.* Lexington: University Press of Kentucky, 1996.

———. "Mrs Mary Trye, Medicatrix: Chemistry and Controversy in Restoration England." *Women's Writing* 1 (1994): 341–53.

Marinovic-Vogg, Marianne. "The 'Son of Heaven': The Middle Netherlands Translation of the Latin *Tabula Chemica.*" In *Alchemy Revisited,* ed. Z. R. W. M. von Martels. Collection de travaux de l'académie internationale d'histoire des sciences, 33: 171–74. Leiden: Brill, 1990.

Matthews, A. G. *Walker Revised: Being a Revision of John Walker's Sufferings of the Clergy During the Grand Rebellion 1642–60*. Oxford: Clarendon Press, 1988.

Mendelsohn, J. Andrew. "Alchemy and Politics in England, 1649–1665." *Past and Present* 135 (1992): 30–78.

Middle Temple. *Register of Admissions to the Honourable Society of the Middle Temple*, 3 vols. London: Middle Temple, 1949.

Nance, Brian K. "Determining the Patient's Temperament: An Excursion into Seventeenth-Century Medical Semeiology." *Bulletin of the History of Medicine* 67 (1993): 417–38.

Newman, William R. *Gehennical Fire: The Lives of George Starkey, An American Alchemist in the Scientific Revolution*. Cambridge: Harvard University Press, 1994.

———. "Prophecy and Alchemy: The Origin of Eirenaeus Philalethes." *Ambix* 37 (1990): 97–115.

———. "Thomas Vaughan as an Interpreter of Agrippa von Nettesheim." *Ambix* 29 (1982): 125–40.

Pagel, Walter. *Paracelsus: An Introduction to Philosophical Medicine in the Era of the Renaissance*. 2nd ed. Basel: Karger, 1982.

Partington, J. R. *A History of Chemistry*. Vol. 2. London: Macmillan, 1961.

Pasmore, Stephen. "Thomas Henshaw, F. R. S. (1618–1700)." *Notes and Records of the Royal Society* 36 (1982): 177–88.

Pereira, Michela. *The Alchemical Corpus Attributed to Raymond Lull*. Warburg Institute Surveys and Texts, 18. London: University of London Press, 1989.

———. *L'oro dei filosofi: saggio sulle idee di un alchimista del Trecento*. Spoleto: Centro Italiano di Studi sull'Alto Medioevo, 1992.

Plessner, Martin. *Vorsokratische Philosophie und griechische Alchemie in arabisch-lateinischer Überlieferung: Studien zu Text und Inhalt der Turba philosophorum*. Boethius, 4. Wiesbaden: Franz Steiner, 1975.

Principe, Lawrence. *The Aspiring Adept: Robert Boyle and His Alchemical Quest*. Princeton: Princeton University Press, 1998.

Ralegh Radford, C. A. *Tretower Court and Castle*. Cardiff: Her Majesty's Stationery Office, 1969.

Read, John. *Prelude to Chemistry: An Outline of Alchemy, Its Literature and Relationships*. 2nd ed. Cambridge: Massachusetts Institute of Technology Press, 1939.

Roberts, Gareth. *The Mirror of Alchemy: Alchemical Ideas and Images in Manuscripts and Books from Antiquity to the Seventeenth Century*. Toronto: University of Toronto Press, 1994.

Rudrum, Alan. "Alchemy in the Poems of Henry Vaughan." *Philological Quarterly* 49 (1970): 469–80.

——, ed. Henry Vaughan. *The Complete Poems*. New Haven: Yale University Press, 1981.

——. "Thomas Vaughan's *Lumen De Lumine*: An Interpretation of Thalia." In *Literature and the Occult*, ed. Luanne Frank, 234–43. Arlington: University of Texas at Arlington Publications, 1977.

——, ed. *The Works of Thomas Vaughan*. Oxford: Clarendon Press, 1984.

Schiebinger, Londa. *The Mind Has No Sex?: Women in the Origins of Modern Science*. Cambridge: Harvard University Press, 1989.

Schneider, Wolfgang. *Lexikon alchemistisch-pharmazeutischer Symbole*. Weinheim: Verlag Chemie, 1962.

Shaw, William A. *The Knights of England: A Complete Record from the Earliest Times to the Present Day*. 2 vols. London: Sherratt and Hughes, 1906.

Smith, Pamela H. *The Business of Alchemy: Science and Culture in the Holy Roman Empire*. Princeton: Princeton University Press, 1994.

Souter, Alexander. *A Glossary of Later Latin to 600 A.D.* Oxford: Clarendon Press, 1947.

Stevens, Michael E. and Steven B. Burg. *Editing Historical Documents: A Handbook of Practice*. Walnut Creek, CA: Altamira Press for the American Association for State and Local History, 1997.

Szydło, Zbigniew. *Water Which Does Not Wet Hands: The Alchemy of Michael Sendivogius*. Warsaw: Polish Academy of Sciences, 1994.

Tanselle, G. Thomas. "The Editing of Historical Documents." *Studies in Bibliography* 31 (1978): 1–56.

Taylor, F. Sherwood. "Alchemical Papers of Dr. Robert Plot." *Ambix* 4 (1949): 67–76.

Thorndike, Lynn. *A History of Magic and Experimental Science*. 8 vols. New York: Columbia University Press, 1923–1958.

Venn, John and J. A. Venn, ed. *Alumni Cantabrigienses: Part I, from the Earliest Times to 1751*. 4 vols. Cambridge: Cambridge University Press, 1922–1927.

Waite, Arthur Edward. *The Magical Writings of Thomas Vaughan*. London, 1888.

——. *The Works of Thomas Vaughan: Mystic and Alchemist*. London: Theosophical Society, 1919.

Walker, D. P. *The Ancient Theology: Studies in Christian Platonism from the Fifteenth to the Eighteenth Century*. Ithaca: Cornell University Press, 1972.

Walther, Hans, ed. *Proverbia Sententiaeque Latinitatis Medii Aevi: Lateinische Sprichwörter und Sentenzen des Mittelalters in alphabetische Ordnung*. 6 vols. Göttingen: Vandenhoeck & Ruprecht, 1963–1969.

Webster, Charles. "English Medical Reformers of the Puritan Revolution: A Background to the 'Society of Chymical Physicians.'" *Ambix* 14 (1967): 16–41.

———. *The Great Instauration*. London: Duckworth, 1975.

Willard, Thomas S. "The Life and Works of Thomas Vaughan." Ph.D. diss., University of Toronto, 1978.

———. "The Rosicrucian Manifestos in Britain." *Papers of the Bibliographical Society of America* 77 (1983): 489–95.

Wilkinson, R. S. "George Starkey, Physician and Alchemist." *Ambix* 11 (1963): 121–52.

———. "The Hartlib Papers and Seventeenth-Century Chemistry, Part Two." *Ambix* 17 (1970): 85–110.